The Gila River Cowboy

By Benjamin Lyle Riggs

Order this book online at www.trafford.com
or email orders@trafford.com

Most Trafford titles are also available at major online book retailers.

Printed in Victoria, BC, Canada.

ISBN: 9781-4269-0411-0 (soft cover)
ISBN: 9781-4269-0412-7 (hard cover)
ISBN: 9781-4269-0413-4 (eBook)

*Our mission is to efficiently provide the world's finest, most comprehensive
book publishing service, enabling every author to experience success.
To find out how to publish your book, your way, and have it available
worldwide, visit us online at www.trafford.com*

 www.trafford.com

North America & international
toll-free: 1 888 232 4444 (USA & Canada)
phone: 250 383 6864 ♦ fax: 812 355 4082

To Shane:
A short life that inspired much

EPIGRAPH

You are responsible for your actions
And
You are responsible for the life that you have.

ACKNOWLEDGMENTS

Deepest Thanks

I had no idea how much time and effort goes into every book by the editor. I express my deepest thanks to my son, Lyle D Riggs for his belief in his father and for the countless hours he dedicated to making this book readable.

I thank my good wife for her support.

I thank my family for providing many experiences and hardy laughter.

I thank my many friends of the Pima Indian Nation for the experiences they provided in my life.

I thank my Heavenly Father for allowing me to live through many of my experiences.

Ben L. Riggs

INTRODUCTION

G EORGE RIBIT CHATTIT was born and raised as a round peg in a square-hole-society. An innate intelligence and an eternal spirit exist in each person. This intelligence and spirit makes each person peerless and possessed of incomparable gifts. If individuals were compared to wood pegs there would be round, triangular, square, pentagonal, hexagonal, octagonal, and a plethora of polygonal pegs. Each peg is unique and designed for a particular function. Yet, in spite of these natural differences, that should be celebrated, we live in a society that tends towards uniformity, but criticizes conformity. We celebrate non-uniformity only in those all too rare instances when one does break free from this push to conformity in spectacular fashion. Such individuals are lauded and praised for being unique. But, we are all unique to begin with. If that uniqueness were cultivated, it is difficult to image the type of society we would have. Instead, when society looks upon an octagon peg, it criticizes, belittles, becomes angry and often inflicts physical, emotional and spiritual damage. We push towards a standardized square peg. This is done in part to excuse our own failure to develop our unique gifts. The criticisms are also made out of pride and ignorance which begets anger which anger begets negative and warlike results.

There exists rare and special individuals that are round, triangle or whatever, who simply refuse to conform. They miraculously choose to remain outside of the conformed society. They do not strive to be a non-conformist for the sake of being a non-conformist, but sincerely and simply live their life consistent with their unique gifts and desires. They have extraordinary experiences that to a conformed society appear to be errors, blunderings or failings, yet to the individual that is true to himself, these experiences are uncomplicated learning moments. These rare lives are repeatedly ridiculed, belittled and battered by the conformist, but are surely the lives that have had the greatest impact on society. Ridicule is followed by admiration due to the eternal fact that each living soul has the right and obligation to fulfill their uniquely endowed purpose. This requires an individual to conform to their

1

own beliefs about himself and to eschew what the rest of the world says. Round, octagonal, or twenty sided individuals that have been true to themselves often have been stoned, shot, imprisoned, exiled or crucified.

These rare and unique individuals also have been leaders that formed new and great countries because they had the courage to maintain their chosen path. They were not superficial rebels, they were eternally true to themselves and they have impacted groups, families, communities and the conforming society.

The desire of this author is that each person, whether laughing or crying with George Ribit Chattit (GRC), will in some manner feel a portion of the life of the "**G**ila **R**iver **C**owboy" and associate with George's individualism, his unconquerable spirit, and his fearless experiences while learning to become a cowboy. The author hopes that the reader will thus be encouraged to seek truth and to honor the reader's own unique gifts.

1—SEE WHAT YOU WANT TO SEE

"What a peaceful and eloquent feeling to be separated from the physical body," thought George Ribit Chattit, as he stood in spirit form on the banks of the muddy Gila River near Black Water, Arizona. My Indian friends had warned me about the soupy, caliche mud that forms after a flood. This mud forms a hard crust on the top, but when the crust is broken an unseen cavern filled with muddy, pancake batter mix is revealed. This cavern is one to fifteen feet deep and offers little or no escape to the unfortunate soul that breaks through the crust. Even if the warnings were at that instance remembered, they would have done nothing to help me. I had walked to the edge of the five-foot concaved riverbank to try and rescue a baby cottontail rabbit. The bank caved and I fell into the innocent looking trap. I was able to help the bunny; however, no one was close enough to provide assistance for me, a sinking cowboy. Only, my trusty horse would be witness to what was happening. As I stood watching, the last few air bubbles from my lungs rose to the surface of the thick mud. I was thinking of a short time back, when I was in New York, how even then I stood apart, not from my body, but from friends and associates. Because of this realization, I had decided to move to Arizona and to walk a new path that I felt was mine alone to tread. I had experienced much and learned to feel and see beyond touch and sight. Now, I stand apart and very alone from my physical body. I still feel and I still recall an eventful life. So, even though my physical body might remain buried forever in the caliche pits of the Gila River, I have no regrets.

GEORGE REFLECTED ON his parents. George's mother, Beth Ann Slade Chattit, was a Rodeo Queen, from Payson, Arizona. She gave lots of time and love to her son. She taught and showed him how to live his life free of the complications caused from negatively judging others. She acquired this knowledge while living amongst the mighty Ponderosa Pines, playing and working with a pioneer mother, and being tutored by Apache Indians who truly honored and revered Mother Nature. George had learned to live with negative and judgmental people, yet he chose and trained himself to see and feel only the positive.

From birth he was different. He had the copper tan skin of a light skinned Indian, and the coal black hair from his father. His deep blue eyes were a striking difference. His mother had some Spanish ancestry, which might have some bearing as to his blue eyes. Those who knew baby George, however, simply said he was born different and this was nature's way of reminding those around him that he was supposed to be different. They hoped that his difference would help influence for good his associates in life.

His father taught him many positive facets of life, while they walked through the Arizona Ponderosa forest. While George's father cuddled the baby boy in his arms or held the boy's little hand, teachings were exchanged through the spoken word, through touch, and most importantly through feelings. Thus, from the innocence of a baby, goodness moved from the subconscious into the conscious. As young George grew, he became aware of his thoughts and nurtured them to maturation, similar to an acorn growing into a mighty oak tree. With these ingrained virtues, George entered the working world.

George's father, Jay John Chattit, was a handsome rodeo cowboy and an Indian. Just before Jay met Beth Ann, Jay won all-around cowboy at a big rodeo. The prize included a huge belt buckle and a brand new half-ton, Ford pickup. When Jay met Beth Ann, he swept her off her feet. It was love at first sight. George's mother loved telling and retelling the story. George could tell that his mother still loved his dad. That always felt good.

His parents frequently spoke of his great heritage and the responsibilities that were his because of this heritage. George felt that he was born to fulfill his great purpose. He knew that part of life's journey was to find and understand that purpose. George's parents lived northeast of Payson, at the foot of the Mogollón Rim. (Mogollón is Spanish for piles or layers of rocks. The cliffs of the Mogollón Rim appear to be layers of huge rocks piled on top of one another.) George Ribit Chattit was born at his parents' home. George was named after his mother's grandfather, George Slade and his father's grandfather, Ribit. (It was originally from the animal rabbit as was Indian custom. People said Ribit was as fast and quick as a rabbit. However, with the mispronunciation that comes from English spoken with an Apache dialect, the word rabbit evolved into Ribit. Ribit became Jay's grandfather's legal name.)

At the base of the Mogollón Rim and among the Ponderosa Pines, George's father began teaching George. George's father taught George over and over that most people have lost contact with or have lost faith in the hereafter that is, the continuation of life after death. He also explained that a curtain or veil separated the living from the dead. Jay taught and rehearsed that mortal death did not end the learning or teaching. It simply ended the physical body. Young George had no doubts about his father's teachings. George believed his father's words.

As a boy George received dreams that taught him as well about accepting others and seeing the positive in any situation. He shared these dreams with his father. His father often helped George to understand the meaning of the various dreams.

George thought differently from other boys at a very early age. George knew that he could learn from his father and mother, from books, from instructors and also from his ancestors on the other side of the curtain or veil. He also learned that in a classroom when he had the correct answer and the teacher ask him where he had learn that answer, he could not say "from my dead grandfather." He was sent to the Principal's Office more than once for giving this answer. He learned to answer, "from my family." This answer was honest and it was readily accepted.

Folks who knew George's father claimed he was the best shot in Arizona and maybe in the western United States. That may have been one of the reasons that George's father joined the United States Marine Corp. During basic training in San Diego, officers realized that enlistee Jay John Chattit, known as J.J., was exceptional in two extremely needed military areas: *One,* J.J. was an expert marksman; and *two,* even more valuable, J.J. had a disconcerting ability to sit without moving a muscle for hours. He was a perfect candidate to be a "specialist" as a sniper. Moreover, he could train many other special operatives as snipers. A sniper trainer was a position that was highly recruited. It required more training than usual, but resulted in a higher rank than normally given a newly trained recruit. Along with a higher rank, this position in the military service also received higher pay. Regrettably, the position was high risk and had a short life span.

After completing basic training, J.J. was stationed at Quantico, Virginia. He immediately began training others how to shoot and remain motionless for hours. Remaining motionless was significantly more difficult, than becoming an expert marksman because it required the marksman to control his thoughts and in other moments ignore his thoughts. By quieting the mind, a person could lay motionless for many hours. J.J.'s ancestors had learned to quiet their minds and lay motionless out of necessity. The Apaches believed that a wild animal such as deer, elk or bear could feel thoughts miles away. In order to hunt successfully, they had to wait until an animal was close enough so they could shoot it with their bows and arrows that had a relatively short range. This teaching and practice was passed on to J.J. as a young man who was taught in the way of the Apaches. J.J. had been trained to rest motionlessly from the time he was a small boy.

Consequently, he was certain that an enemy could do the same, that is, feel thoughts from miles away. Now, his job was to teach grown men, in a few short weeks or months, to alter their way of thinking, breathing, and moving. Even more difficultly, he had to teach them, how to look into the face of a total stranger and deduce that he was indeed an enemy, and then slowly and deliberately pull the trigger that would end a man's life, marriage, fatherhood, son hood, and his past and future with one deadly bullet. Most men could be trained to shoot accurately. A few could be taught to remain motionless. Very few had the capacity to take a life in cold blood.

It appeared J.J. would be stationed at Quantico for the duration of the Vietnam Conflict. Beth Ann loaded the Ford pickup and headed east to be near her husband. After being stationed at Quantico for around two years, J.J. received notice he was being sent to Vietnam for a short time for on-site training. Beth Ann decided to stay in Virginia and wait for her husband to return. It never happened. Jay John Chattit was killed in action.

Early one morning, before Beth Ann and George knew of J.J.'s death, little George left his own bed and climbed into bed with his mother. George seldom did this because he was quite independent. Still more unusual was how this little boy took his mother's head and hugged it tightly.

"Mommy, Daddy wants you to know that he is alright and that he loves you now and will love you forever. He will come in dreams when you need him."

He climbed down and went back to bed. She shed tears of love generated from her young son and how he knew that his father deeply loved his mother. Later Beth Ann asked why he had done such a strange thing? "Daddy came and told me to hug you and tell you, so I did. He told me to be a good man." George went back to playing, but she knew he was no longer her baby.

Beth Ann was puzzled. She felt George had told her something sincere and of grave importance. She spent the next five days trying to understand. Unfortunately, the understanding came in the form of two handsome U.S. Marines. Standing at attention in the open doorway, the marines began to speak. Before they said a word, before they handed her the written notice, she knew. She now knew what her young boy had told her as she buckled and fell to the floor.

She was pregnant at the time. The shock caused a miscarriage. It took her a few months to recover from the shock. She knew she would never completely recover, but her mind often pondered on how her young son knew of J.J.'s death. She felt as most mothers do that her son was special. Well, she said to herself, "I will not be the one to let this boy down. I will teach, lead and exemplify correct principles and behavior."

While in Quantico, Beth Ann worked in a local office of the New York Life Insurance Company in a group whose job it was, as they explained, "to make sure that the "I" was dotted and the "T" was crossed" on each policy submitted. It was not exciting work but she was able to bring much of her work home so she could home school George. She seriously considered moving back to Arizona after J.J.'s death but decided to stay near her husband who had been honorably placed in the

Arlington Cemetery. Along with that reason she also wanted George to experience the many historical sites of the United States and also the culture of various groups, including other Indian tribes, as well as the Mennonites and Amish. She wanted George to learn that each has differences and similarities.

After recovering from the miscarriage, she requested a different position with New York Life. She started investigating claims of fraud and misrepresentation. This position, however, required that she transfer to the main offices in New York City. Much of her work was still done at home. She ferreted out relevant information from hundreds of reports and claims. Twice a month she met in the home office. So, this position was ideal for raising a young son and living on the outskirts of the large metro areas.

Even though the position required that she only go to the New York offices twice a month, she felt she needed to live closer to the office so she could be more available for crisis, either at home or at the office. So, she decided to move George from Quantico. Close to the border between New York and New Jersey and about thirty-five miles from her office is a small Indian Reservation for the Ramapough Mountain Indians. There are about five thousand tribal members. Nearby, was the small community of Mahwah. Living in this community would allow Beth Ann to be close enough to work to respond to emergencies. It would also allow them to enjoy a more rural environment. It seemed perfect for their needs. It would also allow George to stay in contact with his Native American heritage.

Soon after moving to Mahwah, Beth Ann met an Indian family that was a direct descendent of Pontiac, the great Ottawa chief. They took a deep interest in George's ability to dream and claimed that his Indian blood was responsible for his spiritual insight. When Beth Ann had to travel, George stayed with Laurel. Her full first name was Mountain Laurel, which is the state flower of Pennsylvania. She, however, preferred Laurel. Beth Ann was never sure of Laurel's husband's first name, Laurel always loving referred to him as "Ruffed Grouse," which is the Pennsylvania state bird. The couple had eight married children and thirty-nine (and counting) grandchildren. They taught George much about nature and encouraged him to walk and talk with nature. They showed him and taught him to sit for hours to watch deer, birds or other animals. They helped him improve his inner talents.

Beth Ann gave George detailed descriptions of Arizona. She told him of the beauty of the Ponderosa pines, but mostly she would share deep feelings about the strength, power, tranquility, and fear that exist in the living desert of Arizona. She helped him understand the importance of dreams and the importance of finding your place in life and then having the courage to follow the dream. Even as a child of eight he had dreams about his father, not sad or frightening dreams, but dreams of learning. Each dream would end with his dad telling him to "be true to your feelings. Be not swayed by what others esteem as right or wrong. Reach to God always."

Beth Ann also entertained George with stories about Zane Grey, the Hash Knife Outfit, Wild Will Gibson, Slades, Haughts and others and how they survived the heat, the cold, and the lawlessness to conquer the Arizona wilderness and make it fit for frontier families.

"Honor your word to others, but more importantly, be true to yourself." She would relate stories how men would prefer to die rather than break "their word."

When Beth Ann's boss left New York Life and joined the Drug Enforcement Agency, he asked her to change jobs and work with him at the DEA in Washington, D.C. While living in Mahwah, they only made a few visits to J.J.'s gravesite in Arlington. Consequently, they decided to live in Arlington so they could make more frequent visits. The pay was much better and she would have much more freedom to travel. George was in a "Home School" program so he could travel much of the time with her. She was very concerned with his social skills. He could spend hours and days in the Appalachian Mountains visiting with animals but was tongue tied when it came to peers. He enjoyed and seemingly absorbed the historical points of interest throughout Virginia, Pennsylvania, Washington, D.C. and the stock exchange in New York. He became a financial whiz during his teenage years, loved to run but did not enjoy competitive organized sports.

George had just celebrated his twenty-fifth birthday, when Drug Enforcement Agents knocked on his door late one evening.

"Your mother was sent on a drug related assignment and was involved in a terrible auto accident. Her body was burned beyond recognition and had to be identified from dental records."

He thought it strange that they identified her from dental records; he never knew his mother went to a dentist; she had the most perfect white teeth. George also had perfect teeth.

He attended the funeral, which was held in a local chapel of the church they attended. It was closed casket, so George was never given the opportunity to look at her remains or to verify her identity. He watched sadly as, what they told him, her charred remains were lowered into Mother Earth. George felt it strange that he should think of the term, "Mother Earth."

He was alone in the world but he felt no fear. His mother had taught him, "Walk the walk and talk the talk." He knew his chosen path was different from what the majority of society would consider the norm. His mother, a petite woman, had chosen a dangerous path when she entered DEA. She felt that part of her mission was to right the wrongs resulting from the misuse of illegal drugs.

The mortgage on their small home had been paid from a generous life insurance and other DEA benefits. He had a good office job and learned how to invest in the stock market and a few small businesses. He often invested in stocks because he "felt" they would grow. His feelings had been very accurate. He invested the balance of the life insurance benefits, but felt the need to always keep separate accounting of investments of his own money and of the money he received from his mother's death. He was not ready to accept her death and wanted to be able to return the money when his mother was found. Fate and his mother's chosen work had placed him in the eastern United States, but he knew from an early age that his real destiny awaited him back in the wild and untamed west, the land of his birth. Out west where a handshake was a man's bond.

He felt he had acquired most of the historical details about the West in general and Arizona in particular from the dozens of books he read and studied along with hundreds of western movies he watched. He often escaped his real world by pretending that the Louis L'Amour books were factual publications. George had been practicing his "sauntering gate" for years. While others less fortunate hurried past him on their way to work, George took his time, making sure that his legs were slightly bowed and his eyes had a determined look that spoke, without words, "don't mess with this cowboy." He had never really received the respect that he had seen John Wayne or Clint Eastwood receive in the movies, but he knew in his heart it was just a matter of time. Somewhere, deep in his heart, George felt that every person was an intricate part of life and that none were more important than another. He believed that each person should have self-respect and respect others. On this principle he based his own life.

At least once a month, since his father died he would visit the Arlington Cemetery, feel the reverence of that place and kneel by his father's grave. Then at night George would have the same reoccurring dream that came from his father.

"Son, I am with you, you are different, as each of the Master's children are different for a purpose. Always see the best in any person, place, event or circumstance and remain pure from anger, envy, jealousy and pride. Be quick to forgive. If you are offended, stop a moment and ask why you accepted the offense? Then correct the offense from within yourself so you will not be offended again."

George had related these repeated dreams to his mother before her death and never once did she ever display a moment's doubt.

"I am so pleased that you have made contact with your father," she would say.

Each time he recalled a past memory about his mother, he, like most young men, could not believe she was actually gone. He kept waiting for the phone call that would say there had been a mistake and more than anything else, he was dismayed that he had been unable to make contact with his mother, like he had with his deceased father. From the teachings of his father, Laurel and Ruffed Grouse he had learned to abstain from foods in order to get and maintain better control over the physical or natural man. Fasting also served to strengthen the spirit and to improve communication with the spirit world according to Apache teachings that he had learned. Even after fasting, he was still unable to speak to or to see his mother and that left doubt in his heart about her death.

In life it always seemed to him that his mother wanted to say more about dreams and visions, but was waiting for another moment in life when he might have more understanding. After her death, dreams of his father stopped for almost a year. George supposed that his mother and dad were passing the time together in Arizona on the banks of Tonto Creek or the East Verde near Payson where they first lived together. Those thoughts pleased George.

Then early one morning his dad appeared in a dream and repeated the same messages as before with one exception. At the end he added,

"This will be my last visit for a few years. I will come again when you are ready or if you really are in need of my help."

George wanted to ask about his mother, but the dream was gone. He knew he was alone to learn, to gain experience, and to hold true to his feelings.

Every morning George practiced his eye-to-eye contact with himself in the mirror saying without words,

"I respect you, what is your next achievement? Remember always the natural law of abundance. Remember how to attract what you need and want."

On the sidewalks he did the same. He imagined that those who took a moment to look into his eyes became nervous. He learned that most people are unaccustomed to looking into the eyes. George learned of the eyes from a western movie when the hero sheriff was asked,

"How do you know which of the four outlaws will draw first?"

"You see it in their eyes."

Every since that awesome movie, George studied people's eyes. Sometimes it was difficult because he passed hundreds of people every morning and evening. That may have been discouraging to many, but not to George. This just gave him more opportunities to study and to look for the good or the evil eye. He knew it was working because not one person on their way to work ever stopped him and said,

"Draw or die."

It was a good feeling knowing that your eyes were speaking the unspoken words of strength and inner toughness that comes from a hard and experienced life on the western range or in George's case, the life spent studying the hard life in western novels and movies.

Last night when he arrived at his home, which he considered his ranch headquarters, the package he brought back a year ago from his organized tourist bus trip through the lower half of Arizona was ready to be opened. This precious, long-awaited package had been purchased at what was advertised as an Authentic Indian Trading Post on an Arizona freeway. The package had been stored in his closet for almost a year. Waiting to open the package was part of the disciplinary training that he had required of himself. He had heard his mom speak of the patience that his father possessed. In his heart, he knew this package would help him fulfill his true and meaningful destiny and take his rightful place among the great. Now it was time. He had passed the test. With hands trembling from excitement, he opened the package and gazed upon the most beautifully, neatly wrapped and protected white cowboy hat, a 22 X Stetson (The "X" represents the quality furs blended into the hat. Most beaver Stetson hats are three to five "X." A ten "X" is an exceptionally high quality). George had read that the higher the X's the better the quality of the hat. Well, it wasn't really a Stetson. He had really liked the feel of the gray 5 X beaver Stetson but the store manager, "John the Beloved" called John, said to him,

"Try on this great white straw hat with 22 X with two layers special paint."

George tried on the hat and it felt stiff, but anyone knows that 22 X is higher quality than 5 X. He knew also that the two layers of paint would help maintain its shape during the many heavy Arizona rainstorms. In addition, John had explained it was a special paint mixed by the Pima Indians and, most importantly, the white straw was much lighter in weight than the heavy gray Stetson. The Stetson cost much less, but John had given George a "special" deal, because George was an obviously well educated man, in the ways of being a cowboy. The Stetson hat was only $75.00 while the straw hat with the "special price" was $247.00 with the discount included. A full-year later, George smiled at how much he had saved.

The time had come. George, with feelings of nobility of a thousand potentates, stood in front of the mirror, and majestically placed the cowboy crown on his head. He felt the surge of "cowboy power" in every cell of his body. The hat was stiff and rested on both sides of his head but did not touch the front or back. George knew the hat was genuine because John had explained,

"A really good hat requires you to pull the sides apart a little to help it conform to the shape of the head."

There were a few thoughts of doubts about the complete honesty of the salesman John, but George recalled his father's teachings,

"Give every person the benefit of honesty rather than have your heart fall into the pit of non-believers."

As George pulled on the inner sides, little flecks of paint chipped off. That also had been explained. The bona fide design of this hat with "chip scars" causes it to have a western look of having been worn and used in the wild deserts of Arizona. George was delighted.

Next, he reverently lifted the black and white Holstein vest from the package. John was reluctant to part with this vest. He said it represented how the west had accepted the various human races. They had bred their cows to produce black and white calves, so nobody would feel any racism. He also explained that if people were keen enough to observe as they traveled along the highway they would see that the cattle of the west represented every color of human skin. George recalled the bus ride through other parts of the country he saw white animals, some all black, others red and white, red, gray, yellow and spotted animals, which legitimized all John had said. This great man, John the Beloved, knew much about the West and about people in general. He certainly had the talent of isolating a potential westerner such as George. Then he even seemed to encourage the selection of the black and white vest because it could be spotted day or night if by chance someone needed expert help in any given situation.

He looked George in the eye, "You my friend will be of great help."

George recalled the distressing look on John's earnest face as he pulled out a credit card to pay for the authentic cowboy gear. John explained to George that the twenty-five percent discount was available with cash payments only. He pointed to an ATM machine and George withdrew the $2,137.82 in cash to pay for the selected, genuine articles of western wear. The cash register only showed $1,137.82 but John quickly explained that a large percentage of each sale, and in this case one thousand dollars, would be distributed to a needy family. If they placed the money in the registrar, then it would be taxed. With sincerity, John spoke, "if the money is taxed, then less money would reach the hands of the greedy, I mean the needy." Any doubt George might have had about the sincerity of John vanished.

Meanwhile, with the anticipation of a baseball player sliding his hand into his glove before an all-star game, George proceeded to remove the red shirt with the extra large pearl snaps, white trim around the pockets, western tapered cut to display the "wanabe" slim hips and V markings across the back to emphasize the broad shoulders that someday he would have. Snaps were significant on the cowboy shirt because they facilitate the quick removal "if and when" necessary. George did not understand the "if and when" but he felt snaps were a critical part of the indisputable authentic cowboy attire. Consequently, he purchased the largest snaps available. He also bought tight fitting Levis with the original copper rivets in the back, thick gray socks, and a heavy leather belt with the six inch by six-inch buckle. He prided himself on his memory because all cowboy items have a particular reason and vital purpose. Tight pants prevent wrinkles from forming on the sitting side during an all day ride. With loose fitting pants, he was told small wrinkles on the backside would begin to feel like sitting on a one-inch grass rope. This would cause significant pain on the bottom side. The six inch by six inch buckle, which by the way he negotiated a very good deal, much like the hat, is used for defensive purposes and can also be turned over and used to cook bacon and eggs for breakfast while out on the open range, that is if the buckle were not made of "genuine plastic" from Japan.

At last, he took out the three-inch heeled red boots and the still attached spurs with the four-inch rowels. George knew from watching movies that rowels were the rolling part on the back of the spur that is pressed against the horse to make it go. It also made the trademark jingle of a true cowboy as he walked along the wooden sidewalk. The jingle helped to scare off rattlesnakes. The owner of the store explained that a "cowboy" never separates his boots and spurs except on rare occasions that were never talked about, even amongst friends around the campfire. With this important knowledge, George was specific in the shipping instructions that the boots and spurs not be separated for packing and shipping. Even though it was very difficult for John to pack the spurs attached to the boots, for an extra forty dollars he did as instructed. That may seem like a small act to some people, but to George it was significant. This good manager of the "authentic" trading post had not only given George an extra twenty-five percent discount on the $2,137.82 he had spent on this "authentic" western wear, but he also shared much of his hard earned profits with the needy. He also offered the name of "honest Abe" in case George became serious about buying a horse or a working cow ranch or both. John specifically suggested a ranch on the "mighty" Gila River south of Phoenix. After carefully removing and inspecting his authentic cowboy attire, he spent a restless night filled with anticipation of the excitement of the following day. He was as excited as a child on Christmas Eve.

George awoke before sunrise. He joyously, but with a quiet sacredness known only to the "true grit" cowboy, put on each new authentic and significant piece of clothing. This day would go down in history at the office where he worked. Not only was it going to be his last day, he was going to let each and every person see an authentic cowboy and understand what they had missed by not getting to know him better, especially "Pretty Peggy."

George knew this day would be different. Little did he know that it would prove to be even more astonishing than he could ever imagine. He had prepared himself to see what he wanted to see and to feel the joy of standing alone. From the moment he stepped from his car onto the busy sidewalks on his way to the office, George studied the eyes of each individual as they stared with total awe at his authentic western cowboy attire. He could see their respect, not that he deserved more respect than others, but he did feel he deserved respect. Many do nothing to earn it. They just want it. Some were so awed that they immediately turned away or hid their faces. Others were so inspired they grabbed their handkerchiefs to wipe their teary eyes. George was excited beyond measure at the prospect of the wonderment his presence might generate when he would saunter down the hall in the office. He only wished Louis L' Amour could be present to possibly write about this inspiring historical event.

George soon realized why most cowboys live out west in the open areas and why most cowboys are tall. His or her wide brim hats are difficult to wear on a crowded street or in an elevator without bumping the hat against someone else. If he were six feet, six inches tall, or even seven feet, like most cowboys, the brim would not smack others on the shoulders or in the face. Today, even with the three inch cowboy boots the hat rim still hit a few people. It was okay, however, because most of the people gave him plenty of space as they stood back and gaped in awe.

He stepped into the office and as was his custom he spoke with and touched each person in the office, all except one, the unfinished business at the end of the hall. He had written his boss a letter explaining his new interest and the reason he was leaving on such short notice. While he had given the customary two-week notice, he thought he should have given more notice because it would be so difficult to find a replacement for him. He never had the nerve or courage, however, to meet the boss face to face. Actually, he could not meet the boss face to face in the literal sense because George was a tall five foot, ten inches and the boss was a stubby seventy four inches tall. Today would be different. With the three-inch heels on his red cowboy boots and the tall white double painted straw hat with flecks of paint falling, George would look as tall as John Wayne in person and would feel just as dynamic. George tilted the boots back just slightly, enough for the spurs to jingle as the rowels roughly rolled across the painted cement floor. George could see and in his mind interpret the eyes of absolute admiration from every co-worker. His co-workers were in total silence, except for the occasional, uncontrolled, yet muffled burst of what sounded to George like sobbing.

Their envious stares were conspicuous as he sauntered, down the office aisles. Pretty Peggy, who had never even looked his direction, was now gapping wide eyed at this stranger. Yet, he wasn't really a stranger; he had worked five years full-time and two years part-time in the same office delivering mail and supplies to each person almost daily. He knew their names and something personal about each one, but now he looked like an all-new person. Many thought him a stranger. They obviously had heard the news; this was his last day at work. He had not been fired or "down sized." He had chosen to move on to a better life that would more completely fulfill his dreams.

A few of the young ladies became a little hysterical as he moseyed down the aisle. He could hear their sobs and in his mind determined that their hands covered their mouths to muffle the otherwise loud heart-wrenching sadness. Some could not even wait until he had passed. Pretty Peggy, that's what the office staff called her due to her incredibly beautiful smile, sparkling blue eyes, and her self-stated, unequaled organizational ability as the boss's secretary, put her hand over her mouth, turned her back to him and doubled over. She grabbed for tissues as the enormous tears flowed onto the floor. Those less experienced in the reactions between a woman and a handsomely dressed "cowboy" might interpret her doubling over as laughter, but not George. He knew from the moment he purchased the authentic cowboy garb that the girls would absolutely be in total awe. They undoubtedly would enjoy a brief moment in his arms, gaze admirably into his deep blue eyes and wrap their arms around his neck much like the young ladies do in the movies when rescued by Mr. John Wayne from a run-away horse drawn wagon, just before going over the rugged cliff with the jagged rocks.

In front of the mirror, George had practice the Clint Eastwood look, "Make my day" just in case the boss pleaded for him to stay. The "look" worked much better than expected. Before he reached the door the boss stepped out, took one complete look from hat to boots and then again from boots up to the face, when their eyes met the boss immediately returned to his office and shut the door. George could hear the sobs and deep breaths as if the poor man was gasping for air. That was the last time George saw the man, his admiring co-workers or his office.

Nothing more could be said, nothing more could be done as he slowly and with deliberate movements turned to leave. He felt a new confidence as he looked into their eyes, tipped his hat to the ladies and slightly nodded his head in acknowledgement to the gentlemen he had known. This time the silence was different. They realized they were looking at a person that was willing to do his own thing, willing to step out and away, willing to see what was ahead and willing to take the chance. They felt uneasiness in the pit of their stomachs because each of them had wanted to make changes, but lacked the courage. None of them could put on a "cowboy" outfit for fear of ridicule. None of them could walk up to the boss and in a positive way share feelings with him. None of them had felt the joy and satisfaction that radiated from the face of their co-workers and now ex-co-workers. They watched with envy, admiration, shock at their own feelings and puzzlement. George turned, tipped his white straw hat and stepped out the door and out of their lives.

Few people realize what they have until they no longer have it and are unable to get it back. In their minds, they each recalled George's many positive acts, words and actions generated for their individual benefit. Examples of his kindnesses and cheerfulness included a flower

18

or card in time of sadness, a laugh of joy instead of criticism, a pat on the back saying it is okay, the uplifting remark out of a negative situation and his gazing out the window each morning, rain or shine, cold or hot, windy or still, bright or dreary and proclaim.

"Isn't it just the greatest of days?"

They each silently wished him the very best of luck, but fear of what others might think, none dared to speak a word. With the word "luck" on their minds they recalled the non-sermon soft tone of George,

"You don't have luck and you don't get luck, you generate luck."

They were each silently wishing,

"George, we hope you generate endless luck."

Unseen near the boss's desk Peggy placed the flower in her wastebasket; she had never let George know her feelings towards him. Most viewed her as selfish but George always opined that she was kind and gentle. She laughed a little as she saw the look on the others' faces. She thought the man to be ridiculous and he was now gone.

"Good riddance," she said aloud.

She recalled once when he probably thought he was making her feel better as she shared a wish with him about her work. He responded with a smile,

"If wishes were fishes we'd all have a fry, and if horse turds were biscuits we'd eat till we die."

"Off to Dulles International and into the sky away he goes to the unknown he doth fly,"

She said. She smiled as she watched the door close and realized her words rhymed.

2—DULLES INTERNATIONAL

After making a visit to his father's gravesite, George spent a rather restless night. He awoke early ready to enjoy a relaxing day of bus, taxi and airline travel. The seasoned traveler has, on more than one occasion, experienced the numerous and uncanny methods that airports have in generating their own source of authority. These authoritative conglomerates of cement, food smatters, scales, telephones and bewildered people do not require any plastic cards, a PIN (personal identification numbers), other forms of identification or even a name to effect withdrawals of patience, understanding, goodwill and calmness from the depths of the human soul. To the non-seasoned traveler, airports may also activate a reverse withdrawal system, and without requiring permission begin to make deposits of doubts, wrong tickets, wrong lines, wrong levels, wrong terminal, wrong airline, wrong clothing or what was left at home. For the non-seasoned traveler or the first-time travelers who think of themselves as seasoned travelers, airports seem to test the innermost fiber and to expose the deepest frailties and the deepest of unknown phobias. An innocent looking airport can inevitably test a person who views the glass, "half full or half empty." George views the glass as half full and is always grateful. Now he enters Dulles International. There were other airports closer to where George lived, however he chose Dulles for reasons unknown to even himself.

George thought himself a seasoned traveler; due to the many hours he had carefully studied travel instructions sponsored by various airlines on the Internet and from brochures provided by local travel agencies. He learned from the airlines "how easy it is to travel," "the world is yours," "travel as easy as one, two, three" and of course the polite invitation, "please be at the airport two hours early to allow a calm and orderly processing of your travel plans and luggage." Also, it was mentioned, "for your *personal safety* there will be a quick inspection of your carry-on, and you might incur a slight delay at the security check-in area, however, this is only for your *personal protection*." He was appreciative that the airline was so concerned about his personal travel plans, luggage and safety. It was also mentioned to "check-in" all unnecessary items or clothing with your luggage. The various brochures even illustrated the best methods of folding, rolling and ever so meticulously packing a suitcase or in his case, suitcases, with a large plural.

It seemed very rational to him that the probability of finding a nice, clean, and well-equipped ranch headquarters would probably be in a somewhat remote area. So, the logical thing would be to pack a small suitcase for everyday of the week. Thusly, he could unpack Tuesday's clean clothes and put Monday's dirty clothes in Tuesday's suitcase. This was his own genius idea and he was chest-puffing proud. It would be no problem to carry seven pieces of luggage, even though the airlines suggested carrying only two suitcases. He had also read, "if more are necessary for the fullest enjoyment of your trip, you could bring additional luggage for *only a slight charge.*"

George selected an early morning flight believing that there would be fewer people at the airport and that he would arrive in Arizona early in the morning. George felt content with himself because of his ability to reason details, fewer people, less traffic, early morning in Arizona, cool summer mornings in Phoenix and, last, but certainly not the least, the early flight, due to the time changes, would give him all day to explore at least a part of the "Wild West" or the "Untamed" sectors of Arizona.

The evening before his departure was spent packing, rearranging, and packing, then rearranging reading and re-reading the brochures on packing. The brochures were so picture clear. They showed suitcases being neatly packed and shut without needing to sit on top. Finally, George concluded that the pictures distorted that amount of clothes that were really in each suitcase; however, he did see a strap around a suitcase for added security. From a local hardware store, that was open 24-7, he was able to get a two-inch wide nylon strap used for strapping machinery on truck trailers. He wanted leather, which would have been more suited for the west, but no store in his neighborhood seemed to have leather tie-down straps. The manager suggested the nylon straps with a ratchet-type tightening device. With straps connected around the suitcase, he began to ratchet the suitcases closed until each was securely latched, never to be opened again until he was in his ranch house in Arizona. He looked at the suitcases with a sense of accomplishment. All of his worldly possessions packed and wrapped in seven suitcases.

With two suitcases on top, two in the trunk and three in the back seat of the taxi, George headed for airport. At least, George hoped he was headed for the airport. The taxi driver spoke a very foreign language and on the basis of the driver's speed and the number of times he drove through yellow and red lights, he was obviously color blind. George could tell he was not speaking Spanish or Texican, the only foreign languages with which he was a little familiar. With the possibility of miscommunication, George was not sure if the driver had understood his request to go to the airport and the particular gate number. So, he showed the driver a brochure indicating travel and an airplane. He then sat back to enjoy what could possibility be his final ride through the streets of Washington, D.C. He wanted to absorb this street-level view of the nation's capital before arriving at Dulles International. After crossing the third bridge, George became suspicious that the driver was taking the long way to the airport. He attempted to communicate orally, and with hand gestures, fingers, eyes and an increase in volume. Finally, the cabbie pulled to the side of the highway and with slur of never-ending words pointed to the brochure. Indeed there was a picture of a beautiful passenger jet rising to the sky. However, there was also a picture of a saguaro cactus and the name ARIZONA right across the top. The cab was on the wrong side of the freeway heading in the wrong direction towards Arizona.

George remained calm. He had left earlier than required. So, he had plenty of time to unload the seven suitcases, cross the busy road and hail a cab. The first cab that approached stopped; it was the same cab and driver.

"Why did you make me get out?"

"You wanna go bac to Dulles, I drive away so you git out, Now I go bac direction of airport so you git in." That seemed somewhat reasonable to George.

Shortly they arrived at the unloading zone. Security guards swarmed the little cab as the mid-east driver still ranting and raging about the mix up emerged and began to hastily unload the seven suitcases strapped with large ratchet type straps. Then, when they saw the large white hat and the red western leather boots with gosh awful spurs rolling and ringing on the asphalt they froze in their tracks. They looked at each other and placed a hand on their revolvers. George appreciated the help they appeared to offer. One of the men, however, talked into a radio, and when the radio squawked back they all disappeared.

George thought, "Must have been an emergency somewhere."

The security scarcely had vanished, when from within the crevices of the walls appeared men and women from the U.S. Military. It was impressive to witness firsthand how well the camouflaged uniforms blend in with the cement walls; multi-color suits and dresses worn by passengers and the dark asphalt. George stood in total awe as they surrounded the cab. The young driver fell to his knees and then put his face on the concrete sidewalk. Something, he had obviously practiced many times in his native country.

A Marine grabbed each suitcase and carried it into a nearby parked, all steel van. George reached to tip his hat in appreciation, when a young, large, six foot, four inch Marine with short hair and a one inch steel rod for a back and neck bone looked down at the future John Wayne of Arizona and growled. The young marine's size alone was a shock. The first growl spit out the last part of the uneaten portion of the horseshoe that he had for breakfast. The growl caused George to believe that this young warrior had lost his vocal capacity. The second growl rumbled out of the depths of an inner cavern and sounded like a growl that a twelve hundred pound grizzly bear would make. Out with the growl came the commanding words that could not be misunderstood. "Don't move. Keep your hands were I can see them."

George froze with his hand still four inches from the brim of his white painted hat. He thought he was the beneficiary of a marine custom of respect. The young grizzly never lost eye contact, as he slowly reached and removed the 20 X, painted, straw hat that slightly curved at both side brims. "Impressive" was the only word that came to George's mind. George thought this young man, out of admiration for this "cowboy," slowly examined the hat, even looking closely at the brand and the leather interior band. Meanwhile, his comrades reviewed each suitcase with great care. They slowly unlatch each nylon strap. The release of the pressure from the tightly shut suitcases caused them to fly open. This flattened a few marines on the sidewalk. Those not flattened jumped back with apparent delight at seeing Levis, Wranglers, shirts and gray jockey underwear leap from the compressed suitcases, as if they each were alive and happy to be free.

George thanked these young, proud marines for being so helpful as they forced each suitcase shut, and placed it on a cart. They gave him an escort to the ticket counter where each suitcase was weighed. After paying $198.66 for excessive weight and items, he was given his ticket and suitcase stubs. The stubs indicated that his luggage would arrive at nine a.m. sharp at Sky Harbor Airport in Phoenix, Arizona with the adjusted time change. After checking the current time, he realized that the slight miscommunication with the taxi driver and the unexpected assistance by the marines had shortened his "relax and enjoy the airport" time by about one hour and twenty minutes. However, according to the Internet map and printed timetable, he was only about ten minutes from the departing gate. He would just hustle to his assigned area and then enjoy the airport ambiance.

The over-head flashing sign read, "for you security and safety a short delay might occur at the security check point. Thank you for your co-operation." The sign continued to repeat the message as George involuntarily followed the masses around the corner where he witnessed a genuine people traffic jam. Multiple, undesignated lines of passengers stood in front of upside down, U-shaped metal objects. As each person approached they would remove watches, pens, coins, and glasses. The women would have their purses X-rayed and sometimes emptied. George again smiled at his ability to comprehend the information on the Internet and brochures; he did not carry one extra item. With the black and white leather vest, white hat and standing in close proximity to eight hundred thousand warm bodies, he began to perspire just a little. At last, it was his turn.

He purposely bowed his legs a little more than normal, leaned a bit on the heels of the red leather boots so the rowels would jingle on the cement floor, and as he tipped his white hat, he stepped through the metal arch. As security guards and a number of the fine young, uniformed men and women rushed to greet him, he thought: "This favorable greeting is nothing less than remarkable."

They asked him to step to one side. He beamed as they asked him for his hat and spurs, he watched as they studied the hat and spurs with great interest. Next, they asked him to remove his boots. He had noticed a couple of uniformed young ladies intensely eyeing his red boots. He was pleased that they wanted a closer inspection of the fine quality. They were all very polite as they asked one line of waiting passengers to step back and allow him another opportunity to walk through the electronic arches.

Again, the bell and buzzer sounded. He was delighted when the military and security police came to his side to escort him to a private chamber. He wondered if he was the 100,000th person to pass the checkpoint. He wondered what the door prize would be. With big windows and open doors, the room was not very comfortable. They passed over his clothes with some form of a magic wand that generated its own sound. He was asked to remove his shirt. That was very understandable with the over-sized snaps; they probably wanted to enjoy a closer look and touch the smooth pearl octagons. The wand was again passed over the remaining clothes and it seemed all were delighted that the wand responded with amusing buzzing. They gathered up his shirt, boots, spurs and hat and asked him to follow him to the "special guest" room.

The sun light from the ceiling high windows seemed to enter illegally and reveal otherwise concealed occupants. An officer with jaws designed from square steel plates and enough awards to cover his barn side wide chest stood in one corner of the room holding a clear Tupperware tray full of various metal objects. Looking at his size, his face and the way he was grasping the tray, George wondered if those metal objects were a part of his high protein diet.

"Why are you sweating?" were the first guttural sounds that gushed through clinched teeth.

George supposed this was a trick question as he thought, "It is ninety five degrees with ninety eight percent humidity. There are thousands of people packed together and I am wearing a leather vest." That was so obvious; he assumed this officer must have been asking for more profound answer.

"Sir, the evaporation of perspiration helps cool the body and…" The answer was cut short.

"You must be well trained? You remain so calm while trying to penetrate the world's most advanced security check station with highly trained U.S. Military." George thought it a strange question after receiving such an exciting welcome and with such enthusiastic young soldiers attending to his every need. Nevertheless, before he could answer, Mr. Steel Jaws stepped closer and spoke directly into George's sweaty face.

"It is on rare occasions that we get someone with your brass walking so calmly into our reception."

George recalled during a few of his father's dreams: "Son, it is important that you remain calm, never let what others do or say become a negative, there is always good in every existence, every word and every action." These dreams had become such an intricate part of George's life; actually they were a part of his very being. People often misunderstood and could not believe his reactions or his actions.

Thus, he in complete truthfulness felt he had understood the question. Therefore, he was elated that there were truly so few "authentic cowboys" that pass through this area and that he would be considered such a "rare occasion" so as to warrant such special attention.

"Well sir." George spoke to express his gratitude. Once again his comments were cut short.

The steel jaws, just below dark green eyes dancing with excitement, opened and spoke: "remove your belt, your pants and your socks! I would like to review them."

"What an honor! This specially trained uniformed officer would take such interest in a legitimate cowboy uniform," George thought, as he stood barefoot in his gray jockey shorts. He was happy that he had taken the extra time to buy the most genuine western cowboy garb.

Two female soldiers, not in the form fitting uniforms seen on television, wearing baggy camouflaged drapery that indeed camouflaged the female anatomy, entered the room. George smiled and was glad that Pretty Peggy did not wear such clothing.

After five or ten minutes of continual saluting, between the six and now eight soldiers, the young ladies short of breath from running, reported to Lt. Colonel Bones.

"Sir, we found this in his luggage."

George learned that "Mr. Steel Jaws" had a name, Lt. Colonel Bones. George sensed somewhere deep inside that this would not be his only encounter with Lt. Colonel Bones. He felt that Lt. Colonel Bones would fulfill an important role in George's life.

The young ladies handed Bones a pamphlet that George had purchased. "Safety Steps in Using Dynamite." The steel plated face could smile.

Yes, he could smile. As he leafed through the book that explained how to use Dynamite, cut lengths and types of fuse, crimp caps and detailed instructions on how to safely use dynamite to help remove tree stumps, Lt. Colonel Bones smiled. His broad smile was so contagious that all present began to smile, even George Ribit Chattit.

With green eyes sparkling with joy and a grin spreading from ear to ear revealing yellowish teeth, Lt. Colonel Bones stepped close to George. "Is your cause worth the ultimate sacrifice?"

George smiled as he thought, "I left my job, a girl that I cared for, and my apartment and I am traveling into the unknown and into parts of the unchartered west." "Yes Sir!" With that response the commander grinned even more dramatically, causing the upper edges of the smile to actually touch both ear lobes.

"Fellow, you just won a free physical exam from the United States Government." George was astonished at the care offered by these kind gentlemen and ladies. He wondered if all genuine cowboys were treated with such honor and personal service. He was given an olive green bathrobe and escorted by three military men and two military women into another office with two doctors and three nurses.

He marveled, "This is unbelievable, the amount of tax dollars spent to insure that this 'rare' cowboy was healthy." He speculated that cowboys must be on the endangered list. The doctors checked his pulse, eyes and ears, but were particularly thorough with any and all body crevices. The doctor commented to the leader of the camouflaged group,

"No sticks of dynamite anywhere." George understood the comment to be joke and expected a laugh but decided that camouflaged uniforms prevented such displays of humor.

After the physical examination and what seemed to be questions beyond numbering, they called his former boss, checked his driver's license and authenticated his passport. He had earlier obtained a passport, just in case it was required to fly into a foreign destination such as Phoenix International. As information was compiled, these camouflaged soldiers must have earned a "coffee break." They relaxed and even laughed a little as George got dressed with his hat, red western cut shirt with the oversized snaps and dark gray pants with red lined pockets that matched his red leather boots.

Two soldiers and two security ladies had been studying books and computers, all the while holding and examining the large rowel spurs. They kept mumbling something like, "They are not on the list of deadly weapons and I can't find a picture. However, they are made of metal and are kind of sharp."

"Yes, I looked under rowel, spur, horse equipment, cowboys and boot accessories, but could not locate anything under deadly arms or explosives. They are listed in the dictionary so they are legit."

George thought they must have been studying the value of the spurs for insurance purposes because they then requested that he allow them to ship the spurs and the six-inch belt buckle along with his luggage. He agreed and was a little embarrassed; he should have realized that spurs on a passenger plane could cut the carpet although that fact was not mentioned in any of the travel brochures.

George mentioned to Lt. Colonel Bones that he was a few hours late for the scheduled flight.

"Mr. Chattit, we apologize for the inconvenience and will assist you in the earliest possible flight to Phoenix."

The commander, in an extremely serious voice questioned George and then extended an invitation. "Young man, I do not know who you are, what your background is, nothing about your parents or your education. But if you ever decide to make a change in careers, I extend a personal invitation and would be honored to recommend you for officer training."

This gentlemen officer picked up an airport phone, and with great politeness conjured into his gruff military voice, introduced himself, "This is Lt. Colonel Bones of the United States Special Services, you will have a ticketed passenger named George Ribit Chattit accompanied by Sgt. Thins on your next flight to Phoenix and they will be the last to board. They will sit in the front row of first class, they will be fed and served soft drinks and they will be the first to disembark in Phoenix."

George smiled and thought, "One-sided phone conversations are most interesting."

The kind officer continued, "No, they will not be armed. No, they are not known terrorist. No, they were not scheduled to fly first class." He paused. "Then call someone who can authorize this request." Lt. Colonel Bones was used to having his orders carried out to the letter. It was apparent that someone was challenging his request, but more devastating, challenging his authority.

"You ask who my boss is? My ultimate boss is the President of the United States. No, this is not a hoax. Miss I am not accustomed to being questioned in this manner. No, I am not married. What does that have to do with this line of questioning?" It was one of the most perplexed faces ever seen on this steel jawed Lt. Colonel. "What do you mean, I would understand these questions if I were married. Miss it is... How do I know you are a Miss? I guess I don't know. Oh, you are a Miss and your name is B. Hardy. Great, now Miss Hardy, would you please arrange to have them sit in first class? Oh you will because I said the magic word. So if I were to march down there and ask you for a date I would have to use the magic word, please? What, tomorrow evening at 6 pm.? Yes, may I please have the honor of escorting you to dinner and a movie? Thank you, I look forward to meeting you. Are you busy now? Oh you are on the flight to Phoenix."

"Wipe those grins off your faces. You, Sgt. Thins, will disregard the previous order and you will be the officer in charge while I am out of the office. How long? Until I relieve you. I will personally escort this possible desperado to Phoenix. Let's go, and soldiers, try not to be conspicuous!"

George, Lt. Colonel Bones and six camouflaged escorts *inconspicuously* proceeded to the giant American D-C 10 to fly first class to Phoenix. George was honored to have met such fine young people serving their country and displaying such interest in a cowboy as authentic as Mr. John Wayne.

As per his authoritative command with "please" added, all the passengers were boarded. Then a fine looking lady in her mid-thirties approached wearing a spotless blue uniform and, to George's delight, red high heel shoes. She stopped and he supposed she was going to give the usual inspection upon seeing a western dressed cowboy. Instead, she stopped, and gave a detailed inspection to Lt. Colonel Bones, taking in every inch of his six foot two inch frame from his shining black boots, his billboard chest and finally to his perfectly groomed crew cut. Then she fixed her gaze on his astonished, wide green eyes and to the amazement of all present, she winked at this steel straight Lt. Colonel causing him to promptly turn almost as red as her patent leather, red shoes. With no additional introductions and with the simple wave of her white-gloved hand, she dismissed the six young soldiers, who were trying not to demolish their careers by bursting out in laughter. She then escorted the bona fide cowboy and the red-faced officer to first-class accommodations and recharged the glowing red face by brushing her white glove across his flattop hair.

"Do you, Lt. Colonel Bones, have a first name?"

"Name is John Paul miss, but I go by Lt. Colonel."

"Okay John Paul, shall I help you with your seat belt?"

She had him positioned in a perfect upright stance with the calves of his legs tight against the front of the seat, so that with the slightest push with her unringed left hand the broad shouldered, top-heavy Lt. Colonel fell clumsily into the wide first-class seat.

"I asked you, do you need help with your seat belt?"

The square steel jaws were chemically altered to become like Jell-O that could only bounce open and shut without uttering a word.

Without hesitation she bent down to buckle the seat strap, this of course allowed her shiny dark red hair to brush against his face, which in some astonishing miracle became even redder. She gently patted the top of his perfect flattop hair. "Be a good little soldier and listen to what I have to say."

In less than two minutes George witnessed a full-uniformed Lt. Colonel be demoted to a Private and obey every order from a uniformed civilian.

3—SKY HARBOR

THE AMERICAN DC-10 lifted off the runway. George took one last look at the Atlantic Ocean shoreline. The view of the Washington skyline quickly diminished as the plane rose in altitude. At last, George was headed for Phoenix, Arizona.

He remembered riding the bus along miles and miles of what appeared to be Arizona's sandy shoreline. George presumed that roads were never constructed close to the Arizona Ocean for safety reasons. As flat as most parts were on the southern part of the state he remembered thinking, if roads were built very close to the water's edge, one high tide would inundate most of the area. He had planned last summer to visit the Pacific Ocean along California's shore. George took too many unscheduled stops and spent too much time at places that were not on his itinerary. George ran out of time at El Centro, California, so he got off of the tour bus and found a bus headed east.

At least he had seen part of California. Truthfully, he was not overly impressed. It appeared to be mostly alfalfa and sand. At times, he wasn't even sure he was in California as most of the people in that area spoke Spanish.

He was impressed, however, with the Colorado River. When he looked on the map to locate the Colorado River, he also saw the Gila River. He assumed that it flowed like the Colorado River. He was really excited to see a river of that size running through the middle of the Arizona desert. The Gila River must have a large flow as it starts in New Mexico, flows through Arizona and apparently ends up joining with the Colorado and on into Mexico. He really couldn't determine exactly where the Gila River ended. Maybe it just vanished into the desert like some old prospector in movies or stories.

What impressed him even more, just in case nobody else noticed, was that Gila begins with a "G" and River begins with an "R." Likewise,

George begins with a "G" and Ribit begins with an "R." He felt the lump swell deep in his chest as he realized the significance. The name of this river còrrelated with his name. "Yes," he thought, "the Wild West, with a mighty river coursing through the middle, was where he would fulfill his greatest accomplishments." He believed in spiritual life before birth. The matching of his first two initials to the initials for Gila River made him certain that there was a plan that would help him become the "Gila River Cowboy." At once, he also realized that the initials for Gila River Cowboy, perfectly match his own initials. There was no doubt about what he should do and what he should become.

After these pleasant thoughts, he fell into that state between being fully awake and fully asleep. It is that state when dreams are most vivid. In this state, he wondered, "how and where will this huge DC-10 land in old Arizona before a modern airport was built? The dream began to mix with reality. He retraced his journey during the trip last summer. He saw towns like Yuma, Gila Bend, Casa Grande, Benson, and Wilcox as they were in the Wild West days. His thoughts took him back to the special detour through St. David to go to Tombstone where he saw the famous OK Corral. He shivered again as he remembered his feelings standing on the very wood plank walk ways where many of his cowboy heroes had walked. He imagined what it would be like to walk on those planks, bow legged, worn leather chaps, weather cracked boots and spurs. With just the perfect tilt of the ankle the spurs would touch the wood planks causing the metal prongs to vibrate which results in a ringing sound. This sound must be associated with the Diamond Back Rattle Snake which, when it rattles, says without words, "out of my way."

With the possible exception of Tucson, through which he had slept, none of those towns were populated enough to support a large airport, he reasoned in his dream. He could see that each town had sufficient open space to build a fifty-mile runway in any direction. Now he was flying in one of the largest passenger planes that probably required fifty miles to land and it was heading for Phoenix. George wondered if Phoenix, as part of the last western frontier, would have a runway long enough to accommodate such an aircraft. Well, he was hopeful that the American Airline owners would have checked out the possible landing sites before taking off. This was a logical conclusion. So, he felt assured that landing would not be a problem.

Yet, because the dream seemed so real, when he awoke, he momentarily was not sure where he was. The power of the dream left him in doubt as to where the airplane would land in Phoenix. There was not much about Arizona or the Sky Harbor Airport in the many brochures he read. Most of the brochures showed the sun setting behind the giant saguaro. He quickly realized the foolishness of his doubt. Then, he dozed again and fell into the same state as before. His heart's desire was to be a cowboy in the old west. This desire was invading his dream. As the dream continued, he also supposed that there would be thousands of people waiting and gazing at the newly constructed runway to see such a plane land. This size plane would be such a novelty in the west. He speculated about what type of modern hitching rail they built along the airport to tie horses and buggies so other ranchers and "sod busters" could come and see how the east moved their people. He wondered how they could train their horses to cope with such noise created by jet propulsion. He wished he had studied more details about the village of Phoenix. Then he awoke again. He laughed to himself at the notion that Phoenix was still an old west town and that commercial flying was a novelty.

The flight was peaceful and he continued to doze on and off. The multitude of visits from children, who came to see an authentic cowboy and ask questions, interrupted his dream that seemed to continue each time he dozed. Miss Hardy the first class flight attendant and newfound friend of Lt. Colonel Bones announced over the speakers, "it seems we have a relative of John Wayne or Clint Eastwood traveling in first class and would be happy to answer questions pertaining to the Wild West."

Fortunately for George, he knew just about all there was to know about being a cowboy. He had read so many novels and seen most western movies ever made. Later, he realized Miss Hardy might have had an ulterior motive. With the youngsters filling the first class area and asking questions to both Lt. Colonel Bones and him, the commander felt uneasy. He was very pleased when Miss Hardy invited him to the flight attendants' lounge. George was very pleased to see the colonel smile and blush frequently. George was so enamored with Lt. Colonel Bones and Miss Hardy that before deplaning, he invited both to visit his future ranch.

"Just go south of Phoenix. When you cross the Gila River stop at the trading post and they will give you directions. I don't have a specific direction because I have not yet found a ranch to buy."

They shook hands and saluted, "George" the Lt. Colonel spoke, "if you ever need the military, just call me. I have plenty of pull with the military brass and many owe me huge favors." Then with a glowing red blush he mumbled, "I might soon have a little pull with American Airlines too."

George was absolutely correct! He was greeted warmly and everyone seemed to make eye contact and give a nod in his direction. Perhaps, his dream was closer to reality that he thought. Maybe, the western people were astonished to have this giant plane arrive, as if this were an uncommon occurrence. He was thrilled to be a part of this history-making event. Then, he chuckled to himself again. Obviously, the people of Phoenix were accustomed to commercial flying. George was not accustomed to the eye contact and the greeting nods. People in New York and Virginia where he had lived most of his life never acted this way. He was having so much fun with the dream that he continued to imagine the reaction of the other people in the airport who were seeing jets for the first time. There were thousands of people at the airport called Sky Harbor, but few had time to speak because, he imagined, they were all in such a hurry to find a window or try to get a closer look at this magnificent DC-10. The leaders of Phoenix must have anticipated the plane's arrival. They correctly predicted that thousands would want to come and participate and give a warm welcome to the return of the authentic cowboy to the Arizona territory. They had made and were making an effort to construct buildings and add additional parking. They even attempted to construct highways to accommodate the masses. They apparently did not allow enough time, however, because they were still constructing several projects. George surmised that the projects were so enormous that they would not have been finished, even if they had many additional years. How sad, now they would probably stop building until the next jumbo plane was scheduled to arrive. One thing that Sky Harbor had in common with Dulles was the number of police officers, security guards and military personnel. He let the daydream end.

He did find that in reality, Arizonans were warmer than people back east. People in general were thrilled to see an authentic cowboy step from the plane, many shook his hand, others stared in amazement and others froze in their tracks as he took the time to tip his white painted straw hat at the ladies. He was a little disappointed that the western dress code was not required within the boundaries of the airport. It astonished him how many of the young ladies wore very short shorts. He thought that must create a terrible rash on the upper inner parts of the legs on long horse rides. Occasionally, as he made his way through the wide aisles, he would spot another genuine cowboy. He almost got slapped as he closely studied the rear anatomy of three well dress cowgirls in tight fitting jeans. The western novels explained that you could spot a genuine cowboy or cowgirl because their rear ends contoured to the shape of the saddle. He was certain that these three ladies were authentic cowgirls. He knelt to get a closer look at their rear portions that must have been poured into the colorful jeans. After closer appraisal, he was certain that, even though nicely formed, these tight fitted jeans did not uphold the saddle formed look described in the novels. The girls, however, were very interested in George's knowledge and even called a uniformed officer to come and inquire as to his keen interest in their rear anatomies.

George was overwhelmed at the sincere desire these fine ladies, as well as the official, had in learning more about him, his visit, his clothes and how soon he would be leaving the airport. Other security personnel quickly surrounded him, apparently out of curiosity. They suggested that George accompany them to another room for a short visit. He deduced that they would want him to go to a private room. Once others knew of his knowledge about horses and rear compartments of tight fitting jeans, it could cause delays from the large crowds that would gather out of curiosity. Already, there was an enormous crowd gathering to listen and learn what this "authentic cowboy" had to say.

Before the security could move him to a private room, a loud authoritative voice filled the entire terminal and did not require the use of any electronic speakers.

"This is Lt. Colonel Bones of the United States Marines, Special Forces. George Ribit Chattit is at this very moment under scrutiny and being escorted by a member of the Special Forces, thank you for your cooperation in dispersing the crowd."

George had learned that sometimes even when you do not have authority; the voice of authority gives you the necessary authority to over ride the actions of those who do have the authority. The crowd dispersed to allow George, Miss Hardy, and Bones to proceed to the lower level to retrieve George's luggage.

Miss Hardy told George she would indeed visit his ranch someday and Lt. Colonel Bones assured him that the entire U.S. Military service was at his command. The two of them had no luggage so they said their good-byes to George, held each other by the hand and eagerly escaped though the tinted doors.

While waiting for his seven suitcases to arrive (one for each day of the week), he watched television so he could learn more about the local people and local news. Suddenly, his body seemed to shake with the inner excitement comparable to winning a colossal lottery. He was transfixed, as the television screen seemed to enlarge with the commercial of a real cowboy seated on top of a Brahma bovine saying, "This ain't no bull." Right there, with thousands of people trying to see the jumbo jet, "Tex" personally answered George's non-verbalized question. "How does a real western, rowel dragging, hat wearing cowboy with a treasured Holstein black and white vest move around in the vast wilderness of the west?" There existed no doubt that a cowboy needed his horse. Now, George learned that a Ford pickup truck would be just as valuable. He recalled that as he flew in on the giant DC-10 he could see that this "Wild West" had many cement roads that obviously connected to each other and extended for endless miles. With his vast studies and acquired knowledge of horses and keen natural horse sense it was deducted that riding or running a horse with steel horseshoes on a cement road could be very crippling to the horse and in most cases also for the rider. There on the screen was his answer, "Tex."

George knew immediately that "Tex" was authentic. "Tex," owner of the largest Ford dealership in Arizona and possibly the world, was casually sitting astride what appeared to be a 2,000-pound Brahman bull, known to be one of the toughest and meanest range grazers in the west. Tex had mentioned that it really was not a bull, but the camera angle never revealed the truth of that statement. For those

not acquainted with the difference between a bull and a steer. George remembered that his mother explained to him that it had something to do with the way the animal bawls. A bull bawls differently. It is rare to hear a steer bawl. Living in the populated east he was unable to really determine for himself the difference, but he was certainly going to learn.

"Tex" mentioned that an F-150 would do a job perfectly for most people. For the real man, however, the bigger, stronger F-250 was the match. Then, through the mud, dust, cactus, river, mountain, forest, cliffs, snow and rocks, emerged "the truck of trucks" to prove the point completely. This manly of a man's truck, this brute of a brute's truck, after the mud, dust and cactus did not even have a scratch or a speck of dirt. It rolled to a stop in front of a glamorous resort. A gorgeous cowgirl stepped out, apparently having driven the truck through all of the rugged terrain. She took this hunk of a cowboy by the arm and said, "This is my man and this is my man's truck." "Tex" appeared once again and seemingly looked personally into George's eyes and spoke, "George, you are a man's man, you are as untamed as the wild west, you are as independent as a roaming mustang, you are going to operate your own spread, and you want to win Pretty Peggy's heart, you must have this even bigger, still more manly, F-350 Power Stroke Diesel 6 X 6 with dual tires." George was amazed of how personal "Tex" made this commercial. That was the answer to the question, "how do I move my soon to be owned horse from place to place?" The purchase of the horse would have to wait a day or two, right now there was a Ford F-350 just calling for George Ribit Chattit

When he was but a young child walking hand in hand with his dad he recalled a serious learning experience as his dad kneeled to be eye level. "Son, there is much to be learned from books and lectures, however, those are words and interpretations of someone else. Real learning comes from what you experience from life."

George had read much about the intense heat of the Arizona sun and was quite excited to feel the warmth on his eastern winter white face and arms. Stepping from the air conditioned Sky Harbor Airport into the one hundred and ten degree heat mixed with exhaust fumes was a shock that was not explained in the brochures.

"Enjoy the warmth of the Arizona sun." "Feel the pleasure as beautiful sunrays skip across your skin." "Fill your lungs with the healthful warm air." He vaguely recalled the printed lines as his eyes instantaneously dehydrated, his mouth filled with dry cotton and his lily-white face swiveled to a dried prune. "Yes dad," he thought, "knowing from a book is not quite the same as feeling it in person."

4—THE MANLY
MAN'S TRUCK

THE TAXI PULLED to a slow stop in front of the terminal. When the driver saw two loaded carts, a large brimmed white hat, chaps, vest, belt buckle, and red boots, and heard the apparent owner whistling "Home on the Range," he tried to escape. He failed in his attempt. The ever-alert police trying to prevent suicidal bombings blocked him.

Unable to escape, the driver said, "May please I to be servicio for to you."

George smiled, "It seems the taxi drivers in Phoenix also speak a foreign language."

Loading the trunk, the back seat, and then the roof luggage carriage, the small taxi became an unplanned low rider and cautiously proceeded to the infamous "Tex" and to the home of the "no bull."

"I for to take you to my friend Señor 'Tex.' He be known for my family many years now, I tell to you he be good man."

George was impressed by how well known "Tex" was and how quickly the taxi arrived. There were many sparks and loud noise from the now low rider undercarriage of the taxi as it veered off Baseline Road into the drive of the world's largest Ford dealership.

It was evident that "Tex" spoke the truth when he said, "if you don't buy from me, we both lose money." He had every make and model of vehicle that was manufactured, Ford, VW, Dodge, RV, Trailers, Japanese, etc., it was evident that he did not want anybody to lose money.

When George stepped out of the taxi, a horde of salespeople swarmed him as if he were giving out hundred dollar bills. Yes, it was clear that "Tex" did not want anyone to lose money by buying somewhere else. These good-hearted salespeople each grabbed a suitcase and had the taxi unloaded in a matter of seconds and kindly informed the driver that he need not wait. George received a plethora of business cards within the first few seconds and each salesperson offered more cookies and cokes.

Then across the hot blacktop walked a woman that George was certain had been the one that stepped out of the polished truck on television. She was very thin and wore tight fitting pink, western-cut pants. She didn't have a cowgirl swagger or any hint of bow legs. The side-to-side swivel of her hips, however, occupied at least double her width as she walked towards the group. Her smile showed bright shining, white teeth that reflected the sun. They were perfectly framed with radiant, glossy-red lipstick. The other salesmen created a perfect aisle for her to glide through toward George. The young lady held all of George's attention. He stood tall on his three-inch heeled boots. He could not have realized that exciting moments could so very quickly alter the clear and concise picture that one might have in one's mind.

"Hello, Cowboy," spoke the Cowgirl. George was thrilled that the first lady he met in Arizona recognized him as the indisputable genuine article. She eyed him from top to bottom with a pleasant smile. "Nice wears," she spoke with the low voice that seemed to crawl out over her tongue, just a little louder than a whisper. She pointed to a specially design golf cart that was sitting under the shaded canopy.

"Hop in Cowboy and I'll take you for a ride, a ride you won't soon forget."

George tipped his white hat as he felt the skin on his cheeks being stretched back to his ears with a wide uncontrolled grin. "Yes Ma'am," he stammered. His intentions were clear. Broaden his shoulders, hold his head up high and strut with a cowboy sway towards the polished leather seat cart.

He instantaneously gained new knowledge that abruptly altered the very best of his intentions to look like a cowboy in control. He had not noticed that his overly large spurs and unusually long narrow cowboy boot heels had sunk into the softened asphalt. The asphalt softened from the hot Arizona summer sun gripped his boots like a hungry alligator. George was headed from vertical to flat. Luckily for George, the saleslady turned around to investigate the guttural groan she heard above the passing diesel trucks, motorized golf carts and the astonished laughter coming from the other salesmen. With cat-like reflexes, she pivoted on the balls of her high heel shoes, at the precise moment that George's outstretched arms engulfed her petite body. Twenty-two salespeople, well trained to never miss an opportunity, dove behind the young lady to ease her tumble. Two of the quickest moving salespeople were flat on their backs with the young lady lying prone across their bodies. Their smiles of opportunity quickly vanished as the egg cooking, hot blacktop penetrated their once, white shirts and thin dress pants. The young lady quickly arose leaving the gallant gentlemen on the hot asphalt. The eager salesmen quickly pulled the boots and spurs out of the black top and flashed perfectly orchestrated smiles.

The young lady swished her hair back, "I compliment you. This is the first time that particular move, from a sober man, has been tried." He was not sure what she meant but he took her comment as a compliment.

Even though "Tex's" car-lot was only about half a square mile, it seemed she drove about twenty-two miles in the golf cart weaving in and out, in front and behind and side to side of approximately three thousand vehicles without ever leaving the premise, George was about to give up the search.

She understood and softly touched his arm, "Cowboy, when the going gets rough, the real cowboys get tough." With that thought, she sped around the last turn.

Suddenly, the heavens opened and specially sent sun rays descended upon the "truck." Music filled George's ears. He could not believe his own eyes, a bright red, F-350 Power Stroke Diesel, 6 X 6 with dual tires, and polished chrome wheels gleamed and glistened. It seemed to scream, "Here I am." He was overwhelmed that "Tex" had such direct connection with the Almighty to have Him open up the heavens and beam rays of light directly over the truck of trucks. Of course he took this as a sign that it was destiny to own the truck and to become an authentic western cowboy driving the truck of trucks, built "Ford Tough."

He had studied volumes about buying vehicles. One of the first rules of buying is to be calm, act uninterested, show no emotions and never gape at a particular "F-350 red Power Stroke." He felt pleased at the self-control and was certain that the young lady never noticed him jumping out of the cart while it was still moving, causing him to trip and roll twice on the black top without losing his white hat. She apparently was checking her hair as he hugged and patted the front hood, caressed the extendable mirrors and ran his hands over the dual rear tires.

She apologized, "Please forgive me for being distracted for a brief moment fixing my hair and re-glossing my dry lips, I know I should pay closer attention to your reactions." She licked her glossy lips. "My training is to determine how much you desire a certain truck, so I will know how to get you a better deal." George was glad that she had not noticed his reaction, that way he could "make a better deal."

"Now what truck did you like best?"

He casually pointed, trying to control a shaking hand, to the red F-350.

"Oh no" she blurted out trying to cover her perfectly shaped mouth with her small hand, displaying long pink extended fingernails matching her pink Wranglers. George had attempted not to notice that portion of her anatomy but he did notice the Wrangler emblem. "I am terribly sorry," with a weeping tone in her low voice that caused recollection of a baby rabbit peeking out from under a soft pile of leaves, "that particular truck was ordered special for 'Tex' himself."

George was doubly pleased that he had the superb ability to select the best of the best. Now even more so, he had to have that truck. "Please, is there any chance Mr. 'Tex' might sell this truck?"

"Oh, I can see that you are disappointed. Maybe, I could talk to the sales manager to see if 'Tex' might consider selling," she said with the most considerate voice imaginable. Then with pensive eyes and fluttering eyelashes she stood up as if struck with the most brilliant idea, "No, forget the sales manager, I will personally talk with 'Tex' to see if he would consider parting with this special order truck." It was impressive that Mr. 'Tex' with such numerous dealerships and hundreds of salespeople would have time to personally visit with this fine lady about a sale.

George reminded her, "It was 'Tex' himself that invited me to his dealership. If I go to another dealership, we will both lose money."

She smiled her perfect white teeth, "you are so right, I will remind him that you do not want him to lose money by having you go to another dealership."

She walked away, her hips excessively swiveling and her long flaxen hair reflecting the sun. This intentional movement is supposed to maintain the gaze of the client. Any authentic Arizona cowboy knows that when compared to an all-wheel drive, heavy duty bumper, (probably for pushing cows) mounted twenty-thousand pound electric winch, (probably for pulling cows) and a four inch lift, (probably to run over cows) a woman, even a pretty woman, will take second place.

George studied every detail of the truck and almost in audible voice spoke, "Dad, can you see this unbelievable truck? Can you imagine your son, as you last saw him on earth, now old enough to possibly buy and drive this magnificent machine with a huge diesel power horse just itching to work?"

She smiled as George suddenly realized her presence. "Were you talking to someone?"

"Not really, I have lived alone for some time now and often talk to myself."

"Well, 'Tex' was unavailable, but the sales manager says that Mr. 'Tex' is true to his word. He really does not want you to lose money going to another dealer. Additionally, the manager was very impressed with your ability to select the best truck out of the many thousands of units. He is certain that 'Tex' would be willing to part with his magnificent personal truck. Of course, he does not want the dealership to lose money. And he does not want me, as a manager, to lose, but he especially does not want you to lose."

She explained in detail that such a truck is on the books to sell at twenty-five percent over the posted list price on the window. This price assures the dealer a nominal profit. However, with heartfelt conviction, she touched his arm once again and looked him straight in the eyes. "I can see that you are a special breed of cowboy and deserve the best. Let me see if I can do better." She left him with a light touch on the cheek, a sincere wave of her pink fingernail polished hand, and hurried off to negotiate a 'special price' for a special person."

She could scarcely contain her excitement as she returned and exclaimed, "the sales manager, even though he might get in trouble with 'Tex,' agreed to waive the twenty-five percent mark up and let the truck sale at a mere ten percent over list price!" The saleslady mentioned that the offer was unbelievable and she seemed concerned that George was willing to accept the offer. She almost fainted with excitement when he suggested that she add three percent for herself.

With his last three pay stubs, a call to George's bank, a substantial down payment, and mounds of paper, insurance card, a temporary plate and a luminous smile from the saleslady, George drove off the lot in the truck of his dreams. George was happy with himself. He had suggested the extra three percent because he certainly did not want "Tex" to lose money. To George it appeared that the salespeople appreciated him. He thought he saw tears of gratitude as the sales staff bowed their heads and covered their mouths with their hands. They looked humble as he signed the papers and took the keys. He also noticed that they were almost holding their breath, as if, at any moment, the sales manager would suddenly appear and announce, "Stop the sale! We cannot accept thirteen percent over list price."

George looked back through the tinted glass window and saw the group holding each other up, taking deep breaths and Miss Ford sitting down, her head bent down to her lap taking deep breaths between tears of laughter and tears of joy. He was pleased that he had negotiated such a "deal" that brought such happiness to this fine group.

For some reason, the multitude of salespeople, that eagerly greeted him when he arrived, was no longer available to help load the seven suitcases. Skimming through the owner's manual he learned that the Power-Stroke diesel should warm up adequately and should be driven with reasonable care for the first few thousand miles. With this valuable knowledge, he eased onto Baseline Road and headed west. He had no problem on Baseline Road going thirty-five miles per hour as it was considered a side street. He thought that this speed would properly warm up the truck and that it was reasonable care as mentioned in the ownership manual. When he reached the I-10 freeway, he headed south towards the Gila River. Even though the posted speed was sixty-five miles an hour, he felt that forty five miles per hour was better for the truck until it was properly warmed up.

As he slowly drove along the busy freeway filled with after work traffic he was highly impressed with the displays of admiration shown to him by the Arizona drivers. Folks would take time out of their busy schedule to pull up behind the new truck so close they could have almost pushed him. He knew they just wanted a closer look and then they would pull beside him and wave their middle finger wildly in the air. He supposed it was a signal that the truck he bought was the number one truck as advertised on television. He drove a little slower so these good folks could get an even better look. Sure enough, more people passed and waved a number one finger out their windows. He was sure he was going to like the fine people of Arizona.

A short way out of town, he noticed a car parked on the shoulder of the road with the hood up. He read in western novels, which he imagined to be nearly authentic, that ranchers were friendly and helpful. So, he pulled to a stop behind the car just as an Arizona Highway Patrolman pulled up behind the new truck.

Cautiously walking up to the truck, his shoulders about even with the bottom of the rolled down window, "Do you have business here?" a young, well-uniformed officer inquired.

George responded, "I just stopped to see if these folks needed help."

The officer responded, "Are you some kind of a do-gooder or are you an opportunist?"

Thinking about how he was starting a new life in Arizona George said, "Well, I'm an Arizona rancher and I guess I am an opportunist."

With that comment, the officer stiffened and ordered him out of the truck and onto the side of the road.

That would normally not be a problem, unless you are not accustomed to the distance between a raised higher than a normal truck and ground sloping towards the underside of the truck. Even that might not be a particular problem unless you include large spurs attached to boots.

George pushed the door with some difficulty because he was pushing uphill. Then, many simultaneous and undesirable movements took place. George's spurs became entangled in the new carpet on the floorboard. His head, shoulders and body went flying against the partially opened door causing it to fly open. The flinging door knocked the ridged, tanned, uniformed officer to the ground. Because the road sloped down and away from where the officer was standing, the officer proceeded to slide under the truck just in front of the oversized mud and snow grip knobby tires. George's untangled foot twisted and pushed on the accelerator. This caused the large diesel motor to rev up. The young officer, with all the dignity of a screaming monkey, let it be known that he was about to meet his untimely death. A few seconds later, George's tangled foot came free and he fell headlong onto the road only inches behind the officer sliding slowly down the gravel embankment. With the officer screaming for his life, George also began to scream for his life. When he saw the enormous tires only a few feet from his head, George's scream matched the scream of the officer and the two sounded like monkeys in the rainforest. In due time, both realized that the truck was in park and was not moving. Both realized that their fragile lives had been spared. Both realized the embarrassing situation they were in, as they crawled out from under the "Truck of Trucks." Their faces colored just as red.

The two ladies by now had rolled up both windows. It was a hundred and ten degree heat on the outside. In a car with windows rolled up temperatures would quickly reach one hundred and fifty degrees. That apparently would be less gruesome than facing whatever was causing the hollering and blood curdling screams coming from under the truck.

The officer stood, brushed off his not so newly pressed uniform and with a low voice trying to control the fear, anger and shear fright calmly asked George, "Would you please get your registration, driver's license, and insurance card?"

Most, if not all, ranchers or serious four wheeler drivers have experienced opening the large heavy door of a pickup that is built four inches higher than normal and that is leaning towards the downhill side. George, however, had not experienced this before. He was learning so very much in such a short period of time: hot asphalt, sunken spurs, entangled spurs, and officers that are trained to scream. Now, he was about to learn something else. He stretched high and carefully opened the passenger side door to reach into the glove compartment. With only a slight push of the button on the handle, the heavy door flung open causing George to become airborne.

Often the old Indians living near the foothills of the Appalachian had repeated to George, "it is not the fall that hurts; it is the sudden stop at the end of the fall. After being air borne for just short of an eternity, George hit, slid down the embankment and abruptly stopped. Momentarily he realized he had hit something that felt more like an extremely hard and large round pincushion. George now understood the wisdom in the Indian saying. Then he tried to move. The black and white Holstein vest was held prisoner by whatever desert creature had grabbed him. His mind rushed, faster than most modern computers. What was the beast? Would he soon be devoured?

Setting all pride aside, a deep guttural "help" escaped from his throat. The officer, now recovered from being knocked under the truck, in front of the tire with a revved up diesel motor extended his hand to pull George away from the fishhook barrel cactus.

"Mighty lucky you were wearing that heavy leather vest or those hooks would be anchored to the skin of your back," said the officer.

George was very happy with himself. He had planned so well for the unseen, so as to wear an artificial Holstein leather vest.

The door of the truck remained open. George had to literally climb up and onto the truck seat to retrieve the documents.

"I see that your registration was just issued by 'Tex' along with a temporary insurance card for this truck. However, your driver's license was issued in Virginia, and yet you told me you were an Arizona rancher."

Well sir, George took fifteen minutes to explain that he was from the east coast. He lived in Virginia, but was currently moving into Arizona and had been a resident for only four hours. Standing in the one hundred and ten degree sun caused beads of sweat form on his face. The officer eyed him suspiciously and asked why he was so nervous and why he was dressed up in that western outfit.

"I'm not nervous, I am hot. I plan on being an Arizona cowboy. I bought these authentic clothes last summer from the authentic western trading post just down the road a few miles. I was heading to the Trading Post and merely stopped to see if these folks needed some help or some water. I just bought a case of water at a Circle K on Baseline."

The officer smiled, "I just might take one of those bottles if you were to offer." As the officer chugged down one bottle and reached for another, he mentioned, "we have had several calls informing us that a red pickup truck was driving so slow that it was impeding traffic. I know it would not be you because your truck with that Power Stroke could go eighty miles per hour pulling a trailer. Well, you take care of yourself."

As the officer drove off, George thought it strange that he did not check on the car with the hood up. He also considered it strange that the officer had told him to drive eighty with a trailer, even though the posted speed limit was seventy-five miles per hour. He smiled, "I'm sure the officer realized that the ladies were in good hands with me." Approaching the car he found the two ladies sitting with their windows rolled up, scarlet red faces covered with running perspiration and straight hanging wet hair. With some persuasion he was able to convince them that if they would roll the window down at least one inch he could better hear their needs.

"We were driving along and the car sputtered twice and quit. My son usually does the driving, but this time we decided we could manage ourselves."

"Did you happen to notice if there was plenty of gas?"

"Young man, we know enough about cars to comprehend that they need gasoline. We should have plenty because the indicator was on the "E" when we left. June, my older sister, says that means Extra."

Surely, he thought somewhere further down the freeway would be a gas station. This new truck came with vertical black rubber push bars that extended low enough to reach their bumper. "Ladies, it would be my honor to escort you to the next station. If you would turn on the key and put the little white arrow on the 'N,' then I will give you a push."

This was the first truck George had ever owned. He learned to drive with a V W and had always driven compact type cars. Naturally, he was proud of the Power Stroke diesel V-8 as it increased effortlessly the speed. He could hardly feel the weight of the car in front of him. He remembered what the well-dressed officer had told him, "You could go eighty miles per hour with that Power Stroke." It was amazing, how easily the big truck pushed the car. Around sixty-five miles per hour the ladies rolled their windows down and began to wave their hands with great excitement displaying how much they were enjoying the higher speeds. With that demonstration he moved up to eighty miles per hour and touched the cruise control. He determined that the ladies were deeply enjoying the ride because they were no longer waving, but now were honking the horn. The passenger had her face stuck out the open window, so she could feel the rushing air. It was pleasing to see people take such heightened pleasure in life. A few times he thought the ladies were going to swerve into an eighteen-wheeler but the truck changed lanes just in time to miss the ladies.

Seeing a gas station ahead, George slowed to leave the freeway; the power stroke lazily pushed the car into the station. The attendants seemed to become paralyzed as they gazed into the car. George walked slowly to the side of the car and leaned down to visit with the ladies. George again learned amazingly that high speeds and hot air blowing through the windows at eighty miles per hour causes a discoloration of the face. Both ladies had bright red faces and hair seemingly extending straight up. He complimented their skill in passing between the two slow moving trucks. He told them "good-bye" and he could tell that they were so filled with gratitude they could not even say a word. As he turned to leave, he did notice the driver's lower lip quiver a little and a tear seep from her wide-open eyes. He never saw their eyes blink. Even the lady who had her head outside had her eyes wide open and was not blinking. "Amazing" he thought. It felt good to have done such a good deed. He mentally recorded a goal to try and live the Scout Slogan: "Do a good turn daily." He climbed into the high lift truck and headed down the road. He had a horse and ranch to purchase.

5—THE HORSE MUST FIT THE MAN

GEORGE DROVE TO, as was advertised on billboards, the authentic freeway trading post for the purpose of getting directions to Honest Abe's place of business. The previous summer John the Beloved had mentioned the name of Honest Abe's in the event George desired to purchase a horse. Now, he was ready to purchase the perfect horse to accompany this great truck.

He recalled his adventures, his studies and his not so challenging quests while visiting parks and amusement rides on the east coast. With the aid of the Internet, the library, magazines, and talking to the fellows that took care of the children's rental horses at the carnival, George had learned just about all that possibly could be known about horses. George spent a lot of money riding the rental ponies. The ponies were connected to the extended poles, which only allowed the "Wild West Ponies" to walk in a circle. George felt a little embarrassed that he had to lift his feet up off of the ground while riding the ponies. A manager (referring to himself as the Multi State Circus Equestrian Director) had asked George not to drag his feet because "it made the ponies nervous." Since these were the only ponies available, however, George accepted the slight problem." Riding those ponies invited the imagination of a young boy to explore every portion of the vast world. The manager informed George one evening that he could no longer ride the ponies due to his weight.

This was a turning point in George's life. He mustered up enough courage to progress to the larger horses. The horses were tied to each other, which forced them to walk along the same trail day after day. Then after a few months the "Equestrian Director" would tell the advanced riders that the horses would be untied. George knew the routine. On the wall of his mother's apartment hung the plaque, "Nothing Ventured

Nothing Gained," so the first few days, as with any new venture, he was nervous. On the ponies, if he slipped, he just extended his legs to touch the ground. These larger horses were much taller than the ponies. This meant that George would be sitting much higher off the ground. If he slipped out of the saddle, he could not simply put his feet down to regain his balance. So, the fall would be much more dangerous. An ole bystander with a Texan drawl said; "It ain't the fall that hurts son, it's when ya'al hits the ground."

George had started his advanced horse riding and training years before he had made his first trip to Arizona. Now, he was in Arizona and was ready to purchase his own horse. He pulled into the trading post and slid out of his truck. He had not removed his spurs for the short drive from the service station to the trading post. He felt that he had learned his lesson and would not let the spur get entangled in the carpet again. He cautiously slid off the seat maintaining the spurs free from the carpet. *Luckily* for him, his left leg touched ground the same instant that his right rear cheek sat firmly on the rowel of the spur attempting to escape the floorboard. The sharp rowel poked him as bad as the fish-hook barrel cactus had. But now, he was wedged between the floor and the right cheek. *Unluckily* for him, his leg that was touching the ground was not long enough to push him up and off of the piercing spur. *Luckily* for him, the deluxe leather interior cab had a "comfort handle" attached to the inner roof of the cab. He quickly grabbed the u-shaped handle and pulled upwards to relieve the spur/cheek pain. *Unluckily* for him, the upward pull was not sufficient to unbend the doubled knee to release the pinned spur. *Luckily* for him an Indian man from the Maricopa tribe, known for their size and weight, came over to see why the horn was blaring. Unknowingly, while endeavoring to grab the handle, George had pushed the horn button on the key ring. This six foot, eight inch, three hundred pound giant smiled, reached inside the cab, grabbed a handful of front shirt and vest and with unbelievable ease lifted body, arms, legs, boots and spurs from the seat of the pickup truck. This gentle giant stood for a time admiring the truck's interior then stepped back to look at the complete truck. George repeated his thanks at least six times before the giant recognized that this young, rescued man was still about six inches off the ground. Embarrassed at his forgetfulness the gentle Maricopa Indian opened his enormous hand.

Whether a person is suspended in the air one inch or six feet, if he does not know the distance, then the potential of being dropped is frightening. *Luckily* for George the drop was so sudden, that he was unable to scream. *Unluckily* for him, the jolt of hitting the ground caused him to bite his tongue and fall to the ground. *Luckily* for him, having his tongue in between his teeth prevented serious teeth damage. *Unluckily* for him, the tongue has many thousand nerves and the bite triggered horrible pains. He screamed like a banshee, but quickly collected himself and stood up.

With watery eyes he looked up, way up, to this gentle giant. The giant spoke in English with a very strong Indian accent, "Nice truck." He looked down at and saw the watery eyes and simply said, "Hurt like eating ten cayenne peppers to bite tongue." With that he left.

For reasons unknown to Trading Post owner, as George approached the trading post, John the Beloved recognized his former client. Remembering that he had over charged this tourist, John the Beloved abruptly turned to escape. In his haste, he ran head long into the wall and stumbled to the floor. Dizzily John the Beloved gasped for air as he recognized each piece of "authentic" cowboy garb that he had sold George the previous summer. George merely supposed that John was thrilled to see his former customer. The owner came to see if there was a problem when he saw his manager sitting on the floor mumbling something about a thousand-dollar donation and special prices.

George enthusiastically explained to the owner just how kind "John the Beloved" had been last year, including how he had offered special prices. George shook the owners hand for being so generous to a needy family with the $1,000.00 contribution. The owner thanked him for sharing such invaluable information.

"Young man, as the owner I certainly appreciate hearing about the activities of my store manager. When John recovers from his accident, I will have a long visit and share with him what you have shared with me. It certainly helps to answer some accounting issues that have been taking place in my store." The owner asked if there was anything else George might need. The two of them visited for a few minutes. The owner then explained that because George was such a sincere and enthusiastic cowboy and because George had splendidly promoted the Trading Post, the manager John, as a courtesy, would fully refund the $2,137.82 that George spent the previous summer. George was impressed at the goodness of western hospitality.

The owner was not sure of the directions to "Honest Abe's." The owner was concerned that John would most likely be indisposed for a long time and would not be able to give directions to Honest Abe's ranch. So, the owner suggested that George speak with a man sitting just outside the store. "The man would almost certainly be sitting on an old cut off mesquite trunk." The owner told George, "He would likely know the directions to Honest Abe's place."

George walked outside and saw what appeared to be a statue sitting on a tree trunk. When the statue's hand mechanically rose to brush away a menacing fly, George headed in his direction. Judging from the many and the deep wrinkles on his face, this stoic Indian man must be approximately the age of the tree trunk on which he was sitting. The wrinkles moved in a carefully designed choreography when he spoke. His language was a form of English but with a dialect that was very different from the cab driver that took George to the airport.

"You want I help?"

"Yes, thank you, I am trying to locate Honest Abe's corrals."

The directions were very precise. "Go end of blacktop, bout three mile south take left on dirt road, drive towards sun in morning or away from sun if afternoon, be noon do not drive." He laughed causing every wrinkle to form into an upturned smile. "Go maybe see giant saguaro cactus with three arms, arm on left is tallest if you are facing morning sun, if facing you sun in afternoon one on right be tallest. Turn left, going to mountain be maybe hour and half if be riding horse be maybe fifteen minutes miles in big red truck."

He looked in the direction of the George's truck and grunted with appreciation, "Must be okay truck, dog is peeing on new tire." He then continued as if he had not paused to point out the dog's activity.

"Maybe five to twelve miles down wash road," he paused for a few minutes as if in a deep thought. "Maybe use all wheel drive then see pile white granite rocks right side of wash road, turn left next dirt trail maybe you get out wash. If miss turn maybe two to five miles drive more on wash road. Out of wash road drive take to fork, when find fork to left or right, same lead directly to corral, maybe make circle." Again, the wrinkles all danced to accommodate a delightful and contagious laugh.

George was making detailed notes on his Palm Pilot and asking many questions trying to clarify turns, am, pm, mountains etc. but received no answers. The old man simply looked steadfastly into George's eyes. Satisfied that the corrals could be found, George turned to leave. He felt grateful that this good man was willing to give thirty minutes of his day to offer such detailed directions.

The old man slowly spoke again, "Young man, you ask how get Honest Abe's corrals, you follow directions you get to corrals okay, but you want chat with Honest Abe?" He pointed to a man about a hundred feet away sitting on the bench under an old Tamarack tree, "that be Abraham many call Honest Abe."

"These are good people out here in the west."

Slowly and deliberately he sauntered across the gravel parking area. His white painted, twice flattened hat, the Holstein black and white vest with little puffs of hair sticking out the back side from the cactus hooks experience, red shirt and red boots definitely had their effect on others. The spur, one remained caught in the truck mat, he calculatingly let the large rowel lightly touch the gravel, with the long metal tangs striking the pebbles the ringing jingle caused all within hearing distance to stop and look at this rare "authentic cowboy." He was a little concerned about the jingle, pause, jingle then pause as he walked.

Honest Abe heard the distinct jingle, pause, jingle and pause caused by one spur on and one spur off stood and turned to directly face from whence came the jingling tones. George delightfully absorbed the look of shock, esteem or both on Honest Abe's dry Arizona, sun-weathered, leather face. He assumed the man bit his lower lip as his face tuned red in apparent admiration as he witnessed firsthand … His thoughts interrupted, the man said, "You must be a real cowboy from back east?"

It was plain to see that the words were forced through tight cracked lips to prevent a whooping holler of admiration.

"You must be Honest Abe? I am George Ribit Chattit, known as George and sometimes referred to as GRC, which represents the initials for George Ribit Chattit. I am looking for a good horse."

Honest Abe extended his hand in the western way of saying howdy.

Abraham felt a strong grip, but also noted the extremely soft hand without so much as one small callous.

George began to expound the seven virtues that he required in a horse. He rehearsed all the information he had gathered pertaining to horses, their breeding and characteristics. Horse breeds are groups of horses with distinctive characteristics that are transmitted consistently to their offspring, such as conformation, color, performance ability, or disposition. These inherited traits are usually the result of a combination of natural crosses and artificial selection methods aimed at producing horses for specific tasks. George knew that a quarter horse is bred for short distance speeds and rodeo performance, a thoroughbred is best known for racing, the Appaloosa is a good stock horse, and a Mustang has strong bones and hardiness.

George thought it difficult to achieve all the special prerequisites because it would require the crossing of pure bloodlines. "You probably know already, if the breed crossing can be done with pureblood lines resulting breed would better achieve its purpose. So Mr. Honest Abe, I require a horse with purest of mixed bloodlines with the following characteristics." Abraham had no idea as to what this young fellow was trying to say or explain.

George pulled out his computer-generated list and read with a deliberate slow western drawl. After each sentence he would pause and nod his head as if to emphasize the request.

1. The speed and strength of a quarter horse for short runs.
2. The power of a Thoroughbred for long runs
3. The toughness of a line-back buckskin.
4. The last-ability of an Arabian when little or no water is available.
5. The brown and white camouflage of Paint.
6. The durability of an Appaloosa.
7. Black hooves to endure the rocks.
8. There might be a few other items.

Abe stood speechless. He possibly had some thoughts but none would materialize. George could easily observe the admiration in this man's eyes. George asked Honest Abe:

"Please do not mistake me for an easterner that does not understand horses."

George could not remember all the parts of a horse but he attempted to remember enough to astonish Honest Abe and gain his admiration;

it seemed apparent that he had accomplished his first purpose. Now it was time to explain additional details and prerequisites. Honest Abe could not wait to hear what else this novice horseman would tell him. Honest Abe knew the parts of a horse and wondered if George did. For example, a cannon is the part of the leg above the pastern or fetlock commonly referred to as the ankle. (It does not make a noise.) The scapula is the shoulder bone. (No cutting is involved.) The radius is the large bone between the knee and the shoulder. (It has nothing to do with a circumference) The navicular bone is located inside the hoof area under the short pastern bone. (Nothing to do with navigation.) The frog is the meaty/gristle on the bottom side of the hoof. (It makes no noise unless the hoof is placed on a human foot, then there is, most often, a great noise. Not from the horse but from the unfortunate person owning the foot.)

George started to explain what he wanted in the parts of his horse. "It is vital to me that the horse has a good understanding of my personality, that the "Cannon" be loud enough to be heard in emergencies, that the "Radius" fit within the circumference, the Navicular Bone be able to discern direction and the Scapula not be used to cut anything without first consulting the Navicular. And, it is very important that the "Frog" not make any noise at night."

He could tell there was no need to mention any other parts of a horse; he could easily discern the stunned appearance in Honest Abe's eyes at the vast practical knowledge conveyed by this newly arrived cowboy as he related one more vital bit of knowledge.

"The match between horse and cowboy was critical in times of great need or emergencies, and a cowboy's best friend is not a dog but his horse."

It took Honest Abe several minutes to regain his composure and with difficulty due to the emotional impact of George's request. Abe spoke with great restraint. "Young man, I believe I have just the horse for you."

The two men walked around a couple of rustic adobe block homes of local residents to an old pole corral with most of the poles lying on the ground and no apparent gate. George was immediately impressed with the special breeding that was obvious to his trained eyes. He thought almost aloud, "This horse could easily leave the corral but due to extraordinary training this fine animal stayed."

Honest Abe substantiated the observation as he stated, "These corrals, leaky water pipe and fallen shade are all part of the expert breeding and training given to this particular horse. Any dumb horse can stay in a strong corral under ideal shade, but "Thunderbolt" was exceptional."

"Thunderbolt," that was a name that thundered throughout a real cowboy's mind.

It was with immense difficulty that Honest Abe explained the unique qualities of "Thunderbolt."

"Please notice the little thin ears that almost touch at the tip this allows for back, forward, sideways and upward hearing. The four brands on top of each other prove how many astute ranchers have wanted this young horse."

It seemed that the more Abe explained and detailed the uniqueness of this fine animal the more difficult it became for Honest Abe to hold back tears from flowing down his bulging red face. A time or two George actually thought Honest Abe was going to burst the neck veins with the frustrations at having to part with such a matchless, more mature than normal four-year old horse.

Honest Abe knew this horse was almost the exact opposite of what a ranch hand would want. However, a good salesperson will identify the weak points and explain them as positives. Thus, he continued: "Notice the gentle yet deep swayback in the spine. This singular characteristic derives from years of controlled inbreeding which allows the saddle to not slide forward or backward even if the cinch might loosen." Abe further added, "A tight cinch much like a tight belt would inhibit breathing and greatly increase the discomfort around the middle of the horse."

Abe continued, "along with the controlled inbreeding, we have select cross breeding with a quarter horse for fast burst of speed, the bloodline mixtures of the thoroughbred allows this fast burst of speed to continue for miles, the palomino blood helps to blend well with the bright yellow sun, Arabian blood for drought tolerance along with six other varieties of prescribed breeding there is the possibility of the famed Tennessee walker that will give the rider a pleasant journey for the whole day."

George noted that Honest Abe was almost beside himself with grief and emotion when he mentioned the last but probably the best quality.

"Thunderbolt is a tall ten hands high. Many horses are one and a half times taller which common sense would say the tall horse is twice as difficult to mount, twice as difficult to saddle, twice as far to fall and twice as many low hanging tree limbs to avoid."

George tried to control his excitement at the possibility of acquiring a one-of-a-kind horse with such select "in-breeding of bloodlines." He had read in the papers the value of excellent bloodlines in a horse. "Sometimes in the hundreds of thousands," he thought from within. "I really want this fine animal, but I cannot pay that much."

Abe, from years of experience with dealing with "green horns" (inexperienced people) noted what might be a doubt so he continued his sales pitch, "The black hoofs as you requested. Please take particular note of the two natural splits in the front hoofs. This is to allow inner aeration during the long Arizona hot day's ride and also gives better traction for climbing the eighty-degree mountainside. The extra large knee joints are of particular advantage for crawling under low hanging limbs in a sandy wash."

Honest Abe had reached his limit. He was down on one knee with eyes watering and the veins on his neck were about to split the seams from head to toe. Abe had never in his life found a person so genuinely gullible as this young man.

"Please Abe, go no farther, I can see that you are deeply respectful of this unique steed. I will give him an exceptional home and you can come and visit with him as often as you desire. So my dear sir, what is your bottom price?"

"Well young man, I was wanting ten but I would be willing to take nine because I know you will give him a good home."

Abe was having great difficulty with his words.

Now it was time to negotiate price. Compared to prices of racing horses on the east coast or the cost of the F-350 Power Stroke, $9,000.00 was a bargain.

"I feel that nine is a fair price, however…"

Abe cringed and fell backwards at those words. He was sure that nobody would give more than five hundred dollars for this sway back split hoof animal and he would be willing to take three hundred. The word thousand stuttered in Abe's mind.

George felt pleased with his suburb powers of dickering that he had learned from a paperback published by a real estate company. Abe had asked an even nine. However, with keenness of mind and astute observation that only comes from hours of thinking about having astute observations and keenness of mind, George had noticed an old saddle and other equipment next to the fallen shade. He deduced that, due to the saddle being dark weathered brown, rope well worn, rain soaked and sun dried leather chaps standing stiffly against the wood pole and an old saddle blanket with genuine rat holes, this equipment would be worth a small fortune. Such items bring thousands of dollars at antique auctions on the east coast. George had been to a few such estate actions.

Honest Abe stood as fixed as the mesquite post dug deeply into the dry desert soil still unable to fully believe what his ears had heard.

George with complete innocence of experience looked upon Abe as if it were a certain type of tactic of which George had read about. So, before Honest Abe could open his ten-day gray whiskered framed wind chapped lips, he was offered an additional two fifty for the equipment.

"Agreed," Abe said with a shaky voice. He was also thinking this young man has yet to learn many important and valuable lessons. On this hot Arizona day, however, Abe was not going to be one of the teachers. He still was dumb founded over the verbal offer for his horse Thunderbolt. No, someone else would have to be the teacher and explain that in most circumstances it is best to be quiet and observe a way of life before thinking one is an expert.

When George pulled out a large wad of hundreds and fifties and counted nine thousand dollars for the horse and two hundred and fifty dollars for the saddle and equipment, Honest Abe was unable to support his own weight and fell to the ground. George supposed it was because parting with such a fine horse was more than Abe could handle.

Honest Abe regained some composure, stood, dusted his pants and shirt and accepted the money. Abe's light brown glassy eyes sprang wide as if standing in front of a stampede and simultaneously his small chapped-lipped mouth flopped open gasping for air.

George could only assume it was because this professional horse trader realized he had been beaten. Abe just nodded in agreement as he choked back the astonishment. Apparently, he was so ashamed of having been out bargained by an easterner that he had to slip around the old wooden shed. Groans of pain and hysteria could be heard far and near. Abe, in due time returned, tear stained, dusty cheeks and red eyes were evident. George did feel a little saddened with having out "dickered" the man. A bargain is a bargain, however, and it was fair and square. He knew it to be true on his part and he knew it was true on Abe's part. If not true, Abe would never have acquired the name of "Honest Abe."

Honest Abe, still nervous and jittery from the transaction asked George to never tell a soul about the deal. It was clear in George's mind that the reason Honest Abe did not want George to discuss such a beneficial exchange was that Abe had his reputation to uphold. Having been so out maneuvered by an easterner would really have an impact on future business. With the purchase complete there was the task of hauling "Thunderbolt."

Abe pointed to an old pile of lumber, just as the huge a six foot eight Maricopa Indian that helped George out of another too tall pickup escapade arrived. Abe quickly put his finger to his lips to remind that deals were top secret.

"My name Cecil."

George was curious and asked how he pronounced his name Cecil in the Maricopa Indian dialect?

He looked very serious, puckered his large lipped mouth and looked right at George. Slowly he pronounced his Maricopa name, "C—E—C—I—L is name my mother she gave to me."

George accepted the pronunciation and asked Cecil if he had any ideas on how to build a rack for the pickup so he could haul his new horse, pointing to "Thunderbolt" still standing in the corral.

"Oh, you buy horse?"

"Yes I did and felt I received a fair deal from Honest Abe."

"If you pay more than ten, you no get good deal."

Abe's face went into an unfamiliar contortion and it appeared his mouth would open, however, nothing escaped.

In the English dialect there is a tendency to shorten words. So, it is easy for an individual to hear, according to what he is thinking. Cecil would be thinking ten $10 bills, Abe might be thinking ten $100 bills and George is thinking ten $1,000 bills so sometimes the miscommunication can leave everyone happy.

"Well, I won't go into details, but I can say that I paid a little less than ten."

"Good," Cecil expressed. "Horse not worth one penny more."

George felt good about the deal and about himself. He also felt he was learning more about the western culture.

Each had an opinion on how to make a rack for the F-350 to transport Thunderbolt. By the time they were finished with the used one inch thick by four inch wide by various lengths of weathered gray, split boards and what seemed to be a thousand feet of rusted wire that the locals referred to as baling wire or pioneer leather, and two pieces of leather that had to be oiled for it to bend. These pieces of flexible leather nailed to the rack and then to a set of boards that was to simulate a gate function quite nicely as very sturdy hinges.

Abe suggested, "Before you try and load your horse, why don't you walk him around a little."

George, with weather darkened saddle, rope, white smashed, but re-fitted hat and stiff leather chaps that would not bend at the knees led his horse around the Indian village. Every person stopped and gazed at this sight of so fine and rare an authentic freeway cowboy. George was proud of himself. He was leading his horse and wearing his white painted, crumpled straw-hat, black and white Holstein vest with unique strands of cow hide and hair stringing out the backside of the vest, and red boots. The one spur still on his boot jingled extra-loudly, because the strap broke when George fell out of his extra lifted pickup when he stopped to help the women on the freeway. Rather than fitting smartly on his boot, this spur drug behind his boot. The other spur had remained entangled with the new red carpet behind the brake pedal when he fell out of the truck at the trading post.

None of this mattered; George was in Arizona with his newly acquired and trusted bronco. He meandered down their streets. No one dared to make a move and no one dared to make a slip, the cowboy there among them held the lead rope on his hip. There existed no doubt that this swayback, knock-kneed, narrow shouldered horse with cockleburs in his tail did indeed fit the man.

With a powerful rancher's truck and the perfect multi-blood-lined horse, it was now time to acquire a ranch.

George understood that less knowledgeable people might think it is better to buy a ranch before buying a horse. That is easily explained. Most cowboys have their horse and ride for months, years and often a lifetime looking for the perfect rangeland. George learned this from almost every western movie he watched. You can be a cowboy without cows, but you cannot be a cowboy without a horse. This horse is what George Ribit Chattit was after. It had the perfect combinations of bloodlines. He often wondered why these giant men of the west were not called "Horseboys" because they always had horses. Even today, many people own horses, trucks and horse-trailers, but do not own even one cow and yet they call themselves cowboys. Maybe he thought, "Boys with horses would be called Horseboys and those with cows would be called cowboys."

6—THE PURCHASE

JUST SHORT OF a year ago, George had secured a purchase option for a prime piece of ranch land. A righteous minister, Mr. Ladrón, of one of the local Arizona churches actually put George on the trail of this property while eating at the Gila River Café waiting for the tour bus departure. There was a commotion just outside, and some of the Mexican and Indian children were pointing fingers and yelling in Spanish "ladrón, ladrón!" George would later learn that this meant "thief." George did not speak Spanish, so at the time, he assumed that the man's last name was Ladrón. As George stepped closer, he noticed that the man was wearing a white collar, much like a minister. George asked the children to stop bothering Mr. Ladrón. They left, but they continued to mumble something about him being a "ladrón." In the flow of conversation, George mentioned how he wanted to own a real authentic western ranch and live with the coyotes and Gila Monsters. Mr. Ladrón lit up with incredible excitement. He just happened to know a banker friend that mentioned that the bank had recently acquired the Gila River Cattle Ranch. George knew it was destiny that was calling him.

George was astonished. Gila River Cattle has the same acronym as his given name of George Ribit Chattit. This was the second time in his quest that he had found an identical acronym; the first was Gila River Cowboy and a close one with Gila River, which had brought him to this place in the first instance. He also thought that since all of this occurred just outside of the Gila River Café, which also has the same acronym, that this truly was destiny. With that observation George immediately wanted to go to the bank and make the deal. Mr. Ladrón became quite nervous at the prospect of them going immediately to the bank. Mr. Ladrón gave many excellent reasons not to go to the bank: "If the banker saw that George was from the east he might raise the price." "The banker might be out to lunch at three in the afternoon," "If the banker saw them together he might think that Mr. Ladrón was trying to make a three to five thousand dollar commission." There was also the fact that the tour bus was beginning to load. With those excellent reasons, Mr. Ladrón said that for a small fee of $200.00, he would personally go to the bank and have the manager forward all the necessary documents. If by some small chance, however, the documents failed to be forwarded, then Mr. Ladrón assured George he was not to worry.

Mr. Ladrón with absolute sincerity said, "I will personally make the arrangements to guarantee that the ranch will be available, if you return within the year." George assured Mr. Ladrón that he would return.

George happily paid the two hundred dollars for the option, shook hands, and wished Mr. Ladrón a pleasant trip. Mr. Ladrón spun on his heels and hastily departed. George thought Mr. Ladrón must be a very busy man.

After returning home in New York, considerable time went by and the purchase documents did not show up. George was not surprised and he did not worry when the papers never came. He understood how busy Mr. Ladrón and the banker must have been. Now, it did not matter. All of that is forgotten history, because he was here in person and would find the banker. After parking the truck under the shade of a large Salt Cedar so as to protect Thunderbolt from the afternoon sun, he walked to the bank. As he looked at his truck and horse, he had a moment of gratitude. Every once in awhile, he felt he could almost hear the voice of his mother calling him. When his mother was alive and at home needing some help, she would use the same pleasing tone of voice to call for help. Even when George could not understand her request, he could tell from the tone of her voice that she was asking for help. In these serious moments of reflection, George would hear that tone. If it were not for the fact that the DEA director had assured George of his mother's tragic death, he would have thought her still alive her spirit pleading to his spirit for help.

He pushed open the doors of the "Lone Butte Bank." They were heavy doors of aged pine with most of the once white paint worn away with antiquing of time. It was mid-afternoon as the white painted deformed hat somewhat filled the doorway and seemed to reflect the sun as if it were a mirror into the dark void of this old western movie bank. All activity halted, even though there was not much happening.

There were no customers and only one young man seated behind the desk marked "temporary manager."

The young manager jumped straight up. George assumed that the manager probably thought John Wayne or Clint Eastwood had just stepped into his bank. "Good day mister, may I be of…" In mid-sentence the flow of words halted. George stepped from the doorway into the room, and let his now untangled pair of spurs jingle across the old warped pine wood floor. George just knew this act had quieted the manager. This was the same impressive act that Jesse James performed to put "fear and respect" in all present. This young man was impressed, not because George stood his full five foot, ten inches tall plus his three inch heels on the red boots which raised him to six foot, one inch and not because of the tourist type clothes he was wearing, but because this fellow thought himself a genuine, authentic, range-formed cowboy as he spoke with sincere authority. "Young man, are you the manager?"

"Yes mister, I am acting manager for the last four years, ever since I left high school. My father before me was manager, but he retired to get a job with benefits, whatever that means?"

George was awed by the courage of this young man. Most "boys" leave high school and run off to college to avoid having to work. Not this young man, he went right to work, following in his father's footsteps. "If you have been here that long you must recall a Mr. Ladrón stopping by less than one year ago to visit with your bank in my behalf concerning property known as the Gila River Cattle Ranch."

Young Jerry, acting manager, recalled a man whom the Mexicans called ladrón who was caught stealing money from a beggar and was sent to Florence Prison for a few years to "mend his habits." Jerry did not want to lose this potential, and so far this month, the only customer. So, he avoided that detail. "Mister, concerning this prime real estate, this is your lucky day, and it is, at this very moment, still available. We have a few inquiries and there are potential buyers; however, it is strictly on a first come basis."

George felt the depth of his own soul quiver with a volcanic type tremble of excitement with this good news. He knew that it was most likely that Mr. Ladrón had made the arrangement and the young man wanted to take a little credit. He also noticed that this town must be dusty because the papers on the desk marked "GILA RIVER CATTLE

RANCH" were covered with dust. George thought, "They should keep important documents covered so they will not gather dust in so few hours."

The young acting manager, Jerry, was most accommodating in trying to enlighten the new client on the virtues of this ranch. The difficult part of this task was that his father had repeatedly pounded into his young brain: "Do not ever mislead, exaggerate, flower up or lie to a customer. Not only is it against our beliefs, it causes lawsuits."

Thus, poor Jerry proceeded to tell the truth. What Jerry did not know is that George was such an optimist that even when someone would criticize, George would hear a compliment. The truth of truth is that words can be spoken exactly the way the speaker intended them to be heard. But, the listener will hear and perceive something very different. The reason the ranch was still available is that the ranch was almost worthless, according to 99.99% of neighboring ranches. So, Jerry, trying to honest, began his rehearsed sales pitch.

"It has few windmills. There are no irrigated fields. The government has really cut down the number of cows you can have on the ranch. There are no electric or phone lines, so you have to drive up the hill to even use a cell phone. You will have to negotiate with the State Land Lease Department, the Bureau of Land Management (BLM), Gila River Indian Nation, and Arizona Department of Transportation (ADOT), and, worst of all, the so called environmentalist."

George was ecstatic. With just a few windmills, there would not be a lot of maintenance. With no irrigated fields, he would not need a tractor or to plant crops. With fewer cows, he would not need much help. With no electric or phone lines, he would have lots of quiet evenings. Negotiating with several different governmental agencies would give him the opportunity to know important people. George thought that the ranch was perfect. He did have one question.

"Why do you say, so called environmentalist? I certainly want to do my part to protect the environment."

Jerry replied, "All ranchers try to protect the environment because they have to maintain good grass year after year. Many ranchers call certain environmental groups, legal extortionists."

"Well," Replied George, "the ranch must be of significant importance to have that many entities so concerned about one piece of property."

"It is not such an important ranch," responded Jerry, "but it is easily accessible from Tucson or Phoenix. Many of the desk-pounding environmentalist complete their obligations and inspections by visiting the most convenient location."

"Well that is excellent Jerry, I really appreciate the helpful information, and maybe I can soon give them something to inspect."

"Just how large is the ranch," George inquired?

"Well that is a little difficult to answer; the numbers of cows maintained on a ranch normally creates the value and those numbers were determined by how much grass was available. Now, those numbers have significantly decreased each year because numbers are mostly determined by someone listening to the public outcry or by certain environmentalist that count clumps of grass around a watering hole. So, I cannot exactly tell you how many head of cows the ranch currently has or might have. The number of acres of deeded land or State Lease land also determines the value of property. This property has never been totally surveyed to determine the exact acres that exist, but it is not so important. Because the BLM, the Gila River Indian Nation, ADOT and the environmentalists say you have no rights. Any rights that you think you might have, the environmentalists will spend limitless amounts of taxpayer or donated monies to block those rights.

"As near as the bank can determine, you have four old abandoned homesteads, each consists of original forty acres. So, you have approximately one hundred and sixty acres of deeded land. Of the other so-called legal use, there are about twenty sections of six hundred and forty acres. This amounts to 12,800 acres of land with limited rights, limited access and doubtful ownership, but you are required to pay annual grazing fees based on a per cow assessment. The fees do not amount to much, because each bureaucratic group will spend thousands of dollars trying to collect hundreds. So, the results are never accurately published. Well, I should not say that, most groups would publish how much they have collected, but would never publish how much it cost them to collect. With the latest report, the ranch can only have one cow per section which means you can have 20 cows on the 12,800 acres plus what you have on your own home place."

Then Jerry became very serious. "George, this ranch really is not worth much. It will take tons of hard work, and probably will never pay for itself. The good news is that you can buy it for nothing down, pay 6% interest only, and the balance of $40,000 at the end of twenty years or whenever you choose to pay off the mortgage. If you decide not to pay anything, you can simply return the "deed of trust."

George could not believe his good fortune. This young man must realize from the red boots or maybe the white painted distorted hat that he was looking at a cowboy that would take a pile of dirt and create a mountain, see a pile of horse manure and find a horse or take something worthless and make it valuable. "Sounds good to me, where are the papers?"

Jerry wanted to know if George would first want to see the property.

"Jerry, I have not met a person in the west that has attempted to take advantage of me and I do not expect you to be the first. I will take the ranch sight unseen and it will be my future and the future of my children and grandchildren."

"Oh, are you married with a family."

"No Jerry, I am not married, have no children, but I suspect *if* a certain young lady accepts my invitation, *if* she pays me a visit, *if* she sees what I have done with the ranch, *if* she enjoys ranch life and *if* she accepts my proposal her short visit may become a permanent visit. And then *if* she wants children, we will have a family." Jerry was not sure how many "*ifs*" it would take before whatever he had said would become a reality.

In his heart, George knew that no person would dare take advantage of him. His cowboy attire would discourage such a thing and besides, he would quickly recognize such an act. George returned to his truck and horse and with contract to his ranch in his hand. "This had been a very eventful day" he thought to himself, "I am certainly looking forward to a nice quiet and peaceful night where there is no electricity, no sirens, no telephones and nobody checking to see if he would be to work on time. Yes sir, this would be a peaceful night." With explicit directions in hand, he left the bank to drive to "his new spread." He was grateful for the longer day light hours of summer.

Between Jerry and the two Pima Indians, George learned the difference between mesquite, palo verde and ironwood trees along with prickly pear and cholla cactuses. This knowledge was important as the turns on the hand sketched map indicted turns by a forked mesquite or a dried palo verde or the large prickly pear along with the gas line or high voltage power line that crossed the property.

George had traveled for about three hours, even though for two and a half hours he had no idea where he was or had been. He justified the experience in that he was taking the time to learn more about his spread and probably that of his neighbors and anybody or anything that might be in the area.

Having driven through the desert on rough roads, George was elated with the relatively smooth sandy roads in the bottom of washes. The sandy washes result from the infrequent, but torrential rainfall. Unable to soak into the ground the water quickly accumulates. This creates small flash floods that race across the desert floor and cut deep grooves into the desert hard caliche. The water washes away the lighter clay particles and leaves the heavy sand behind.

George was also excited because the soft sandy road allowed for the maiden test of the all-wheel drive on his new F-350. He quickly learned that seat belts were necessary, not because of a crash, but simply to keep the driver somewhat attached to the seat. The large pickup truck was made for hauling. The heavy duty springs caused the truck to go air borne when the tires bounced over a pile of dirt, a clump of grass, or a rut caused by a cross flow of running rain water. Nevertheless, after going over the thousands of not so gentle bounces, he now stood at the gate that would open to the Gila River Cattle Ranch and that would open to a new future. He was holding his breath in awe, with an excitement he had never imagined possible. He stood in one of the deep ruts caused from a combination of truck tires causing a small indent on the desert floor creating a crevice for accumulated rain, which deepened the tire tracks with each rain. There he stood, leaning on the old pole gate, gazing at the two tire track-rutted lane leading to the homestead, corrals, barn but most significantly those dry ruts will guide George Ribit Chattit to a new and electrifying future.

Arriving at the ranch gate, he stepped out of the truck uneventfully, leaned against an old twisted mesquite stump, and he paused with a new level of thought. "Few people ever experience the passion or enjoy the thrill of a 'deciding moment,' a 'fulfilling dream' or a 'switch point' in the ecstasy of life." To George the moment of being a man's man or a cowboy of cowboys was this moment. He had an F-350, 6 X 6 Power Stroke, loaded with one of the most highly trained and selectively bred horses with a pre-formed saddle. He looked at the pole gate held together with wire and leather straps as the sun set over the rusted tin roof of his own ranch house. The "Gila River Cowboy" was absorbing a once in a lifetime flash. He was feeling depths of life, inner vibrant joys and gentle powers within that he had never experienced. With such feelings of euphoria, George said aloud,

"I desire that every man alive could feel what I feel at this moment, the authority of endless strength within his own thoughts and choices. I wish they could understand the natural laws of abundance."

He looked upward to the clear heavens, waves of air that come from the exchange of hot and cool from the open desert, "Thank you God for letting me, for a brief moment, be aware of the dynamic spiritual power within a man willing to take risks."

He knew that he still had much to learn; in fact, he had so much to learn that he was trembling with excitement. Many people shun a venture into the unknown without adequate knowledge or a detailed plan. He remembered a good friend who desperately desired his own accounting business. He was an excellent accountant, worked for a large international company, and had a good solid income. He just wanted the challenge of developing his own business, being his own boss and succeeding or falling by his own efforts. Yes, he really wanted all the results that come from owning your own business, but he just did not want them badly enough to take the risk. Men have walked on the moon. There was no great economic windfall from this venture. These types of men with an undefeatable character are the ones who keep the world spinning. They are the ones who create new frontiers and then set about to enjoy that which they created. George, soon to be the Gila River Cowboy was proud to feel like a noble character. This ranch was not the moon, but in a literal sense, it represented as much to him as a walk on the moon. His desires were being put into action. Would he succeed? Maybe he would be like the stories of Thomas Edison when asked how many times he had failed and he responded, "Never, I have learned over six hundred ways a light bulb does not work, but I have never failed." It has been stated that you only fail when you cease to try. George knew he would never cease to try. He would never cease to learn and he would continue to see all that was good. This was what his mother had taught him. That is what she said was the corner stone of his father's strength. With a loud voice that could span the universe George Ribit Chattit could feel his father's spirit and thanked him aloud. He thanked his mother for her love and support. Yet, questioned why her spirit could not be present?

He looked across the desert, broken fences, pole gate, rusted tin roof and the missing fan blades on the windmill. He spoke aloud as if these objects were living souls, "I am grateful to each of you. I know you are here doing your best and I am here to help you do better than your best. I will learn from you and you will learn from me."

With those thoughts and comments he approached the broken pole gate that would willingly begin the teaching process. It has been spoken, "Before the learning comes the teaching." The teaching was about to begin. It was as if the gate, post, windmill, house, corrals and animals had previously decided that this young man was worth teaching. So, they in conjunction would teach and train him in a most immediate fashion.

7—THE ENTRANCE

THE EUPHORIC FEELING vanished more quickly than a quick view of a skinny coyote crossing a narrow road. George had seen the old rusted hinges attached to the opposite end of the pole gate. Often a person sees something and assumes it is what he or she is supposed to see. Hinges are supposed to pivot, the hinges on the gate to Gila River Cattle Ranch had rusted and been broken years earlier. So, when George attempted to untwist the wire holding the pole gate shut. The old gate was theoretically supposed to swing open when the barbed wire loop attached to the fence post and holding the gate pole was untwisted. That might have been what someone might have expected, but the surprise came when the heavy pole gate fell toward its new owner. It was similar to a young lady hastily jumping into the arms of the man whom she loves, except the man was not awaiting the jump. This ole weathered pole gate seemed to jump onto the lap of an unsuspecting George who crumpled like the unsuspecting boyfriend.

As fast as the wiry coyote disappeared, the Gila River Cowboy, in his white hat, black and white vest, and red bandana tied around the neck was knocked from a confident vertical position onto his posterior; it was a humbling experience to say the least. George Ribit Chattit had been taught from early childhood that every experience could and should provide a learning moment. This precious moment lying on the ground with a heavy weathered pole gate held together with an assortment of wires lying across his waist and legs was one such moment in life that resulted in multiple learning experiences for the Gila River Cowboy.

As he looked at his crumpled, white painted hat and the underside of the front bumper of his pickup truck, he grew in wisdom. He learned that you do not park close to a gate that falls towards you instead of away. He mentally registered that cowboy hats not only protect the head from weather, they heroically place themselves between the cowboys head and a hard chrome truck bumper. He quickly understood that the dreadfully hot desert rocks and sand do not cool down at sunset. He noted that he should first check gates to determine if they are connected to a post on the opposite end of the latch. And, last, but not least, he painfully realized that gates wrapped with barbwire are not easily pushed off the top of a now dust brown and red shirt.

He had not previously taken the time to review the underside of the F-350. So, he was thus given the opportunity. As he struggled out from under the gate, he also crawled out from under the front of the truck. Consequently, as he crawled out, he studied in close detail the front axle and differential of his manly man's truck, which was still hot from the extended tour of the Arizona desert.

As George crawled out from under the truck, he looked up to see Thunderbolt peering over the side of the make shift rack with a bewildered gaze. This look only comes from a horse that had just witnessed an event that neither man nor beast, especially not a horse, should see. George, however, felt that Thunderbolt recognized the worth of the gate incident and the newly acquired experiences. Thunderbolt stomped and whinnied. Some people might think him a fool, but George felt that Thunderbolt was telling George that he agreed the experience was valuable. From infancy, George was taught that the real fool is the man that will not attempt something new for fear of ridicule. So, with that understanding he was elated about the gate incident. He had not even entered the ranch site and already had gained valuable experiences. He felt grateful that "Honest Abe" had sold him such an astute horse that naturally understood his new owner and friend.

In the back of George's mind he recalled that in every western novel the cowboys had leather gloves. George's use of gloves on the east coast or mountains was to keep his hands warm during the cold winter months. Now, he realized that trying to push, pull, lift and drag a weathered pole, barbed wire gate with uncountable splinters and barbs all intent on finding and penetrating the tender skin required gloves. Mentally he recorded, "get good leather gloves."

He drove through the gate and closed it without incident and securely wired it back in place, George entered a task in his palm pilot to repair the gate. At minimum, he would replace the barbwire with smooth baling wire. In the future, this would make it easier to crawl out from under the gate in the event another unsuspecting cowboy ended in the same predicament. He also thought, as he looked at the century old ranch gate, that he should probably replace the rusted off hinges and four of the five poles, redo the wire cross brace, and reconnect the loop latch. Other than these minor repairs, the gate was in fine operating condition

He also mentally noted to smooth the road between the gate and the ranch house. He would have entered the note in his Palm Pilot but it had bounced out of his shirt pocket on the first or second sharp bounce. He would have tried to catch it but due to the short and safe distance from the gate to the ranch house, he had not "Buckled up." As his head thumped the top of the truck cab he remarkably recalled a very recent teaching, "seat belts on a desert road are not needed in case of a crash, they are needed to keep the driver attached to the seat and somewhere in the vicinity behind the steering wheel."

George parked the F-350 between the front door of the house and the corral. Thunderbolt stomped the metal floor of the pickup truck letting it be known that it was time to put hooves on solid ground. "Honest Abe" suggested putting some dirt in the bottom of the pickup, but no one had a shovel and no one volunteered to shovel the dirt. So, Thunderbolt was loaded slipping and sliding on the perfectly corrugated and newly painted floor of the truck bed. As a result, the bed was no longer corrugated and no longer painted. George was pleased that the new truck was getting "broke in." As he studied the tailgate and the gate of the make shift rack he was not sure if he should first open the wooden gate or lower the truck tailgate. He decided to lower the tailgate first. As it turned out, lowering the tailgate first saved him the effort of "unwiring" the rack gate. The moment the tailgate was opened, the rear legs of Thunderbolt slipped backwards and burst through the rack gate. Legs and all quickly followed. George hastily dove out of the way and avoided another learning experience. Thunderbolt's quick and unorthodox exit combined with his weight smashed the weathered one inch by four inch boards which splintered into a thousand uneven toothpicks. George saw the wisdom of using old lumber. It easily shattered without doing any damage to the horse. He thought, "It is impressive how much one can learn in such a short time." Thunderbolt tried to recover from his backwards summersault caused by his reverse exit out of the pickup. He rolled onto his stomach. This left his front legs crossed, his head down, and his ears forward as if to cover his eyes in shame for the unprofessional exit. George stood in the mist of the huge cloud of dust that rose as Thunderbolt landed in a heretofore-unseen position from the magnificent exit. George viewed this as conclusive proof that his horse was from the best of bloodlines.

Thunderbolt required about fifteen minutes to uncross his front legs and locate the outstretched hind legs before he managed to stagger towards the corral or at least what appeared to be a corral. It was once made of a native desert plants called Ocotillos. These long stems with protruding thorns every inch or so make great corral fences. These stems are planted just inches apart with wire woven between to hold them upright.

As GRC looked he could not determine if the stems were woven through strands of wire or wire woven through Ocotillo stems. Now, it seemed to only be patches of Ocotillos. Some stems had small green leaves showing that they had survived the prolonged years of drought. Other stems looked more like dried sticks mingled with a few coils of rusted wire. Thunderbolt walked around and over the once existing fence. When he felt he was in what was once a corral, his special breeding and training seemed to rise to the occasion preventing him from running astray. He promptly lay down and rolled on one side and then the other. The extra high and peaked withers were valuable. They prevented the horse from rolling over completely. As "Honest Abe" had explained, the high bony withers would keep a cowboy from being crushed if the horse fell and tried to roll over.

When George opened the truck's rear door he saw the bag of horse grain he purchased at a gas station that also doubled, as a local feed store was broken. Apparently, the trip across dry washes, ruts in the road, a few small boulders, and the minor collision with an unseen mesquite tree stump caused the bag of oats and a bale of hay to become a little discombobulated. Rolled oats mixed with molasses had filled the floorboard and now was spilling freely onto the ground. The odor of molasses, oats, and hay masked the new truck smell. Additionally the famed leather seats with a name brand of "Eddie Bauer," would have done the brand proud. There were only a few scuffs, small alfalfa stem punctures, and a little molasses stain on the seat and floor. But, they were proof that these genuine leather seat covers were well worth the extra money. Now the new interior carried an authentic cowboy look and smell.

Thunderbolt immediately recognized the problem of the broken bag, left his unclosed enclosure and promptly began to clean up the spilled oats accompanied by a few bites of green alfalfa hay. George thought, "He is such a great horse and well trained to help." George figured that a horse that smart would surely know not to over eat. Little did George know that the average horse, smart or dumb, pure bred or inbred will eat as long as there is grain to eat.

When George purchased the horse feed, he put all of it in the back seat. He did not want Thunderbolt to eat while he was riding in the truck. George feared he would get truck sickness. Also, George wanted Thunderbolt to have his head up so he could get the lay of the land. He put some of the suitcases in the front seat. Because he had brought seven suitcases, he could not put all of them in the cab. George put the remainder of the suitcases in the back of the truck.

In spite of his excellent breeding, Thunderbolt was shorter than a normal horse. Consequently, he had stood with front legs on the suitcases, so he could better see the road over the extended cab of the truck. George was overjoyed in having purchased such an intelligent horse that had figured out how to see over the truck cab. He was sure that Thunderbolt was getting an excellent view of the lay of the land.

The suitcases, however, were a little worn or better-said really beat up. He was disappointed that this famous Samsonite luggage did not withstand this test. All of the advertisement portrayed the suitcases as having great strength, durability and protection of garments. He could not understand why these suitcases were so easily destroyed with two small hooves from a small horse.

He dragged the suitcase for his first day from the front of the truck bed back to the tailgate. When he opened it, he was doubly disappointed. The suitcases allowed large amounts of sand, dust, dead mesquite leaves, and some kind of smelly yellow moisture to get inside. He studied for a moment and determined that the suitcases were damaged because of the newness of the luggage, combined with the cold altitude of the airplane, and the heat of the desert must have caused some kind of yellow smelly condensation to seep in on the lower side of the suitcases. He decided that it did not matter at least his clothes and other possessions had arrived to his new ranch. But, if the occasion ever presented itself he would explain to the Samsonite engineers that this condensation smelled a little like horse urine. It probably came from the fermentation of green mesquite leaves and the warm weather.

So, with Thunderbolt cleaning up the mess, George proceeded towards what appeared to be the ranch house. He approached the doorway with two suitcases and smiled at the absolute honesty and hospitality that existed in the west. There was not even a door to stop any stranger in need of help. He wanted to keep that hospitality. Anyone in need would be welcomed at the Gila River Cattle Ranch. This would be his slogan. He swung the first suitcase up to place it on the old kitchen table. The sudden extra weight caused one leg to collapse, which caused the suitcase to slide down the newly formed incline and strike an old wood crate that apparently had once been used as a cupboard but now was being inhabited with a very unhappy badger.

Badgers do not appreciate being disturbed in the early evening or probably during nighttime or, most likely anytime. This very unhappy creature quickly demonstrated that his enormous open mouth could easily consume a red cowboy boot along with the foot inside the boot. It didn't take a second look to easily see the mouth was loaded with bloodthirsty teeth. It also had long ample claws, which looked like miniature pitchforks that could easily be used to catch and rip to threads any object, whether made of steel, plastic or a frail but delicious human leg and stuff into the drooling mouth. Gratefully the fierce looking badger decided to make his exit through the open doorway leading to the outside. George decided it best to watch the badger's departure by quickly retreating backwards in the opposite direction. With two hasty retreats occurring simultaneously, the angry badger through the front door and George running backwards through an open bedroom door. He unknowingly fell over the old metal frame bed and onto an old worn mattress. He took a moment's pleasure thinking how his natural instinct led him to fall onto the bed and not onto the floor.

What his natural instincts did not convey to him, however, was that an old worn mattress in an abandon house was an ideal location for the home of a couple of coyotes. Many people believe that wild animals cannot be scared. George learned very quickly that this belief is erroneous. The two coyotes, rudely awakened by a chill-producing howl, which sounded like a mixture of wolf, coyote, and wildcat, were now standing up on their home, the worn mattress. The coyotes were wildly staring towards the door when this large object with the apparent form of a human entered their room. They had seen many humans from a distance, however, they had never seen one with skinny looking wings waving wildly in the air, but unable to lift the body. This mystic form came flinging through the door, backwards, and landed squarely on the two peaceful coyotes. Normally coyotes are very timid and tend to sneak unseen away from danger, however, when something so large with a mixture of sounds escaping as if it were part of wolf or a cougar and with the large flapping wings as if attached to a scarecrow but beating at the speed of a humming bird lands squarely on top of two untimely awakened coyotes, it was not a time for coyote bravery.

The coyotes sprang from under the fallen intruder. At the same instant, George felt something moving that he could not see. The coyotes were attempting to flee at the same time George was trying to increase the distance from whatever he had fallen on. George rolled from the mattress onto the floor and was crawling on hands and knees trying to get through the door. All three knew that there was only one exit from the house. All three were moving as fast as they could. George was a little closer to the door. The pair of coyotes saw a strange looking creature with a crumpled white hat and with eyes slightly larger and whiter than two boiled eggs. This creature was crawling and howling. The coyotes redoubled their speed and charged toward the bedroom door to make their escape. Meanwhile, the badger was lumbering his way through the outside opening as well, but turned when it heard the commotion coming from the normally quiet bedroom. When he heard the most unusual howl, the badger turned around prepared for battle. He saw something that would be discussed for years to come, when badgers join together to relate experiences.

The badger saw a human on hands and knees crawling close to the speed of sound. His eyes were wide open and had the look of rabid animal. As if that did not astonish him enough, two coyotes came jumping through the same opening. One of the coyotes landed on the back of this growling snarling wild human. The other sailed right over the back but straddled the neck and head kicking the white hat towards the badger. With a million years of instincts the badger, surmising that this white object was initiating a fierce attack, lunged towards the hat, grabbing it in his massive jaws just as the coyotes plowed squarely into the badger, fortunately for the coyotes the massive jaws of the badger were fiercely clamped on the useless crumpled white hat. Normally this would never occur, however, it seems that when George becomes involved, the abnormal becomes the normal.

Even though this sight or event had never been seen, even a badger will run from a terrifying unknown that is ten times its size crawling on all fours like a bear and then falling flat on the floor and lumbering wildly like an alligator with growling, howling and grunting sounds never before heard. So with hat in mouth out through the front door at top speed fled the badger and two coyotes. So, George's first entrance will never be forgotten.

Thunderbolt, standing lazily on the far side of the pickup parked in front of the door opening, was diligently cleaning up the excessive piles of spilled oats and was surely thinking how pleasant it would be to leisurely return to his unenclosed corral. He would then lock his leg joints (as horses do while resting) in the up-right position. He would have horse dreams about anything to help him forget about the ride over the rough desert road, the gate breaking from the wood rack of the pickup, and the backward somersault, as he not so graciously exited the pickup. He was prepared to sleep away the night. With those peaceful thoughts, he raised his head to take one final look at his new surroundings. The excitement of the day, however, was not over.

Hearing the strange commotion coming from the house Thunderbolt raised his head with perfect timing to see two coyotes in midair using the top of the truck as a vaulting ramp. The two coyotes did not anticipate that, as they sailed speedily over the top of this truck, a horse would rear his head. Even though coyotes are extremely agile, they cannot change direction in midair. The coyotes and the big eyed horse instantly knew there was going to be a collision even though none of the participants desired or planned this forthcoming activity the simply knew it was going to happen. The coyotes wanted to escape the monster from inside their normally peaceful sleeping quarters and the horse wanted to do absolutely nothing. One coyote parted the tips of Thunderbolt's ears with his belly and rear legs, the other landed on the sway back of the horse and used it as a trampoline to vault into the desert. Thunderbolt was in the reactive process of having his rear legs buckle, apparently preparing for a newly practiced backward somersault. However, before this could be successfully maneuvered, a white crumpled hat in the jaws of a badger dashed from under the pickup and literally crashed into the buckling rear legs of a trembling Thunderbolt. The hind legs did the only thing that hind legs do when they are scared beyond any sensible controlled reaction. They jump. Not just a normal jump, but also a jump with enormous quantities of adrenaline pumping through the muscles. This creates another perplexing problem. Thunderbolt, reacting from the coyote parting his ears, had just ducked his head inside the rear space of the pickup. In this odd position, when the badger hit Thunderbolt's back legs, entire body was propelled forward.

George was certain something had knocked him dizzy because when he was finally able to crawl through the kitchen doorway he saw the head of Thunderbolt sticking out the rear driver side window and the tail swishing frantically out the open door of the rear passenger side. Regaining some composure in a typical positive fashion, he squeaked out words from a still trembling throat.

"Well ole boy, you decided that riding in the back seat would be more comfortable than riding in the bed with the make shift stock rack. I wonder if the Eddie Bauer leather seat covers were made to carry horses."

At this point, it mattered not. George thought to himself, "I have learned and experienced in one day what it takes many people a lifetime to learn. I am tired of flying, tired of driving and tired of learning. I believe I have earned a little rest. No complaints Thunderbolt, I just wanted you to know."

George managed to get the driver side rear door open and Thunderbolt thrust forth his front legs and there he was, high centered in the back seat of the truck. Front legs hanging out on the driver side, rear legs sprawled out on the passenger side and an overstuffed belly perched on leather seats. It was soon evident that Thunderbolt had seriously assumed the job of cleaning up the fifty-pound bag of oats and any loose hay.

When a horse eats too much green hay, molasses, and rolled oats at the same time, it can seemingly produce enough natural gases to operate an alternative fuel vehicle. George's eyes were tearing dramatically, as escaping gases engulfed him. Also, when this type of natural gas permeates the air, there exist few, if any, mosquitoes. Yet, in his positive fashion, he thought of how much this fine horse cared for his new owner. First, Thunderbolt cleaned up all of the oats and hay, the very first night. Second, Thunderbolt used natural gas to chase away any lingering mosquitoes. He could tell from the loud moaning of Thunderbolt that generating that much gas and thrusting it out of the overstuffed belly resting on the Eddie Bauer leather seat covers required much effort and sacrifice.

"What a great and noble horse I purchased" were the exact thoughts that filled the Gila River Cowboy's mind as the sunlight exchanged itself for total and absolute darkness void of mosquitoes, also void of the ability for the human eye to see.

"Where did I leave the flashlight?"

8—FIRST NIGHT

THERE ARE HUNDREDS, maybe thousands, of books and pamphlets explaining that the desert floor in the Southwest can be deadly hot during the day and drop forty to fifty degrees at night. With that in mind, George purchased a down filled sleeping bag to keep the cold from seeping in from the top and a six inch foam pad to keep the cold ground from penetrating the lower side. When he asked for a down sleeping bag with full zipper, water proof exterior, and flannel lining, the young sales assistant built like Atlas asked if he were going to camp in Alaska. George reported with a broad smile, "better warmer than colder, better dryer that wetter." He had not heard that in a movie, but he was sure that is what Charles Bronson would say.

Now, he was set for the cold air. He was sure that cold nights are a major concern of any Arizona desert camper. What George did not fully comprehend was that although the summer daytime temperatures can drop twenty to forty degrees during the night, is that the daytime temperature might rise to 120 degrees. The nighttime temperature, consequently, drops to eighty or might even remain near the one hundred degree mark. The nighttime temperature in the Arizona desert is about the same as the average daytime temperature in portions of the eastern coast of the United States.

He was beginning to realize that some details are not printed clearly in the travel books. Thus, realizing that the desert's nighttime temperature in the summer is still very warm and that a down filled sleeping bag is unnecessary, he smiled, "Another detail learned from experience."

He dedicated a difficult hour to the unsuccessful endeavor of removing Thunderbolt from the rear seat of the truck. Being so preoccupied with Thunderbolt he failed notice the absolute darkness. The interior dome light was ample for pushing and pulling a high centered horse.

Then he realized another detail. Once the sun ploddingly sets behind the Estrella Mountain Range, the desert becomes extremely dark. He would come to realize that this was especially true at the Gila River Cattle Ranch. He suddenly realized that there was no electricity. There were no artificial lights to disturb the darkness.

The sun, that was so generous with its light during the day, after ducking behind the distant western Estrella Mountain Range, seemed to become a vacuum that sucked all remaining rays of light. For someone who spent most of his life under the bright city lights of the east coast, the darkness was almost scary. When he thought about his encounter with the badger and two coyotes, his apprehension grew exponentially.

At this moment, however, he noticed that the darkness lessened. The moon was inching up from behind the San Tan Mountains with its much-welcomed glow. The lights of the stars quickly followed further easing the darkness. George's apprehension was fractionally reduced. He did not feel, however, the need to have some artificial streetlight shine in the darkness of the desert. Even though he was a little nervous he felt a large artificial light would be an intrusion. The moon and stars were there to help guide this wary earth traveler. At this particular time of the year, George felt that the "Sun God" made a deal with the "Moon God" to make sure that this newest arrival was able to see every star.

He had not been where there was no electricity, since he was a small boy in northern Arizona. He could not recall since that time ever being where there were no lights that automatically strutted and magically lighted each night. He realized that he had never stopped to appreciate that simple fact.

After this moment of feeling appreciation for electricity and absorbing the natural night lights, he remembered the whereabouts of his six-battery flashlight. He purchased the flashlight at "Popular Camping" because he could adjust light to be a very long-range spotlight or to be a wide-angle light for seeing everything close. He was happy he had remembered. He was unhappy that he could not reach it. The flashlight was under the seat that Thunderbolt currently occupied.

It had been less than a couple of hours pushing and pulling Thunderbolt but it seemed like forty. He leaned against the hood, realizing that he did not have enough strength to free his horse.

Thunderbolt could not be enticed with grain. He had eaten most of it. From the look of his overly bloated belly, he most likely wanted no more hay. George decided the best approach for the moment would be to simply leave his special multi-purebred cattle workhorse in the back seat and use the two battery double AA pen light in his suitcase that was on the kitchen table, or most likely on the kitchen floor beside the broken table. While he was quite certain that neither the badger nor the coyotes were in the house, with some trepidation he started to enter the house. Besides he thought, "What else could possibly go wrong the first night?"

George had studied about the desert animals and insects. He recalled that almost all of them ate and moved around at night. This is especially true in the summer time. So, he cautiously moved toward the doorway without a door. While he was not frightened, every shadow that moved or sound that he heard had his complete and undivided attention. Of course, George had studied in detail the behaviors of desert animals, so he reminded himself that most desert animals are afraid of men. But, as with the majority of inexperienced travelers trying to feel their way back into a blacker than black, and darker than dark area that has recently caused them a slight scare, he was not in a hurry. He told himself that what had happened earlier was not really a scare, but more of an impressionable experience. Already, as often happens with a frightening experience, he was forgetting how scared he had been when he had had an up close and personal encounter with the badger and coyotes. He was also failing to remember many of the things he had studied about desert animals. His brain seemingly was stalled in a "freeze mode."

What was locked in the "freeze mode" was that during the early evenings, millions of spiders emerge from their hideouts and create beautiful masterpieces in web designs. Their beauty is misleading. The intricately spun webs are traps for unsuspecting insects. These intricate designs are important in helping maintain nature's balance of insects. They are not fabricated to trap anything larger than a horsefly. They especially were not spun to catch a beast like a human.

George edged towards the entrance of his house. This same entrance had served as an exit for the badger, the coyotes, and a screaming and crawling George just a few hours earlier. Now the screaming and crawling would never be retold as evidence of fear. Instead, those events would be used as evidence of a highly trained frontiersman. The deliberate loud voice was to frighten any other varmints in the area and the crawling to prevent someone or something from attacking a standing human.

Stepping through the doorway, his hatless head and clean-shaven face were seemingly attacked by a newly formed spider web. Within the already nervous mind this was no ordinary spider web. No, the web seemed to be spun by some giant treacherous, never before seen spider. Very few Arizona desert spiders hurt or even have the ability to hurt a man. But, when the sticky silk threads of a large spider web engulf a person, that person forgets that supposedly common knowledge about spiders. Instead, his mind is riveted on the notion that this web has come from a spider that is capable of devouring a human. Even though he would never admit it, he was still shaken by his earlier run in with his uninvited houseguests. Thus, he could only imagine that this web was produced for the exclusive purpose of trapping large animals or humans.

This spider web consisted of finely spun, extremely weak, hair like threads. However, in the mind of an innocent intruder the threads seemed to be larger and stronger than a one-inch nylon rope. George's imagination ran wild and he was sure that each thread was committed to his mortal destruction. The more he flailed his arms, the more George became entangled in the web.

He imagined himself completely wrapped in the web, lying on the porch, and watching as at least a dozen giant, carnivorous spiders lick their chops in anticipation of this ultra fine, eastern human meat. Within moments this extreme, near-death experience passed. The extremely powerful cobweb was totally destroyed by the same flinging arms that attempted to fly when escaping the Badger. George was extremely red-faced from the adrenaline rush. After he collected himself, he slowly looked around to see, if there had been any witnesses to the destruction of some extremely large and sturdy spider web. All he could see was the extreme blackness of the night and the extreme heavy snorting of an over-stuffed horse in extreme advanced stages of pain. George was momentarily disappointed that no one saw his extreme bravery in warding off a potential threat. George realized that "extremes" were constantly present in the Arizona desert.

Once again, for the third time he mustered the strength to reenter the house. He located the suitcase. Opening the suitcase required excessive effort. He finally forced open the hoof imprinted and damaged suitcase latch that had failed the guarantee that it could never be damaged. Opening the damaged Samsonite, he began pawing through the clothes. Suddenly, he remembered the unpleasant odor that he had encountered before. This time his bare hands felt the repulsive wetness that was causing the dreadful smell. With hands wet and nostrils flaring, he located his penlight practically floating in one corner of the suitcase.

Few individuals have experienced standing in a cave in a darkness that prevents him from seeing his own hand. George experienced this when a he visited the Carlsbad Caverns. The guide jokingly turned off all lights as part of the tour of the cave. Even fewer have stood in a dark cave that may be home to rattle snakes, carnivorous spiders, or other predators. George had not previously faced this situation. While George recalled again that humans frighten most animals, he also remembered that any animal that is cornered would become unusually aggressive towards its perceived captor. George quickly turned on his penlight. The small flashlight cast an enormous beam of light. This momentarily soothed George. He, of course, had already rewritten this experience in his mind to show that all of his actions were the calculated efforts of an experienced rancher.

As the light from the flashlight, broke the darkness, George appreciated, from the depths of his soul, the invention of stored electrical energy in batteries. This prized light could solve so many problems, remove so many needless fears, and simultaneously reveal a whole new set of problems and fears. It is one thing to imagine prehistoric monsters lurking in the darkness. It is quite another to actually glimpse what you thought only could dwell in one's imagination. The light skipping across the old wood floor showed ample gaps between each of the slightly warped planks. Gradually, this synthetically stored light revealed movement on the floor. It appeared, at least to an already nervous newcomer, that he had placed a spot light on prehistoric monsters. His fear induced heightened awareness and along with his frequently used imagination estimated that there were three million of these critters immersed in his light. There were only at most three or four.

These were not the rubber monsters that you buy at the store or the plastic varmints advertised on TV to falsely scare the unexpected. These were real. These were alive. The low angled light cast twelve-inch shadows along the floor. George could see that their tails curled up and over their backs. These were predators on the hunt, and would, without doubt, attack any moving or non-moving, warm or cold-blooded and living or non-living entity. George's first response was to jump and run. But, he wondered, jump or run to where? Can scorpions climb? Can scorpions eat a human with those dreaded looking pinchers? Can they jump like the cholla cactus or like a rattlesnake?

He noticed a slight vibration coming from the old wooden floor. Then, he realized that the noise of the vibration was indeed coming from the floor. The cause of the vibrating floor was his boots. He suddenly realized that he was shaking in his boots. He also noticed that his teeth were chattering. He calmed himself. He was sure that scorpions could not climb his red boots. He made a mental note that the part about him shaking in his boots would never be told. Considering how scared he felt after the giant cobweb incident, he considered he was handling the scorpions quite calmly. He was indeed pleased with himself at how quickly he calmed down. He remained quite calm until the penlight drifted to his pant leg and spotlighted what looked like a six-inch scorpion. It was then that he learned another bit of vital information concerning the desert; boots do not prevent a scorpion from crawling up the pants in search of a nice tender leg.

Clint Eastwood certainly would have calmly brushed the varmint back to the floor and, with a twisting boot, ground it into the already stained wood floor. The floor for the moment ceased to vibrate. However, legs sometimes do what legs sometimes do. They jump, stomp and bounce, run or some simultaneous combination of these movements without going forward or backwards. They do not bother to even consult the brain, which in most cases has already gone back into a freeze-up mode. This leg movement, devoid of any brain thought, continued for what seemed like five minutes before the monster fell to the floor, shrunk to its original two-inch size and disappeared into one of the many crawl spaces.

Grinning at his responses, he said out loud, "It is amazing how one learns from such a variety of situations." He was now certain he knew the exact origin of the famous "western stomp" and he wondered how Pretty Peggy would look in a pair of "tight fitting jeans" doing the western stomp. Of course, he did not want her to learn the dance the way he had just learned it. It would be okay, however, if she learned the dance. "My" he thought, "how quickly the mind does wander." He was pleased that he never let his imagination take control of his actions.

George realized that he now had a new problem. After seeing the scorpions on and under the floor, and then seeing them disappear completely after his western stomp caused some alarm, he was sure that as soon as it was quiet, they would return to their hunting grounds. He was unsure where to unroll his sleeping bag. He was certain they undoubtedly would be highly discontent to find a sleeping bag placed in a location that might interfere with their hunting. The questioned loomed into the darkness, "Where do I sleep?"

He slowly ventured into the previously, but briefly, seen bedroom. The bright moon was now shinning through the glassless window onto the old worn mattress. The western stomp in the kitchen did not appear to molest in the slightest the scorpions occupying the old mattress in the absence of the coyotes. Turning to leave, he saw "it" on the wall. The moonlight back dropping a creature unknown and unseen by George created a shadow approximately six-foot long. George was positive that this was a Jurassic Park escapee in search of an evening meal. This shadow seemingly moved up and down as if doing push-ups in preparation for some type of battle to obtain a nightly snack. George realized that he was the only possible snack. George felt he was in control of his extreme fear. So, it must have been the continued heat of the night that facilitated the large drops of salty sweat to roll from his forehead into his oversized eyes that were not blinking. His legs, which he recently learned to function independent of the brain, chose to remain as if embedded in a ton of dry concrete. The six-foot shadow began to move towards him. But, in no particular hurry. George tried to move his gaze to see the source of the shadow but his eyes would not leave even for a moment the shadow. The monster seemed to sense its prey was unable to run. The shadow moved towards George. Even with this eminent threat, his legs remained steadfast. The legs seemed indifferent to the prospect of having George's upper body devoured by this ever-growing monster. Even as the mind was giving commands to race away, the legs remained frozen.

With the shadow moving closer he repeated in his unfrozen mind, "Monsters do not exist, Monsters do not exist, Monsters do..." even before he finished his last plea for sanity, the wall became totally encompassed with darkness. Had the shadow outgrown its creator? Had the moon moved away from the window opening? Still, the legs refused to move. If the legs will not move, maybe the neck and head with sweat burning eyes could slightly turn to face the monster. He recalled, in his slow functioning mind, how many times the great authentic cowboys had starred down an evil opponent. Davy Crockett, the famed frontiersman, so the story reveals, even stared down a bear. Slowly, ever so slowly, George turned his neck with smooth jerks. His eyes tried to race ahead of their sockets, so they could more quickly face the opponent.

Slowly his shaky arm lifted the small flashlight that been uselessly pointing to an undetermined part on the floor. His salt burning eyes focused on the predator clinging to the wall papered wall. The predator's eyes fixed on the human. The human jaws and mind finally coordinated.

George softly spoke, "You probably thought you scared me with your colossal shadow, but I knew all along, you were only a small lizard. Your shadow reflected on the wall. Did you actually know that the moonlight would cause a bigger than life shadow to be cast in front of you? Any other person might have displayed fear, but not George Ribit Chattit. You perhaps noticed that I did not attempt to run."

At that precise moment, looking eye to eye with a five-inch lizard, and understanding that there was not one ounce of danger; the legs decided it was time to run. Miraculously, he shed what had felt like a ton of cement that was holding his feet. His legs moved with alacrity, practically leaving behind the neck and head. His legs took twelve-foot leaps, over-stepped the scorpions, and jumped through what remained of the spider web. He made a grand attempt to fly through the doorless door. It was during this hasty exit and somewhere between dropping the penlight, hitting his head on the weathered wood porch, twisting his legs to an unusual position, and slamming his heels and spurs into the door jamb, that a question was formed in his mind.

"When is it appropriate for an authentic cowboy to remove his spurs? He is not riding, so he does not need them to encourage the horse. There is no one to impress with the rolling jingle of the rowels on the wood floor." He thought of this for those milliseconds between the start and the finish of a headlong fall. His conclusion was, "It surely is best to remove the large rowel spurs before they become immovably wedged into the door jambs.

George now understood that often the needed knowledge to avoid a situation comes after the situation has occurred. He also grasped that this newly acquired knowledge would not likely be needed in the future, especially, if the event were unique. As he was falling towards the porch, he wished that the last few minutes could be repeated and the new knowledge used retroactively. Alas, this was simply not possible.

George's face, not so gently, became acquainted with the rough-hewn, dusty planks of the porch. While the pain in his face began to spread, he fleetingly thought of the badgers, the coyotes, the scorpions and the lizard. He was comforted that the badger and the coyotes had fled the scene. He was less sure about the residential status of the scorpions and the lizard. He knew from recently gained experience that his running, stomping, and spur jingling, along with his verbal expressions (screams of terror), that were still echoing off of the desert mountains twenty miles away, and his precipitous fall on the wood planks, that he had created adequate vibration and disturbances that the scorpions and the lizard had scurried to some obscure part of the house. This comforting thought only lasted momentarily. He knew that the scorpions and the lizard would soon come out of their hiding places to resume their nightly hunt for food. With his face discomfortingly resting on the porch and his spurs embedded in the doorjamb, he was once again in a situation that made it difficult to move. He was also at eye level with the scorpions when they began to re-emerge. With keen focus, he began to contemplate how to get out of this situation.

As a rule, cowboys want their boots on their feet during times of danger or even death. They are notorious for even sleeping with their boots on so as to be able to flee quickly a situation if unexpectedly awakened. But, as with most rules, there are exceptions. George's current situation invoked one of those exceptions. When a cowboy whose boots and spurs are tightly wedged in a door jamb and the cowboy is in a prone position in scorpion hunting grounds facing scorpions that delight in whipping out their nicely curved tails and inflicting terrible pain on the human anatomy, the cowboy may shed his boots.

It could not be timed, but it would be guesstimated that the duration of the boot removal and crossing the thirteen feet between the porch and the side of the make shift horse rack was one ten millionths of a second. He clung to the side of the one by four inch sideboard and wondered if he could ever gather enough nerve to let loose of the weathered lumber tied together with rusted baling wire to drop to the dusty ground and recover his penlight and boots. A cowboy becomes somewhat helpless when he has no boots on, because it would mean either taking off his socks or getting his socks dirty, both options are unacceptable.

It was in the haze of this decision-making process that he noticed the penlight on the ground move, then it moved again to reveal what materialized yet another desert monster of the night, but approximately a thousand times larger than the scorpions he had seen already. The limited light from the moon exposed a large gleaming white shank tusk that should have been attached to an elephant at a zoo. Then the small flashlight rolled and shined directly into a black nose with two large nostrils, guarded by lion type teeth hanging out on each side of the mouth. From the warning grunts that threatened life around the monster, George realized that just below his perilous grip on the loose and half decomposed boards was a family of javalinas. He pondered for a moment, "Does this desert have anything besides pre-historic creatures?" These fierce looking animals, from fables are believed to be a mix of wolves, lions, elephants, pigs and bovine. There are also as many brutal myths about javalinas, as there are javalinas. These stories include legs being ripped apart, German shepherds torn to pieces, grown men gutted, and rattlesnakes eaten for lunch and their fangs used as toothpicks. These were mean creatures. They were approximately three feet from a bootless foot clinging to boards that were beginning to creak.

With the cracking sound of a whip, the boards and the rusted baling wire gave way. George feared that he was about to be sacrificed to these javalinas and to become one more fable told around the campfire. Some may say it was the bloodcurdling scream of a dying man, or, as he later explained, "My controlled verbalizations actually frightened the savage beasts." There never seems to be an acceptable truth in life threatening matters. It may well have been the many pieces of boards striking the animals on their backs that caused them to scatter.

To those actually experienced with javalinas, they are not as fierce as they look, are not meat-eaters, and are nearly blind. However, these kinds of facts are rarely mentioned or expounded while sitting around a campfire. Most truths are camouflaged with slight or more likely excessive exaggerations. The slow, deliberate, cowboy swagger ceases when the cowboy lands on top of a mama javalina. Amongst the controlled movement of a hysterical human, the squealing of a mama javalina with babies, some decisions are readily made. The Gila River Cowboy chose to spend the night in the front seat of his F-350 with his trusty horse in the back seat. With two open doors and all windows down.

When the belly of a horse is aching it means nearly all of the horse is aching. The escaping gases, the groans, and the rumbles should have blocked the other normal sounds of a living desert during the night. But, they did not. George was accustomed to life on the east coast with sirens, traffic, garbage dumpsters, fender benders, and blaring television sets. He was not used to the desert. At first, it seemed disturbingly quiet, then disturbingly filled with sounds, strange sounds, sounds far away and then sounds very close. He could recognize the yelps and howls of coyotes and smiled at their loneliness, but as the howling became closer and closer the smile grew smaller and smaller. He would have rolled up the windows but for two reasons, smell and the fact that both rear doors were propped open with horse legs. He took comfort that maybe coyotes liked horses more than humans. This limited comfort was short lived as the grunts of the Javalinas returned. Apparently, they had decided that the smell of fresh, eastern human flesh was well worth the risk of returning. Unknown to him, javalinas were enjoying the new found feast of the remaining rolled oats mixed with sweet molasses. The grunts and snorts, mingled with visions of tusks and teeth, highlighted with images of stories filled his mind. It was at that precise moment that he felt a crawling sensation on his neck, which caused him to jump straight up in the front seat. What followed is a memory he would prefer to forget.

Beyond his expanded powers of logic, beyond all understanding, he could not comprehend how quickly, how deliberately, and how accurately a desert spider could select a site that might efficiently trap the prey. He was amazed at how extremely fearless this spider was of the size of the victim. Inside the cab, connected to the visor, the hook for hanging cloths, the rearview mirror, and the dome light were spider webs that matched the super strength NASA built cords. They waited for the innocent victim, which, for a brief moment, might be distracted and enter into the web. George entered with his head, face, ears, nose, mouth, hair and eyelashes, all of which were encapsulated. Once again he reacted as calmly as he had the first time. His mind did not recall the percentages of non-lethal spiders. His arms and legs quite defiantly refused to remain calm. His arms became entangled with steering wheel and his elbow hit the horn. The blaring of the horn caused the poor javalinas to bump the underside of the truck. The addition of the noise from the javalinas bumping into the truck caused George's already over-active adrenal glands to release even more adrenaline.

The events of George's first night as a rancher can only be re-told by an eyewitness. The only viable eyewitnesses were the animals, insects and other critters, real or imagined. Fortunately, for George, none of them could speak to humans. But, if a human could over hear the spider explaining what happened that night to his mother it would probably have been something like the following: "You will never believe what happened to me tonight. I nearly died of fright and then of laughter. This huge man got caught in my web two different times. He was not really caught. He just walked into my webs first at the doorless door of the house and then the one in the truck. The way this man cast about, you would have thought the web was made of super strength cable." The story would continue as follows: "This human slowly attempted to walk through the door opening, at the moment my beautiful web was just completed. When the web touched his face, my goodness mama, you should have seen the flailing of arms, the yelling, and the rolling on the porch, it was hysterical. You would have thought there were hundreds of carnivorous bugs eating him alive. When he realized that neither the web nor I was going to hurt him, he stood and with intense dignity and quickly brushed the web from his entangled body. I am quite new at web building. I decided that an opening as large as the doorless door would attract prey much larger than I could possibly eat. So, I left the house and located a site near a horse, resting in the back seat of a pickup. No mama, I am not making this up. The horse was in the back seat of a brand new four-door pickup. I do not know how fast it was going, or why it decided to cross from one side to another through the back seat. Do you want to hear my story or not? Okay, I was sure this site with the resting horse would attract many flies and gnats as the horse was creating an awful smell. I was sure that I would have my fill of small insects and that they would not destroy my well-designed web.

"I worked extra fast and extra hard because I was getting hungry. I connected the first part of the web to the mirror, next I propelled over to the visor and finally over to the hook by the door. I was so excited and was eagerly waiting for my first insect. Then, I noticed that the same ugly man crawl into the front seat. Yes, this truck has two seats! He seemed to be nervous and was looking all around. I should have quit right then, but I was almost finished with a splendid web and I was certain that he had learned that I was not going to eat him and that my beautiful web was no match for his flinging arms.

"I listened to the songs of the coyotes and was watching Beauty, you know, the mama javalina, bring her precious little piglets joyously grunting and eating, practically making hogs of themselves. I thought how kind this man was to have put oats on the ground for Beauty and her children.

"It was at this moment with these kind thoughts that I spotted a small gnat on the human neck. I dropped down to see if I might catch the pest and have a little supper. The moment I began crawling across the neck he must have thought I was a giant poisonous reptile. No mama, I only think he thought I was a snake. I did not see a snake. Suddenly, this man began to yell, honk the horn, jump up and down, and turn a complete somersault in the front seat of the truck. Then, just before he banged his head on the roof for the fourth time, with his twisted face and wide-open mouth, his waving hands destroyed my beautiful web.

"One thing I learned tonight is that human monsters learn very slowly. Maybe, because he left his boots in the house he was unable think or to learn from the previous experience. My splendid web was again destroyed. That is why I am here. I have not had dinner. No, I am not sure where the man is at this time. Yes mother dear, this is the complete truth. How could I make up something so unbelievable?

"I climbed up and out of his reach. Then the truck began to shake as if were a bird nest in the top of a tree during a windstorm. The man must have thought some unknown monster was trying to steal his precious truck. He grabbed the steering wheel, honked the horn again, put on the brakes, released the brake, all the time hollering. What he did not see or understand was that the horse that was sleeping in the backseat. Yes Mama, it is the truth! No Mama, I do not know why the horse was in the backseat. Anyway, the screaming and honking must have caused the horse to wake up. He must have been as scared as much as I was because he jumped out of that backseat with one long panic jump and disappeared into the night.

"Somehow, this erratic behaving man did not know that I was a harmless little spider. He managed to get out or fall out of his truck, land on his rear only to be face to face with Beauty, the mama javalina. The javalinas were in a high speed run from being scared by the runaway horse. And, you know Mama how Beauty runs with those long gleaming white tusk when she's scared. With no malice intended, she showed the human those long tusks. Then she let out with her deep guttural grunt and her two piglets jumped across the legs of this human. He just disappeared. He seemed to go straight up into the sky faster than a scared quail. No, I told you, I did not make up this story just to get something to eat. Please believe me, I have worked really hard and didn't even get the gnat"

George stood on top of the cab for some time trying to find where his heart had gone. He heard more than saw Thunderbolt rubbing against the one solid post in the corral. What a smart horse. He got himself out. Finally, George was able to lie on top of the F-350 and looked to the star filled heavens. "Had I stayed in New Jersey where it was secure, I would never have had such amazing experiences." As he dozed, he again had a vivid dream of his father. This time he merely saw his father's face with a radiant smile and knew he was pleased with his mortal son. George still wondered why his mother never appeared with his father. Was there any possibility that she was still earth bound? His mind assured him it was an impossible thought. So why did his heart still cling?

Drifting to sleep with the pleasant thought, "what will the morning bring?"

9—FIRST MORNING

THE FIRST BRILLIANT rays of the early morning sun crawled over the rugged, dark, agglomerate boulders, but held firmly to the sun dried and windblown Arizona Mountains. Slowly, the light crept over the San Tan Mountains and began to fill each and every crevice. Streaks of light beams skipped from boulder to sand and then brilliantly silhouetted a giant Arizona Saguaro. Streaks of light then bounced across the desert floor and to seemingly ignite the almost invisible needles of the famous cholla "jumping cactus." For its climax, the sunlight created dancing shadows on the Prickly Pear. All of these seemingly daily events occurred, before the life-giving rays actually reached George Ribit Chattit's messed hair.

George wished that he could have awakened with the majestic look of the morning sun, but today was not such a day. Instead, the new owner of the Gila River Cattle Ranch was found standing on top of the cab of this new pickup truck with no boots on his feet. With momentary embarrassment, he recalled the events of the last night that seemingly catapulted him to the top of his truck to sleep.

He remained optimistic, "Tomorrow I will rise as majestically as the mighty sun does every morning."

Even with recalling last night's events and having had an almost sleepless night, he still felt genuine excitement as he absorbed the early morning rays. He vigorously inhaled the raw and massive desert air and gazed towards the rising sun,

"You must be well rested my friend. You certainly took your time in getting here. I was awake most of the night, waiting for you and while you were away there was much activity, however, I thank you for coming."

He looked around and half-muttered, "my how things look different in the daylight." In all the night's excitement, he had forgotten that his incredible horse had climbed out of the truck without any help.

He climbed down from the truck. Peered into the rear seat compartment and concluded that the Eddie Bauer seat covers must have been tested better than the Samsonite luggage; there was not even one tear in the seat covers. A few stains and small puncture wounds but nothing major.

He turned and gingerly walked towards the doorless door, he reverently observed a small spider busily developing a magnificent web with intricate and uniform designs high in the corner of the porch. He smiled, "I see that you have learned to build your excellent web out of my reach." A small hole in the rusty tin roof over the porch allowed a delicate funnel of sun to glisten on the newly formed web. George, in awe and wonderment, offered a verbal and sincere apology, "Little one, I am sorry for destroying your beautiful webs during the night." In fact he said, "I destroyed two webs and I hope they weren't both yours?"

He paused and listened to the creaking and groaning of the rusted corrugated tin roof expanding from the heat of the morning sun with almost a musical rhythm. He mused, as he picked up the shredded, white straw hat, and thought how much fun the badger and the baby javelinas must have had playing with this strange, imported toy.

Yes he thought, "Everything looks different in the daylight."

He made mental notes and recorded each item he saw. He would be prepared for nightfall, when darkness again crept across the living desert. He would see with his mind what he only could see during the day. He remembered what his mother once read from his father's letter.

"My dear one, far away, you are never alone. Never let the fears of darkness overcome the joys of light; never let the beauties of darkness be faded by the light." George look upward and simply said, "I will endeavor to remember."

He stood on the porch that he so carefully dusted with his body last night when he fell face down onto the porch, while engulfed in a spider web. The web that enveloped him last night seemed to be at least one hundred times larger and stronger, than the one he observed a moment ago. He stepped on the wood floor with ample gaps, leaned over and slipped on his abandoned boots. Stomping on the floor he verbalized a heart-felt thanks to his boots, the old plank floor and his pickup: "Thanks for helping to keep me safe last night."

He walked a few steps into the desert, "You scared me last night. Nevertheless, you afforded me new experiences, and now, Brother Desert with all your inhabitants; you and I will become friends. I will learn to appreciate your strength, your endurance, your patience and your ability to live and let live."

Something stirred deep inside his very soul. Maybe it was a teaching from his mother or a teaching he learned in a prior life. He understood that prior knowledge was a part of present mortality. He was not sure, but he took pleasure in this newly found emotion. It radiated from the hard life of the desert to associate with a feeling deep within his soul.

He stood in the shadow of a mesquite tree exaggerated by the low angle of the early sun and smiled as he recalled the experience of the small lizard portraying a giant shadow.

"I wonder if all creatures try to portray a larger than life shadow? Why not?" He answered his own question.

He pulled a green seedpod from the sturdy and thorny mesquite limb, split open the long skinny pod and popped a seed into his mouth. The mesquite pod has uniform lumps protecting the seed much like a green pea pod, in the produce section of a grocery store. When a mesquite bean is yellowish-brown, the seeds are hard as river pebbles, but have a very sweet taste and an extremely high protein content. When the pods are green, they have a very bitter taste. In less than a split second, he experienced the bitter. He quickly spat repeatedly to get the taste out of his mouth and attempted to dig out the green seed from under his tongue with his index finger. This was the same finger he used to break off the mesquite bean. Unknowingly, a mesquite thorn had stuck to his finger and now was stuck in the inner corner of his mouth. The bitter seed was stuck under his tongue. So, he ran to his truck to get a bottle of "fresh spring" water.

Where there should have been a full case of this life giving, crystal water, now there was only one partially filled bottle with the plastic lid smashed from a bite from the large teeth of a thirsty horse. He twisted and broke off the remaining portion of the lid and rinsed his mouth, spit out the thorn and looked at the satisfied face of Thunderbolt, "What a smart horse, he knows how to drink from a bottle."

Of course, the lack of water presented another problem. He was smack in the middle of the Sonoran Desert in the summer time. He would learn in painful detail that a man in the Arizona desert without water poses the same danger as a fish out of water.

He knew he must shortly get supplies and ample water. Before leaving for town or a nearby store, however, he figured to check out the plumbing from the windmill to the storage tank and from the storage tank to the kitchen sink. Then he would check out the windmill. He was nearest to the kitchen, which seemed the most logical place to start.

With a high degree of caution, he entered the kitchen. He made sure and hoped, that neither the coyotes nor the badger had decided to re-occupy their previous living quarters. Of course, in his mind, he would not jump or be frightened, if they were to leap out at him. He was almost certain that he would not jump. Yet, he was very careful, because he did not want to *scare* the poor, defenseless animals.

The kitchen faucet was a valued antique on the east coast with white cross handles engraved with "water." It did not indicate hot or cold. In time, he would learn that the same faucet furnished him with hot and cold water--hot in the summer and cold in the winter. He twisted the handle counter clockwise and to his surprise the faucet turned. He was impressed that the previous owner must have bought quality merchandise because the cross handle still easily turned. No water flowed, however, not even one drop. He decided to check under the sink; kneeling on the well-worn wood plank floor, he opened the cupboard doors with spooky, squeaky hinges.

With his extensive reading, and hours of studying, he should have recalled with exactness the detail, that some desert creatures of the night enjoy quiet, dark places in which to spend the hot sunny days. To his utter amazement, kneeling on his hands and knees to better inspect the underside of the sink, he had the rare opportunity of looking eye to eye with one of nature's most enjoyable creatures. At least that is the portrait that Walt Disney so humorously developed in the movie Bambi. Many famous cartoonists have put pink ribbons on or around the cute little varmints, and caused their eyes to flitter with love, as they scampered over the green meadow grass. When a man, however, on bended knee looks into the dark brown eyes, all those furry little cartoon characters seem to quickly evolve into a nightmare. Eyes to eyes, and nose to nose, Mrs. Skunk saw the first man she had seen, since she was a baby. For this imported Easterner, he was seeing a skunk up close for the very first time. Looking a skunk eye to eye never caused any problems. The problem comes, as George was about to learn, when the cute little skunk with super-sonic speed makes a one hundred and eighty degree pivot. Now, George was eye and nose to the skunk's backside. He could only hope that the liquid he felt on the side of his face, down his neck, and on this pearl snap shirt was water from a broken pipeline. That was the hope of hopes.

Alas, the smell quickly told him that his hope would be unrequited. He quickly rolled over backward to escape another spray. The extreme odor from a skunk at close range will cause a man's lungs to cease function, extract tears from his dry eyes, and cause his nostrils to close and his mouth to open. All of this occurred concurrently. He was positive that nothing worse could possibly happen to a man. Then he remembered that his faithful and super smart horse had consumed the water. So, worse than being sprayed, is being sprayed where there is no water or soap available. George could barely see. Yet, at this moment, when all seemed to have gone wrong again, George thought of something good.

He conjured up only one thought, "There is not a varmint, snake, spider or lion that would bother a human directly sprayed by a skunk." All these grand experiences and it was barely 6 a.m.

After spending almost two hours rolling in the dirt, rubbing sand on his face, washing with the sponge like substance hacked from a barrel cactus with a rusted shovel spade, and changing into clothes that had been dampened by what he could only imagine came from his trusty horse, it was nearly eight o'clock. The smell had been partially resolved, he thought. In truth, the nostrils, after receiving two sprays from a close range skunk, simply gave up in defeat. He did not realize how grateful he soon would be for the odor emanating from him created by the mixture of skunk spray, sand, cactus juice, and horse urine soaked shirt he wore. He would come to appreciate it more than the finest blends of perfumes sold in best stores in New York City.

Being able to see a little more clearly, after another two hours since the spray, and knowing he had to drive into town for supplies, he hoped the old, paint faded, and rusted water storage tank might have a little moisture left. The water tank rested on a cement slab and was about ten feet tall. While the top of the tank was covered, there was an opening about one foot by two feet on the side and near the top. Climbing up the rusted pipe ladder, he peered into the hole of the tank. He could hear dripping water. It took a moment to focus and see that there was about six inches of water in the bottom of the tank. But, it took another moment for him to realize that the drips were coming from his own eyes, which were still burning and watering from the skunk spray and odor. After surveying the situation, he realized that if he got into the tank, he would not be able to climb out, as there was no ladder inside the tank. As he was trying to figure out what to do, he looked down and noticed a drain valve at the bottom side of the tank about three inches above the ground.

"All I need to do is climb down the rusted ladder, open the galvanized valve and wash my face at least a dozen times." He enthusiastically spoke aloud.

Filled with delight and anticipation, he scurried down the rusted ladder, ran to the rusted galvanized outlet, and knelt down to utilize the water. When the handle refused to turn, he noticed small drops falling from the valve. The dripping water had washed away some of the dirt under the valve. It had created a small tunnel that led under the tank. So, he flopped flat on his stomach to suck what little moisture might remain and cup enough in his hands to wash his face.

Whether the eyes or ears recorded the first message of his next encounter is debatable. In reality, it is matters not whether George first heard or first saw the next critter. The sun was up and proceeding to create another notorious one hundred and ten degree day. With that kind of heat, the eyes see waves rolling across the desert floor. Yet, his body froze as solid as the icebergs that the Titanic struck. He quickly accepted that he was in just about the same trouble as the great ship.

Without daring to even move a lip he cautiously thought to himself. "I am looking at a triangular shaped head with black deadly eyes and a forked tongue slipping in and out of a mouth that definitely appeared to have a slight mischievous smile that seemed to say to me, 'You have just made my day.'"

When this happens to an individual, whether from east or west, north or south it goes way beyond the very word of unnerving and enters into a complete muscular, emotional, skeletal and mental dysfunction.

"Okay George, you have experienced a badger, coyotes, javalinas, and a skunk, and now you are quietly literally face to face with a diamondback rattlesnake. Just move away, just move away, just move away," he told himself. He quickly realized his mind had shattered and was functioning like a broken record.

The night before, when he wanted his legs to stand still, they ran. Now, he wanted them to run and they were perfectly frozen stiff, even with an extremely hot Arizona summer morning.

He should have remembered, from his reptile study book, that Arizona rattlesnakes like moist and shady places to rest during the day. What is learned from a book does not press upon the mind as much as the actual experience. He would never forget again where snakes like to hide or to check such places before laying on the ground again. He should have realized that the small space just under the tank and six inches from the dripping water was an ideal location for rattlesnakes. He was able to see the black tongue darting in and out and back and forth just inches from the cheek that that skunk had sprayed. He still reeked with skunk odor and horse urine.

His brain slowly returned to function but only in fragmented thoughts. He was able to recall that snakes taste and feel odors with that wicked looking tongue. Apparently, the large diamondback decided that this very enormous skunk was the result of cross breeding with a horse. The different creature was simply not worth trouble. Besides, he had just had a couple of plump slow moving desert mice for breakfast. So, he retreated farther back under the tank.

Still unable to thaw his frozen legs he muttered silently, "God bless you Mrs. Skunk"

Although it was probably only a few minutes that George's heart was racing at three hundred beats per second and his blood pressure was 220 over 160 it felt more like an hour. Ironically, with everything else running at high speeds, his brain worked as slow as molasses in a cold winter. It seemed to take even longer before the upper and lower limbs began to function enough to move away from the tank.

George managed to put about twenty yards between him and the tank. He lay on his back in the dusty sun baked yard for a period of time. He realized he was breathing erratically. During the encounter and for several minutes after the encounter he was breathing quickly, like a sprinter after crossing the finish line. Now, he was breathing so slow that it was almost not perceptible. While resting in the sun, he felt gratitude that he could still feel the heat. He mentally noted not to drink from that faucet without getting permission from the snake.

He was startled when he heard laughter, a deep guttural laughter. With great determination he was able to crawl into a kneeling position and turn to see an Indian couple perched on the dry-wood feed trough. They were laughing and pointing at this dusty young man.

Pima Indians have a close-knit society and pretty much know what is happening on and near their reservation. This couple had been visiting relatives near the town of Blackwater. Walking back towards their home the day before, they saw the new red and white pickup and were curious. When they saw a young man have a gate fall on him they became more curious. Having nobody awaiting on them at home they spent the night in the old barn, which gave them pretty much a full view of the night and morning activities. They normally would watch a short time and be on their quiet way. This morning they concluded that this young man without water would soon become delirious. Plus they appreciated how this man expressed gratitude to his horse, spider and desert.

They spoke with their delightful dialect. "You maybe have much experience already in one night and one morning, maybe stay alive for one week you have long life. You met spider, coyote, javalinas, mesquite, skunk and snake. You dirty and stink, but you still live. You do good." With those words spoken, they laughed aloud for a long period.

"Me Jesse, dat be Chula have one gallon water, leave by post, you smell like skunk, we no like smell."

They both looked, "Who be you?"

"I am George."

They pointed towards the low hill. "George go to caliche watering pond, wash in caliche mud and rub with chaparral leaves, better than skunk perfume." After each brief statement, they had a good laugh. He was confident he would like these good people.

"Jesse say you no have food, no have water, do have broken house, do have broken horse, do have pretty truck, be plenty happy person talk plenty to trees, talk plenty to animals, talk plenty to self, do have good spirit and good heart. Jesse help."

With those words spoken, they seemed to perform a disappearing act, except for the occasional laughter heard amongst the dry desert vegetation.

The gallon water jug was wrapped in Burlap, probably from a feed sack. He took a good hardy swallow of cool water before he staggered in the direction indicated by the Indian couple. He had read about the innate ability of caliche to heal wounds and reduce swelling. Caliche is a type of soil layered like sheets of paper piled on top of each other. These layers of soil are cemented with Calcium Carbonate or Magnesium Carbonate. When moist the layered particles expand causing the cracked looking soil often displayed in desert movies. This mixture of caliche and water forms a mud that in texture is like play-dough only stickier. As the mud dries, it contracts and creates a sucking or absorbing process that can remove poisons. This type of mud is often used by Hollywood Stars in their "mud baths." George doubted if any of them ever used real mud from a drying watering hole in the middle of the Arizona desert.

He was ready to try anything at the moment. The combination of skunk spray, snake induced fright, and excess adrenaline caused him to be a bit woozy. The old watering hole still held a few small puddles of water with ample slick and gooey mud. He literally lay face down in the soft mud, clothes and all. Then he slowly rolled over and rested on and in the cool mud and slathered his entire body including his burning face.

"I have never had anything feel so great."

It was apparent that he had not slept much during the night as his breathing became slower and deeper. Even though it was late morning, the bright sun can quickly change soft moist mud into dry layers of cement. He awoke with a sensation never before felt. His mind was talking but his jaws and lips were not moving.

"What has happened to me? I can hear, but I cannot move. My body is paralyzed! Has my heart stopped from fright, or does enough skunk spray paralyze a man?"

What he was hearing, had never heard before. The noise was frightening, but being unable to move was even more shocking. With effort he could move his restricted feet a little side to side. What was the most frightening was that one or a combination of experiences, possibly the skunk spray, seemed to have left him blind.

"I cannot move, I cannot see, but at least I can hear. What is the matter? What has happened? What can I do?"

When a person is unable to see, and unable to move, while in a strange place in a desert with which he is unacquainted, he tends to create a million thoughts or no thoughts and both actions occur simultaneously.

"Will I ever drive my new truck again? Will I ever ride Thunderbolt? Will I ever see Pretty Peggy?"

He wanted to laugh at his priorities, but his chest felt as if it had a hundred pound steel anvil sitting right in the middle. The strange noise, a cross between rooster, turkey, and screeching tires on a pavement began to get closer. He, at least, wanted to see what was about to devour him. He rolled his eyeballs in their sockets that felt like heavy grit sand paper. The grit under the eyelids caused tears to form. He had not realized that the thick layer of caliche mud had dried, literally gluing his eyelids shut. Now, with the tears oozing out, the dry mud began to soften and with agonizing effort one eyelid was able to open a fraction.

"I am not blind." With great effort he moved his lower jaw.

"I am not totally paralyzed, I can speak."

He determined that his body weight on the mud and his rhythmic breathing caused his body to sink half way into the mud. The heat from the sun, the heat from the body, and the dry clothes soaked up the moisture. Now, his body form was cemented into the dry caliche.

"I cannot believe that I am stuck in the mud. I wish some Hollywood actor would show up, I would gladly let them have my place."

This amusement stopped when he recalled an incident in upper state New York. A farmer broke through the ice on a shallow pond. After struggling, he was able to crawl free of the water, but was totally exhausted. He decided to rest a moment before returning to his house. Within a few minutes his clothes had frozen to the ground. He was unable to free himself and would have died if not for his worried wife. When she found him she had to use a shovel to break him loose and then drag him inside to thaw.

"Is hardened caliche mud as binding as ice?"

He could not move. "Someone needs to come and find me. That is very unlikely. Maybe, it would begin to rain." He thought, "That is even more unlikely."

Body strength greatly increases when one is placed in eminent danger. The adrenal system injects a powerful ingredient that gives the strength to lift cars or other incredible feats of strength. But, for George that much desired effect was delayed.

"I am stuck in this mud and there is no way I will ever get enough strength to break free. Yet, I will never give up."

Moisture from the eyes continued to soften the caked mud. Finally, he was able to open both eyes and begin to focus. As his focus grew, he made out something short and black. His eyes strained to see, but was not sure what.

Finally, he saw standing a foot away, over his super glued body were a number of black, ugly birds. They were patiently waiting for his demise. He would then provide the main course for their feast. Buzzards! He had seen them in movies a few times circling high in the sky, but never this close. The close up shots in the Westerns showed their curved beak and an ugly head. They had beady eyes and the long curved necks. They had dark black and feathered bodies. With their grotesque looking legs, they circled or stood nearby in western movies as they waited for something to die. Hollywood contributed to their deserved reputation of being ugly, nasty birds. In truth, up close, they made ugly seem pretty.

"Wait just a precious minute," his mind raced, "those buzzards are waiting for me, I am to be their lunch and maybe dinner."

As mentioned, the body generates strange and super strength in the face of fear. Before focusing on these awful and grotesque birds, he had not been sufficiently frightened for an adrenaline rush. But, now he was facing the prospect of being a main course for these rough feathered scavengers. With superman powers, he busted loose from his quasi-surface grave. He left behind a perfect imprint of his complete backside. The large buzzards generated a miniature tornado flapping their wings in upward fright and flight. They squawked loudly enough for all the desert creatures to know their meal had miraculously risen from the almost dry water hole and had been restored in the form of a mud man.

Every experience in life has some form of silver lining. One need only look. George had always tried to see the good in every situation and this was no exception, as he laughed aloud.

"The mud almost became my grave. But, it also prevented me from receiving a severe sunburn, as I slept in the hot sun."

Locating creosote bushes, he broke off some limbs and began to brush off the dried caliche chunks. He laughed a little as he recalled the flying buzzards' dusty whirlwind. Now, with the flinging limbs and dust flying from his clothes, he created a similar spectacle.

He looked overhead and smiled at the circling birds, "Are you still waiting for me to keel over? Well my friends it is now eleven o'clock and I'm still breathing. I have work to do, Adios."

The plumbing still needed to be checked. The kitchen unrelentingly held onto the heavy smell of the skunk perfume. This time he took an old broom handle to beat away the smell and to poke cautiously around and under the kitchen sink just to make sure that all was safe.

"Yes," he said to himself, "given time I will learn the ways of the desert as well as the ways of an Arizona cowboy. Look at what I have learned already this morning."

The sink fixtures and underside plumbing appeared to be in working condition. The drain was unusual. It connected to the sink drain a pipe that was approximately one and one-half inch pipe. Then it curved about forty-five degrees and went through the wood siding. It then turned with a ninety-degree elbow and finally connected to a hose. The hose initially was blue and of uniform color. Now, the portion that remained constantly under the shade of the porch was still bright blue. The portion on the porch that received part of the sunlight during the day was a light blue. The portion of the hose that was in the morning and afternoon sun had no blue coloring. This portion was also extremely brittle.

He mused, "I become darker in the sun and the hose becomes lighter."

The hose proceeded to an area on the north side of the house that must have been the garden. He looked and pondered how efficient the simple system was and how well the precious water was utilized.

"I will soon have a garden with vegetables and flowers, just in case Pretty Peggy ever decides to come and visit."

George was grateful his Palm Pilot still worked. The list continued to grow, "I need *water*, hay, grain, *water*, hinges, nails, *water*, baling wire, bolts, *water*, food, bottle gas, *water*, fry pan, utensils, *water* and then of course I better remember to get *water*."

Parking the F-350 Power Stroke a safe distance from the broken pole gate, and remembering how the gate fell the opposite way than it was supposed to open, he carefully unlatched the rusted barb wire loop holding the gate shut. The loop is fixed securely to a post permanently placed a few feet into the ground. The wire loop is then placed over the post that is not permanently fixed in the ground. This pole is also attached to the swing gate. It is a simple, but highly effective latch that does not wear and takes years to rust away. On the other end of the broken pole gate there should have existed two hinges. He had learned the night before that the hinges did not work.

He lifted the latch; careful to help support the weight of the pole gate, swung the gate slowly open. Seeing the distance between the open gate and his truck he took a moment to reflect how the first time he opened the gate, it fell forward, pinning him under the truck.

"My, how quickly a person learns from the desert!" He paused, "When I first opened the gate, it fell forward, this time I will carefully swing it open." He turned to look at the heavy pole gate, held together with wrapped barbwire. He was in the middle of the turn, one foot in the air, when the massive pole gate decided to once again fall, only this time in the opposite direction. However, this did mean that it would again fall in the direction of the person opening the gate, or, once again on George.

Scientists and university professors probably will disagree that inanimate objects have minds of their own. They likely will say, "There is no scientific proof." However, many, very intelligent people will swear that azoic objects such as brooms, pots, pans, doors, computers (especially computers), and cars, and the like have a mind of their own. Such was the case with the ole pole gate. George muttered under his breath, "If the gate had waited one more step or reacted one step later, then I would have had both feet firmly planted on the sandy granite road bed. As it was, the gate patiently waited until I was half turned with one foot in the air to act. Knocking George once again on his humble posterior." George asked, while laying flat on his back, "How does this gate know these things?"

Moreover, this inanimate object showed the keenest of ingenuity and aim. There was only one protruding knot on the horizontal pole. The gate matched this knot up perfectly with his electronic partner, his

Palm Pilot. He knew from the inevitable crunch escaping from his shirt pocket that he no longer was the proud owner of a Palm Pilot; it was now a crashed pilot. He cogitated, "If a pilot in the Air Force crashed there would be an immediate rescue effort made; I hear no helicopters coming to rescue my pilot."

Roads with two ruts caused from the combination of tire and water erosions crisscross all of the United States. They have been the subjects of numerous studies financed and supported by government and environmental grants, land management groups, and universities all attempting to enlighten local citizens (ranchers and farmers) how to drive without causing these ruts so as to eliminate the erosion. These costly studies offer many solutions, however, when vehicles or animals pass over the same tracks or trails sufficient times, they will create ruts. Ruts are a natural consequence of man, insect or animal traffic. The only permanent solution is to eliminate traffic, not just vehicle traffic. The world, as we know it, would be altered drastically, if there were no ants, lizards, deer, javalinas, cars, trucks, and the like. So it is logical that the world will continue to have trails and roads with ruts. Well, George's humble posterior was located in one such rut.

A simple fact about ruts is that they are always located in unappreciated spots. The fallen gate rested on the high side of the rut. George mumbled, "Is it the gate or the ruts that has a mind of its own? Or do they actually conspire to facilitate new and unusual experiences?"

George's rear fit perfectly in the lowest part of the rut, while his shoulders rested on the high middle ridge of the rut. Then, as if to completely authenticate the non-scientific truth, the head flops into the second rut. Of course, he had no hat to offer protection for his head against the sharp edges of the granite pebbles. He sheepishly recalled that the badger and javalina used the painted white hat for a play toy the night before.

"Nature is a very patient mother. How many years did she plan and assist in the eroding of this particular spot to create this perfect trap for George's body?" He chuckled, at the very possibility.

Yet he thought, "My boots are pinned on the high side, my rear is in the low middle, my shoulders rest on the middle high point, and my head is in the second." He laughed aloud, "Not only are you long-suffering you have a delightful sense of humor."

As previously established, many, if not all-inert objects have minds of their own. Thus, it is logical if they have minds they can hear. They may not listen and they may not do as requested, as is the case with most teenagers. But, it is an accepted truth that it does no damage to talk to an inanimate object.

George said politely, "Mr. Gate, would you please get off me?" Would you please stop poking me? Would you please not touch me?" The gate must either be a teenager or really old because it did not hear and it did not heed the request.

"If only I had parked the truck closer I could at least grab hold and pull myself out from under the gate." Every time he moved, the barb rips became longer and the pokes deeper. "Use your brain not your brawn," he said to himself for the 900th time. Then he heard the familiar guttural laugh of Jesse and Chula.

"You must like to study underside of gate." The laughter grew nearer. The woman knelt down by this strange human.

"He no hurt, he no dead. No need buzzards,"

With that comment they both enjoyed a good laugh. The man on one end and the woman on the other easily lifted the gate and propped it against the pole anchored in the hard desert soil. Before he could thank them, they spoke,

"You give my woman ride to town, I come also." The Indian way is simple and direct, a deed for a deed.

Words like "Thanks" are easily spewed out of an open mouth. Thanks by deeds, however, require an effort and are much more meaningful and appreciated.

"Get new hinge, no need to study underside of gate, young George now study both side." This again resulted in a good laugh as they bounced along the rutted road.

"Where you go?"

He explained that he needed water, grain, parts and water.

"You go to R-Country Store or you go to Co-op, R-Country Store no have hinge, but have good people, Co-op have hinges but no have help." Again a heart-felt laugh.

"R-Country Store people laugh much with your experience, they all have many good experience much laugh very important, two day later get hinges, very good people, much laugh."

With that bit of information the F-350 headed towards the unknown store with three passengers.

"It is amazing how much a person can learn when they get their head out of the sand." George thought as he reviewed his first morning at the ranch.

10—THE BRIDGE

JESSE, THE PIMA Indian that always happens to appear when needed was busy instructing George on the variety of desert plants and their uses,

"That is Ocotillo, cut limbs when green, stick one foot in soil and it grow, make good fence."

Chula, the round Indian lady, began to laugh.

"What funny to Chula?" Jesse asked.

"Jesse short man, think Jesse plant one foot in ground, maybe grow taller, but no make good fence." They both laughed even harder.

Jesse explained, "Jesse not mean Jesse plant one of Jesse foot in ground, Jesse mean plant ocotillo stem one foot in ground maybe only six inches if ground hard, ha, Chula see Jesse with one foot in ground. Maybe Jesse plant two feet in ground, then who take care of Chula?" They both laughed.

George was almost in tears of laughter watching and listening to the conversation. He noted with interest how they seldom used the word "I" but refer to themselves by name. They never seemed offended or defensive at another's remark, but simply laughed at the possibility of self-error.

"We stop here," Jesse spoke as he waved his hand, "Cousin live over there." George looked, but couldn't see a house. "Where does your cousin live?"

"He live over by Black Water and by Berg where old bridge cross Gila River."

George had no idea where either of the places might be. He stopped the truck and asked, "I have no idea of either place? Can I take you closer?"

With that offer the couple sat back in the leather seat in the luxury cab that still smelled with a combination of oats, molasses and horse.

Jesse commented, "This very good truck, have nice seat, make good cowboy taste in nose."

George did not know if the smell was so bad that they could taste it, or if ole Jesse had lived around snakes too long he developed the ability to taste with his tongue.

Leaving the rutted dirt road for a wide two-lane blacktop was refreshing, but only lasted a few minutes then on to a narrower blacktop well worn with potholes that led to a narrow bridge. There were no cars in sight and the bridge looked very old.

He chuckled to himself thinking of the scorpions, spiders and snakes, "Even the bridge is pre-historic."

Jesse spoke, "Jesse tell you some about Old Berg Bridge."

George saw a sign that said "Olberg" and could not decipher if Jesse was saying Olberg or Old Berg, but in reality it did not matter, the bridge fit either name.

"Mr. Charles Old Berg (Olberg) be good engineer and be good Indian Commissioner, built bridge so people who stay at great Hotel San Marcos could come visit Pima and old Indian Big House (Casa Grande Ruins) over for to direction Coolidge."

"Jesse, this truck is heavy, can I cross the bridge?" George asked.

Jesse laughed. "This only bridge for many year that connect Phoenix to Tucson, all truck, big or little cross bridge, you truck very small and cross bridge easy much like horse and buggy."

Slowly the new F-350, with the molasses smell, crossed the bridge, which was well worn from thousands of crossings, and the passing of time. Places of superficial cracks from tires, rain, cold and heat were visible on the cement. The oversize rugged mud grip tires rumbled noisily on the pitted cement and thumped with a jolt on every section of the bridge.

"Maybe bridge break" Jesse said with a chuckle, "truck not too heavy but big tires, big diesel motor make sound like big eighteen wheeler, maybe bridge spirit think too heavy and fall to sand, maybe."

George was really enjoying the humor of this couple.

"Jesse tell you much history of bridge, you stop at store buy Chula and Jesse strawberry soda and Jesse tell much."

With that invitation, they continued crossing the bridge, from south to north, and pulled to a stop in front of an old store. The store could have easily been a set for an old spaghetti western. They stepped up to the screen door and felt the cool air generated from an evaporative cooler. It was cool moist air and felt good on the dry skin.

"Me need three strawberry soda."

The polite gentleman handed Jesse three Nehi strawberry sodas that had the combination pop off or screw off lid. George tried to twist the lid, but the rough corrugated edges felt as if they would bring blood to the thumb and inner index finger.

Chula laughed, "George have hands like young girl, but soon be tough like pig skin unless momma pig Beauty eat him first."

The fellow at the store spoke, "Oh you have had the privilege of meeting Beauty." He then looked at Jesse, "Does she have piglets?"

"Jesse say have piglets yesterday, not know if have piglets after cowboy fall in middle and scare many piglets, maybe they still run, Beauty maybe no find."

They and the fellow in the store laughed heartily. George quickly determined that this man had lived around the Pima and appreciated their humor. The three walked out the door.

"Chula, you be sure and bring the bottles back."

George smiled, not only had this fellow been around the Pima, he knew them personally.

Jesse led the way, then George and then Chula. With most Indian tribes it is customary for the woman to follow behind the man. It made George a little uncomfortable because his upbringing was to escort the woman. Which is right and which is wrong is a matter of custom as he recalled the saying,

"When in Rome do as the Romans." Well he is with the Pima and he will do as the Pima.

Under the shade of the bridge Jesse began to explain the history. George was very impressed with the knowledge of this old man.

"Many years back, maybe late 1800 the white man come to Pima, Pima friendly so white man tell Pima, this is your land to live, Pima always laugh a little. Pima chief say, yes this is our land, thank you for telling to us. Then white men begin to farm. Indian has little farm and live on farm, white man have big farm and sell much. Pima and white man work land, plenty land, plenty water. Then year come when no rain in mountain. No rain in mountain no water in river. My father he tell to me many time, always the same. Indian history talk from father to son and grandson, repeat often. One year no rain, white man up river has little water, red man down river has little water. Great men in Washington tell to Mr. Olberg, you make dam so Indian have water. Mr. Carl Hayden, I think important man in Arizona tell to Washington, God make rain and river have water. Jesse think he no think Washington is God. I think Washington think they God. Soon, because Washington think they God, many mules and many horse come. Indian man and white man work with many mule and many Fresno."

Wait, George interrupted, "What is a Fresno?"

"It be much good question, Fresno is scraper to move dirt. Man hook chain or rope or leather to Fresno scraper then hook chain to many mule or few mule or one mule. Maybe use horse. Fresno like pipe but no is pipe, maybe think pipe too much understand. So pipe be maybe sixteen inch to thirty inch in round with maybe one-quarter cut out full length, maybe look like one-quarter moon or maybe like the letter "C" in alphabet and maybe two foot to four foot in length, maybe depend on how many mule. Steel rod hook to each end of pipe, end of pipe have weld plate with pivot pin like maybe a rolling pin, rod from each end go forward maybe 14 inch then bend and go to middle and make hitch where chain hook to mule strap. Long rod or mesquite or oak handle hook to middle of Fresno backside, man on back lift handle up like to sky and Fresno scraper tip and put one-quarter open part forward, lower lip of open part now cut into dirt, mule pull hard and fill pipe Fresno almost full then man pull long handle back down towards earth and open one-quarter now point to sky. Dirt stay in Fresno and mules pull long way and no lose dirt, then man lift long handle to sky and let go until handle almost hit mule on rear, now one-quarter opening face the ground and all dirt fall out. This done many times for many many months and right here the white man and the red man made a dam be call diversion maybe in 1916."

George again interrupted, "Was Arizona a state then? People for years called her the 'Baby State.'"

"Yes, Arizona state on Valentine day back 1912."

"So, Jesse where is the diversion dam?"

"The diversion dam was very good work, make road on top. Dr. Chandler, man who own big Hotel San Marcos much happy. Dr.

Chandler built famous hotel, San Marcos in little town of Chandler, Jesse think Chandler name for Dr. Chandler or maybe Dr. Chandler name for town. With road across top of good dam cross Gila River that no have water when no have rain. Tourist okay travel down visit great wonder named 'Casa Grande Ruins,' You read history about ruins later, Pima think big pile of fall down caliche but white man say to Pima, no you think Great Spirit might live in old ruins. Pima think, why Great Spirit live in great pile of adobe when He have all creation, have pine trees, have all desert, have all mountain and have all sky? All maybe happy but still very little water, me think Washington Town no is God. Then rain come to mountain and rain come to valley. Maybe Washington take credit for rain, but Pima know it Great Rain Spirit."

"Maybe in George language some words mean many things. Sometimes diversion is when have good time with much laughter. Pima man on south side of river and white man on north side watching when much muddy water hurry down from mountain rain and much muddy water from flat valley pour into Gila River. Pima have great diversion watching water jump over little dam and wash road and rocks and dirt down to meet with the Santa Cruz River. White man not having diversion on north side, they think diversion dam mean change direction of water into much irrigation, but diversion dam only divert much money down Gila River. Maybe Pima have much diversion see water running free like Indian should run free."

Jesse waved his hands across the desert.

"Mr. Chandler tell to Mr. Hayden, we need good bridge, we need build dam up river. Mr. Hayden talk to Washington who maybe learn they not God, then all talk with Mr. Olberg and soon bridge being built. Bridge finished on June 30, 1925, my father one of first to walk across, many people walk many times before car cross. Maybe think better for many people fall into river before car fall into river. President Calvin Coolidge do much talk in newspaper maybe like he do all work with own shovel. No matter, very good bridge, Mr. Olberg very good engineer and know very good spot for bridge. Old engineer learn very hard change direction of water. Years pass, maybe new engineer think they God, like Washington think they God. New engineer build new freeway with bridge. Maybe many engineer with many book, we tell engineer and many farmer who see many times how Great Gila get

116

mad. Maybe tell engineer that water from Gila runs very fast and not like to make sharp turn. Engineer maybe think very smart and have all figures and numbers. My father, very young when Olberg Bridge built now old man, he laugh many times, maybe engineer want to sleep on bridge when mighty Gila get mad."

Both Chula and Jesse enjoyed a good laugh, apparently recalling the incident.

"Many year not pass when much water come down Gila very angry. Much water come down Santa Cruz, he start in Old Mexico, and maybe much water run over flat valley. Jesse not know if smart engineer have shovel to help but when big muddy water crash to freeway, Gila River Spirit not like big road in way of much water, big water look and look, go round and round, not find where new bridge built so much big water take road, much like diversion dam, and push road down river and hide her. After freeway wash down river, engineer not have much pride, then ask and Pima help him to build bridge for river, not build bridge and then ask water to find bridge. Water Spirit is big medicine, wash away dam, wash away road, and not like to be told what she should do. Very much like Chula, ha ha."

Chula poked him in the rib. "Jesse say Chula not like be told what to do, like big water. Yes, big freeway bridge wash away but Olberg Bridge still here. She be good bridge. Chula still here, she be good woman. "

With that history lesson George looked with greater admiration at Jesse. They walked to the south side of the bridge and could still see the great cement structures with massive steel gates used to divert Gila River water into the canals for irrigation of Pima lands. He climbed up and around picturing in his mind how all of this functioned. He wondered if some of the lands he had just purchase might ever be irrigated?

Walking under the bridge there were piles of trash, beer cans and plastic bags.

"George be much careful, many drug people come thru ranch."

George understood why the very mention of the word drug caused him to stop. His mind quickly recalled that because of illegal drugs his mother was not with him. He gazed across the sandy river bottom with a flash of sadness.

Chula apparently sensed this change. "George have heavy sadness, maybe tell to Chula?"

George felt such a close kinship with these two good people, yet he was not ready to share his feelings, however, he sensed that Chula and Jesse would be an important part of his life.

Jesse interrupted the thought, "Let's go look north end of bridge, have big gate and still use some time. New canal about forty mile long bring water from east of Florence through many canal. White farmer and Indian farmer live like neighbors. White man in Washington and wife of Washington man come to Pima little town and tell to us Washington be big help. Washington wife build many pretty house that hot in summer and cold in winter but look good on outside, make Washington wife feel happy. Indian build ugly house out of mother earth. House is cool in summer and warm in winter. Pima have many laugh about white man house. White man not learn from Indian."

"Oh no," Chula interrupted, "Jesse tell bad joke."

Jessed laughed and continued. "Indian laugh at first white man. Indian man go hunt and fish all day, woman wash, cook and have children, all very happy. White man come and say to Indian, white man have much better life and come to teach Indian. White man work all day to make much money but only he hunt and fish one day during each moon. Indian have but little money but hunt and fish every day, no think white man have better life."

George laughed aloud at Jesse's logic. They walked across the bridge, back to the north end, and George could see another structure of cement that consisted of steel gates that open from the riverbed to a large and very deep canal. There was a little water in the bottom of the canal.

"Jesse, why is there water in the canal? Where does it come from?"

"The river is very dry on top but under dry sand is always water moving slowly. The canal is much deeper and some river water seep under rocks and cement. Always some water in canal. Jesse tell to George, look at canal side and bottom, what earth do you see?"

He walked over closer and smiled, "That is super hard caliche."

"That is good, remember my teaching, when caliche wet, swells tight, no water leak, now caliche have crack along side but when rain or when irrigate, no cracks, no water leak."

George proceeded to climb down under the cement bridge to look closer at the gates and the architecture of the bridge that had stood firm for so many years and still carries some traffic. He was very impressed with the structure of the bridge. One end of the reinforced concrete bridge was butted up to and into the small rock mountain. Thus, there was no way the river, no matter how raging or how high, could wash around the end of the bridge and wash out the bridge. He was not an architectural engineer, but it was easy for him to understand the strategic location of the bridge. The wide span of the bridge, he guessed, was five to six hundred feet across and was anchored in the solid caliche soil that had been deposited for thousands of years. This rock hard caliche was additionally protected with large boulders hauled down from the nearby San Tan Mountains.

"Yes," he spoke to himself, "this bridge is here to stay." He chuckled at his own remark, as if it were some important prophetic proclamation. "Time, rain and floods have already established that historical fact."

He remembered that rattlesnakes like the cool moist areas. So, he was very alert. He was studying so intently the ground, every shaded place, and each crevice where a snake might lurk, that he failed to see the large gray nest of yellow jacket hornets overhead. They are generally harmless, unless their nest is disturbed. Once the nest is disturbed, these big, mean flying machines attack with the ferocity of a United States Air Force strike. The yellow jacket hornets are armed with their own version of a stinger. They are hard to defend against. They change directions in mid flight, stop in flight, and remain air borne. They have some sort of a sense almost like a laser-guided beam that leads them to a precision attack. While they cannot penetrate concrete, these stingers can easily puncture a man skin and leave behind welts and pain that a man will not soon forget.

If George were not so afraid of what might lay on the ground at his feet, he would have seen these fighting machines perched on the large multi-perforated nest. They looked like planes on an aircraft carrier all facing into the wind before takeoff. Each plane generated unmatched noise from the jet engines warming up for a speedy take off. These unmatched flying hornets actually turn towards their target, exercise their wings, and in doing so they create a vibration that normally warn possible invaders. If the invader understands or hears the noise, he will smartly move away from the nest with great haste. However, when the invader, in this case George, is looking for another possible ground attack and intently listening for the warning sound of a rattlesnake, the real air attack may well go unnoticed and unheard until the well equipped and highly maneuverable yellow and brown aircrafts (resembling hornets) are well into their flight pattern. When the first two lead hornets make a strafing run, even the blind and deaf will know that they are in big trouble. In a foxhole a soldier will holler, "incoming," never for certain which way to run or hide. It seems the alert only serves to elevate blood pressure, increase breathing and prepare the legs for something yet unknown. So was the case with George, when the buzzing bombers passed within millimeters of his head, he knew he was in some kind of major trouble.

He was not even certain what caused the miniature jet stream, but he knew he was in the wrong spot at the wrong time, once again. He began a very hasty retreat. He thought for a moment that he was successful. The lead pilots must have relayed through wasp warp communication that this was an easy target and a few hundred fighters would enjoy a safe and needed practice with quite possibly zero casualties.

A new speed record for climbing from the riverbed to the road on top of the bridge was without doubt set at that very time and place. Jesse and Chula saw him coming. They also saw the fighter pattern making the slight turn in order to deliver a deadly air to human bombardment. If not deadly, at least the pain would be enough of a deterrent that the intruder would lose all desire to ever return and bother their home and landing base.

Just about as quickly as the hornets were maneuvering, Chula, the short, well-rounded Pima, whipped the well-worn blanket hanging around her shoulders and covered George. The yellowish/brown fighters were confused as to their target. They jetted around the hump on the ground and then they saw two other targets. The yellow fighters made a couple of strafing runs. They soon determined that these targets were unafraid. In the tiny, meanest, and unforgiving brain of a hornet, it seemed to instinctively discern that only one possible conclusion was possible: These two additional intruders had greater firepower than the yellow fighters. Further, the intruders were no longer an immediate threat to the carefully hidden nest. So, on some unknown, hornet, flyer frequency the broadcast was aired, "Return to base, return to base, repeat, do not attack unknown target, do not know their strength, return to base."

The hundreds of yellow flying fighters made a quick one hundred eighty degree turn and flew out of sight.

"You can come out now." Chula said as she lifted her blanket.

Bright red swellings were easily seen on his right cheek, neck and forehead.

Chula gave her normal chuckle, "You plenty fast, but not faster than Yellow Jacket Hornet. This night when work done, Yellow Jacket talk much about protecting home from intruder, big celebration, brave fighters honored for making perfect score, you must be happy for them."

He could feel the burning pains increasing. "What were those things? Why were they mad at me?" he asked.

"Hornets not mad, hornets protect home, you go close to home, now not go back near home? Yes. You need make friend with mean yellow ones, they do much harm, many bites kill man, kill calf and kill horse."

George looked puzzled, "How do I make friends with them?"

The two Pimas laughed, "When you learn make friends with angry hornet you please to come teach us," another round of laughter.

"Now you go down to canal and put cool caliche mud on stings, you lucky only three make good shot."

"What should I do if I do not have a blanket to hide under?" He was expecting some great wisdom on how to run or hide from the yellow hornets. Indeed he received sound wisdom.

Jesse and Chula said, "Always look for nest, find nest and go away before big hornet make big attack."

They laughed and continued, "If no blanket, hide in mud and put much mud on face and arms, do not move, yellow hornet think you maybe dead, you wait for buzzard to come before you get up." A hardy laugh and they led him to the caliche mud and plastered the swelling welts.

"You drink much strawberry soda?" This sudden switch of questions in behalf of his welfare intrigued him.

"No, this is the first Nehi soda I have ever drunk." The two chuckled, "Hornet no hurt Chula, maybe she drink many red soda pop, maybe you need drink many red strawberry soda pop hornet no bite."

He was impressed at how quickly the burning eased with the cool mud. In a short time, the drying of the caliche seemed to ease the pain completely. The two went over to a prickly pear cactus; cut off one of the pear shaped, thick leaves, and scrapped off the numerous thorns. Then they cut a two inch square piece and split the square as if to make a sandwich. The moist meaty part was placed on the sting.

"Not good like Nopal or Aloe, but help."

He wondered if these good people ever stressed. He just escaped a possible very painful death, and they could still laugh. Thinking to gain a little sympathy he suggested, "I could have been stung a thousand times and possibly been killed."

"Yes, but you only stung three, thank always for good things, bad things go away but good things stay, yes thank always for good things."

"Chula," he asked, "It is so hot in the Arizona desert, why do you always carry a heavy blanket with you? Surely not just to swat hornets or protect a green-horn cowboy?" They all laughed.

"Chula carry blanket for many reason, maybe to hide from hornets, maybe lay under shade of mesquite, maybe gather much dry wood, maybe hold prickly pear apples when ripe, maybe put over Chula to protect from hot sun, maybe hide Chula from Jesse, maybe Chula like color of blanket."

For any number of reasons, George was profoundly grateful that she had the blanket to throw over him. He recalled the teachings of his father that explained that the Indian way was a more simplified life. His dad, however, had expressed concern that the business of the white man would probably soon overcome the Indian families.

They were climbing in the truck when Chula laughed,

"Must return Nehi bottles, Chula think store refill bottles with more red strawberry soda, no find Nehi in other store, only in Old Berg store." Jesse laughed, "Jesse return bottles while Chula climb in tall truck, Chula take long time, Chula legs short." All had a good laugh, as they again watched the short, good-humored lady stretch to place a knee on the floorboard, grab a seat belt and pull herself upwards and on to the seat.

Driving along the seldom-used black top road, he could see grass squeezing up through the time-weathered cracks extending from one side of the road to the other. What once was the connecting artery from Phoenix to Tucson now had mesquite tree limbs hanging to touch both sides of the truck, as it rolled down the middle dotted white line now scarcely visible. To the right, adjacent to the road, was an old railroad track that had been abandoned.

Jesse picked up his line of sight, "New railroad go through Queen Creek, Magma and cross to Florence." Jesse lowered his window,

"Please to turn off blowing air, please to go slow, always much to see and hear. Water in canal, much tree, much grass, much mice, much bird, much to see and hear."

Driving slowly, along the potted blacktop, as Jesse spoke, "Much better on horse or on foot, diesel motor make much noise, we stop."

He stopped the truck and turned off the Diesel Power Stroke. The afternoon sun was still very warm, but the shadows were beginning to grow longer as the rays lowered behind the variety of plants and trees.

"George must learn listen, hear to quail and mourning dove, hear to rabbit running through grass." Then he laughed as if remembering a funny story.

"You must hear Mr. Diamondback before get close enough to kiss." They both laughed.

"We get out now, you safe in truck, no snake, no spider, no skunk, no badger, no wasp. Jesse maybe think George safe to go store."

They stepped out and walked into the mesquite thicket. He wondered how they manage to disappear or reappear so quickly. He waited a few moments, watching through the passenger side window into the mesquite thicket, the direction of their departure. He allowed his mind to wander and recall all that he had learned in such a short time.

"I would have never known this life existed, if I had not stepped away from the normal routine of life. How many people go through life always wanting to, but afraid to even attempt a change? What prevents a person from changing? Is it pride, fear or both?" He was in deep thought wondering where his two friends were heading. He almost jumped out of his skin when Jesse touched him and spoke on the driver side.

"Jesse speak more to teach friend George. One, in desert, *not worry where went, always worry where are*. Two, someday friend George meet Bapchule, he see much spiritual things, he talk much to desert, he talk much to spirit not in body, he dream much and tell what friend dream, much good man. George listen and learn much. Answer much George question. Now leave friend, important remember. *Always worry where are.*"

In his rear view mirror he could see *"Where are."* He laughed to himself as his new and loved friends walked down the old abandoned historic road and he continued to head into a new and exciting future and to meet "good people" at the R Country Store.

11—STORE AND SACATON

THE OVERSIZED MUD grip tires rumbled unto the gravel parking lot of the feed store, hardware store, pet store, hay store and antique store with a big sign overhead, "R Country Store" and on the door way a smaller sign, "Family Farm since 1948." Actually, a couple of the Riggs families were original desert homesteaders just a mile from the location of the store. Thus, the reason the name of the store has the initial "R." George parked his truck and up until this moment he felt that he might be one of the exclusive men in all of Arizona driving such a powerful truck, now he looked at the feed store parking lot. There parked were new and old dual tired trucks some Chevys, but mostly the Ford Power Strokes, there was a white, a blue, a tan, and a red and white.

George said softly to himself, "This family must be friends with "Tex"; they all own Fords and most are Power Stroke diesels."

One truck was connected to a gooseneck trailer. It was a long trailer that has a goose looking neck hitch attached to the frame of the trailer and extends over the tailgate of the pickup and into the middle of the bed. There it attaches to a ball that is attached to the truck frame. He was fascinated. As he studied the trailer and hitch, a man looking like a professional tackle for the Dallas Cowboys walked up and gave a brief explanation. George later learned he was one of Riggses that worked the store.

"By attaching the trailer to the middle of the bed directly over or a little in front of the rear axle a pickup becomes a miniature semi truck and can pull much heavier loads with better control and safety."

George thought to himself that someday he would have need for a large "gooseneck trailer" to haul his cattle.

The folks at R Country Store were extremely helpful. They merited Jesse's praise. He said these good folks would laugh with him, as he explained his multiple experiences including the swollen cheek, the lump on the neck, and the over-extended forehead that the yellow jacket fighter planes with "Stinger" missiles caused. All had a great laugh when he related that Jesse suggested that he become friends with the hornets. They responded, "if you can make friends with the yellow wasp you need to be sent to the military department to make friends with the Middle East."

When discussing the scorpion problem they suggested chickens, peacocks, turkeys or guineas. One of the friendly patrons mentioned, "Only problem with poultry is that they make mighty fine dinners for the coyotes."

Suggestions to pen poultry inside of the house raised another decisions, "Do you want scorpions or the mess chickens make in a house?"

They also suggested a mixture of Diatomaceous Earth, and Sulfur powder scattered around the house, floors and doorways. "This is a non-toxic mixture, so it will not harm the environment or other wildlife."

George reviewed his list, which included several bales of hay for his horse Thunderbolt. George backed the F-350 to a pile of baled hay and eagerly climbed in the back of the truck to load five bales of alfalfa-oat hay that was recommended for horses. They also suggested that scattering a few flakes of hay around the corral and near the barn that might entice a few of the stray calves to wander in and be corralled. As stated earlier, one fellow looked like a pro-lineman and his son walked out five inches taller, both were going to help load the three twine bales of hay. Alfalfa is cut green, allowed to dry naturally, rolled into windrows, let dry a little more and then baled with a machine that picks up the loose hay, pushes it into a compacting chamber and forms a bale. To keep the compacted bale together, two or three strong nylon twines are automatically wrapped around each bale and tied. Two string bales weigh around eighty pounds while three string bales weigh around one hundred and fifty pounds.

George had never loaded baled hay. As he was pulling in by the store, he saw the "Pro-lineman" grab a bale by the twine and toss it onto the bed of a truck. He watched the other take two metal hooks, hook them on each end, and pull the bale from the stack.

"Looks easy enough" George thought to himself.

He grabbed the twines on a bale about head high on the stack. If he had been paying a little closer attention, He would have noticed that all activity, in and around the store, had stopped. All were intently anticipating what would happen when a 135-pound inexperienced man grabs a 165-pound bale of hay, which would have been entertainment enough. But, the bale that George grabbed was a little higher than he was even with the three-inch heels on his red boots, so their anticipation was even greater.

Precious few folks have had the rare occurrence of having a large object falling towards their faces, but even fewer have had the experience of a bale of hay rolling in a downward spiral with both of their hands securely pinned between the twine and the hard scratchy alfalfa/oat hay. Newton's First Law of Motion is that things in motion tend to stay in motion until acted upon by an unbalanced force. George had never studied this particular law. All who were watching and who had listened to George's other experiences concluded that this oddly dressed, "so called cowboy," prefers learning from experience. As the bale fell, George was pulled right along with the bale. As mentioned earlier, the bales are tightly compacted, but not tight enough to prevent a good bounce when hitting the ground (the unbalanced force). As the bale bounced back up, it hit George squarely in the face as he was still on his way down. This collision of opposing forces sent George rolling, hollering and spitting out alfalfa hay leafs. As anticipated, the on-lookers had a good laugh as the neophyte cowboy learned another lesson.

"Ya have to give him credit, while others stand and look, he jumps in to help and seems eager to learn. Yup, learn first-hand." One of the Riggs men mentioned: "You can still smell the skunk. Probably another first-hand experience."

After a couple of bounces and collisions, George finally came to rest lying on his back, arms in a tight twist, and hands tangled in the twine of the bale of hay. The bale was now draping across his stomach. Most men would have exhausted themselves being angry, blaming, making excuses, stomping the ground, and throwing a tantrum. Not George, that was not his way. In spite of being from the east coast or a foreigner as the locals would call him, he won their hearts, when with a big grin as he enthusiastically spoke, "That went quite well for the first try."

They all had a good laugh, quickly helped him up, and loaded the pickup with hay, grain, four cases of bottled drinking water, and a fifty gallon poly barrel filled with well water for Thunderbolt. They helped him tie a new two-hundred-gallon galvanized water trough with automatic shut off float valve. They explained to him about replacing the old galvanized, rusted water pipe with a heavy schedule #40 PVC, a type of hard plastic pipe that does not rust. Different ones took time to draw maps to various stores in the area where he could buy additional supplies and offered any additional help he might need.

He shook hands with everyone there. They seemed to be related to each other and seemed to be happy working together. He thought how he would someday like to have his family living and working together and caring for each other. He was never sure who was who as they talked about a Grammy and Grampie homesteading, and Grandmother and Granddad farming for more than fifty years. Then, there were numerous aunts, uncles, cousins, nephews, nieces, grandsons, etc. It was a great pleasure to meet them, but a little intimidating to be standing at five foot ten inches and have a twelve year old already four inches taller, his dad a full ten inches taller, his Granddad and Uncle an easy hundred pounds heavier. He was most happy that they were friendly.

He easily could imagine, "You fight one you fight all" or "You are friends with one, you are friends with all." He was certainly hoping that he would be called a friend, especially as they shook hands, the one dad or uncle or Granddad had hands that could have crushed George's. He felt the strong and calloused hand and recalled Chula's comment.

"Soft hand like young girl." He thought, "my hands will not always be soft, they may be small but they will become strong and tough." He climbed into the loaded truck.

"Hello," He turned to see a tall, about six feet, strikingly beautiful young woman with radiant light bronze skin, long black hair and a vivacious smile.

"I'm Carin, please excuse me for asking, do you have Indian blood?"

"What an interesting question," he thought.

"Yes, why do you ask?" He had never been asked before and he did not have many obvious features of his Apache ancestors.

"I have Indian blood, you might tell from my dark hair. I watched you pull the bale of hay on top of you and you did not get angry or embarrassed. I watched you kneel and pet the dogs and talk with them as if they were your friends. I watched my young daughters go right up to you and visit as if you were a relative. This is why I ask if you were part Indian."

"Yes, my father was Apache from the White River area in northern Arizona."

He was glad he was sitting in the seat of his lifted F-350 so he could at least look eye to eye with this smiling Riggs lady as she mentioned, "Please, I would like to hear more."

He was amazed at his own inner desire to share a little bit of his history.

"My father was raised by his Apache mother in a town called McNary where there was a big sawmill. I did not know my father very well. He liked to rope, steer wrestle and ride in the rodeos. He met my mother; she lived in Payson, at one such rodeo. They were married and lived just outside of Payson. When I was young he joined the military. My mom and I moved from Payson to the Quantico, Virginia to be near him while he trained. He was sent overseas and was killed in combat. We stayed on the east coast and later moved to Mahwah, New Jersey, close to New York City. My mother said he was a very good man."

This tall young lady suggested that George go to Sacaton where the Bureau of Indian Affairs is headquartered and talk to Edna Antone. She would help him locate his Grandmother, if she were still alive. He also could register his Indian blood. This would allow him many additional privileges and acceptance on the reservation.

"Thank you so very much. You and your family have been very helpful. I hope someday to invite all of you to the Gila River Cattle Ranch for a dinner."

"We will accept, but only if you let us bring most of the food. Our family is known for the Pit Bar-B-Q, Dutch Oven Biscuits and Dutch Oven Cobbler."

He had no idea what a Dutch oven was, but his stomach growled at the thought of warm peach cobbler with a little vanilla ice cream melting slowly from top to bottom. She smiled at the sound of his stomach. She was not embarrassed, so he was not embarrassed. She simply smiled and asked, "Have you eaten? We are about to cook some hamburgers over mesquite coals." He had barely nodded his head when about five or ten young children, grandchildren and great grandchildren appeared from atop the large haystacks, from under the old antique buckboard wagons, out of cement pipes, and between old farm equipment sitting around the yard.

"Who are these people that have a hamburger fry on a hot summer's day with no particular holiday?" He looked at the activity in the nearby yard. "Then," he thought, "invite me, a total stranger to eat with them."

He watched as all gathered and waited. A new, bright red Suburban pulled in the yard and the youngsters ran over to greet Great Grandmother. Each one hugged and kissed her with a great affection. He thought she must have traveled a long distance until he realized that she lived only a couple hundred yards from the store. This show of love was something that this family did quite naturally. Not just the youngsters, each adult went to her, bent over and kissed her, and expressed love. Each helped her. Some helped her out of the car, with her walker that she used, and with her food. They frequently asked if she needed something.

"I want to have children that learn to love." Suddenly, he missed his mother and father. He wonder how his father died, was he a good soldier? Did his mother die alone?" Yet, even as he asked the question to himself about his mother, his heart still refused to believe.

He watched as this loved Grandmother managed to get a moment with each individual. "Did you get your weeds chopped? Did you play your soccer game? My you grow an inch every day? Is your show steer getting nice and fat?" She knew each of them and kept well informed about their lives. She hugged each and they were off to eat or on to another adventure. They made no special fuss over George; he just seemed to be a part of their group.

"Go get another hamburger! Get another pop! How's the ranch? Where are you from? What's your name? Why are you called George? My cousin is called George, but my uncle is called B.J.," so went the questions and comments.

A big hand attached to 245 pounds of body grasp George's shoulder, "George," it is getting late, would you like to spend the night here, and finish your purchases in the morning, before heading back to the Gila River?"

George stood, faced this giant of a man with a big tender heart to see if he were serious. He was. George wondered to himself, if all people of the west were this friendly, just the old time rural people, or just this type of family.

"Thank you so very much for your kind offer and I am certain I would have a much better rest, however, my good horse 'Thunderbolt' is without water or feed so I must head back."

"Take care of your horse, and he will take care of you." He turned and walked back to his family.

A couple of miles before he reached the ranch, Thunderbolt came trotting up; his whinny was heard as a welcome committee long before he actually appeared. George was certain that this special bloodline horse had come to see him personally and the smell of the hay was an insignificant motive. Thunderbolt was able to grab a few bites of hay as the truck rolled along the rutted road.

He backed into the barn and in his thoughts, "I will use my acquired skill to unload the hay. I will pick up the 165 pound bales and toss them to form a neatly organized stack in the barn."

In reality, he would wait until Thunderbolt grabbed a big mouth full and tug to break the tightly compacted hay from the bale. As the horse pulled to get a large bite from each bale, George pushed with his legs to offer assistance from the topside. Each bale slid out of the truck. Where it fell, he decided, was exactly where he wanted each bale. Especially, since he could not lift or move these tightly compacted alfalfa bales that felt like lead weights.

Thunderbolt apparently had learned about overeating, something that most humans never learn. When he had managed to take a few bites out of each bale, he left the barn and returned to the non-enclosed corral.

George slid the galvanized oval watering trough out of the pickup and emptied the fifty-gallon barrel into the trough. Thunderbolt attempted to drink the entire fifty gallons with one complete gulp. Satisfied with the hay and water, the gallant steed walked a few steps and flopped on the ground. Horses have the unique capability of locking their leg joints while standing, which allows the muscles to relax and enjoy a total and complete rest. Other horses with special breeding, such as Thunderbolt will lay down completely, with neck and head outstretched, ears flopped to one side, legs and feet extended and tail engaged in the auto-pilot position to slowly swish across his body to unnerve a resting fly.

He studied his gallant steed, "You and I have special talents, and we were made for each other."

The night passed without incident. He had decided that, rather than disturb all the natural, night creatures and varmints in the house, he would sleep in the plush and comfortable soft leather seat of the truck. He once again took those few moments at the end of each day to express thanks to his mother, his father and to his God. It was a good day and he slept with a contented smile.

The sun inched over the majestic mountains, and the first rays spotted the Gila River Cowboy. He was sitting under a mighty mesquite at the edge of the drying catch pond. There existed sufficient moisture to form small puddles of water for the quail, roadrunners, and a desert mule deer to take a sip.

He whispered, "Good morning" to each.

They seemed to sense his presence, but felt no fear. He slowly moved his head upward, "Thank you for early mornings in the desert, these unique mornings afford a spiritual high. Please always help me take the time to sit, listen and feel."

Today he would drive in to Sacaton, the Pima Indian Capital. He would rent a postal mailbox, so he could mail a letter to Pretty Peggy and invite her to come for a visit. To accomplish the latter, he would have to finish the letter. He felt the hardest part was already written on the letter pad he had purchased at Sky Harbor Airport,

"Dear Peggy" the words fit next to the drawing of a hat, rope and spurs in the upper left corner of the page.

He was not sure what to write. He really did not know her very well, but he remembers how she gave him the special glance each time he passed her desk. He certainly attempted to let her know that he was in love with her precious smile.

"Early in the morning with the rising of the sun,
The rabbits and roadrunners have such fun.
Near the water pond, I saw a desert mule deer,
And my heart whispered quietly, I wish Peggy were here."

"Enclosed is a round trip ticket for you to fly to Phoenix. I will meet you at the airport. So, you may visit the Gila River Cattle Ranch. I will have a room reserved for you in Chandler. It is a famous hotel, called the San Marcos. The ticket has an open date, please send me the date you are coming to Post Office Box 7 in Sacaton, Arizona. I know this is a brave thing on your part to come here. However, we have known each other for many years, working in the same office. I do hope you will come and visit. Your admiring friend, George."

"P.S. You will love my horse Thunderbolt."

Slowly folding the letter, he thought, "I truly hope her heart beats as fast as mine when she reads this letter."

The town of Sacaton is not much. The largest business and source of revenue is the Bureau of Indian Affairs. There is a grocery store, a modern hospital, a parts store, a service station, and a memorial for Ira Hayes. There is also an old (really old) Catholic Cathedral (built with adobe bricks), and the U.S. Post Office.

Centuries earlier Indians established small villages along the Gila River. Most have vanished with time. However, with the oncoming tide of white settlers in the late 1800's, the need for horse feed became more demanding. When the stage line was developed between Tucson and Phoenix, one reliable source of hay was the "Pima Village" on the Gila River. They produced grass hay called "Sacate." Soon large wagons with long teams of horses would leave Phoenix, travel to the "Pima Village" and load a ton of Sacate. The Indians had learned much from the Mexican travelers; in Spanish, the most explicatory word is always spoken first. English would say "big house," but Spanish would put "house" first as it was the more important of the two words, thus "House Big." In due time, with the Indians referring to the wagons as needing a "Grass Ton," the Spanish name of "Sacate Tonelada" was abbreviated to "Sacaton." The name became a site of American history, and the capitol of the Pima Indian Nation.

At the main intersection in Sacaton, the U.S. Post Office occupied a corner, a service station another corner, a parts store another, and finally, the Ira Hayes monument the fourth corner. Entering the Post Office a grouchy face attached to a white male postmaster looked at him and turned away, a short round Pima face flashed a bright infectious smile that is, infectious to all accept her apparent boss.

"It is a good morning, may I help you?"

"Thank you, it is a good morning. I would like to rent a post office box."

"Do you want small one or big one?" Again, the delightful Pima accent and the no nonsense direct speech.

"Small one three dollar each month, big seven dollar each month, pay eighty one year, save four dollar, how long you want box?"

"Well, Miss."

She giggled, "I no Miss, I Cecilia, I marry Ernie."

Mr. Grouchy face reentered, "Why do you want a mail box in Sacaton? Do you live here? Are you an Indian?" The questions came in rapid-fire succession.

"Well, I would appreciate getting mail. I live at the Gila River Cattle Ranch east of here."

"Are you from New York?"

"I was born in Payson, Arizona. But, I was raised in Virginia and New Jersey."

"I knew it." Grouchy said, "I am from upstate New York, and I recognized your accent. I couldn't take the cold anymore and was offered a transfer to a city near Phoenix. I did not realize that in the West 'near' might mean fifty miles between watering holes so I ended up in this God forsaken village."

With that negative comment the postmaster turned to leave. He made a complete pivot, "Wait just a minute; did you say you lived at the Gila River Cattle Ranch? You must be mistaken. No one lives at the ranch."

"Well good sir, there is now. I am George Ribit Chattit."

With that, Mr. Grouch turned and hurried off.

Cecilia helped fill out the forms, which included previous addresses and current physical place of dwelling. As Cecilia looked at the forms, she grinned at George, "You good owner of Gila River Cattle Ranch, maybe you now be Gila River Cowboy, your name have same initials of GRC." With that observation Cecilia covered her mouth and giggled joyfully.

George was filling out the second page with directions when her comment began to sink in. Before he could react she spoke again.

"You no need all direction, everybody know Gila River Cattle Ranch."

That saved about forty sentences of explanation.

"You have box seven, big box on bottom."

He signed the paper and received the key. He was about to tell Cecilia that she was, other than himself, the only person to notice the initials, when Mr. Grouchy returned with a stern face.

"Would you wait one moment? I have doubts of your authenticity." The words had not finished escaping from his mouth, when two uniformed Gila River Police Officers walked in. The average weight of the two would be approximately two hundred pounds. However, the short one only weighed about one hundred thirty pounds. The large one was not exceedingly tall, but would approach a square with little difficulty.

"Why you tell Postmaster you live at Gila River Cattle Ranch?"

"Well," feeling a little bewildered, "I live at the Gila River Cattle Ranch, I just purchased the property a few days back."

"You have paper say you buy?"

"Yes, in my truck."

As they walked out, the postmaster seemed very pleased that he had helped apprehend a possible drug criminal.

George smiled back at Mr. Grouchy and thought, "I shall someday bring him a very sweet watermelon, so he can enjoy something sweet."

The officers were polite but dreadfully official. Cecilia stepped out into the parking lot.

"Hern, you be much careful, Ceci think this man GRC be nice, I no want to hurt my brother for do wrong to nice GRC." Hern, the big officer, was her brother. If he did not treat new GRC nice, his little round sister, with the radiant smile, would hurt him. At that thought, George laughed aloud.

"Why you laugh?" George sobered immediately.

He produced the papers. "Papers not good for me must show to judge." Hern pointed to the truck,

"Hern ride in big red truck."

A few hundred yards down the road, the patrol car, with flashing lights, that was leading the way, pulled in a parking lot adjacent to a large single story red brick building.

"We stop here."

A traditionally dressed Indian lady in her late forties stood outside the door. It was clear she was in charge.

"What is it you boys need?" Just a hint of Indian accent was detected.

"Miss Edna, Hern bring young man to office, Postmaster think he not speak truth, young man say he live on Gila River Cattle Ranch."

At the mention of the name Edna, George perked up. Could this be the very lady referred to him by the tall young lady at R-Country Store?

He blurted out with excitement, "Excuse me, are you Edna Antone?"

The officer released his arm, as if he had just received a shock of electricity. Both officers placed their hands on the large pistols strapped to their side.

George was surprised at their reaction. He later learned that at a nearby freeway rest stop there had been violent drug activity and the judge, Edna Antone, had been threatened more that once.

"Who might be asking?"

"I am George Ribit Chattit the new owner of the Gila River Cattle Ranch."

They appeared to be a little surprised, maybe because of the ranch or maybe the rareness of his name.

"A young lady from the R Country Store suggested I visit with you."

"That would be Carin."

"Yes," responded George.

"Thank you Hern," Edna smiled at the officers. "This young man needed to see me and probably did not know how to find my office. Thank you for being courteous and bringing him here. Please inform John the Postmaster that I also appreciate his alertness."

The officers departed and George recognized that he stood in the presence of a grand lady, which he already admired for her kindness. With kind words in one sentence she effectively patted the two officers on the back and complimented the Postmaster.

"Please sit and tell me about yourself. Why did Carin suggest we visit? You were able to meet the Riggs family? Did you meet Grandmother?"

He related the hamburger fry, the bales of hay, and the offer to spend the night.

Edna smiled, "They are good people that have been in the valley for many generations. They worked many Pima Indians, both male and female on their farms and always treated them fair and honest. They would tell each person, 'An honest day's pay for an honest day's work.' Sometimes it is difficult to get an honest day's work out of the Indian men, some would rather sit under the shade of big tree that use a shovel."

She covered her mouth with her hand as she softly chuckled.

Edna continued, "The Riggs family are very busy people yet they seem to live a slower life than most white folks and are always willing to help."

Her large dark brown eyes danced in amusement.

"I think Riggs men absorb blood from the Maricopa tribe because they are all very large men and have large hearts, much like the Maricopa Indian."

George explained about the ranch purchase. He explained in sketchy detail his life and a little about his father.

"First, let me see the documents you received from the bank." She read each detail including the fine print. She was in no hurry and did not excuse herself for taking time to read. George was learning that Indians have enormous patience.

"You have good papers but are not valuable until they are recorded with all the agencies. Your piece of land has little value because no one has been able to record ownership. Edna has never helped because no one ever asked."

Again, her large eyes had a mischievous sparkle. "Edna will help George, not because you have Indian blood, but because I think there is a happy future in this area for you."

Every so often a Pima dialect slipped from Edna. Beyond the dialect he detected something in the way she smiled and said, "I think there is a happy future."

"Could she predict the future?" Wondered George.

"George, you come here tomorrow evening at seven o'clock and you will meet the tribal leaders, if they like you, and I am sure they will, they will tell Edna to help you obtain proper documentation and record your deeds. Your ranch has many deeds and they must all be recorded with each agency or you will have trouble in the future. Do not worry about drug traffic or so-called environmentalist. If they trespass, you call Hern."

He shuddered; this was the second mention of "so-called environmentalist and drug traffic."

The next evening, he arrived early for the meeting, and was busy shaking hands, when Edna arrived.

"You have met some tribal members? Have you met Governor Antone Soke?"

A short man in what appeared to be in his late hundredth year of birth with a bush of white hair approached with his hand extended.

"You are George Ribit Chattit. I am Antone." George noted that none of governing board used any titles when introducing themselves. They were common men and women asked to represent various families or groups. It did not make them special or a cut above. He liked that concept.

The meeting was conducted as any business meeting, agendas were followed, and presentations kept short and to the point. Those who had not made previous presentations were given instructions on how to present documents a day or two prior to the meeting or to see Edna to be placed on the agenda. There seemed to be nothing of such great consequences that could not wait to be presented properly. The point or points of each assigned topic were clearly stated and then a brief explanation followed. The Governor, just prior to the meeting had told George that he had been placed number three on the new business.

George was a little surprised that he was on the list since he had no presentation and was not even certain why he was there. The Lt. Governor was conducting and when he announced that the item on the agenda was related to Mr. George Ribit Chattit, George just sat in silence. Edna started to stand, when a man from the dark corner behind the table of the Governing Board rose.

"Bapchule will verify the motion to give Tribal support for Mr. George Ribit Chattit soon to be Gila River Cowboy. I think we call him "GRC." Bapchule says cowboy GRC talks to animals, plants and rocks and they communicate with cowboy, that why Bapchule say to support. Bapchule watch young man much, Bapchule will teach and train young man much. Bapchule say young man be good for Indian people, maybe have happy future."

George was not certain who this Bapchule was or what he represented, but he just witnessed an uncommon passage of a motion presented to the Board. It received a hundred percent vote of approval. He still did not have a clue as to what it meant. He remembered that Jesse had stated that George would meet Bapchule.

George stayed the reminder of the meeting to learn more about his neighbors. Disappointingly, however, before he could visit with Edna or Bapchule, they had both vanished.

"Who is Bapchule? Why did he help? How did he know that I talked with the plants, animals, Thunderbolt and everything else including the gate that had penned me twice? What did he mean he would train me?"

Again, that night he looked upward and smiled at the greatness of this day. He smiled even more when he thought of his new name, "GRC." George Ribit Chattit, the Gila River Cowboy and the Gila River Cattle Ranch or the GRC Ranch had become one and the same.

12—LEARNING FROM THE DESERT

G EORGE'S FAVORITE TIME of day is early in the morning. He enjoys watching the sun peek over the mountains and reintroduce itself to the awakening earth, plants, animals, and birds and even to the most minute of insects. This particular morning was a glorious Sunday morning. George had not made any particular plans, except to spend the day thinking, reading, and appreciating all that he had learned in such a short space of time. He was peaceful for the moment because no extraordinary experiences had occurred for some time. In the cool of the morning, sitting on the old mesquite stump, his "thinking stump," he thought he would reflect on his adventures since arriving in Arizona and have a couple of good laughs. His mother used to say to him, "If you cannot laugh at your own follies, others will and that might cause embarrassment." As George was thinking, he observed, at a distance, an old man.

The old Indian walked slowly through the desert. He exuded a spiritual peace. George could feel the old man's reverence for life, as the old Indian looked, touched and talked to the plants and animals.

They, in turn seemed to revere him and to respond audibly, "Welcome dear friend, it has been awhile since we have seen you."

There was an unknown feeling worming its way through George's very being. It was not an alarming feeling, but it was not completely pleasant either. The old Indian paused, looked his way and began to narrow the distance. The unknown feeling grew in strength and power as the man drew near. Anytime an unknown, but very desirable, feeling develops from deep within a person's being, he endeavors to identify it by associating it with something from his personal history. Was it fear? Was it love? Was it anxiety of the unknown?

"Hello, you be the George, I know?" spoke the old man. He uttered with a low tone and heavy Indian accent. It was interesting how he asked, answered, and acknowledged in the same sentence.

"Hello," George responded. George now recognized the elderly gentleman as Bapchule. So, he was surprised that the Bapchule called him George, after stating at the tribal meeting that George would be known as GRC.

"My name is Bapchule, I am from over there." The old man motioned with his right arm and hand as he swung it over the desert in the direction of the distant Estrella Mountains, but pointing nowhere in specific.

George thought that Bapchule's name should be Atlas, not the super strength Atlas, but the road map Atlas. This man had major and minor highways along with many rutted wagon roads crossing in every direction across his weathered face.

"Some of my friends told to me that you be crazy like to me, you talk to Brother Badger, you talk to tree, you talk to Sun and you bathe in mud. Yes, come I to visit with white Indian with blue eye. Other blue eyes must think you crazy."

Trying to interpret what was being said George inwardly smiled of what "other blue eyes" often called him. Crazy was one of the mild names.

While it could be difficult at times to understand an Indian who is speaking English, George remembered reading that native languages of the Native Americans were very useful during World War II. Many Indians were used as code talkers, especially in the Pacific Theatre of the war. None of the native languages were written languages, so it was almost impossible for the enemy to understand what one Indian was saying to another in their native tongue. In addition to being great code talkers during the war, many Indians were true warriors during the "war of wars to end all wars." The day that George opened his postal box in Sacaton, he made a short visit to a monument that was across the road from the post office. The memorial honored Ira Hamilton Hayes, a Pima Indian Marine. He helped raise the flag on the island of Iwo Jima. George felt he was about to learn more from Bapchule about the local Pima Indian Nation and its people.

"Yes, come I to share some knowledge and gain some knowledge. You come now with Bapchule. You leave past George in big pickup, now, new GRC come with Bapchule."

The hand gesture indicated a return trip into the desert from whence to ole man had just traveled.

"White man talk, you forgive me for say 'white man', truth be, many man, not all man but many man write book, have class and pay much American dollar to have man who not know Gods teach other men about Gods. I no understand this man way."

George mentally was left in the truck as GRC walked into the desert with a stranger. Yet, he strangely felt as if he were one of the oldest and dearest friends anyone could have. Thoughts filled GRC's mind, "Yes men who know nothing of God are busy making thousands of dollars telling others about God, then they wonder why so many doubt the existence of an Eternal God."

> "Many man of many color make big talk and big program about Cristo but do not want to know Cristo. Bapchule, do not know the big God and I do not know the little God, Cristo, but when a man produce good cattle, when a man take care of family, when a man have good crops, Bapcule thinks he is a good man. Bapcule like to think of big God as a good Big Man. Big God make earth, sun, wind, rain, moon, stars, plants, animals, insects and man. God say earth, sun, rain, moon, stars, plants, animals and insects all obey his rule but earthman creation got big choice. Big choice is for earthman to make choices, even against Big God. Maybe God make big mistake letting man creation choose? Bapchule show Cowboy about Big Desert Spirit. Maybe help GRC creation choose more better."

The old Indian led GRC away from the barn and corrals then stopped under the shade of a mesquite tree. He brushed away the fallen stems, thorns and leaves from the dry ground and squatted cross legged next to the trunk of the old weathered natural wonder of the Arizona desert and indicted with his eyes and head that GRC should do the same.

"GRC wonder in small head why Bapchule come talk to GRC? Bapchule tell GRC. Bapchule listen much to people and listen much to Spirit. Tells Bapchule that GRC is pure spirit. No get mad when airport take off clothes. No get mad when police stop big truck. Why not get mad? GRC not judge others do wrong so GRC not get mad. Big Book from Big God tell earthman creation not to judge, even earthman judge Big Book to be false before read Big Book. Bapchule tell to GRC many things, GRC chose if words good or words bad. Big Book say good orange tree produce good fruit, bad orange tree produce bad fruit. If not know orange tree and just know fruit, can tell if good or bad tree, yes? If GRC no know Big God but know Big God fruit, then know if Big God good, yes? You have talked to tree?"

"Yes sir."

"Bapchule, not your sir, I brother. Do you call brother sir?"

"No, I wish I had a brother."

"GRC have many brother. Brother Snake, Brother Badger, Brother Tree."

"Could it really be that simple? If I am a brother and if all living creatures are my brother… If an individual does not like oranges, then they think God is a bad God. If an individual sees the beauty in life then they will see the goodness in God."

"Tell Bapchule about Brother mesquite." He felt the trunk and touched the leaves.

"Well, its bark is rough, limbs are brittle, its thorns are long, however, Mr. Mesquite does make excellent charcoal because its dry wood is hard as steel. His seeds are sweet when dry and bitter when green and it appears to be very hardy."

When he had finished George was expecting a little admiration for the detail in which he described the tree. The old man sat very quiet, penetrating with serious brown eyes into his very soul.

"First my brother, you call my brother, Mr. Mesquite, an 'it' several times. Would you like me to refer to you as my 'it friend'?"

He shook his head sideways.

"Second you do good to exhort white man teaching. White man fast to judge and compare, tell me how you think bark is rough? To think bark is rough you must judge another tree bark. To say Mesquite produce little shade you must compare to other tree. To say green bean is bitter you must relate to sweet. Can you not appreciate Brother Mesquite for being Brother Mesquite? He do better at his work than any other tree. Do you not want to see Mesquite for being Mesquite?"

George recalled many writings in most great books, "Judge not." He had never realized how many times he judged for the mundane sake of judging.

> "If you were walking in the hot desert would you not appreciate the shade offered by Brother Mesquite? Would you say, 'mesquite I will stay in the sun because you have not big shade like big Pine? Would you not appreciate that mighty Ponderosa Pine does not grow in hot dry desert? Would you see and love green Cottonwood tree for growing by the wash or irrigation ditch where there is much water? You begin to learn from desert, you learn of Big God and you learn about friends. You untrain George earth mind so to absorb spiritual atmosphere that exist under great Brother Mesquite Tree."

George realized that Bapchule was not talking about a tree; he was talking about people, their work, and their personalities.

> "Does GRC not see that two-thirds of Brother Mesquite is not seen. Roots extend hundreds of yards into mother earth. Mother Earth rewards tree spirit for the gallant effort; she gives to him of her hidden moisture, her stored nutrients and minerals. Brother Mesquite humbly receives gift of each item and transports through the miles of unseen roots. Millions of big lives and little lives now able to do nature good because Brother Mesquite make great effort. Each life completing task in which it has been assigned. Do you feel the harmony my brother? Look

now at the life on, around, in and under this grand God creation."

Above his head was seen a small bird nest, he could both see and hear small insects busily working around the tree and armies of ants marching up and down the tree trunk. However, he did not see how "millions of lives were given existence." The old man then led him to a dry sandy wash with exposed rocks, boulders and something that George had not really noticed, exposed roots from an old mesquite tree.

"You have looked at roots with natural eye, now, let spiritual eye follow the root into the unseen womb of mother earth. See the struggle that small root has when it finds a pebble, rock, salt or toxin in its path. Does it go through, does it go around or does it quit. Can you see with spirit eye that some roots do quit, some stop and but most build new roots in other areas. Some of the tiny roots are very diligent and split a massive rock. Which root is right?"

Unconsciously he had closed his eyes and let his imagination penetrate the hard dry earth.

"You see Brother GRC, people in life have same challenges. When the root faces the challenge they become stronger and more productive roots. When people face challenge, they become stronger and more productive. You must see root struggles with spirit eye because the struggles are not seen with natural eye. You must see people struggle with spirit eye because most struggles are not seen with natural eye."

It was difficult to maintain concentration; "I will practice in solitude until I can envision the unseen."

"One root meets with many pebbles and rocks and another in soft soil. Root in soft soil grow three hundred yard while one in rock soil only grow one hundred feet, which root better? To often man judge good and bad, success or failure, by what see with natural eye, should see with spirit eye."

Soft eastern grown fingers were reverently touching the exposed roots. Letting his imagination peek into the unseen earth and watched the struggles, the successes, and the persistence of each root, large or small, long or short.

The old man sat motionless, observing the physical reaction and feeling the developing spirit in his Brother.

"Your Big God Bible book says, 'Man cannot see God with his natural eye. You begin see God with spirit eye. What is living? If you see only with natural eye, is that living? You see maybe one/tenth of Brother Mesquite with natural eye; you see nine/tenths with spirit eye. Is seeing one/tenth called living? Bapcule think seeing all is living. Bapcule cannot see Big God with natural eye, must see with Spirit Eye."

"How many times have I heard that verse? I thought it meant to see God face-to-face or person-to-person. Now I have learned to see the handiwork of God and more fully appreciate living."

He slowly turned away from the eroded bank of the dry wash that had exposed the tangled roots and looked intently at Bapcule. This old Indian man was looking beyond the natural eye and seemingly with a spiritual talent looking into and possibly through George.

"What was he seeing in me?" George wondered to himself.

"Cowboy GRC always walk a different path. Now make path longer and wider."

His use of the word cowboy was with reverence. George knew that this good ole man respected the word "cowboy" and its meaning of independently depending on a greater power for their existence.

A quick flash of insight passed through his head, "cow is representative of nature and boy representative of the human. However, boy is used instead of man, because a boy is still adventurous. A boy still is not molded into what the world expects, and still uses the imagination or as Bapchule says, "Seeing with the Spirit Eye."

"Yes, I will be more respectful of the words Cow and Boy or better yet, Boy still with Nature." George inwardly promised.

"Your path has been a good path, it has kept you from falling or sliding into man traps. Traps that say a man is only worth what he owns. Traps that say a man must dominate. Traps that say a man must look and walk like other man look and walk. Traps that say I must have much like Jones have."

Bapchule smiled, "I do not know who is Jones. I do not know what Jones need. I do not know if Jones have much problem or few problem? How can Bapchule know Jones if Bapcule only look at Jones house, car, boat or clothes?"

He climbed out of the wash and walked towards the mesquite tree. "Remember my Brother, you see Mesquite tree with man eye, you see root and need of tree with spirit eye. Do not ever want roots of one mesquite to be same as another. Each must find its path."

Bapchule took him by the arm as if to lead him, the ole man was going to continue his teaching.

"You my brother are to be like cactus, when there is much moisture, cactus absorb plenty water. When desert dry, cactus use moisture to help many survive and help self survive. You learn plenty good, your spirit whisper to my spirit. This thing not done much with man, man mostly talk with tongue. Remember the mesquite tree, most tree seen by spirit eye, not man eye. Your arm tell me spirit want to learn see with spirit eye, Bapchule teach brother GRC more."

Still holding the arm, the old man guided GRC to squat by a two-foot cactus with thorns that looked like the hook of Captain Hook's steel hand.

"Every plant in desert can teach man to be better man. Many men, even many Red Indian choose not to look, listen or learn. Cactus now has no flower, when rain come cactus suck in all rain possible, soon after rain cactus put one or many flower so bee family can come and enjoy more moisture. Look at big cactus over there. Big cactus have many holes in side. Many men see hole and say, poor cactus."

Cactus say, "come my little feather friend, I have water inside, little bird must make hole in outer skin and I give stored moisture. Cactus say, Big God make plenty for all. Cactus say, Big God make law of abundance for all to share, all have plenty."

"This big lesson for man. When man have opportunity to store up much, must store, must then make opportunity to share with others. Man, red, black, white, yellow or tan often store plenty, make big flower or many flower to show world he has plenty but not share. Cactus have faith Rain God will send more rain when needed. Not all plants are cactus. Not all plants have great capacity to gain much storage during abundant moment of moisture. Great Mesquite tree no have capacity to store, must put much root down very deep. Which is greater? Which more important to Great God?"

Reverently the old man rose and proceeded towards the small hill a few hundred yards distance. He nodded to each plant as if acknowledging their individual importance to the life of the desert. He bent down a moment to observe a small lizard, similar to the one that scared George so desperately the first night in the dark and lonely house. This small creation did a few push-ups as if to acknowledge the presence of a spiritual leader.

"Bapchule, my spirit seems to tell me that you are in a Grand Temple."

"Bapchule please that GRC learn listen to his spirit. Many religions build spacious and beautiful buildings for special worship. Bapcule has a spacious and beautiful desert."

George thought, "Yes, what a glorious temple."

"This great boulder we call Malapai. Mala is Spanish word for bad or bitter, Pai is sweet; all nature is bitter and sweet. Leave choice to all. This boulder is hundreds of tons and has been around for thousands of years. It no bad unless fall on Bapchule."

He looked seriously at George and said, "Bapchule make a funny for my brother."

With that comment he allowed himself a deep rumble type of laughter that seemed to roll out of his soul like the pleasant sound of distant thunder.

"The desert tells us to laugh much. The desert is a hard place and when no moisture exist and no cloud, it not a time to shed tear and waste moisture, no, it time to laugh and tell Rain Spirit, you make funny with us, you make fat barrel cactus have small belly, you make us not grow so fast, you make mesquite have deeper roots, you make us hide flower, however Rain Spirit, we still have laughter. Ancient Indian felt that when desert laugh very loud it sound like thunder, Rain Spirit enjoy thunder and begin to laugh. Sometimes laugh so hard produce tears of joy. Desert then enjoy tears of joy and Skinny barrel cactus become fat once again. You understand my brother, life in desert is hard but desert learn to laugh."

Looking at the rock, the crooked little grass stem or a fleeting lizard a vibrant laugh erupted with energy. Bapchule was showing George how to laugh.

"Sometime man life become hard and man waste much energy feeling how hard is life. When desert dry it does not waste moisture with tear, when life is hard for man, he should not waste energy with self-sadness, it is good time to laugh. When man laugh, he gives joy to others and the Great God of Spirits hears laughter and begins to laugh, when man or God laugh he more willing to give. Is that not true my brother?"

The old man stood and walked into the desert. George looked at the giant size Malapai boulder and touched it.

"You are dark, have pits on the surface and to most eyes appear to be mean, bad and ugly because they look at you with man eyes and only see what is outside. What are you like inside?" George found himself talking to this massive boulder.

"I believe you are good. Yes? I know you are good because God created you for a purpose. Each creation has a purpose and thus each creation is good."

His hand with open fingers on the surface of the boulder, felt its hardness and roughness and then spoke reverently.

"Brother Rock, thank you for being a part of my life. Thank you for being an example of strength and silent power. Thank you for your patience. Thank you for enduring for such a long period of time."

He lifted his hand and turned to leave when he felt a shudder through his body and heard an inner communication. He wondered if it was just his imagination or if the rock, as Bapchule had explained, really did have a spirit. George felt the rock communicate.

"Brother GRC, what is time? What is patience? How have I shown thee strength?"

This feeling and these words hit a seldom-used portion of the brain sensors causing a shock that almost paralyzed the body.

"Wait just a minute. I have talked to plants, computers, trees and horses but I never expected them to answer."

George felt his physical body slowing in mortal time. Yet, the spiritual portion sped up to learn and partake. Yes, much like the Barrel Cactus soaks in the rain in order to have moisture when it is not raining. His spirit was soaking up spiritual knowledge.

"If this great boulder really has a spirit and if it really was created by the same greatness that created my own spirit then you my brother rock could indeed communicate with my spirit."

149

Recalling a thought, "The native languages were used in war time because others could not understand but God created each spiritually so any spirit, no matter race, color or creed can communicate spirit to spirit."

Pondering this possible truth, "that is not a thought to share with office friends or Peggy. They would have me see a psychiatrist." He stood as immovable as Brother Rock.

Bapchule approached with an ear-to-ear smile.

"Brother Rock spoke to you did he not? What did he say? Are you going to answer?"

Bapchule, normally speaking with a low slow tongue, was enthusiastically spitting out the questions. Then a reverent peace replaced the questions and seemed to replace every desert sound occurring in the early morning. George looked at this grand ole spirit housed in the human form of Bapchule, his new found and greatly appreciated friend.

"I thanked Brother Rock for being my friend and for being around for such a long time."

"What did Brother Rock say to your spirit?"

George was amazed that Bapchule understood and so easily accepted the fact that there had been some form of communication between a human and a huge rock.

"He simply asked me a question?"

"What was answer?"

Astonished how easily the conversation flowed, he was concerned that he was losing his mind, and this kindly gentleman was extremely excited that there had been spiritual communication with this Malapai Boulder.

"I have not answered. I am not even sure it was the rock or my imagination. I am not sure of anything at the moment."

"Yes my young brother, Brother Rock did speak with you, I know, Bapchule spirit eavesdropped." He chuckled a bit.

"I know not polite eavesdrop but Bapchule think Brother Rock spoke loudly because George spirit ears very deaf. Bapchule bring GRC to big Malapai spirit because has loud voice, think maybe GRC hear. It not hard question he asked? 'What is time?' I ask to myself many occasions?"

Speechless was a mild explanation as a million thoughts; ideas, questions and teachings flooded the mind of his trembling physical form.

However, the most predominant thought, "This man, this old man, this man with little formal education had heard the question, he was standing twenty feet away and heard the question from the rock, but was only a few feet away when I was talking to the rock and he did not hear a word. How is it possible? Who is this man? Why did I hear the spiritual voice of Brother Rock? Have others passing this way heard the voice? Am I just crazy?"

He wished he had his bright white hat. In the movies when a cowboy does not readily have an answer he slowly raises his hat and scratches his head, much like a professor taps a pencil or pipe smoker will slowly lower his pipe and fiddle with it a moment while he is thinking. He was thinking but did not have a hat to lift so he did the next best, he just scratched his head. Except for the brain and hand, nothing else was functioning. No legs, no heart and no lungs. It was as if the physical portion of life ceased to function. The spirit portion of his soul seemed to be so overly excited that it totally dominated the physical, allowing a greater spiritual communication. His eternal spirit seemed a continuous ricochet inside the physical entrapment. The Spirit felt excitement for being utilized.

George mumbled, "I have been found, yes, another mortal has rediscovered that he is composed of two parts: the Spirit and the Physical." He mumbled to himself a bit more. Not a negative mumble but a mumble from talking to oneself. "Maybe the 'Being' is like the mesquite tree, a third seen by man and two thirds seen by spirit."

"Well?"

"Well what?"

"Answer Brother Rock?"

"How do I answer, what do I say?"

"Open your mouth, speak what you speak I do not know?"

Bapchule respectfully placed his hand on George's shoulder,

"You have chosen a path few men choose, you listen to your spirit now. Bapchule see you again sometime."

Between the effect of tears and the ever-brightening sun, the giant of a spirit housed in a small dark brown structured man disappeared into the university desert campus.

George sat and leaned against Brother Rock and conversed. Tears of joy, tears of sadness, tears of loneliness, and tears of recall, but mostly tears of a newly discovered or rediscovered art of spiritual communication graciously flowed. He smiled to himself: he had faced a badger, coyotes, skunk, rattlesnake, scorpions and fierce looking javalinas without a single tear. Now, with this new experience he sat talking and crying with a huge dark Malapai boulder.

"How does one explain a toothache if the one listening has never felt pain?" He smiled, "How does one explain time to a Malapai boulder that has never experienced the need for time?"

He thought as he placed both hands on his new brother Malapai, "This might possibly be the best experience ever."

He was beginning to understand why his mother had so diligently taught him to keep his spirit, emotions and body clean. His father, in a dream once told him, "Son, remember, you cannot comprehend pain or joy until you have personal experience. Do not fear either, they are good."

This experience with Bapchule was delightfully uplifting which caused him to reflect much on his mother's teachings. "It is not wise to drink from a dirty glass, it is not wise to put pure water in a dirty container, remember that the Spirit is wise. Keep your inner container pure."

He looked upward, "Thank you Mother and Father."

Much like special days of childhood, a baptism, a birthday or graduation, George felt the presence of many family members. He could almost visualize his father. He found himself looking around to see or at least feel the presence of his mother. "Where was she?" A mother would not miss something this incredible, unless she was in a condition that prevented the visit.

He would anxiously anticipate the next visit from his friend called Bapchule. Maybe with his insight into life he might shed light on why his mother could not attend.

13—WINDMILL AND CHULA

I F THE TALL windmill had been built centuries earlier and in another continent, then it could have been called the leaning Tower of Black Water. On the Gila River Cattle Ranch, it was just a galvanized angle iron structure that had two support legs sunk a foot into the desert soil causing one side of the pyramid looking structure to lean about a ten to fifteen degrees. The four legs of the tower had once been anchored on a three-inch thick cement slab. The corners on the east side of the slab provided shade from the intense western afternoon sun for small animals, including a family of prairie dogs. Each hot afternoon, they would dig a little farther and deeper under the cement in search for more shade. When enough of the hard earth had been removed from under the non-reinforced concrete, the constant weight of the windmill broke the cement. When that occurred, the weight disbursement was now on about ten square inches instead of a ten square foot pad. Each rare rain softened the dirt a bit more until the two legs had sunk over a foot. The sinking of the east two tower legs put increased strain on the ½" bolts anchoring the tower to the cement on the west side causing, sometime during the past several decades, six of the eight bolts to pull out of the cement or snap from the strain. George could easily deduce that the windmill structure could topple at any time it chose or with a little help from the wind. The "Leaning Tower of Black Water" was good for post card photos, but if it were to pump water it had to be straightened, new footings poured, the gearbox repaired, the blades straightened or replaced.

He had previously bought pre-mix bags of concrete; this meant all he had to do was mix with water. He had borrowed a large tank of water from R-Country Store, and bought a wheel barrel and a shovel to mix cement. He was ready. Two problems existed: One, how to straighten up the Leaning Tower of Gila? And, two how to keep it up while making necessary repairs to the cement footing?

He could climb the leaning tower and attach a rope to the higher portion of the tower and pull the tower straight. A one foot drop at the bottom of one side of a thirty foot tower meant, without doubt, the weight of a man on the top of the tower would be sufficient to cause the leaning tower to fall. The man foolish enough to climb to the top would most certainly let out a blood-curdling scream on his way down.

The other option was to place a jack on the lower leaning side and lift until the tower was level again. This of course added two more problems: One, operating the jack would place George on the falling side of the tower. And two, was the ground sufficiently hard enough to support the base of the "High Lift" jack from sinking into the ground?

He was in deep thought when he heard Thunderbolt whinny.

"Good friend GRC, Cecil (the very large Maricopa Indian George met in the Post Office parking lot) and Jesse think you try and fix windmill, decide easier to help to fix than to dig friend from under heavy windmill." They both laughed.

"Cecil tells to me maybe pickup truck have big cable winch maybe attach on front truck frame. Cecil tell to me that Cecil think GRC no ever use big cable winch, maybe not know how."

He was profoundly grateful to see his two friends arrive and Cecil was right. The winch was installed on or in the front bumper. George had never used it. He did not have the slightest idea how to use the electric machine.

"Cecil say park truck in no good corral, ask Thunderbolt let use corral with no fence, take cable from truck and throw high to tower. Cecil say he good to fish in river, maybe good to fish on tower?"

With the truck in position and enough three-eighths inch high strength cable pulled from the spool of the winch Cecil began his fishing expedition. The first throw of the cable completely missed the tower and all had a good laugh. The second hit the tower, causing it to shake; each held their breath thinking the tower would fall. On the third try the open hook caught a cross brace of angle iron near the very top of the tower.

"Cecil good to catch, maybe try for fish next time be water in Gila?" Cecil held tension on the cable and guided it across the spool on the winch.

Slowly the cable tightened as the electric winch evenly wound the cable around the rotating spool. He was so engrossed in the winch that he missed the tower as it began to straighten itself. Both Cecil and Jesse whopped with delight.

"Go very easy my brother, do not want tower on top nice truck." When the tower reached the desired vertical position Cecil motioned with the imaginary cutting of his throat with his hand that signaled stop. The three stood with a newfound pride. Jesse spoke,

"Three Indian better than one half Indian, two Indian plus one-fourth Indian with cable on truck better than many Indian."

George thought from various ancestors that his percentage of Indian blood might be about one fourth even if his birth documents showed one-half. He also knew he weighed about one fourth of Cecil's weight; so they had two reasons to call him quarter Indian.

What would have been an insurmountable task for George alone became easy work with proper tools and proper knowledge. Together, as brothers from different paths of life became one, Cecil from the Maricopa Tribe near Phoenix, Jesse from the Pima Tribe south of Chandler and George a mixed blood Apache from the East Coast. They looked at their accomplishment. They had a good laugh and started mixing concrete.

George thought, "My dad died in a war because different people from different walks of life could not figure out how to work together." Maybe, he wondered, "What the world needs are more old crooked windmills."

The three simultaneously looked up as they heard a new squeaking sound come from atop the windmill. The old Dempster Mill manufactured wind fans; now free from the bind in the pipe from leaning so far, was starting to turn. At least a third of the blades were missing. It had been years since it rotated and more years since it was serviced. Dempster Mill was founded around 1886 and the wind fans became a frequent sight throughout the Midwest and Western plains. Now after all the many years, this old faithful machine was trying to pump water again.

George thought back to New York City and remembered many men and women living on the streets. They were also bent or leaning, so as to be non productive in this life. They, like the old windmill, were created to be productive. Maybe, someone needs to help pull him or her up straight, so they can become productive once again.

Cecil hurried over to the tower and moved a lever, which caused the tail fin to close ninety degrees into a locking position. This caused the turning to stop. The tailfins' purpose is to keep the large rotating blades facing the wind. However if the wind changes direction, the fin has a braking system to stop the blades from rotating. Cecil applied the brake. When the large blades are spinning they create a powerful gyroscope force, which does not easily permit the fan to change directions. That gyroscope action is what causes most windmills to tear apart.

"If old pump lift water into pipe, water get heavy, make weight of tower heavy and make cable pull hard, good to stop. Good to see "Dempsi" (nickname for the Dempster Mill) turn, good to mix cement fast."

Before pouring any cement, a footing was dug along the east side to connect the two loose tower legs. The old pieces of cement were broke loose, and the dry ground was wetted. Wetting the ground, as Cecil explained, "Always good to make dry ground be wet, keep dry ground from soak much moisture from new poured cement, no moisture in new cement make new cement to become weak." George watched the two men working without pay as perspiration dripped from their faces and soaked their shirts.

"Cecil like much work but Jesse like much talk, both like much red soda."

George had not anticipated Cecil or Jesse coming to help, but he learned from the Riggs family, "Better to have too much, than not enough, God has plenty for all." So he had purchase a large ice chest with plenty of red sodas along with other varieties then filled it with ice. He decided to play along with Cecil. "It sure is hot, a cold soda pop would really taste great or a big glass of ice water."

Finally, Jesse could no longer stand the thought. "Little quarter-brother talk much about water, maybe make Jesse more thirsty, maybe want more water." He walked over to at least have a drink of warm water from the bottle. George motioned to Cecil who came closer to the pickup. As Jesse was about to take his first drink of one hundred and twenty-degree water, Cecil opened a bottle of cold Nehi strawberry soda, the fizz caused Jesse to make a one hundred and eighty-degree turn and raise his fits in jest.

"GRC make funny to Jesse, but Jesse no mad, Jesse want cold pop." The three sat in the shade of the old barn as the cement dried.

Night creeps in very late during the summer and the working body is always ready for the slight change in temperatures. The tank of water brought from R Country Store had plenty in which to wash. GRC decided to fill Thunderbolt water trough and bathe.

"Water plenty good, but think maybe Thunderbolt no like to drink much muddy water with much human salt," Jesse mentioned.

Cecil responded, "When horse thirsty, horse drink." They all felt and looked better as they looked to the sky and watched a few falling stars before the moon appeared.

Jesse and Cecil became very somber as they gazed to the eternal heavens and then fixed their gaze on George.

"Our brother," Jesse spoke, "Cecil and Jesse do much work, much favor for our brother GRC, and Jesse make big request. Chula very sick, GRC know Chula, Chula very strong, now very sick. Bapchule say something maybe bites, Bapchule say GRC have gift to talk with rock and tree and Great Spirit. Maybe GRC talk to Great Spirit and ask to help Chula."

They all sat in total silence.

"GRC not to answer soon, think and talk to Great God then speak to Jesse."

Most of the night, GRC rested on the seat of his truck looking out the side window. His two friends sat in the back, worrying about a sister and a wife. He found no answers, only more and more questions. With all his soul he wanted to help his friends, but they had asked something of which he knew so little.

"A clean vessel can do much good." Words from his mother crept in and out of his mind.

"Yes, but is my vessel clean enough? What gifts do I have? How do I know if I have a gift?"

"Opening a gift, even a Christmas gift, requires the faith that the giver of the gift is wholesome. The gift must be opened or it is of little value." He recalled a dream from his father years previous, "When given a gift, when possible, always open the gift with the giver, thus both the giver and the receiver are happy."

Sometime during the early morning he dozed. He had several dreams of which he had no interpretation. The sun was up when his tired eyes were pried open. His friends were gone and only the early morning sounds of life greeted him. No matter how difficult or sleepless the night, nature always welcomed a new day, as if yesterday no longer mattered.

As George sat under the shortening shadow of Brother Mesquite, he asked, "Brother Rock, I have been asked a very difficult favor, can you give me an answer?" Brother Mesquite, can you give me an answer?"

"Neither responded, which was not a surprise. It is very easy to doubt, and very difficult to believe. Anytime a person begins to believe, that person must be willing to make changes. That is why it is easier to doubt, it requires no effort. Yet, he so desperately wanted to help his friends.

"I heard and felt the rock, or was it my imagination? Bapchule said he had heard the rock? Was it his imagination?"

He recalled a few of his mother's teachings. She had spent many months and years with her Apache mother-in-law.

"Son, you can be different, but not special, you can be special, and not different, or you can be different and special, but you must always be true to you."

He pondered this teaching. He had accepted the fact that he was different, actually very different from most of his acquaintances. He just never thought of himself as special. Maybe, he was not special and not different, just himself.

"Always be true to you."

"Which is more special, the little stem grass or the giant ponderosa?" Bapchule had recently asked of him.

Deep in thought, he forgot himself. His body stayed, yet it seemed as if he had been carried into a different sphere. He no longer wondered about the hundred questions. He seemed to be suspended outside of his physical body and was surprised to see Brother Diamondback coiled up between the legs of his human form. In this spirit-like form, he spoke to the spirit of Brother Diamondback, housed in the snake body,

"Brother Snake, why do you make your rest between my legs?"

Spirit to spirit the snake responded, "I come to apologize for my cousin. He bit Chula. Chula did him no harm. My cousin reacted in anger and struck your friend Chula. Now Chula is very ashamed. She thinks she did something wrong and desert Spirit punished her. Chula thinks she is evil because my cousin struck her when she could not see. Chula is a good human and my cousin is very sad. You must take leaves from the Nopal and place on the bite for one full day. Please tell Chula that she is not bad. My cousin is very sorry and if Chula desires to crush his head, he will understand. He will come to her again for it is the law.

He jumped as if emerging from a bad dream. Hours had passed since he sat under the tree. He slowly looked between his legs and saw no rattler. He looked intently and could see the definite markings in the soft soil of where a snake had coiled between his legs and then departed towards the old water tank. He jumped up and rammed his head into the large solid branch protruding from the main trunk of the tree.

"What a way to end a spiritual experience," then he laughed,

"How easily a man feels something spiritual and thinks he is special. How quickly nature restores humility!"

He rubbed his sore head. "Seek and ye shall find" just emerged with a whole new meaning.

He stood by the truck trying to decide what to do? He wasn't sure if the cable from the truck attached to the windmill tower could be released. Yet he really wanted to give Chula or Jesse this possible answer.

"When you are ready to learn, you will be taught, maybe you have answer." George jumped at the voice of Bapchule.

"Yes."

He turned to face his spiritual friend.

"All answers exist, but they must be found. A baby finds answers in the touch of his mother, later in her voice, eyes, breath, each question is asked before the answer is found. Some find answers in a book, is this not a gift? Some find in nature, is this not a gift? Some find in the spoken word, is this not a gift? Some find in the rocks, plants or animals, is this not a gift? Some find in the heavens, is this not a gift? Which is different or which is special? Is not every living creation something special? Come, you talk to Jesse."

George hesitated, "Jesse left early this morning and I don't know how to find him."

"Last night Jesse hear scratching of Scorpion, did you hear? Last night Jesse hear soft patter of small cottontail rabbit, did you hear? Last night Jesse hear plea of Chula many miles away, did you hear? GRC have talent to hear spirits talk, Jesse not hear spirit. Jesse hear rabbit foot, GRC not hear rabbit. It okay, GRC go to desert and speak to Jesse, he come soon because he hear the words of GRC. Does GRC understand? Which is more needed in the desert, the sun or the rain, the wind or the rocks, the plants or the animals? All needed? All great worth. Now go speak to desert and come back fix windmill, cement good and dry."

George walked into the desert, stopped to speak then walked farther away from Bapchule.

"Jesse," he spoke aloud, "Jesse, this is GRC your brother, if you hear my words come soon, I have an answer."

He stood alone and listened. He could hear a jet plane passing overhead, but could not hear a word from Jesse. He could hear the truck tires from the freeway fifteen miles away, but he could not hear a rabbit eating grass. He returned to the pickup as Bapchule was leaving.

"Remember my brother, you see what you want to see and you hear what you want to hear, choose wisely."

When a person has had a spiritual experience, many times the physical body becomes very exhausted. Combine that exhaustion with forty-five minutes of sleep the night before and that person becomes a disaster waiting to happen. George was trying to remember how Cecil let the cable loose. It seems he moved some lever on the winch.

For those less experienced than George, there is a release lever on most winch spools. When the lever is released the cable can be unwound (free spinning spool) without wearing out the electric motor. However, on most gear drives it is clearly stamped, "Do not disengage while cable under pressure."

In the direction manual it will go on to say that serious accidents could occur. The sad truth about laws, natural laws or manmade laws, is the innocent are not exempt.

He saw the lever and pushed and pulled with no success. They had previously used a large hammer to break away the cement.

"I have no idea why the company would make the spool so difficult to disengage."

With that he swung the large hammer and stuck the lever; the lever has one or two large male cogs or teeth attached to a shaft that rotates with the electric motor. When engaged with the female countersunk part that is on the spool there is no rotation unless the motor is rotating, thus the cogs are either in or out, there exists no slow release, it is all or nothing. When struck with a large hammer the disengagement is quick, instant, complete and most often extremely dangerous.

There exists little reaction time or recollection during the split second it took for the cable to instantly be free from thousands of pounds of tension, the tower to bounce only a few inches backwards, but with sufficient rebound to free the cable hook that had been attached to the tower and to send the hook flying through the air aiming at an undetermined target. Unlike the movie versions, in real life there is no slow motion.

As was previously discussed, innate objects seem to develop minds of their own. Those who have worked with cables and hooks will testify that these so called innate objects do indeed have a mind and will of their own and often do spiteful and outright mean things just because they so desire, maybe in retaliation for the abuse humans give to them. If a free flying cable has the choice of falling harmlessly on the ground or striking a human it will almost inevitably hit the human. At first glance the flinging cable hook saw the innocent windshield, and then it discovered an innocent human head. If a person turns a cable hook just right, it forms a full smile. The hook now turned to form a very sadistic grin, and seemed to find a new target, a vulnerable head and a windshield, both supposedly waiting to be shattered. As mentioned, innocence provides no exception to the law. This law is simple, a metal object flying at near supersonic speeds will not be damaged upon striking a human head, however, the human head might well receive considerable damage and still allow the steel hook to continue towards the destruction of a brand new expensive windshield. Thus, apparently with its own mindset, the hook destroyed two targets before recoiling fast enough to wrap the body holding the head even before it could fall to the ground. There exists no doubt that the hook and cable were both satisfied with those great accomplishments that in real time required less than two seconds. When cable, also referred to as a wire rope, is wrapped very tightly around a spool and the tension is released, even though it is pulled with tension in a straight line, the cable tries to recoil itself as if around the spool. In this event, the innocent Gila River Cowboy became the spool.

When water is splashed on an unconscious face, there is always a start. However, when the human eyes from the startled face opens to see the muzzle of a horse two inches away, there is mass confusion relayed from the small human brain.

"What happened? Did I fall from Thunderbolt? Was that why the horse was standing there? Why am I lying here?"

He tried to move but something seemed to have his head and body tied to the ground. He focused on Thunderbolt and could see that the splash of water was coming from the horse's mouth.

"Why would my horse drip water on my face? Why am I looking at the underside of the bumper on my truck again?"

He recognized the sight because he had in detail studied the underside of his truck the first night when he endeavored to open the gate. He wanted to smile, but some glue like substance had dried on his face, preventing a smile. He seemed to reenter a dark tunnel only to have another splash of water fall on his face and look up once again to see Thunderbolt standing directly overhead.

Slowly the mind began to remember. It was not pleasant because as the memory began to increase, so did the pain in his head. Near his hand he could see a large hammer. "What am I doing with a hammer? Why can't I move? Where did Thunderbolt go? Why was my horse letting water escape from the mouth and fall directly on my face?"

Questions without answers continued to form.

"My brother, I came as quickly as I heard your voice."

Jesse froze as he came around the front of the truck and saw the dried puddle of blood, a head and face covered with blood and a large and open gash on the upper forehead still bleeding. He fell to his knees,

"My brother what has happened to you? Why are you bleeding? Why are you wrapped in cable?"

"Jesse it is good to see you. I don't remember what happened." George's mind was spinning. "Jesse, I have an answer for Chula, we

162

must find Nopal leaves to save her, cousin snake is very sorry, crush head if…."

He faded into darkness.

When focus and feeling returned he was untangled from the cable and lying in the rear seat of the F-350.

"Jesse, I didn't know you could drive."

"No drive very good but faster and easier than carry GRC."

It was good to hear that even in a crisis Jesse still had his sense of humor.

"Jesse take little brother to hospital."

"No!" George protested, "I am alright for the moment, we must get Nopal leaves to save Chula!" He struggled with every word. "I don't even know what Nopal is."

"Jesse think maybe Riggs man have Nopal he bring from Mexico. Jesse take little brother to Riggs, maybe they put head together, maybe know Nopal."

"Thank you Jesse, you are a…" Again he faded into the darkness.

Jesse knew where the Riggs families lived. The only problem was that there were a dozen Riggses living in the area. He recalled that one of the men had a Mexican Hacienda looking house. He was hoping that he would have Nopal or at least know which family would have it.

It should be about a thirty-minute drive to the Riggs' house that Jesse thought might have knowledge of Nopal. Jesse was driving faster the normal and as he pulled onto the gravel lane leading to the house, he began honking the horn.

Benjamin had been working in the shop repairing equipment.

"What in the world happened to George?" The look of astonishment filled his eyes.

"Get him out of that truck and into the house right now!" It was a plea and a command in the same breath.

George was on the bed when he awoke to a new set of faces.

"Where is Jesse? Must talk to Jesse. I know how to save Chula." Tears of emotions and tears of pain mixed with oozing blood fell onto the clean white pillowcase.

"It is okay, Jesse told me something about Nopal, snake and Chula being sick. I have worked and lived in Mexico and know that a Nopal poultice on any poisonous bite will pull out the toxins. It is best to apply immediately after a bite or sting, but it will still help. My son returned with Jesse to help, they took plenty of Nopal leaves. If Chula can travel they will bring her to our home to spend a few days. Now young man, you need some rest."

He was not for certain but he was quite sure this had to be the most comfortable bed he had ever experienced, especially after having slept several nights on the seat of his truck.

Early the next morning, he awoke to the smell of bacon and hotcakes. He tried to get up, but his head felt like a hundred Yellow Jacket Hornets had made two or three dive bomb attacks each and had successfully hit strategic nerve endings.

"Well how are you this fine morning? Hope you slept well? Can you get up or do you want breakfast in bed?" Then as if he were reading George's thoughts,

"You know Clint Eastwood could get up the next day after being ninety percent beaten to death, shot twice and drug behind his horse, of course that is only a movie."

He took the challenge and sat at the breakfast table.

"Where and how is Chula?"

"She is fine. She stayed in her own home because she did not feel like moving. She kept the Nopal poultice on the bite all night. My son left a cell phone with Jesse, he called this morning and said she was doing much better and was able to get out of bed. Someday you must share your experience with me on how you learned about a Nopal poultice?"

After a good breakfast he felt much better but his head was still pounding.

"I am curious. Who splashed water on your face? Most concussions like you received cause a person to go into a coma for days and sometimes permanently"

"I am not sure, each time I was able to open eyes my horse was standing over me and letting water fall out of his mouth. I could not understand at first, but the third time, I realized that he was doing it deliberately."

There was a chuckle from those near enough to hear. One of the ladies commented, "I hope your horse practices good hygiene. That water probably kept you from going into a coma, but it also fell into an open wound and could cause serious infections."

"Don't worry," one of the delightful daughters commented, "Dad has had plenty of practice being a doctor with five sons and hundreds of bike, horse, trampoline, three-wheeler and sporting accidents. Last night he washed and disinfected, shaved some hair, disinfected, pulled the skin back in place, disinfected and taped the wound in place and disinfected. You will probably not even have a scar."

Trying to get up and sit in a chair almost caused another collapse.

"It is okay, another of my sons volunteered to go to the ranch and make sure that your horse is fed and watered. By the way, did you scatter any hay around for the strays?"

That evening, after resting most of the day, George reluctantly rehearsed the profound life-like dream experience. Learning what Chula needed, seeing the snake between his legs and having the snake talk to him. He was certain most families would have had him thrown out that very night upon relating such an out of the normal experience.

"Young man, you have had a very profound learning experience. Regard the experience as sacred. Do I believe? Yes, it is easy for me to believe because I have had similar experiences. I firmly believe that all things are created spiritually and then housed with a physical body. You have a gift, please use it wisely or you will be mocked. There are many with similar gifts. Gifts of healing, gifts of understanding, gifts of teaching, etc. are granted to those who seek or those who will best utilize the gift. Gifts can be lost. Have you heard of King Saul, King David or King Solomon? All these great men had great gifts and lost them because they did not hold them sacred. Remember, you find what you look for. Look for the very best," explained Benjamin.

George's head continued to ache, but these words and thoughts easily entered his mind. They were like water being poured on sand that moves around the many grains of earth and stops where it finds a suitable location. He could almost feel the ideas gently moving through his mind. Like cool water, they were very soothing.

Benjamin continued, "The world is selectively strange, if a man has a gift to sing he is applauded, if one has a gift of leadership he is esteemed, if a young person has a gift to play the piano she is congratulated, if person has a gift of a particular sport he or she is paid well, however, if a person has of gift of spiritual nature he or she is ridiculed."

Pondering the ease in which this family received this unusual experience he felt a relaxing sleep approaching. Tomorrow he hoped to return to the Gila River Cattle Ranch, his home. He had an immovable feeling of concern.

14—FAMILY AND FRIENDS

FTER A COUPLE of days of recuperation, George was anxious to get back to his ranch. He had been under the care of the Riggs family and had special nurses that ranged from two years old to the Grandmother that, according to her, had seen many a horse and buggy and a few brand new Model A Fords. The young nurses were full of questions. "Why did you hit yourself in the head? Why didn't you just duck? We sometimes tie each other up but we use a rope not a cable?"

During the few hours that he was left alone to rest, his mind envisioned his mother. She had never lost her youthful looks and carried with her a pleasant smile at all times. She made his life and the world a happier place in which to live. Sometimes, he felt that he could hear her voice. For a moment, he really felt he had heard her spirit voice much like Jesse had heard George's voice after the cable accident in the wide expanse of the desert. "Why does she not come to me like father has to let me know she is alright?"

George learned the meaning of genuine hospitality and hoped one day he could return the favor. Mark, one of the sons simply said, "You can return the favor by helping someone else in need. That is what our Granddad always taught us." One of the younger Riggs sons drove George back to the ranch; they did not want him to leave their care so quickly. Yet, they understood his desire to get home.

"I have a concern that something is wrong."

They had stopped to check on Chula and found her outside feeding chickens. She handed George a bag of fresh eggs and insisted she and Jesse go to the ranch. Along the road, they saw big Cecil. He climbed in the rear bed of the truck even though it had two very comfortable seats. Chula laughed,

"He is so big that he no fit in most cars so ride in the back, Arizona make law say no ride in back, patrolman he stop driver to tell no man ride in back. When Cecil stand up and look way down at small patrolman, patrolman just say, 'have a nice day,' he gets back in car and no stop Cecil again."

They all laughed at the image of this big Maricopa Indian standing in the bed of the truck. He would then be at least four to five feet taller than the officer. Each one in the truck laughed as they repeated the words,

"Have a nice day."

George could feel every bump on the blacktop. It was worse when they turned onto the dirt-rutted roads. The bumps were magnified ten times in his swollen head. The cable and hook had left a large gash in George's forehead that in most cases would have required stitches, but, with years of experience of repairing their own children along with dozens of scouts and neighbors, the Riggs family had learned that a good clean wound held firmly with tape, would heal quickly, properly and seldom leave a scar. With each bump George wanted to groan, but he had learned enough from his Indian friends to understand that groaning was a sign of weakness.

Before they arrived at the ranch, they saw a couple of Gila River Indian Pickups and one Sacaton City Police car parked along the dirt road and in front of the ranch house. An officer approached the pickup even before anyone had time to get out.

"Sorry GRC." The officer handed George a one-sentence note in large bold red printing.

"George Chattit, go back to New York before you really get hurt."

"Who wrote this? What does it mean? How do they know me?"

"This area is a passage for people entering illegally into the United States and the Phoenix valley. The rest area on the freeway that is fairly close to George's ranch house had become a drug exchange point. We believe that drug smugglers provide the illegal families with help in crossing if they will bring drugs into Arizona. The families and men are so desperate to work and to improve their lives that they are willing to take the chance and even risk their lives. I have no idea how they know your name or that you are from New York."

This was a shock. "What should I do?"

"Well," the officer looked around, "It doesn't seem to disturb your friends."

People, some he recognized, but others he did not, were moving in and out of the house. It looked like a small dust storm escaping from each open window. In his few days of absence, the Riggs family and friends had filled the water tank, fed the animals, and repaired the corrals. They had apparently scattered small bunches of hay around which attracted a number of calves and cows that belonged to the ranch, these animal were now in the repaired corral. They had cleaned and were continuing to clean the ranch house, which was the cause of the miniature dust storms twisting out each window.

George eased himself from the pickup. He had bit his lower lip to prevent the scream that he really wanted to release to relieve the head pain. He could taste the blood from his lower lip. Then he stood staring at the flurry of activity. This kind of help with no monetary reward was new to him. Deep inside, he always felt that people should support each other emotionally, spiritually and physically, however this was the first time he had seen and felt the words in action. When one of the young granddaughters spied a tear seep from his swollen eye, she hugged him,

"It is okay to cry when your head really hurts, I cry when I am hurt." The tear was not from pain, but from gratitude. He had recently met these people. They were not family, and yet they were taking time from their own busy work schedules to come and help.

"Western hospitality" he said to himself. "To bad it is not worldwide."

"How can I ever repay you for your kindness?" These men all had grand spiritual experiences in their lives, yet they joked and laughed at every opportunity. So many people seem to think that to be spiritual, one must always have a sober face.

"Just get well, you were never the most handsome man in the world and now with your black eyes half swollen shut, cut lip and bald spot where the cut was taped together, you are approaching ugly," Benjamin teased.

They laughed and another said, "Don't say such a thing! I saw him before he failed to duck the hook shot. I say he looks a tad more handsome in his current condition."

They helped him inside and led him to the bedroom. The shock of this clean room was about as great as when the coyotes jumped out at him the first night or the shadow of the "giant lizard." The room was clean, no cobwebs, no lizards and no coyotes. The bed was made, a candle and lantern sat on the small table next to the bed and the cutest little girl, one he had not previously seen, was standing with a hand full of flowers she and her cousins had picked in the desert.

"I hope you like the flowers; they are from the desert gardens."

He wanted to bend down and give that precious smile a kiss, but he did not know if it were appropriate or even possible with his pumpkin size head.

"Thank you so very much, the flowers are almost as pretty as you." With that she blushed slightly.

"My daddy gives me a hug, when I bring him flowers."

With that beautiful invitation he slowly knelt down on one knee and received the warmest and sweetest hug.

His mind whispered, "Oh my dear mother, I so wish you could meet these good people. They are in the stories you used to tell me as a boy. At least Lord, let her spirit visit for a moment."

He lay on his bed and listened to the activity outside. He wanted to be helping. He wanted to be learning the how, why and what of the activity that was taking place just outside. He made a mental note,

"I will help someone every opportunity that arises just so they will feel love as I feel it now. I wonder if Peggy could adapt to this life of giving."

Outside one of the Riggs men could be heard,

"Cecil, we need to pull the pump out of the well and replace the leathers."

Leathers are used in the pumping mechanics of the well. They are round and formed like a cup facing upwards inside of a pipe that is located in the underground water supply. This pipe (pump) has a small foot valve at the bottom, which allows water to enter but automatically shuts to prevent water from escaping from the small cylinder housing the leathers. The leathers are attached to a rod that is attached to the windmill overhead, as the rod goes down the leather flexes inward allowing water to pass around the outer edges and as the rod pulls the leathers upward the cup designs opens until it presses against the inside of the pipe (pump) which prevents the water from escaping. Each movement, down and up, lifts ground water up from the ground and into a reservoir tank. As the leather cups rub against the pump wall they wear and need replacing. The tower holding the windmill fan also serves to attach a block and tackle (pulley set up) to lift the entire pump system from the underground water so the leathers can be replaced. The frequency of leather replacement depends on the type of water underground. Some water carries sand or excessive minerals. This underground water supply had the Gila River underflow for a source, which slowly ran through natures "sand filter," thus the water was constantly cool and clean.

"Cecil, we can hook the pulley to the tower and use the winch on the truck to lift the pump from the underground water which is a slow process or we can see if Maricopa Indians are as strong as they claim. Can you pull (lift to the surface) the pump by hand?"

Cecil walked over and stood on the cement inside the tower. "Cecil lift easy, pump not heavy like front of cousin pickup."

His cousin had been doing mechanic work under his pickup when the jack stands collapsed and pinned him under the car. While other family members were trying to locate additional jacks and stands, Cecil grabbed the front of the truck and lifted it up while they pulled his cousin out from under the truck. Then he told them to replace the jack stands before he lowered the truck. From that time forward his cousins have not teased him about being six foot eight and weighing over 300 pounds.

"Excuse me," George asked, "What is that strange smell?"

"Oh," one of the wives answered, "That is the organic pest control spray that has been applied in, under and around your house to rid the many scorpions and bugs. It is a natural control and if the birds eat the dead or dying bugs they will not be harmed."

"You mean I won't have to sleep with those predators that wanted to have me for a main course the first night I was here?"

They all laughed. "Well let's just say there will not be as many and they won't be as famished."

"Cecil, we don't know how deep the pump is, but we did bring the pipe clips."

In Arizona, ground water is usually very deep, even if the well is located relatively close to a river. To reach the groundwater a succession of pipes are lowered down the well. Each pipe is about twenty to twenty one feet long. Each end of the pipe is threaded on the outside. A coupling is a piece of pipe that is about four to six inches long. The inside diameter of the coupling is the same as the outside diameter of the pipe. The coupling is threaded on the inside. Two ends of different pipes are screwed into the coupling until the pipes reach the groundwater. When the pipes are pulled out for repair work, a pipe clip is slipped under the coupling. Pipe clips are small plates with a U cut out, when a joint of pipe, about twenty-one feet long is pulled, the clip is placed around the pipe, the coupler that connects one length of pipe to another is slightly larger so the clip fits snuggly around the pipe and the coupler sits on the clip keeping the reminder pipe and pump from falling back into the well while the joint of pipe out of the water can be unscrewed and laid on the ground).

Cecil lifted the pipe and pump, placed the clip under the coupler and the upper joint was unscrewed. This process was repeated a couple of times until the pipe and pump with the leathers were lifted out of the water and placed on the cement slab for repairs.

Cecil wiped his hands and forehead the commented, "Cecil say Maricopa Indian faster than electric winch."

"We all agree Cecil, you make it look easy. You are not only faster you may well be stronger."

"Maybe, good thing, Cecil no have steel hook to mash GRC head."

Overhead, the youngest of the sons had changed gear oil, cleaned the gears and serviced the pivot points of the 1914 Dempster Mill gearbox; he was now replacing the missing blades on the large fan. In the "good ole days" changing the blades was a time consuming process due to the numbers of 5/16 inch galvanized bolts required to be removed from each blade. With the bolts placed on the inside portion of the angle iron, each tight nut loosened with a wrench was a potential "knuckle buster," however with the fine battery power DeWalt impact wench the time was cut by three fourths.

Once the pump was out of the well, it only took a few minutes to replace the worn leathers and the lowering (putting pump back into the well) took less time than the pulling. Cecil replaced the pump and pipes with such ease even though the pipe and pump combinations weighed in excess of three hundred pounds.

George was feeling better after his rest and periodic naps. A little blond blue-eyed girl ran into the room,

"Granddad says ole Dempsi will be working soon."

Who is Dempsi? Which cousin, uncle or friend was named Dempsi? Then he remembered that the windmill was a Dempster and he supposed that Dempsi was a nickname known to most of the ranchers. Ranchers and farmers seemed to relate to each piece of equipment and to every animal as something personal and have names for most.

He really wanted to get out. He wanted to see the Dempsi and Thunderbolt. The splashing of water from the mouth of this horse probably saved his life and he had not been able to thank his good horse.

He had not noticed the change in his "cowboy gear"; none of the family members had mentioned his attire but some of them had looked with the astonished admiration at what he had received in New York or at the airports. That afternoon he ate hamburgers with the family. One of the young granddaughters did mention that he looked like a toy cowboy doll she had seen in the movies. He did not understand if that was or was not a compliment. Later Grandmother, spoke to him,

"Young man, you do not have to dress differently to be different. Difference is in the heart and you have a different heart." That was all that was said.

When he awoke this morning, his only focus was the head pain and his determination to not moan and groan. Even though he had not been shot with a Colt 45, or hit with a Mike Tyson hook shot, he had totally lost his fight with the cable and hook. He was determined to be as tough as John Wayne.

Now, he was a little more focused and a little more conscious, as he slowly bent over to reach for his clothes and boots and even though his head pounded with the rush of blood, he did not moan. As he pulled on his pants, he noticed that these were not the pants he purchased from the trading post last summer. These pants had no dangly fringes. Then he quickly realized that he had an entirely new outfit. His boots were not his red leather boots with three-inch heels. There were no spurs attached. His shirt was a light tan western cut shirt with normal snaps. He pulled the leather rough out Justin boots and they slipped easily onto his feet, he stood very comfortably without the three-inch extended cowboy heel. Physically, he had lost three inches in height, but emotionally he had gained a foot.

"You don't have to dress different to be different," he recalled the words of advice.

Standing in the kitchen, gathering enough nerve to walk alone down the two weathered board steps and to the corrals, he heard a great cheer. He noticed that with all the previous activity, now there was not a soul in the house, the cheering was outside.

As he edged towards the steps leading from the porch to the dry barren yard, the cheering stopped. Suddenly, it erupted again, but this time it seemed closer to him. He looked and saw all present clapping and cheering in his direction.

"Way to go!"

"Good going!"

"Be Careful!"

Words of cheer filled his heart. The younger ones ran to his side and helpfully hindered his decent from the porch.

"What was all the cheering?"

"The Dempsi is working and the Gila River Cattle Ranch once again has a source of water."

The pipe had been diverted away from the storage tank and water made slow spurts to the dry ground. He had never seen water flow from a pipe in slow low-pressure spurts; he realized that the sporadic water flow was directly related to the upward lift of the windmill pump. When the pump rod lowered itself into the well, the water flow stopped only to start as the newly installed cup leathers lifted another portion of water.

"How did you fix the pump? How does it work?"

He gazed in awe at the small puffs of dust being created by the water striking and flowing out over the parched earth. He always thought that water was used to squelch dust. He smiled to himself,

"Only a few hours home and already he was learning new and interesting bits of information."

His intent puzzlement at the puffs of dust was interrupted when he felt a nudge on his shoulder. He didn't know if all activity around the windmill, yard, barn and house actually ceased or if his look and love for this horse actually shut out all other sounds of the activity.

"Thunderbolt!" He could scarcely contain the tears of joy and love as he held the thick jaws of the horse that probably saved his life.

"Thunderbolt, thank you, thank you and thank you. What caused you to bring water from the trough and drop it on my face? What caused you to stand over me, creating a shadow from the bright burning sun? Some people have laughed at your sway back and have mentioned that I paid a high price for you. Thunderbolt, I knew you were the horse that fit this cowboy! Thanks once again."

The noise from the activity resumed and Thunderbolt went back to his flakes of hay.

"How did you get the windmill pump repaired so quickly? The pump company said it would take two full days to pull, repair and install the new pump."

"It might take days for them, however, they do not have a Cecil."

George wondered, what is a cecil? Was a cecil part of the hoist or derrick? Was a cecil a large gripping tools that increased leverage? Was his friend named after this special equipment used to repair wells? George started to ask, but quickly saw that they were all laughing, except big ole Cecil. Even under his dark skin, a reddish blush could be detected. George realized that Cecil was the Cecil.

"Uncle George you better go sit on the porch in the shade."

One of the small girls dressed like a miniature cowgirl mannequin with bright blue eyes, blond hair, and a smile to compete with the bright sun had taken his hand and lead him back to the porch.

His head was whirling, not from the accident, but from the activity and love these people were showing and then to have this precious little lady refer to him, as "Uncle" was almost more that his battered brain could comprehend.

"What a wonderful place the world would be if people actually helped each other instead of just preaching about how great it would be if the other person would help or if the other person would help me."

He was sitting in an old rocker that one of the sons had already repaired when the words of a phrase he had heard suddenly changed.

Instead of "Love one another" the words come out "Be of service one to another." "Love" he thought is not a mere word, it is an action."

Not one of these family members had mentioned that they loved him yet he felt something inside that reminded him of his mother when she held and cared for him.

"We are going to repair the roof on the barn. It will begin to rain the end of July and part of August and the inside of the barn needs to be dry."

George smiled, that was not a question, "Would you like us to…?" No, they saw the need and they fixed it.

The heat of the desert was surpassing the 110 degree mark, even though the young children continued to play in the mud or under the partial shade of a Mesquite tree, the adults were finishing the repairs and looking for shade. With water now available from "ole Dempsi" the women would soak towels or dish cloth in water and hang them over the open window, the hot dry breeze would pass through the moist cloth and create a miniature evaporative cooler. George was impressed how much cooler the house was with this new idea. They laughed at the remark that it was a new idea.

"In the late 1800's when our family first came into the Salt River Valley in Arizona there was no electricity, no running water and no blacktopped roads. So, this cooling method was used, probably by all hot, dry, desert dwellers from the beginning of time, so we would not refer to it as new."

A couple of the Riggs brothers were sitting by the table where George was seated. They had seen the note that told George to go home. These two were big men, big in strength, big in emotion and big in spirit.

"George that note is probably from drug trash, however, we will be checking in on you from time to time and the Gila River Police will also check. Our questions would be to understand who would know you were from New York that would be meddling in illegal drugs. Any ideas?"

"I have not had much time to think, because I had the same question. My first thought was that my mother worked for the Drug Enforcement Agency. Almost a year ago she was involved in a serious accident and … he could not say the word died."

They looked at him with puzzlement, but did not press the issue.

"It is best that you be extra careful and look for any strange signs such as car tracks, cigarette butts or beer cans. A few illegal Mexicans pass through here but they rarely smoke and do not drive. Most are very friendly and very willing to work for a little food or a drink of water."

Hern, the Police officer brought a big gray German Shepard as a get-well gift.

"Big dog train for drug but no good. No find much drug, find much children, like play with children no sniff suitcase. Be good for little half-breed brother have big dog. Bark loud and have big bite when want to bite."

Within a few short minutes, each gathered their tools and children and in a cloud of dust much larger than a herd of cattle could cause, the pickups disappeared down the rutted dirt road.

With the wet towels over the windows the bedroom was more suitable for sleeping. Often during the night the big dog, Bert, would growl.

"How did they know I was from New York? Who are they? Why do I dislike so much the very mention of the word drug? Why am I thinking so much about my mother?"

He questioned, "Even to myself I cannot mention my mother as if she were dead? Is it because I would want her and my dad to see the ranch, see me and meet these good people? How can my heart be so heavy and yet so grateful?"

15—THE VISIT

I T WAS A strange letter, at a strange time, with a strange invitation, and from a person she always considered strange. Yet, strangest of all, it had two roundtrip airline tickets from Washington, D.C. to Phoenix, Arizona. Peggy Penderest showed the letter to many at the office. They all remembered George because most felt he was always a bit strange. He spoke to each person in the office, knew their names and something about their families. He did his work okay but there was something strange about how he always tried to be friendly. Most had a good laugh recalling how his last day at work he came dressed in a cowboy outfit that should have been in "Toy Story." That was a strange day, but most strange was how he just kept smiling even when fellow workers were laughing at him. He seemed to think that they were laughing with him or admiring his cowboy clothes. Yes, those were strange occurrences, but this invitation with plane tickets was the strangest of all.

"What are you going to do Peggy?"

"You aren't really going to go?"

"If you get out there alone you will be in his trap like a fly in a spider web."

If they only knew how a spider web at night could make a grown man feel wrapped and trapped. If they only knew of the experiences that George, the Gila River Cowboy, had received while they in the office continued the same life month after month. If they only knew how much and how long this young man had admired "Pretty Peggy" they would not be laughing at this moment. She would not be laughing.

"Well," spoke Peggy, "he did send two tickets, so I guess I will take my mother or cousin." With that thought they all became Peggy's best friend and each desired to accompany her.

"Dear George, You cannot imagine the great surprise to receive your letter, invitation and two tickets to visit the Gila River Cattle Ranch near Phoenix. We never became close friends, but I did see you each day. I have thought of you a few times after you left. When I received your letter, I hope you didn't mind, I shared it with many in the office and most of them remembered you quite well.

"I have invited my cousin to go with me as it is a long trip and I have very little knowledge of the Arizona wilderness. In your letter you mentioned that I should bring jeans to wear and some lightweight blouses. I am excited and so is my cousin. I hope we can visit the Grand Canyon, as we have heard much about that attraction. We will arrive at the date and time posted on the ticket.

Regards, Peggy Penderest."

"Chula," George spoke with excitement, "Peggy is coming to visit me and you will see how pretty she is. Here is the letter."

Chula and Jesse read the letter silently and said nothing. After George had left Chula softly spoke to Jesse, "I no like lady already, she no say happy to visit ranch, no happy to see GRC, no happy to ride horse, come only to see Grand Canyon. Chula think maybe GRC be very sad after two day visit."

George made the rounds to R-Country Store, Co-op, Trading Post and everyone in between to let them know that his "Pretty Peggy" was coming to visit.

A lot of work had been done on the ranch home. One of the Riggs had showed George how to build a smaller wind machine and installed a 12-volt alternator to charge two large tractor batteries that were capable of starting an enormous Caterpillar Crawler. With the batteries charged, the house had lights and a small twelve-volt evaporative cooler normally used on a motor home. To George this was like living in a grand hotel. In the comfort of a soft bed, reading light, a cool breeze from the cooler, the singing of the Arizona Quail in the evenings and the songs of the coyotes was as close to heaven as he ever expected to get. He was so excited to have Peggy be a part of this life. Somehow he was so sure she would love the ranch and the activities just as much as he did.

Peggy arrived on schedule; she stepped from an air-conditioned plane to an air-conditioned terminal down to the air-conditioned luggage area. He wanted to hug her but refrained and was content with a handshake with Peggy and her cousin, Susan.

"It is not as hot as I thought it would be. Everyone kept telling me that a visit to Phoenix in the summer is preparatory to visiting Hell."

"You have not stepped outside yet. The university students here are called the 'Sun Devils' so you are pretty close in your explanation."

He smiled to himself, as he saw the number of suitcases each had brought.

"Maybe Peggy is planning on staying." He thought to himself.

As they stepped from the air-conditioned building into the 118-degree summer heat, the shock on Peggy and Susan's faces should have been recorded for "Americas Funniest Videos." They fanned their faces and tried to say something, but the oven like heat engulfed them head, shoulders, knees and toes.

"It feels like an oven, how do people live here?" "Why do people live here?"

"Gosh, oh gosh" as she gasped for breath, "I am going to die," Peggy repeated several times. "I cannot breathe. George, did you bring me here to let me die?" The faces of both young ladies changed from a pale eastern lack of sunshine white to a bright glowing red. There was a constant flow of adverse verbiage from the time they left the terminal until they reached the truck. Because of the size of the F-350 with dual tires and the limited parking spaces, it had to be parked in the open parking area fully exposed to the sun. The first few moments inside of the 145-degree cab made the outside temperature feel much better.

"Here are some bottles of cool water, I never go anywhere without a few bottles of water."

He thought they were cool; at least they were cool when he left the ranch house. He had purchased a small propane gas refrigerator for the ranch and it really kept water, milk, etc. cold. Ice-cold water, however, sitting in the cab of a red pickup in the hot summer sun becomes warm, actually just under the boiling point.

"Thank you," as Peggy and Susan gulped down the water. They had at least two to three large gulps before the hot feeling in the throat registered with the brain. Once they realized how hot the water was, they immediately spewed a portion of the warm liquid all over the inside of the windshield on the dash air vents that George had previously turned on super high for cooling purposes.

Those who have had the occurrence of having the first blast of air fleeing from the air-conditioning vents know that the first few minutes of air is not really air-conditioned. The blast of hot air is exactly the current temperature that exists in the cab of the vehicle. When the hot water that Peggy and Susan spat out collided with the hot blast coming out of the not yet cool air condition vents, it blew back on their faces and hair. George did not, could not or maybe dare not say a word as he looked at the astonished faces with matted wet hair hanging down over their eyes.

"This is not a good start." He said silently under his breath.

After a few miles in silence and with the air-conditioner working extremely well he ventured his first words,

"I thought you would like to run out to the ranch and ..."

"We will go to the hotel, we will cool off, we will unpack, we will eat in an air-conditioned restaurant and we will sleep in an air-conditioned room," interrupted Peggy.

When first confronted with an Arizona Diamondback Rattlesnake, even without any prior knowledge of snakes, the deadly sound of the rattle warns that trouble is nearby. George had never dated. His only female relationship to this point was with his mother. Yet, instinctively he knew that trouble was nearby. Without a word spoken, he took the ladies to the San Marcos Resort located in Chandler, Arizona. He checked them in, hauled in their luggage before he dared speak a word.

"It would be best if we visited the ranch early in the morning when it is a little cooler. There is a two hour difference, so if you normally arise at seven am that would be five am here, I will pick you up at five and we can have breakf..."

"You will not pick us up at five am, you will pick us up at 8 am and then we will have breakfast in an air conditioned restaurant and then we will decide," interposed Peggy.

"It is okay, you are probably not used to traveling and I am certain that you are not used to the extreme heat. I believe that tomorrow will be different. When you see the beauty of the desert, when you meet Thunderbolt, the horse I told you about, and when you visit with Jesse and Chula, you will understand why I like this country so much."

George spent the night tossing and turning. The first impressions were not so good. He was so hoping that the morning would bring a delightful change in Peggy and Susan.

It was a typical summer morning filled with hot dry air. It is interesting that he had not noticed the heat or the dryness. Now with the visit of Peggy he saw many things differently. He was at the hotel waiting for the clock to finally reach eight.

"Good morning Peggy, how did you rest? Are you ready for breakfast?"

"It is not a good morning, I did not sleep well and I am not hungry."

"Well, let's go for a ride and then we can eat later."

"Susan is not feeling very well. She decided to stay in the room. Is it okay if I go alone with you?"

He inwardly jumped with excitement, "Yes, that will be fine. We should be back in about four to five hours."

"Four to five hours, where are we going? You said the ranch was only about 45 minutes from Chandler." I told Susan that I would not be gone more than a couple of hours. "We will be back in two hours." George knew better that to speak this time.

Driving down the rutted desert road was a pleasure for George; it wasn't the same for Peggy. She was gripping the overhead handgrip and squeezing the door handle as if the lock was not working.

"Isn't this just great! That is a grand ole Mesquite tree, there is a palo verde, there is a cholla, there is a Prickly Pear and there is the granddaddy of the desert, the Giant Saguaro."

"What was God thinking when He made this desert?" Peggy interrupted. "Had He run out of green paint? Did He use up all the big leaves? Was this Hell's waiting room? Is this the desolate world?"

The big gate swung open on the newly installed heavy-duty hinges. He felt a sense of inner achievement with how easily the gate now opened and closed, but nothing was said to Peggy. They drove up to the front of the newly painted house with the newly hung front screen door and stopped. He eagerly jumped out and opened the pickup door for his Pretty Peggy.

Peggy was looking with astonished eyes at the windmill and old barn as she slipped or rather fell from the high seat to the ground before George could help her.

"Ugh! What is that stuff? It stained my white 'Reeboks' green."

"Oh, I am sorry, I think Thunderbolt got excited while waiting," George said as he rushed around the front of the truck to help not so pretty Peggy.

"George, Oh my gosh, George," Peggy was screaming at the top of her lungs and each scream got louder. "George, I am going to be trampled by this wild horse, he is trying to push me back to the ground, he is going to kill me, George, do something!"

"Thunderbolt," George made a kissing sound with his closed lips and the ole horse turned and trotted over and protruded his big lower lip waiting a lump of sugar.

Peggy again could be heard for miles, "George, he is going to bite you!"

"No, Peggy, he is just wanting a lump of sugar."

"You feed that thing sugar? You put your hand by his big ugly mouth and then you touched me? I have only been here ten seconds and already my shoes are stained, that dreadful animal tried to kill me and I see that you have no hygiene. What else can go wrong?"

He smiled to himself remembering his first night and hoped that Peggy would not experience the spider, the coyotes, the scorpions, the skunk or the javalinas. Yet all of these experiences taught him to appreciate the greatness of this grand country. It is interesting how the same experience in life can be seen and felt so differently by dissimilar people.

"This is where you live? For this you moved away from New York? You are crazier than what they said at the office. Take me back right now!"

George, looking at Peggy thought, "She has a bright smile that was not utilized very often; she has bright eyes, long hair that glistened in the sunlight and a beautiful physical body, yet she is not so pretty at this moment."

"Wait a few minutes and I will get you a cold drink. Would you like a Coke, Pepsi or Sprite? With or without ice?"

He was hoping to impress her.

"You mean you at least have electricity out here?"

"Well, no not exactly, the refrigerator works with Propane Gas."

"Do not make fun of me, never make fun of me. Do you think I am stupid? Propane gas if for heating."

The more he explained how the heat exchange creates an expansion of a Freon type liquid, which cools coils, the more she interrupted. She flatly said, "Nothing gets cool from a fire!"

"Well it really keeps things cold." He realized he was just making things worse.

The remembrance of the beautiful smile, the sparkling eyes, the smooth delicate skin on her cheekbones, and the small dimple on her right cheek, he had so often admired in the office seemed to vanish into the hot desert breeze. She was a beautiful girl in New York, but in the Arizona desert and on the Gila River Cattle Ranch, she was as plain as the old fence post. Yet, even the fence post had developed certain admirable characteristics. Sometimes in one's mind a beautiful panorama is developed without considering the personalities or characters of others.

He thought, "I was out of place in New York and Peggy is out of place here. Which is right or which is wrong? Neither."

As Peggy was leaving the house, she froze just as stiff as a fence post and in a low, almost whisper of a voice. George jumped to be her rescuer, thinking there was a large rattlesnake in the doorway.

"George, George, come here quickly, there are Indian savages looking at your pickup."

When he reached her she was trembling with fear as uncontrolled tears poured down her face. He, for the first time in his life, held her close to him and calmed her fear.

"Those are my dear friends, Chula and Jesse. They walked over so they could meet you."

"I don't want to meet them, look at their dark evil eyes and quit holding me. Do you think I am some little girl?" She jerked away to hide in the kitchen.

Jesse and Chula seemed to sense that Peggy did not want to meet or visit with them and they did not want to put George in a more awkward position. When Peggy looked up they were gone.

"What do you mean, those are your friends? They looked like Indians to me."

"Yes they are Indians. They are from the Pima Tribe that has lived along the Gila River for hundreds of years."

"Well you can have them. I want nothing to do with them because they cannot be trusted."

"Peggy, you have never met an Indian and yet you formed a negative opinion. How could a person do that?"

He could hear Chula, "Maybe now GRC forget pretty girl and look for Chupa Rosa."

"Peggy, please let me show you just a little more of the ranch yard, barn and livestock."

She stiffened at the thought, but at least she agreed. With that they walked to the barn and for a brief moment he thought she might have a growing interest.

"How does the windmill work? Where is the grass for the livestock? Why do you have chickens running loose in the yard? Is that huge dog very dangerous? How did you learn all of that stuff? Did you know all of this when you lived in New York?"

Her beauty was beginning to seep out once again and his heart began to beat a little faster. Sometimes the spirit of life plays mean tricks on a person. Within a matter of seconds poor Peggy lost all interest.

"What are those?"

"Those are bales of alfalfa hay use to supplement the natural desert feed."

"Are they very heavy? They look real heavy"

He recalled the first time he moved bales of hay at R-Country Store and had them fall on top of him. At that time each bale seemed to weigh about five hundred pounds. Now with daily loading, unloading, George easily moved the bales from the barn to the feed bunk.

"This is my chance to show her how strong I am."

Lifting the bale of hay was not so difficult even though it weighed one hundred and fifty pounds. When a screaming one hundred and ten pound frantic girl jumps on top of the bale that is being carried, the weight becomes extreme.

"Snake!" was all she could scream.

Before he could turn to see or help, one of the nylon twines wrapped around the bale of hay broke. Peggy hit the dirt floor about the same time the loose hay scattered all over the barn floor. Nature has a unique sense of humor. Peggy could have landed in any one of the 360 degrees, but no, Peggy, quite accidentally, landed very near the snake, which had curled up in a striking position.

The scream could be heard for distances yet unknown. George was impressed that Peggy knew some form of the western stomp, but at extremely fast tempo. Before the dust cleared, and before he could react and explain that it was just a harmless gopher snake helping to control the population of mice, Peggy was in the truck still screaming. Sometimes nature can and does play a few mean tricks.

On the trip back to the San Marcos Hotel in Chandler, George wondered how this young woman sitting on the far side of the pickup, clinging to the door could be so different than the one he had known in the office.

"Maybe" he thought, "she is not different, maybe I am seeing her with different eyes. Much like Jesse and Chula are my friends and yet to Peggy she saw hostile Indians. Maybe that is why one person can look at a sunrise and have tears of joy while the next person can only complain about the early hour. The sunrise certainly does not change to accommodate an individual, so it must be the way that a person chooses to interpret circumstances."

Back at the motel, Peggy related her horrible experiences to Susan.

"I had a horse that tried to trample and bite me, I stepped in fresh horse manure that stained my new white shoes, George made fun of me over a gas refrigerator like I was an idiot to believe that with a propane fire something could be made cold, I was almost attacked by Indians that were intent on stealing the truck or scalping my hair and the worst, I was within inches of dying a horrible death from a rattlesnake bite."

He rarely felt sadness. Yet he was feeling sadness at the moment. He did not feel sadness for himself, but sadness for Peggy and Susan for their narrow thoughts and closed vision. In one brief breath she had used the word "I" four times.

"How quickly the world would change, if it thought in terms of 'we' or 'you'."

"George, we want to see the Grand Canyon with or without you. You promised that if I came I could see the Grand Canyon."

George agreed and commented, "I believe you will have a much more enjoyable time on a tour bus. Most of those fine tourists are from the east coast and will better explain the sights and scenes, and the bus is air-conditioned."

He returned to the hotel early the next morning to help the girls find the right bus. They seemed to be in better spirits and were the first to jump in the bus to find the very best seats. They did not offer to help the numerous older couples. He hoped they were good seats, as they would be sitting for quite awhile before they even started the tour. The older tourists required more time for loading.

He made arrangements with the San Marcos Hotel staff to have the girls taken to the airport and he knew he would never again see or think again of "Pretty Peggy Penderest." She was another experience in his life. She will always be a pleasant memory and her visit encouraged him to finish painting the house, to fix the gate, to get a larger propane refrigerator, to install an evaporative cooler, but most of all she helped him realize that only a few people enjoy walking a different path. Not a right or a wrong path, just a path fit for the person. Like a horse must fit the cowboy, maybe the cowboy must fit the path.

That evening he climbed up a nearby hill to watch the sunset. It was hot and dry, yet he felt excited, as he looked over the barn with a new roof, the corrals that actually kept animals in, the cow that were gaining weight, the Dempsi pumping cool clean water, a painted house and last but certainly not least stood his horse Thunderbolt looking right back at him. Again, he wished every man at least once in his life could have the feelings of accomplishment and grandeur that he was having at this moment and would continue to have. He felt that as long as he was determined to live to help others he would continue with these satisfying feelings.

He smiled at the recollection of what Chula had said, "GRC like initials to his name but Chula smile when think of initials of Peggy Penderest, P.P. not such good initials."

George smiled then wondered in a soft breath, "What did they mean? Maybe it is now time look for Chupa Rosa."

Back in the ranch house he looked in his Spanish-English dictionary.

Chupa Rosa he found to mean Humming Bird. Why would Chula want him to look for a humming bird?

16—THE FLOOD

BAPCHULE, JESSE, CHULA, Cecil and Benjamin had been discussing the ranch, feed-grass, animals, and weather. Those who had lived in Arizona for a long time explained to George that it is normal for summer rains to start around the end of July and last until the end of August or mid-September. Most of these rains have very little impact on groundwater levels and seldom cause dry rivers, like the Gila River, to run. These late summer rains are generally a short respite from the stifling summer heat. Every few years, however, there are sufficient rains in the mountain basins that surface water runs into the Gila River. This mountain water combines with rains in the valley areas to cause severe flooding. George recalled the related history of the Olberg Bridge. While the newly engineered freeway bridges washed out from these floodwaters, the old 1925 Olberg Bridge stayed intact.

He had begun the process of proving his percentage of Indian blood. It was not difficult. His Father had been in the military with Apache nationality. It was not apparent whether his Father was full blooded or three-quarters. There were some records of his Great-grandmother marrying a soldier in the U.S Calvary, which would have made his grandfather half Apache. There was no record, however, of the soldier and many of the Calvary Scouts were Apache or from another tribe and few records were kept on the Indian Scouts. His grandfather's marriage to George's full-blooded Indian Grandmother would then make his Father three-quarters Indian. George did not find any records indicating whether his Grandmother was Apache, Navajo, or Hopi. Nevertheless, with his Father's marriage to his European mother, George would be at a minimum three-eighths Apache. If, however, the soldier, George's Great-grandfather, were a full-blooded Indian then George would be a half blood Indian, even though he showed very few Indian features. His blue eyes were definitely not Indian origin. Many early Spaniards that entered Mexico and the lower U.S. had blue eyes. Edna

Antone suggested that he claim the half blood until someone proved differently.

With most of the paper work done at the Pima Tribal office, George then had to make a couple of trips to White River, Arizona. White River is the headquarters for the Apache Tribal Offices. He made these trips to sign papers and present final documentation.

On one of the trips, Edna Antone, from the Pima Tribal Office, rode with him. She was very pleasant company and explained more of the history of the Pima Indians and how there were approximately four thousand living along the river when the first white man came to the area. The Indians were known as the Akimel O'odham Tribe. They were very good small-acreage farmers. They have always been a peaceful people, which is one of the reasons they have been able to stay in the same area when other tribes were scattered to distant lands.

She told of many Pima folklores. One was about "Tall Flower," a beautiful maiden, and a young warrior, who enjoyed her company. When all the young warriors were gathered to hunt rabbits, Hick-vick (Woodpecker) returned to see Tall Flower. Instead of finding Tall Flower, he met the wicked witch disguised as a young maiden. The witch enticed Hick-vick to drink some Pinole (a fermented drink), after he drank his fill he began to notice feathers growing all over his body and large talons replace his feet. He flew off to the high mountain, but soon became lonely. One day "Eagleman," as he was now called, swooped down from his cave and carried Tall Flower to the high mountain home, where they had a son. This son was very mean and very hungry. Eagleman began to daily catch a Pima Indian child from the village and carry him up to the high cave to feed his son.

The Village chiefs sent for Elder Brother. Elder Brother is another legend of an Indian Warrior that protects innocent children, and comes to their rescue. He climbed to the high mountains, found the dark cave and set a trap, which led to the death of Eagleman and his son. The beautiful Tall Flower was returned to her valley home, married and had many brave sons and beautiful daughters.

Edna knew much of the Apache history and related many amazing and true stories about Chiricahua, Mescalero, Cochise and Geronimo. She also shared many of the legends about the creation, fire and wily foxes. He found all of these stories very fascinating. In every legend, the good prevails. George liked that part of the culture.

With Edna's help and with George's completion of the previously sent forms and requests for information, the registration process was painless. As the two of them were returning to Sacaton, Edna began to talk about the flooding of the Gila. She discussed that some of the Elders felt that maybe this year there would be flooding. She explained that the Santa Cruz River flowed north out of Mexico, through Tucson, south of Picacho Peak and on the west side of Casa Grande to join with Queen Creek and Salt River coming from the north. The Gila Rivers flow mostly from east to west. When flooding occurs with two or more of these rivers it becomes very serious concern for the Phoenix valley. In 1980, and again in 1983, the flooding washed out many homes and killed many people.

Most people who were killed believed they could walk or drive across the raging rivers. When the rushing waters strike the side of a car, it is like a huge caterpillar dozer pushing the car off of the road. Once off the road, the car begins to roll, like an alligator death roll, until for some reason it stops. Usually it stops because it hits a protruding tree, rock or a submerged hill. The stopped car then creates a whirlpool and as, the water flows over the car, it creates a waterfall. The waterfall washes away the dirt immediately down river of the car until a large crater is formed. Then the car rolls once more and becomes embedded in the crater to be covered by water and then by mud. Quite often it is never found.

Edna related a couple of news articles that she had read. The articles stated that witnesses saw the car wash off of the low water crossing. They knew the exact time the car would begin to roll. The witnesses described the two people in the car and there were enough witnesses to assure the truth. Yet, the car or the occupants were never seen or found. She verified what Jesse and Cecil had both warned about the river after the waters recede.

Sometimes when the water begins to swirl, either because of a curve in the river or an implanted tree, a similar excavation occurs. The very muddy flowing water stops which causes the mud to fall out of temporary suspension and the crater is then filled with a soupy caliche mud that takes months to dry. However, the top of the crater, exposed to the hot sun will form a dry layer which is almost impossible to detect and if a heavy object such as an animal or a human walks across the dry layer, the layer may well break open much like ice on a frozen pond. Often, whatever falls into the caliche soup is unable to get out. Escaping this desert trap depends upon the depth of the crater. This strange phenomenon in many parts of the nation is known as "Quick Sand," but in the Gila River and amongst the Pima Indians it is known as "Death Pits."

Edna talked about her family of three boys and two daughters. They are all grown and all married except her youngest daughter, Victoria. She is getting her Master's Degree at Brigham Young University in Utah. Edna smiled at the very mention of her daughter.

"Victoria must be a special daughter the way you lit up when you mentioned her name."

"She is very special. She was only four when her Daddy was killed in a train/car collision and she was the person that helped me through the sadness. We called her "Little Humming Bird" because she was always humming a song, sometimes the very songs that her daddy used to sing or hum for her has a baby. She still hums beautiful tunes and has the ability to cheer up the sad. One of her songs goes something like, "Have I done any good in the world today, have I cheered up the sad and made someone feel glad.""

Edna had a faraway look then she turned and faced him. "I told Victoria about your Pretty Peggy and how sad you were that she did not like the desert or the ranch. Victoria said she wished she were closer to home so she could help cheer you up. I think you will like Victoria."

A few light rains in late July cooled the temperature a little, but increased the humidity. Arizona is known for its dry heat but when the temperature is one hundred and ten degrees and the humidity is fifty percent or higher, life in the Valley of the Sun becomes quite miserable. George soon learned why people invest in air-conditioners instead of swamp coolers. The swamp cooler depends on evaporation to create cool air and when the humidity is high the evaporation is low and thus the only thing the cooler did in the house was circulate hot humid air. A couple of nights, it became so unbearable that he actually reclined the driver's seat of his pickup, turned on the air-conditioner and fell asleep. He learned that one of the advantages of a diesel motor is that it does not spew out carbon monoxide.

The days passed quickly with looking for cattle, mending fence and patching roofs before the hard rains began. After each light rain the refreshing smell of the desert was beyond description. The creosote bushes seem to store their entire aroma for months just waiting for a rain. Within days after the first rain the desert began to change to a green carpet. The desert grasses, long dry from lack of moisture responded with haste. The skinny Saguaro began to grow plump with renewed water storage and the dull lime green leaves of the mighty mesquite turned to a bright green. Animals scarcely seen began to scamper freely in the early morning rays of sun and birds of all species were hammering away at the cactus or palo verde trees.

Old tracks are washed clean with each rain. One morning he found two sets of vehicle tracks about a half-mile off the road. Many boot and shoe tracks indicated there had been some sort of scuffle. George, as promised, notified the local police.

Hern and his partner came to investigate. "We think maybe people sell drugs. Phoenix say one man is shot and die. Body found on road by Phoenix. Maybe dark spot be dry blood. No need for test."

Later, back at the ranch, Thunderbolt was enjoying the fresher air and seemed to be waiting each morning for a good ride looking for strays or mending a fence. Many areas of the ranch were inaccessible for even a four-wheel drive. A few of the locals suggested Quads (all terrain vehicles), as a way of getting to the hard-to-reach places, but George preferred the quietness of Thunderbolt. Beside it seemed more logical for a cowboy to talk to his horse. How would it look for Charles Bronson to climb off of his Honda and tell it to stay put or later whistle and have the Quad come chugging over. Maybe someday he would own a four-wheeler, but for now he just loaded his saddlebags with staples, pliers and baling wire for fence repairs.

He found several pairs (cow with calf) that did not have a brand. George spoke with an Arizona State Livestock Brand Inspector. The inspector explained a process whereby George could acquire clear ownership to the livestock within twenty to forty days. The inspector suggested that he hold the cattle in his corral and provide adequate care. If no one comes forward to assert ownership within twenty days and pays for the cost of the feed and care George provided, then George could initiate a proceeding in court. George would need to post a public notice of the found animals and the pending proceeding in court. A hearing will then occur within ten to twenty days of the notices being posted. If no one comes forward to pay the feed bill, then the court can award George lawful ownership of the cattle. George said he would do this and that he would contact the inspector in twenty days if no one came forward to claim ownership and pay the feed bill.

George was happy to feed the animals. He would have done it even if there were no method for collecting payment for caring for the animals. But, he was also pleased that he could acquire ownership by this procedure.

About mid-August, the rains became serious in the northern counties of Arizona. It also began to rain in northern Sonora, Mexico from whence comes the Santa Cruz River. The valley had already received a few inches of rain, which is high for the flat land valley. When rain comes slowly the ground can absorb much of the moisture, however when it falls fast it churns up the caliche, this muddy liquid seeps into sandy pores and seals off absorption. When that happens, a small amount of rain can accumulate to form running washes and many running washes form rivers.

The entire Valley of the Sun (Phoenix area), the Queen Creek Valley, the Gila River Basin and the Casa Grande basin were all formed from flood-waters bringing mud, slit and top soil from the high mountain ranges. Thus flooding was and is creative. Small washes begin to flow, carrying silt and trash and when the trash gets too heavy it simply stops and forms small dams, which stops the water. The moment the water stops the silt settles out and the wash is now filled with topsoil and silt brought from another location. This activity repeated time and time again over thousands of years can fill a large canyon to form a very fertile valley. Many of the washes fill with sand deposits and then are covered later with the silt and caliche. These underground sand washes become aquifers where pumps are placed to lift the water, providing irrigation for farming.

George was like a sponge as he absorbed the ever-flowing bits of information furnished by neighbors and magazines. He also had the twelve-volt converter that provided the 120 volts necessary for his computer, which he connected to his cellular phone, which provided Internet. Every chance he had, he would visit the local libraries, but George's most enjoyable and educational events were his visits with the old-timers that still farmed in the area.

The rains continued and soon the big truck could no longer cross many of the washes. The rutted road became two continuous steams of water and the waterproof roof on the barn proved to be not so water proof. He drove over to Sacaton to check his mail and visit with Edna. As he stopped at the crossroad near the Ira Hayes monument, he noted a lot of activity. He also saw Edna Antone talking with Cecil and a few of the tribal leaders. They were enthusiastic to see him and hurried over to talk.

"GRC, there is a family of five near the river, but cannot leave because of the high waters between them and the road. The river is rising and probably within thirty minutes will reach the stranded family and carry them to their deaths. We have no boats and it will be over an hour before we can get a helicopter or a big farm tractor to help with the rescue. We hate to ask you to risk your new truck, but Cecil thinks with the big tires, the four-inch lift, and the diesel motor, and with plenty of weight in the bed of the truck you can drive though the water covering the road. If you get stuck, Cecil says he will pull the winch cable to the big tree and you can haul yourself out."

They were nervous and by then even Governor Antone approached, (Elected Governor of the Pima Indian Nation)

The governor was well dressed. George smiled as he thought, "This man looks more like a cowboy than an Indian. He spoke perfect English with no hint of an Indian accent, "We don't really want to risk your new truck, but would you please be willing to help?"

Big Cecil spoke, "No worry little brother, Cecil plenty weight and Cecil not let little brother get hurt, Cecil plenty like big truck, not let water hurt truck."

The first aid group quickly loaded the back of the truck with fresh drinking water, food, cold Pepsis and a few Nehi strawberry sodas. Then Cecil and six other men got in the back of the truck. Each man seemingly weighed three hundred pounds or more. Edna climbed in the cab with George. She told George the story of when a Pinal County deputy sheriff stopped him for having people riding in the back. When all six of the Indians in the back stood up and looked down at the officer, the officer looked up at the six gentle giants that were standing in the bed of the pickup which made them about four feet taller than the deputy. All he could muster was, "Have a nice day!" This gave Edna a little laugh and a break from the tension of the flood.

The water was much higher than anticipated and was still rising. There was an old adobe house across the wash. It looked like at least six inches of water was in the house. The family was standing on the highest part of the hill near the road and frantically waving their arms with the hopes of a rescue.

"The rushing waters deafened their verbal pleas, but they could see the mother clutching her very young baby. It now was a matter of minutes before the rushing, muddy water would engulf both the home and the family. Without any hesitation George put the truck in all wheel drive and headed into rushing waters flowing over the vanished road. No one knew for sure how deep the water was, or where the edge of the road was, or if there was even a road that still existed.

Big Cecil stood leaning over the cab. "Cecil give little brother directions. Cecil see better see ripple who say is road edge. When nose of truck go under water, Cecil tell little brother that there is no more road." With destruction on every side, the big Indian never lost his sense of humor.

The advantage of a Power Stroke diesel is that there is little risk of an electric short normally caused when spark plug wires become wet. Diesels do not have sparkplugs. Another advantage is that the intake is located on the high part of the front grill so even if the fan grabs the high water it will not spray water into the intake and drown the motor.

It took about ten minutes for the truck, food and passengers to ease across the fast rising water. During that brief period of time the floodwaters had risen six inches causing the family to be standing in swift muddy water. Cecil and the other men jumped out of the truck bed and helped the woman and children into the truck. The man of the house wanted to stay and protect his belongings. There was no time for an explanation so big Cecil simply picked him up and walked to the pickup.

On the return trip, Cecil was once again giving directions. He pounded on the roof, which means stop.

"Little Brother, Cecil see part of road wash away, Cecil not know if place where road was is much deep, Cecil walk now."

"Cecil, take the cable in case the water is too deep, you can pull yourself back to the truck," George shouted.

"Little Brother have good idea, Cecil no throw hook back to hit Little Brother in already sore head." They all had a chuckle.

With that caution, Cecil held the hook, the same hook that had almost decapitated George when it broke free of the windmill and struck him in the head.

"Hook," George found himself talking aloud, "if you can save Cecil and help save this family you will be totally forgiven."

Cecil edged into the deep water and when he was about belly deep he was having difficulty maintaining his footing. George shouted,

"Can we drive though that deep of water with slick mud on the bottom."

Cecil managed to climb out of the deep cut in the road and continued along the flooded road until he came to a large Cottonwood tree that had been there for many decades.

"Cecil, the flood is pushing the truck sideways"

With the cable securely wrapped around the tree the electric winch mounted in the front bumper was engaged.

"We are moving forward." George spoke enthusiastically.

Slowly the cable began to tighten and the truck had moved just a few feet when the nose began to slant downward and water began to seep in around the doors. The small baby girl began to cry, probably not from seeing the water itself but from feeling the fright from her mother.

"Cecil, the big Cottonwood tree is shaking. Will it hold?" George hollered above the roar of the river and the chatter of the diesel motor.

The cable became extremely tight. Twelve thousand pounds of winch slowing turning trying to pull the truck up the steep embankment caused by the section of road washed away.

"Oh God of all the heavens, please help me get these people to safety." George found himself pleading because he had never been responsible for lives. It was a humbling experience and he pondered how pilots, captains, and other similar people could ever get used to the responsibility of safely overseeing many lives each day.

Cecil could be heard above the roar of the water. "Drive big truck, use four-wheel drive, help cable pull truck up washed away part."

Cecil had much more experience with cables and he knew that if the cable broke the truck with all the passengers would soon disappear in the raging waters. He stood at the edge of the waters holding the cable as if he alone could pull the truck to safety.

Increasing the diesel speed the oversize tires began to spin trying to grab any possible traction. The Cottonwood tree, with massive roots reaching into the water soak earth began to topple forward with the pulling pressure from the cable.

"Cecil, the tree!"

Except for the furious muddy water, time stood very still. Cecil tightened his grip on the cable as the bed of the truck filled with water and trash.

Jesse hollered, "Family much afraid."

The cable suddenly went slack and Cecil turned to see if the tree had indeed been uprooted. The tree stood firm as the deep mud/snow cleat tires found footing on the bottom of the wash and the side of the old road. Slowly the truck filled with passengers began to inch up and out of the possible watery grave.

A great cheer could be heard from the back seat and bed as the truck stopped on the high portion of the flood free asphalt road and allowed what seemed to be a thousand gallons of water pour from the cab and rear of the truck.

"Cecil pulled GRC, his little brother from the truck and gave a bear hug that would shame most bears. Cecil think little GRC okay, think maybe this be good truck. How people thank GRC?"

No answer and no thanks could top what followed. Chamita, a four year old, with her bashful bright smile framed by her dark luminous brown skin walked up to George. She looked up at George; her smile was perfectly punctuated with the large sparkling Apache teardrop black eyes. She was dressed in a crimson red dress soaked with the muddy water. Standing next to George, she threw her arms around George's legs and hugged his legs. This was remarkable. Little Pima girls are extremely shy.

"May I hug you," George said and then not waiting for an answer he picked up this living doll and hugged her. With another unprecedented reaction, she hugged him in return and for a brief moment the people, the birds and the raging river were silenced in respect for the pure exchange of love they were privileged to witness.

George, Cecil and the big red truck became legends overnight. As with any exploit, when repeated, the water becomes deeper, the wash wider, and the heroes bigger. No one, however, believed that Cecil or any of the other men could get any bigger.

There were reports of cattle stranded on small islands formed by the raging Gila and many cattle were lost. Southwest Phoenix and Buckeye were really flooded after the Queen Creek met the Gila and then the merged rivers met the Santa Cruz. Homes, vehicles and lives were lost.

"When Water God gets muddy, gets angry," Chula brushed her long jet-black hair. "Chula no understand white man, white man see big river very dry, not think dry river made from much water so white man build many house near river, river water not like close company and take away earth that hold house, house fall in river, white man get very mad and say government to blame, white man have eye to see river but no have brain to think, why white man think government have better brain? Government have no brain. Government just many people. Chula no understand."

Solutions to the majority of life's most critical problems are often solved with food. Groups gathered around the Ira Hayes monument. The smell of mesquite limbs and hot grease filled the humid air and almost by magic the grills and pans began to produce the delicious Pima Fry bread. A special mix of flour, water, oils, salt, and little baking powder and the love from the ladies' hands form to shape a pancake like form. When dropped into the super hot grease, within minutes the raw dough is transformed into a fluffy golden brown bread that truly begs for a little butter and mesquite honey. Once the first piece enters the mouth, the brain relinquishes all control to the hand and arm. As self-control is regained the most common response is,

"Oh, I shouldn't have eaten those last four pieces." George moaned.

The laughing response was, "No my friend, it was not the last four, it was the first eight that are beginning to swell in your belly."

With water raging, bridges floating away, roads washed away, and television blasting the disaster, the Pima were eating, laughing and reverencing Mother Nature and the God that gives her direction.

Big Cecil stood, "If no ever flood, no have fertile land, no have big valley, no have much TV news."

"Where is Bapchule?" George inquired.

"Bapchule maybe by Olberg Bridge, he like strong bridge and like watch big river squeeze to pass under bridge." Jesse answered.

Chula, Jesse, Cecil and George drove through miles of shallow water crossing over the black top road before coming to the bridge. The Pima Indian Police were directing and diverting traffic. The bridge was stout and strong but was not necessarily designed to carry the weight of the modern eighteen wheeled trucks. The bridge could accommodate passing model A'. But the narrow bridge was not designed for eight-foot truck trailers. The police had the big trucks turn around and go back to Phoenix, back to Tucson or over to the Coolidge Bridge about 20 miles east. Most people were respectful, but there are always the few that feel that they are important people and all others should respect their selfish ways. These selfish few are quickly calmed when a few police officers including Cecil's six foot eight 345 pound brother walks over to the vehicle.

The officers allowed only three cars at a time to be on the bridge, thus reducing the vibrations cause from heavy traffic. The freeway from Phoenix to Tucson had been restricted due to the flooding of bridges and erosion of roads. The road south of Chandler was about five feet under water near the river so the traffic was at a virtual stand still.

Bapchule was sighted on top of a nearby rock ridge overlooking the water.

Jesse pointed towards the mountain, "Bapchule like watch water, Bapchule learn much about life while watching much water. When water no has control, do much damage. When man no has control, do much damage. When water move fast tear up good things. When man go fast tear up good things. When water slow leaves new dirt, new life, and new nutrients. When man go slow, leave good family and future. When water controlled do much good for many life but water no like control. When man has control do much good for much life, man no like control. Water and man much like."

Chula poked Jesse in the ribs, "Chula tell Jesse. Chula good, give Jesse much control, make Jesse good man."

As they approached the edge of the rocks overlooking the raging Gila River, Bapchule approached the group, "Bapchule speak with GRC."

With no offense taken and with reverence the other two walked back to the truck.

"Bapchule have vision." The old man had never moved.

"Bapchule see darkness on Gila River Cattle Ranch, see darkness for GRC. See light not far away. GRC lose something, then find, then lose then find forever." The old man was perspiring much more than normal.

"Great worry and sadness for George must have great test so to grow much but then much light. George told as warning, but no can change path. Will follow and find great joy for which was lost."

George could feel more than see that there was an enormous emotional strain and not much more explanation would follow from this humble man.

"GRC go now, talk much to Spirit. Be very careful of dark one."

With that statement, Bapchule walked into the mountainous area known as the San Tans. An area where until vandals destroyed them, held many hieroglyphics telling of the Indian tribes and Mexican families that passed this way before the white settlers made their way.

George sat motionless gaping at the rushing muddy waters being channeled to a reduced width to flow under the Olberg Bridge. His mind wished to have a moment to be idle, but the words spoken by his friend and spiritual mentor left his aching head with many more questions than answers.

"Lose something and then find." George squirmed a little to adjust to the hard rock. "Great worry and sadness, what did Bapchule mean? What did I lose or what will I find? How can I find what I do not know what is lost?"

George felt perspiration forming on his own head. "Why didn't this wise man stay and explain more of what he was saying. Talk much to the Spirit but be very careful of the dark one. Was he talking about the color of skin or the adversary or what?"

George was so tired all of a sudden. Was it from the rescue, the hit on the head or the spiritual energy just extracted from his soul? He was unable to answer.

17—STRAY TEACHERS

FOR THE NEXT few months after the flood, life was fairly uneventful for George. He spent time fixing fence, painting, nailing sides on the barn and making general repairs that never are completed on a ranch. Each week a few stray cattle wandered onto his property looking for feed and water. George thought he had truly found the good life he had always desired.

Life, however, seldom follows the path that one designs. Sometimes there are slight detours. Other times there exists a wait and hope. Then there are the moments, when life is going full speed in one direction, and due to some unplanned circumstance, the straight arrow path turns one hundred and eighty degrees. Such was the case for George on that bright Thursday morning.

A number of crossbred cattle he had purchase at the livestock auction and been grazing and a few had been corralled. The assistance offered by the neighboring ranchers had been most helpful. Actually, they had been the ones that had located and corralled many of the animals after one of the neighbors had discovered the outer perimeter fence had been cut.

The combination of an inexperienced horse (Thunderbolt) and an inexperienced cowboy (GRC) offered a high degree of comedy for the other experienced riders. The neighbors would say, "It's okay GRC, we all had to learn, just keep on trying and you'll get the hang of the horse, rope and stray."

What a person learns in their youth seems to remain with them throughout life. George had watched little boys coil and throw a loop just like they had been born with one already in their hand. Adults can change. Bapchule had said to him on one occasion, "Adult change like river, someone need insist on change, many time insist, many time old river go back to original course. When River Spirit want change, it change."

They were patient in demonstrating how to turn the calf away from the mother cow or how to get ahead of the cow to turn her back to the direction of the corral. They coiled the lariat a dozen times showing the proper procedure. He had been practicing for days and months on how to rope a bale of hay. At R Country store he was able to purchase a molded plastic calf head with short horns that could be stuck on the end of a bale of hay. Coil, make loop, twirl overhead two or three times and throw the loop hard. They insisted that you had to throw hard because when riding the horse on a fast run chasing a calf it will feel like you are in a wind tunnel. So day after day, coil, loop, twirl, throw and jerk slack.

"Do this a hundred or a thousand times until it became so natural you will not even have to think." They repeated the statement, watched and laughed.

It is quite simple if the coil stays in the left hand while the right hand is throwing. It is simple until the loop hits the hat or wraps around the exposed skin of the neck. It is simple until you jerk the slack, that is jerk the rope back towards you, so the loop will catch and close around the horns of the animal or your own fist pounds your nose as the roper jerks the rope. All in all it is simple. He felt he was becoming reasonably skilled at catching the plastic dummy head attached to the bale of hay. There are always the comments that "any dummy can catch a dummy."

Now he was astride his gallant steed, all circumstances seemed to abruptly change. The animals moved forward and side-to-side and once in awhile when the horse finally got himself into a full run, the ole wise cow would decide she wanted to suddenly stop and rest under a mesquite tree. On one such occasion, the neighbors had all attempted to turn a straggle eared cow that looked like a cross between a donkey and a jackrabbit and that displayed much of the same skills and temperament. The cow gave the impression that she precisely understood the location of the weak link and headed straight towards Thunderbolt.

"There she goes George, get your loop ready and throw."

He was excited; this was his big chance to display his skill and gain the confidence of the other cowboys. The coil is set, the loop is already made and all that is left is to twirl and throw. His petrified hand and arm held the open loop along side the horse; he had not practiced with an animal running directly towards him. He had not practiced with horns attached to an angry locomotive rapidly closing the distance between his leg and the shiny horns.

He recalled when he was on his stomach by the water tank looking eye to eye with the diamondback rattlesnake and his mind was screaming to his arms and legs to move, run or at least jump but they refused. He now realized that similar reactions were occurring with a horse called Thunderbolt. George was confident that he was kicking his horse to urge him into action. He did have the large spurs firmly attached to his boots. Even though the local cowboys assured him rowels that large would do more damage to the rider and would do little to encourage the horse. He wondered which could possibly do more harm to the rider, a set of rowels or a charging cow. He continued in his mind to persuade his gallant steed to turn, run, back up or at least jump. The soon to be famed Gila River Cowboy, however, recognized the fact that his legs were not moving and neither was the horse. The rope remained with the loop end dangling from his hand and the other end coiled (dallied) but not fastened to the saddle horn. At least one end of the rope was doing something correct.

The other cowboys had explained to him, "If you tie tight the rope (small loop around the saddle horn) it is very difficult to turn loose of the rope in the event you catch an animal that is bigger or meaner than your horse."

They showed him a dozen times how you throw the loop, catch the animal, then dally (wrap) the rope around the saddle horn a couple of wraps, and pull tight the loose end. The friction of the wraps around the saddle horn will prevent the rope from slipping. In the event previously mentioned about having an animal that is bigger and meaner, the cowboy can release his end of the rope and let the animal run away from the cowboy's horse. The heavy-set neighbor called Slim also pointed out that you must dally fast and tight and never let the rope slip around the saddle horn or you could easily loose a finger. With that explanation he raised his hand and displayed a stub finger,

"Once the finger gets caught between the slipping rope, the solid saddle horn and the pulling cow there is only one thing left to do."

He waited until George asked, "What can you do?"

His response was brief followed by loud laughter, "All you can do is yell and cuss then try and find your lost finger."

These thoughts plus another thousand were rushing through George's mind, yet his horse would not move. He looked at the charging animal and saw her veer a little to one side so as to not plow directly into the horse.

"Smart horse, knew that if he stood firm the cow would not hit him, yes this is one smart horse," George mumbled to himself.

With the pleasant thoughts of success floating in his mind, he did not realize that the animal had veered a little to one side, which put her directly in the path of the open loop dangling harmlessly at his side. When an angry cow is charging at what seems to be two hundred plus miles per hour and passes within inches of your leg, there is little time to react to the circumstance and there is no time to form new thoughts to calculate an action or reaction to this novel experience.

Frequently, several sets of eyes can view the same event and see the event very differently. George saw that he had roped the cow, but the other cowboys saw it more as the cow having roped herself. Her speed gave the same results as if the slack in the rope had been jerked tight. The loop tightened perfectly, but only around the cow's right horn. George released the loop from his right hand just as he had practiced. Like a broken record, he repeated, "I caught the cow, I caught the cow."

George suddenly realized that he needed to complete one more step after the blur of the cow passed his horse. His mind was racing frantically similar to a computer trying to locate a file previously stored. When after several attempts the computer flashes a small note, "Cannot locate file. Please exit." This computer note would prove prophetic.

The problem was that the other end of the rope had wrapped around his leather glove with his hand still in the glove. A moment too late, he remembered he had not dallied the rope. The momentum of the cow and the sudden jerk of the rope caused an immediate exit from the saddle. As George flew through the air and before he hit the ground, he knew he had no file to locate to help him out of this situation. He had no control over the outcome of this event. He surmised that he would have to "cowboy up" and see how this experience would end. "Help" was the last desperate plea that came from the unsure, airborne cowboy.

The other cowboys helplessly watched their young friend being drug at high speed across the desert floor and plowing through grass, weeds and bushes. When he rolled onto his back, the large spurs spun like truck tires and made nice furrows that could easily be planted in the future. The cowboys could only sit quietly on their horses. If they gave chase the cow would run faster and farther. All they could do was sit and watch, knowing that soon the cow would tire, the rope come loose, or the glove slip off.

Because George's loop had tightened on the right horn, the cow's head was in a forced turn, causing her to run in large natural circle. To keep up with the action, the cowboys were turning their horses or pivoting their heads to watch the whole show. The cowboy's heads spun like a Hoot Owl as they hooted encouraging words to George.

About the eighth time around the same circle the cow tired and stopped, gasping for air. Still the cowboys did not move. George began to wonder if he was going to get any help. The cowboys, however, did not want to approach the animal for fear she would run again. Yet, they too, wanted to do something to help because they feared their friend and neighbor was hurt.

"Can you believe what we just saw?" They were all talking at once as they dismounted and slowly attempted to surround the fire-snorting cow. Yes, the cowboys saw one thing; however, George saw something very different.

After sliding two or three time down a hill, the sled run becomes smoother. About the seventh time around the desert he realized that he was not sliding down a snow slope in New York and began to focus on the means of his transportation. Once he realized that he was being drug by the cow the remainder of the blur began to clear.

When the cow finally wore herself out and stopped, GRC untangled the rope from around his hand and wrist and was very grateful that the cowboys had insisted he wear good leather gloves while working. He grasped the rope with both hands and pulled himself to his feet, brushed the dirt, weeds, grass and thorns from his shirt and leather chaps.

Amazed, astonished, joyful and stunned were words that filled each cowboys head as they watched this "newly initiated cowboy" stand with rope in hand. He had indeed "cowboyed up." They were not sure if he would simply drop the rope and run, or if the cow would suddenly charge. He stood with rope in hand facing the cow that was still heaving from want of air. He remembered what Bapchule had told him,

"Speak to the animal spirit with your spirit." In his mind he spoke softly, he apologized for causing any alarm to the cow and then he walked slowly towards the animal.

The cowboys thought about yelling words of alarm, words explaining that the cow was still mad and would probably charge him. They did nothing, however, but waited with dumbfounded expressions.

"Easy lady, I am just going to loosen the loop from around your head and point the way to the corral. The corral has good hay and fresh water." The old, long-horned cow stood and looked just as dumbfounded as the cowboys. The rope was removed and a gentle hand pushed the side of her head turning her in the direction of the corral.

Slim scratched his over sized belly and commented, "This young cowboy has a way with him, I do believe he talked to that crazy cow and she understood. Can ya beat it all?"

George then turned towards his neighbor cowboys and stammered, "When one does not know what he is doing it takes a little longer. I did catch the cow, however, with my first loop."

Each cowboy knew that this was one of those strange occurrences in life that would be repeated over and over. It would become part of the oral traditions that make up cowboy and Indian folklore. As with all folklore, each time a story is repeated it becomes a little more embellished. At this particular moment, the cowboys doubted that the story could be retold in a fashion anymore interesting or unbelievable than what they had just witnessed.

George began to caress Thunderbolt who continued to stand knock-kneed, sway-backed and ears lopped over to one side in the exact spot where the scene was initiated. "Good boy, you did really good and thanks so much for protecting me." That is what he was saying.

The other cowboys were saying something very different. They muttered, "You sway-back, worthless animal. You didn't move and you almost got your rider killed." Even though they had all seen the same event, George noted again the different observations.

The day was cloudy and cool, perfect weather for working cattle. George made a number of spectacular catches during the course of the day; however, none involved cattle.

Each time the group joined up with George, "Well what'ya catch this time."

With joy in his tone of voice, "I threw a perfect loop over a tree limb. Caught a creosote bush. Caught the front legs of my horse."

Thunderbolt seemed to figure out that when a calf or cow ran away from the direction of the corral that he was supposed to speedily get ahead of the animal. This he was able to do quite easily, but it took George a number of attempts to get the horse to stop once he passed the animal. He determined that it was Thunderbolt's intention to pass the animals and then let them rest for a period, "Smart horse, yes sir, very smart horse."

Sometimes if a calf is injured, has an infection, lost an ear tag, or needs a horn nipped, it is more practical to rope the animal, treat and release rather than herd it back to the corrals. (Ear tags are like earrings. One is put in one of the calf's ears to help identify who owns the calf and tracks a breeding program. Nipping the horn entails cutting the horn off while it is short so the calf cannot feel any pain. (Also it protects a cowboy's leg from the sharp point when the calf gets older.) A cowboy effortlessly ropes the calf and holds him while another cowboy wrestles it to the ground and performs the needed treatment.

It seemed effortless to George as he watched how quickly the cowboys routinely completed the task. One occasion Slim caught a calf and motioned to George,

"Throw the calf to the ground, so we can put on an ear tag."

When a one hundred and forty pound, inexperienced cowboy tries to "throw" a three hundred and fifty pound experienced calf to the ground there will be a variety of results most of which lands the cowboy on the ground with the animal still standing.

"Grab the front leg, lift it up high, and then push the calf over with your knee," was the first set of instructions. It sounded mathematically correct. If the calf weighs 320 pounds the one leg would carry about 80 pounds so it seemed feasible.

"I will grab the leg, shove my knee firmly into the rib cage and shove forward with all my strength, no problem," George repeated.

With the rope dallied firmly on Slim's saddle and the loop end holding the head of the calf, the momentum of cowboy's body weight and the weight of the calf combined, being unable to stabilize his front feet the calf falls to the ground. The ground stops the momentum of the calf, but the momentum of the cowboy is higher in the air and continues forward. Normally, that would not be a disruptive predicament, because the experienced cowboy would simply double his knees, land on the calf pinning it down. The cowboys failed to give George this instruction.

Once again George was able to experience another first in his short life on the open range. He toppled over the body of the calf and into a sage bush. The calf regained its composure much more rapidly than the crumpled cowboy in the bush. If the cowboy does not get his legs out from under the calf, then the calf with its four legs will inflict additional injury and humiliation to the cowboy. It will stomp on the cowboy's legs until the cowboy moves them out of the way. Somehow, one of George's legs ended up under the calf with the other on top. As a rule, the calf would step once or twice and run off. But, because the rope still firmly held the calf's head, the only recourse the calf had was to stand in one spot and jump up and down, it mattered not to the calf that this same spot was occupied by the crumpled cowboy.

Slim, in between laughter, eased his horse forward enough so the calf could back away from the spot George occupied. The crumpled cowboy managed to crawl, and then he stood and in true cowboy fashion reached for his hat and dusted off his shirt.

With a smile, the ever-optimistic George said, "Well, I thought that went quite smoothly, I got the calf down on the first try."

His positive attitude was appreciated, but short lived. The calf, realizing that there was slack in the rope made a swift dash to one side and away from the horse. This small act would have gone unnoticed, except that the rope lay between the boots of the now momentarily standing cowboy. The rope jerked tight sweeping George's feet very smoothly out from under him. If this were a wrestling match, then once again the small calf would have been awarded points for a takedown.

One is never defeated until he gives up the effort. George jumped to his feet, grabbed his hat, and wiped the dirt from his eyes, just in time to see three hundred and twenty pounds of irritated calf running straight towards him in another effort to take him down.

George reacted and jumped straight up in the air. The jump, however, was not high enough to clear the animal, but it was high enough to prevent a direct collision. It was also high enough to land

George squarely on the back of the bucking calf. George was face down and his head was at the back end of the calf. In this precarious position, George could only see where he had been and not where he was going. His dangling legs, furthermore, also blocked the view of the running calf. The calf proceeded to run directly under the belly of the young gelding Slim was still training.

Cowboys attempt to train their horses to have many sets of skills. Saddle, bridal, turning, stopping, maintaining a tight rope, not brushing against a tree trunk, and standing are some of the needed skill sets. A horse, like a cowboy, must also learn from experience. One can only imagine what Slim's horse saw and felt when the head of a calf with flaying legs and boots sticking out from the calf's face ran towards him. Then, to add to the perplexing situation, the calf was not bawling like a normal calf, but was screaming like a wild javalina. Before the newly trained gelding could resolve the matter, and before he could make a quick move, the calf, charged unswervingly towards the colt, and proceeded to duck under the belly of the wild eyed horse. No training or experience had prepared this young horse for such a happening.

It was instantly apparent that Slim's horse did not like the calf, the rider on top, or the possible humor involved. So, he did what any frightened horse would do in these unusual circumstance. He jumped straight up on all fours, did a semi-roll with a half a twist, and parted company with Slim, his rider. (Strawberry Roan, the horse made famous in ballad for throwing every cowboy who tried to ride him, would have been envious.)

One must not overlook the natural reaction of the cowboy when his horse makes a wild jump. He instinctively holds on to the reins and grabs for the saddle horn with his free hand. In most situations, this is a correct procedure. When the free hand, however, is also holding the rope dallied around the saddle horn, and when the rope's loop is taunt around whatever is on the other end of the rope, a pristine experience is about to occur.

The calf veered away from Slim's flying horse and the loose rope wrapped around the horse's rear legs. As the calf stretched the full length of the rope, the sudden jerk caused the calf to do a perfect somersault, which would have resulted in ten points in any gymnastic competition. This beautifully executed flip separated the calf and

George. Additionally, it tightened the rope around the horse's rear legs. That is an act that is seldom, if ever, appreciated by a horse, and certainly never by a young horse on his first field trip.

When Slim's horse came down on all fours again, he began to kick, jump, turn and rear in simultaneous actions. While he was no longer on the horse, Slim was still too near to the action. Slim, who was a petite five foot ten inch carrying two hundred and fifty five pounds, did his best imitation of an Arizona Jackrabbit. He was on all fours crawling and jumping jackrabbit style in an effort to distance himself from the horse. Since most of his weight was in his mid-section, it was all he could do to lift his body off of the ground. Still, Slim could easily have distanced himself from his frightened horse, but for the conditioned habit of grasping the end of the rope that by the mischievous quirk of nature had half hitched itself on the saddle horn. The horse jumped up again. The roped tightened and jerked Slim, but he did not perform a perfect flip like the calf did. In a matter of seconds, all of the participants (George, Slim, Slim's horse, and the calf) in this not so flamboyant exhibition were flat on the ground, as were all of the spectators, who fell to the ground from laughter.

When the dust settled, George stood up, dusted himself, spit out dirt and Creosote leaves, and untangled the rope from the calf, horse, and Slim, who was still trying to get dirt out of his eyes. They completed the task of ear tagging the calf without further exploits. Then, they all sat under a large mesquite tree recalling and retelling the event. This too would pass into cowboy and Indian folklore, but the embellishment, while once again unneeded, began immediately. Cowboys can be shot, drug, stomped or lose their girlfriend and never shed a tear, but when they relate hilarious events they can laugh until tears flow from their dusty eyes and streak their faces. It was only noon and they still had the rest of the afternoon to be with their friend, George, The Gila River Cowboy.

It was previously mentioned that George made some spectacular catches; the best and the worst was the perfect loop over the long arm of a cholla cactus. Very carefully the rope was removed, the cowboys actually suggested that he abandon the rope, but since it was his first rope and the very rope he had used to catch his first cow he really wanted to preserve it. After carefully removing the rope it was strung between two palo verde trees and with the use of some dried limbs and leaves the cowboys made a torch and preceded to pass the flame under the rope to burn off the eight million invisible thorns that were stuck to and in the rope. Twisting the rope so as to burn all sides Slim told George,

"Don't ever use this rope without gloves, those little invisible thorns will continue to creep out of the rope strands and will get in your hands and fingers." Slim passed the torch under the rope several more times.

"If you get thorns in your hand..." Slim suddenly moved the flame towards George's hands. George flinched at the thought that Slim might just grab his hands and burn off the thorns.

Slim was good natured, but was having a difficult time swallowing his pride for getting thrown from his horse, doing a somersault in front of his buddies, letting his horse get tangled in the rope and then crawling like a baby trying to escape his falling horse. Cowboys seem to take most events quite personal.

It was getting towards evening when George noticed that all of the cowboys had stopped what they were doing and were looking in the same direction. As he emerged from behind a tree, he also stopped and gazed, then he noticed that all the cowboys were now gazing at him. "Hey, who is your guest?"

Riding towards them on a small Paint horse was a young lady with long black hair that was waving in the breeze. She had a bright turquoise blouse and a white hat. Most impressive to George was the ease and smoothness with which she was galloping her horse across the desert.

"I have no idea," was all that he could manage.

She waved to them, as if she knew them; they all spontaneously waved in return. She approached with a vivacious smile that displayed a perfect set of teeth. She appeared to be Indian, but as she rode nearer he fixed on the deep blue eyes, which are very unusual for any Indian. She was strikingly pretty and her blue eyes seemed to enhance the beauty. She had no noticeable makeup and no lipstick. He thought it strange that he would notice these details, but he recalled how Peggy had always had so much skin makeup and lipstick.

"Hi, I am Victoria, Edna's daughter. I am home from school for Christmas break and Mom said I might be able to come and help. Sorry I am late but my horse had to have her hooves trimmed from being in the corral so long without being ridden and that took me a little longer than I expected."

Beauty, school, rider and a furrier wrapped all in one package. The other cowboys seemed to sense the electricity in the air and moved off to continue working.

"Hi,"

There was a vast difference between this pretty lady and a rattlesnake, yet both left George's mouth extremely dry and non-functional.

"May I presume that you are George or as they call you, 'GRC'?"

"Yes," That is all that came out of George's dry mouth.

"Do you have some more work to do and may I help?"

"Yes work more and yes, help may you please and calves move cows to corral," George stuttered.

George could tell that his words were mixed; yet she just nodded her head and rode towards the other cowboys.

"Dear Lord, dear Spirit, dear Mesquite, dear Desert, dear brother rattler and whomever else might be near, help me to at least talk coherently and not fall from my horse while in the presence of this young lady."

She approached the other riders and, out of George's earshot, Slim asked, "Aren't you the one they call Humming Bird?"

"Yes, my mother says I used to hum all day and I could mimic the sound of the Humming Birds wings while flying."

"I hear you are good with cattle and know how to handle a horse."

"Well, I started riding while still in the womb of my mother and I have a picture of me sitting alone on a horse when I was one year old. I have been riding since, that is, whenever I get a chance. I love working with cattle."

"They say you are pretty good with a rope?"

"I have won a few roping and barrel riding events in a few rodeos."

Slim decided to venture a comment or maybe a suggestion, "It seems that GRC is quite new at riding, roping and working calves and it might be awkward to have you out do him. However he takes experiences with great humor."

"Thank you Slim."

George trotted up on Thunderbolt and saw how easily Victoria pulled on the lightweight leather gloves from her saddlebag, slips the rope from the sling and flip the rope into a perfect loop without even a thought. He could tell that she was doing the movements out of pure habit, without so much as a thought. When she saw him looking at her she became a little self-conscious.

"No, please don't be hesitant, I would love to watch you rope. These cowboys can tell you some hilarious events that have occurred this very day. I am learning from each of them and I want to learn from you. Besides you are much more pleasant to watch than Slim." He became red faced at his own remarks.

She was pleasantly embarrassed, yet very impressed at his total honesty and humility. Most men she knew would try so hard to impress her with their outstanding abilities, few if any ever expressed a desire to learn from her.

Slim shrugged his shoulders, "I told you this young man is a different breed and we all respect his honesty and his positive attitude. He would end up on the ground under a stomping calf, stand up, brush off the dirt and proclaim how much he had learned."

Victoria and Slim were visiting trying to catch up on families and friends when they saw a frisky calf slip away from the main herd and run full speed in the opposite direction of the corral. Before any could react, Thunderbolt seemed to sense the urgency and bolted into a dead run after the calf. GRC, like a professional cowboy threw a perfect loop that landed perfectly over the young calf's head, perfectly jerked the slack, and perfectly dallied the rope.

When a cowboy catches a calf, it calls for an immediate response of another cowboy to come, throw the calf and do whatever is necessary. They all, including Victoria, sat motionless on their horses. None of the cowboys could believe what they had just witnessed. They thought they had seen it all, under the calf, over the calf, in the bush, through the bush, in a mesquite tree, over the creosote but never the rope thrown that actually caught the calf. George, under his breath, was expressing a profound gratitude,

"Thank you Lord, thank you Spirit, thank you trees and plants and desert Spirits, thank you calf for dodging into the loop and thank you rope and horse." He sat quietly astride his sway back horse with the knocked knees, he knew that for a brief moment he was a hero and he basked in the feeling.

Back at the Ranch House they all sat around with hot chocolate or cold sodas and laughed until their sides ached. Victoria observed intently this strange cowboy that laughed at his own experiences, laughed with others and unashamedly expressed his own terrified thoughts. She knew that he knew she was watching and listening to him, yet he easily accepted his own weaknesses and showed no sign of pride.

She thought, "I would really have liked to have met his parents to see what kind of people could raise and train up a young boy to have the sincere, not boastful, desire to walk his own path." She recalled an ole Indian saying,

"Before you judge a man, walk in his moccasins for a week." She knew that George did not need to walk in another's moccasins before judging, he simply did not judge. She noticed her pulse rise a little when she looked at him.

They heard the tires crunch the gravel in the yard and George stepped to the front porch.

"You George Chattit?"

"Yes, who is asking? May I be of help? Can you come in a minute?"

"You the one that reported the car tracks near the highway? You the one the reported the camp by the bridge? You the son of Beth Ann Chattit?"

"Yes." Before he could say another word.

"We told you to get off this property. Now we are going to help you."

The stranger pulled from under his windbreaker a rather large pistol and shot a hole in one of the Dempster Mill's blade. Shot twice in the air and sped off leaving behind cowboys, a young lady and George stunned and shocked by the gunshots. George was not only shocked and stunned from the gunfire, but also from the fact that this person knew his mother's name. He had not mentioned her name to a soul since he had arrived in Arizona six months ago.

With these thoughts filling his mind, he did not realize that upon the first shot he unconsciously had grabbed Victoria and placed his body between her and the shooter. He was not sure how or why? He had never dreamed or even imagined doing such a thing and yet he was so inwardly thrilled. When reality returned, she was looking into his eyes and he into hers. His arms did not automatically release and for a brief moment he could see that her eyes were as dark blue as an unexplored ocean, yet bright as a midnight star on a clear night.

She felt her heart beating fast and heavy, maybe from the gunshots or maybe from standing so close to this newfound friend. From her youth, when Victoria would become nervous, scared or excited the pleasant sound of a humming bird would slip from her lips.

George released her and stepped back to make sure this sound was coming from her and not from a humming bird. In the spectacular George fashion he stepped backward off the porch and sprawled on the dry and dusty ground.

Victoria was alarmed for two reasons, she feared he might have been shot and if not shot and the other he would be so embarrassed that he would never speak to her again.

She was wrong on both accounts.

George sat in the dirt, crumpled hat; dusty face streaked with mud and looked up with a bright smile. "Please, Victoria, please hum that tone again. It sounded just like a..." He stopped in mid sentence, stood up, put on his crumpled and dusty hat and walked closer to her. "Are you the one called Humming Bird"?

Before she could respond, Slim was standing by her side. "Oh my young man, I apologize, I thought you knew she was called Humming Bird. She has been called by that name for years. Have you ever heard a tone so beautiful?"

Suddenly Slim's face turned the brightest red anyone had ever seen when the thought and words escaped, "Bout as pretty as she is."

"Why thank you Uncle Slim, that was very kind." She again turned to George, "Thank you for gallantly standing in front of me."

Almost in unison they all stood on the porch and gazed at George, "What was that all about, why did he warn you, why did he shoot, why do they want you off this land?"

George was just as puzzled but had many more questions.

Victoria broke the silence, "Better call Hern."

Slim rumbled with thunder like anger, "Someone better catch that stray, hog tie him and drop him in a muddy river."

George's mind reviewed again, "How did he know my mother's name?"

18—DROPS OF SPIRIT

ERN, BOUNCING ALONG the rutted road in his four-wheel drive, arrived in about thirty minutes. He quickly made plaster of Paris castings of the tire treads, and talked to each cowboy and also to Victoria. There was no explanation. As far as anyone could determine, there was no connection between any drug groups, environmental groups, or any neighboring angry landowner.

George explained that his mother had died in a fiery vehicular accident and that she had worked for the U.S. Drug Enforcement Agency. That idea did not present a logical connection or explain why someone would want to spy on the ranch or try to scare off the new owner.

The windows of the shooters' Jeep Cherokee were tinted dark enough to hide the occupants. Perhaps, thought the group, since the house had been abandoned for so long, some young people were playing a teenage prank. They didn't shoot to hit anyone and they didn't damage any property, well, maybe a new hole in the windmill fan.

"Maybe just a prank," responded Hern, but not convincing anybody.

George felt a similar uneasiness when they found the tracks and garbage near his house, while he had been away recovering from his head wound. He was even more concerned now that his good friends had been threatened. He wanted to find and visit with his friend Bapchule; more than just a visit, he desperately needed to share and feel the spiritual strength of his friend.

He wondered, "Was there a connection?"

Bapchule was located sitting quietly on the side of a hill that was beginning to show shades of winter green grass sprouting. Nothing was said, just nods from each other acknowledging with a silent, "hello friend."

After sitting for a while, the old Indian softly broke the silence. "Dark cloud have silver lining to tell man that sun still shine behind darkness." Speaking with seriousness, "Big rain and big flood go but leave new life, leave new grass, leave new seed, open new path." Each short statement was followed by a long wait as he looked out across the desert and waited for an understanding of his words to show on George's face. "Big trouble and big experience go but leave new learning, leave new growth, leave new idea and open new spirit."

George was beginning to understand, not just the words, but also some of the life and spiritual implications plainly hidden behind the words of Bapchule.

As they sat side by side on a gentle hillside slope, George listened and tried to feel what life was offering to them. They were sitting quietly, as if, they were indeed a part of this desert landscape while a cool Arizona winter rain gently fell on them. The brief sprinkle instantly increased the fresh aroma of the desert plants.

Bapchule pointed to a miniature drop on a leaf, "Look at the tiny raindrop on the leaf, young mind might think drop no importance, drop join with other drop, two drop join with twenty drop, twenty join with thousand to make small stream in desert. Small stream join with other small stream, two stream join with twenty, twenty join with thousand to form mighty river. One river join with other, two join with twenty, twenty join with thousand to form mighty ocean. Mighty oceans evaporate one drop, one drop joins with twenty drop, twenty join with thousand to make big cloud. Big cloud release one drop. Which drop most important, first, fourth or one hundredth?"

Thirty minutes passed as both men observed a drop, then two, and then probably a thousand that formed the small stream that fed the muddy river.

"Small drop like idea. One idea join with other, two join with twenty, twenty join with thousand to form man. Understand young GRC that one idea important. Man not just one idea, man not just physical. Mighty river is physical but also is spirit formed by spirit of many drops."

Bapchule picked up a small twig from the ground.

"Bapchule touch drop and move stick across leaf, drop follow. Drop have spirit but no have power to choose, must only follow. Man has idea and man have power to choose. Many idea not so good, many idea very good, man have right to choose. No good idea must be sent back to Great Spirit, He have power to change no good idea too good. Many man let no good idea stay. Build small nest in man brain. Man think very little nest do no harm. No good idea very small but invite other no good idea. They join with other small no good idea then join with twenty and form power. Big power grow from no good idea spirit that come from many small no good idea. Many 'once good man' let no good idea grow and form powerful no good spirit, then 'once good man' now loose choice to no good idea spirit and no good idea power now make choice. Very hard conquer no good idea power."

So much deep soul impacting information was being squashed into crevices of his brain that had not been used before. George sat on the slope and pondered how many ideas floating in his head were "no good" and how many were "good."

Bapchule continued, "Young heart have many good idea, let good idea join with other good idea and Great Spirit develop Good Spirit in GRC. Good Spirit Idea invite more good idea, many good idea hide in human brain, human brain no find, but Good Spirit go deep to human brain and find good idea to make big good idea. Bapchule think Good Spirit look for GRC to have much good experience. Often good experience seem bad or difficult for man to understand. Later good experience reveal why be good experience. Bapchule now quiet, wait for GRC to talk experience."

The light rain stopped, allowing the desert to strut its colors like a royal peacock. Rains in the desert are few and far between. The desert seems to store colors and fresh smells. Like people who dress in their best clothes, jewelry, colognes, and perfumes for special occasions, the desert puts on its best colors and smells for those special occasions when rain falls, even if it is only a brief rain.

The predominant smell comes from the creosote bushes, which are the most populous plant in most desert areas in Southern Arizona. The smell is so unique that it cannot be described. It can only be experienced. The effect of the smell is very relaxing; even the most troubled soul can feel the calming influence of the creosote bush. George's troubled soul was finding relief from the creosote bush aroma and spirit.

Bapchule had verbalized many thoughts and now he sat as immovable and quiet as the rock upon which he perched. He had looked at the physical drop of water, he had looked at the physical desert, he had looked at the physical clouds and he had looked at the physical world. With closed eyes it seemed he was now looking at the spirits of these same creations. George recalled from their very first meeting.

"Look at the mighty mesquite tree. What do you see?"

George described the leaves, stems, thorns, seedpods and bird nest. Bapchule nodded as if pleased with the keen observation.

"Very good my young friend, you have seen the physical creation of the tree, open other eye, spirit eye and look where you cannot see."

That had been a new thought to George. "What did he mean? Look where you cannot see." Now it has become a common practice to look at objects, life and people with a degree of spirit eyes. It has become a natural response and has made his life much more pleasant, fulfilling, rewarding and meaningful.

When his dream with Peggy vanished, he did not feel sad. Strings in his heart were tugged, but mostly for this fair young lady who had succumbed to the typical mortal that feels uncomfortable when spiritual happenings draw close. He took advantage of moments to look with his developing spirit eyes. He wondered if there might be a conflict in Peggy between her inner spiritual life opposed to living a life that others might expect. He felt empathy for her and wished he had been able to open her spiritual eye much like Bapchule opened his.

Yet, as he thought he realized that he had been searching for truth. His dad, in one of the last letters, explained to his young son. "There are universal laws such as gravity, sun, moon and stars that all operate under laws. One such law is a law of attraction. Man with his great inner powers granted to him can attract what he most desires."

When George found or actually when Bapchule found George, George, more than any other desire wanted to learn of the desert, land, animals and plants. Maybe Peggy did not want the same?

He pondered and wondered if many good people have accepted drop by drop the confused world in which they lived. Believing that clothes, make up, perfume, hairstyle, shoes and income were the elements that make up the real person.

He recalled his mother's wise words, "People change only when they are ready to change, and the desire for the new is greater than the old."

He was still learning how to be true to himself. He released all past thoughts and only thought about the moment. He smiled trying to control his conscious mind as if it were ball bouncing from place to place. After much effort and time his spirit thoughts sped up and his desire was that one drop of his good idea could join with one drop of another true idea, and grow to become a spirit power within.

He recalled the many times he had read and re-read about Gandhi. This lone man fasted a country into independence. "If his calling upon the Spirit was so powerful that it influenced more than one nation then maybe I might influence at least one person."

He studied intently the spiritual form housed in the body of an ole Indian called Bapchule. He knew that not only was this spiritual leader absorbing the vibrations of the desert, he was also giving GRC time to organize his thoughts and feelings to verbalize a recent spiritual, emotional and physical experience.

The rains and flooding of last summer had brought new life to the desert. Some of the neighbors had attributed the good fortune to the positive attitude generated by the "Gila River Cowboy" George. However, he did not take any credit. The calves had grown and fattened nicely during the fall and sold for a good price. The cows held over produced some excellent spring calves and the grass was green and growing.

One of the large electrical power companies needed to cross some of the Gila River Cattle Ranch lands and not only were willing to pay easement fees but also willing to install a transformer so the ranch could have actual electricity. He had gotten along very well with the twelve-volt light, the wind, and batteries, but it would be nice to have electricity. One of the Riggs family in-laws worked for the power company.

He was able to get permission to allow George to visit and watch the electricians install the huge towers and pull the lines. It was all fascinating. Men hanging from suspended cables high in the air. Tractors, Caterpillars, trucks and backhoes filled the desert route. George, for the first time, realized how much work and effort is needed so we can simply flip a switch and have lights, cooking, cooling, heating and all other conveniences associated with electricity. He remembered spending much of one night on the hill near the ranch house expressing gratitude as he looked down and saw a bright shining light bulb.

These and other thoughts were flashing through his head when Bapchule came over and sat near George. George had been yearning to visit with the old man. George needed as much as he had ever needed anything, to verbally share a recent event. George was concerned, however, that what he was going to share would appear so preposterous that even this spiritual man would not comprehend or would he simply dismiss the story and say, "That is a nice story, but it cannot be true." George felt a small inward reassurance because he realized without realizing, he had used the law of attraction to invite Bapchule to come and sit next to him.

As the gentle ole Indian graciously sat, George stood, then sat, then stood and walked then returned to sit beside the revered man sitting motionlessly.

George blurted out his first question. "Bapchule, is it possible for a mortal man to leave his body, be in only his spirit body and then return to his mortal body?"

"You please to answer to me your question. Bapchule feel you have plenty good answer."

"Yes, I think it is possible, I just don't know if it were real or only my imagination."

"What you feel in heart is real, what is real to you may never be real to others."

George sat beside his new and old friend and poured out his soul. "After the river had flooded I was riding Thunderbolt along the bank on the south side, mostly thinking of how much my life had changed in such a very short period of time. I had stopped several times trying to listen to the desert and what it might be telling me. My emotions were mixed and I contemplated many inner feelings. Some of the feelings I understood, some feelings I did not comprehend. I felt the silent desert voice wanted to share something with me, but I seemed to be carrying too much inner turmoil. I learned that it is the person's responsibility to clear his thoughts, clear his mind and open his heart before any of the beneficial spirits can communicate. I stopped Thunderbolt and tried persistently to clear away the many thoughts circling through my head. I knelt down and finally in desperation I lay flat on the ground. I have found the ground seems to be capable of absorbing many negative frequencies stored in the body."

He stood once again and walked a few steps, then returned to perch on the rock beside Bapchule.

"Finally I felt the desert would once again accept me. I had tears of joy from that tremendous positive feeling. 'Welcome, but believe and prepare.' I can't explain if that message was felt or heard. I rose to my knees to thank the desert and God when I heard the same message, 'Welcome, but believe and prepare.' I stood to get back on Thunderbolt and he backed away. I again approached and he again backed closer to the embankment. As I approached the second time he stood perfectly still, then I heard what seemed like a baby crying so I walked to the edge of the embankment and saw a baby cottontail rabbit that looked as if it were trapped in one of the cracks caused from the drying caliche. I was impressed and honored that the desert would invite me to save one of the little cottontails. I moved closer to the edge of the embankment trying to decide how to get down into the riverbed to rescue the little fellow, not realizing that the water had eroded the underside of the river bank, suddenly the ledge crumbled and I was flung down to what I thought was a dry riverbed. Seconds after I landed I could hear the cracking of the dried caliche crusted flakes that had been formed from the last flow of water. I was not concerned until I felt my knee quickly sink, then my other leg and both feet. Before I could react I was up to my hips in mud. It must have been one of those "death pits" I had been warned to avoid. I was able to reach the baby rabbit and toss him over to the sand but I was unable to reach the old tree trunk or any overhanging limb. My only hope was that the naturally excavated pit might only be a few feet deep. The sinking was a very slow process but the more I moved the quicker I sank. I look upward and saw Thunderbolt standing on the riverbank close to where the ledge had broken looking down at his trapped friend. I softly talked to Thunderbolt, trying to coax him down the river's embankment so I could possibly reach the lose reins. Then I pleaded out to God, to the Great One, to my own Spirit or to anybody who might be listening. I wondered if I would ever see the ranch again, would I ever eat with the Riggs family, would I be able to learn more from my friend Bapchule or would my body be lost in these depths. I was not so concerned about dying because I know that the spirit lives on but I was concerned about what I would miss during this life. Then I felt even sadder when I thought that my dead body would be so buried that the poor Arizona Buzzards would not even have a small feast. I wanted my last portion of mortal life to at least be beneficial to the buzzards. My arms were spread to give more support but only a part of my arms and head remained above the soupy, yet deadly, mud. I wondered if my mother and dad might meet me. I saw the little bunny hop safely away. With my head tilted back I was able to get the last few drops of air to fill my compressed lungs. I heard some quail expressing love to each other and then I heard and saw a small humming bird inches from my face. Oh dear little one, please tell each of my friends how much they have meant to me and tell them that I have no regrets, the Arizona desert gave me a new life and thus it has a right to take that life away. Much like God gives life and has the right to recall. I gulped down the last deep breath as the mud engulfed my face. It was darkness, void of any light."

George was sobbing as he looked into the eyes of Bapchule. Those eyes moved and the head nodded, as if to say, "continue."

"I do not know how much time elapsed, there was no shining bright light; there was no soft music, I was just standing once again on the embankment yet all was different. There existed much communication between all living creatures and the feeling of joy was over whelming. I walked along a path and realized that I had to adjust to various tones to understand different groups. The mesquite, the chaparral, the lizard and each and every living insect greeted me. Bapchule, the love felt for each, the love felt between each was so majestically powerful. I knew each one individually; they all seem to respond to a greater source of power. I looked and tried to absorb all the knowledge that was so easily attainable, I saw plainly the spiritual root structure of the giant mesquite and the millions and millions of microscopic life required to sustain the life of that stalwart tree. Each organism was thrilled to be a part of the greater life and each was filled with gratitude for the great opportunity to serve. Each and every entity was ecstatic yet respectful of my power as a human. They spiritually relayed to me that man was the esteemed creation of the Great Father and each of them had pledged their support of man, thus they were supporting the Father. I recalled what my mother had taught me, 'when you are in the service of your fellowman you are in the service of your God.' I looked back at the pit and could see my one hand still protruding out of the mud. It wasn't franticly waving. It was just there as if marking my own grave with my hand.

"Almost as if time stood still, I reflected on all of these events and teachings. I recalled in detail the many experiences I had and the things I learned from those experiences. I remembered my friends, new and old, and how much they had taught me. I considered my life to be a rich and full life."

George paused to organize his thoughts, and then continued, "Then I saw a man walking towards me and from the pictures my mother had shown and from the dreams as a child, I knew him to be my father. I wanted to embrace and have him hold me. I suddenly remember how secure I felt when he held me in his big arms when I was but a youngster. I recalled many moments with him and I remembered all his teachings even though I was a baby. I remember how he changed my dirty clothes and would look into my eyes, bend over close to my face and with such a pleasant smile whisper, 'let all the dirt be on the outside, let no dirt get on the inside. Keep your spirit pure.'

"With those thoughts I wanted to go to him, feel secure with him, however he indicated with his hand that I was to stop, he explained that I was not yet ready to enter immortality. He shared some experiences he had during combat and how he had spent much of his time as a spirit trying to help his comrades from both armies. We did not talk as you and I are talking at this moment; we seemed to exchange feelings quickly without misunderstanding so in a very brief time there was an enormous amount of communication. My father shared, 'If man would merely live the basic rules of love and learn the joy in service to one another there would never be need for war, there would never be reasons for a father to be separated from his son. When one nation attempts to enslave another, often war is the only means to overthrow tyranny and allow men the opportunity to choose. Having the freedom to choose is one of God's greatest gifts. Now my son, you should return, nevertheless it is your choice. Each child of God is responsible for changing itself.

"I wanted to know what would happen to me? What was my future? Who would save me from the pit?" He lovingly looked into my eyes, and spoke,

"Son, all is accomplished through the faith of a higher power. The more you learn how to live His teachings the more fulfilling is your life. I have come to you with a critical message. Find your mother, she yet is mortal and she needs you."

"Bapchule, I was so shocked. I responded 'Father, she is with you.'" He looked at me with the deepest of any loving eyes I have ever seen. Without another word I spoke,

"Father, I will find her and tell her of your love."

With that thought of mortality, the need to find his mother, George instantly felt the pressure of the liquid mud squeezing his lungs; he could feel the burning and the desperation from lack of oxygen. Yet he felt no panic. For a brief moment he wondered what would happen. He was penned under the mud with no human to help. George wonder: "Would an angel come and lift me out? Would God command the mud to regurgitate this almost dead human form? Suddenly I felt a warm inner feeling, I actually thought I was dying so I relaxed and thought, Father, Thy will be done."

At that moment of complete surrender, the moment he allowed the Father's will to direct him, he felt something near him move.

Suddenly, he was being thrust upward until his head emerged from the muddy grave. He felt a powerful push that propelled him until he felt the sand. He swung his arms hoping to find something to hold. He touched the lower limbs of a tree; he grabbed with all his physical forces and pulled himself free. He lay on the ground gasping for air. Wiping away the mud from his mouth, nose and eyes and then and only then did he look back at the pit to see the calm eyes of Thunderbolt sinking slowly into the "death pit."

Recalling and sharing the experience caused George to tremble. "Bapchule, what made him jump into the pit? What made a horse willing to sacrifice his life for his master? I openly cried aloud, Oh God, help me save my horse? Where are you oh Great God? I again, through eyes blurred with tears and mud, stretched out to touch for the last time the face of this grand horse as he disappeared into the deep pit. Father, I cried out, please be kind to this horse, let him be bigger, stronger, with powerful straight legs and with a long straight back because he was in mortality a horse that certainly fit the man and he was the horse that saved the same man."

George sat quiet for a time with his kind friend Bapchule giving comfort. "Bapchule, I cried for that sway-backed horse, I cried for my dad and wondered what he meant when he said, 'Find your mother, she yet is mortal and she needs you.' I pleaded for help and understanding. Bapchule, is my mother really alive?"

Bapchule put his arm around George and they sobbed uncontrollably. "My son, the Great God was with you, your father was with you and Thunderbolt fulfilled the full measure of his creation. He died in the service of his fellowman. That is the most we can expect and attain in this mortal existence, his spirit is now with the great ones and he is telling and retelling the experiences of mortality and with the short life lived with the Gila River Cowboy."

"Bapchule, I have told no one of this experience and yet some look at me with different eyes. One of the Riggs men looked at me and asked if it had been a pleasant experience? I have told no one and yet many seem to know, why is that so?"

"Maybe they have similar experience. Maybe they see little inner man George become big inner man Gila River Cowboy. Bapchule now speak of other experience. Experience important also to GRC. I speak. Victoria, your little Humming Bird prays much for GRC. Victoria has much good experience, maybe she tell much to GRC, maybe GRC learn much. She learns great power to pray with much love for other people. More power in love prayer for other person than prayer for one self. Great Father listen to love prayer. Bapchule not know how all work but maybe think Thunderbolt stand on side of bank looking at GRC, not know what to do, humming bird poke horse on rear side and cause horse to jump. Thunderbolt get all credit but humming bird is good promoter. Most times something very small do big things. You asked Bapchule if GRC experience is true? Bapchule say yes. Bapchule already see much experience in dream. Now GRC find mother. Dream say mother very sick, maybe die soon in hospital, must come to Ranch House to live. GRC must go soon. Must tell Victoria your experience. She believe and help find sick mother, very sick, Spirit speak many time, very sick."

He was relieved and impressed that Bapchule accepted this experience with such ease, and without doubts and ridicule.

George, with some frustration said, "It is most interesting that churches and ministers talk of spirits, talk of love, talk of life after death, talk of creation, and talk of God, yet when someone actually has a spiritual experience the ministers get angry and ridicule. Why don't' people…?"

Bapchule answered before the question was asked.

"Great Spirit of Great God want all have many good spirit experience but most people much afraid to have spirit talk. Sad, very sad, many let No Good Idea stay in spirit body and be happy with No Good Idea. When Good Idea or Spirit Idea come very close maybe make people afraid, make unhappy, maybe people think better ridicule or kill Good Spirit Idea so No Good Idea not be unhappy."

The sun was arrayed in a brilliant sunset and cheerful colors darted across the sky in the western horizon, just to the east of where they stood was a complete rainbow and soon thereafter the second array of beautiful colors arched across the vast sky.

Bapchule smiled, "Me think great God very happy today. Maybe have one more to believe Him. Now go my son and tell Victoria and then go find George mother that be hidden from GRC. Edna, Humming Bird mother, very good to find people hidden in computer. Ha, Bapchule no think GRC mother hidden in computer, maybe find name hidden in machine. Bapchule not know how machine work, how hide much information and how Edna find? Bapchule look one day, no find nothing, and look in back, no find nothing."

Bapchule silently disappeared into the desert. GRC sometimes wondered if the man was truly a man or was he a spirit that sometimes appeared as a man. He wondered how this man crossed the river? How he was able to be in the right spot at the right moment.

George Ribit Chattit sat for hours pondering his experience and the retelling of the experience and the more he thought the more questions filled his mind. "What did Bapchule mean the prayer of love? Why was Victoria praying so much for me? Why would she believe this crazy story? How does the spirit leave the body and then return? What does the humming bird that might have poked Thunderbolt have to do with anything spiritual?"

The answer to the last question came quickly and clearly as a thought in his mind.

George spoke aloud so as to not lose the memory of the thought. "The poke from the humming bird could well represent in human life as a kind word, a word of encouragement, a smile or a pat on the back. Many souls want to fulfill their righteous desires but just need a little encouragement. Much like Thunderbolt, he knew he wanted to help, maybe he couldn't decide how maybe he just lacked a little courage. Once he was in the quick sand and once he saw you safe he was happy he had accomplished this great task."

George was humbled and thrilled; he had just received, heard, or felt an answer from the spirit. His physical body was exhausted from the spiritual experiences.

With a heart much lighter and a spirit filled with joy, He headed towards Sacaton to find Edna. Then he would call Victoria and see how soon or when she could come or if she would come?

"What did Bapchule mean?" 'Great Father listens to prayer of love.'

"Was he talking about Victoria? Was he talking about Victoria's love for the Father? Was he talking about the love of prayer? Was he talking about Victoria's love for George?" His heart jumped at the possibility. He knew he cared for her, he could not forget nor did he want to forget the evening of the gunshots and how he held her in his arms and looked into her eyes. He had prayed often for answers about what was in those deep sparkly eyes but he had learned that even though the Spirit might know all things. That does not mean it will tell.

"I enjoy visits with Humming Bird, in fact, I delight in hearing her name."

He remembered when Chula had attempted to meet Peggy. As Chula was leaving she said something to the affect of, "Maybe now look for Chupa Rosa."

"I never did understand that comment, even after I looked it up in the Spanish dictionary. Now I believe it has much meaning for me."

19—JOY

GEORGE VISITED WITH Edna; she had not talked with Victoria for almost a week so she placed a call to Utah.

A roommate of Victoria's answered. "She is not here, she talked to her professors and said it was an emergency and took the bus late yesterday after classes. Is there something wrong?"

"No, I merely wanted to visit. Please tell her to call home when she gets back."

The roommate agreed then added, "She has been acting really strange these past few days and each night when she prays aloud she pleads for the spirit to protect George. I am worried about her."

Edna slowly pushed the end call button.

"Young man, I suggest you tell me what has happened and what is happening?"

"Yes, you are right, you need to know all and I will share with you, first give me a couple of minutes, I need to go outside and try and get my anxieties under control so my puzzled spirit won't up and leave my body."

Under his breath he whispered as he stepped through the door. "I am so worried that she is so worried and I feel I do deeply love her."

The voice was soft and delightful. "Who do you deeply love?"

Edna and George were speechless.

"Victoria, what, how, why?"

They both grabbed and hugged her.

It was a special moment for the Gila River Cowboy; he had never hugged his beautiful Humming Bird in a display of affection. The one and only time was at the Ranch when shots were fired, then it was for her protection. Then it did feel very good, however this time it felt about ten thousand times better than good.

"I suggest you tell me what is going on."

Edna and George both laughed.

"What is so funny?"

"Little Humming Bird, I just asked this cowboy the same question verbatim."

"I must speak to you and your mother together, then I have something to say to you, but not until I speak with the both of you."

Both ladies noticed a stronger more mature young man. They, especially Victoria, like what they saw and heard. Without hearing a word, they knew that this young man that was so "green from Washington, D.C." had had experiences that caused a fast and permanent maturity that would continue to develop. As with most events or subjects, the more you learn and experience the more you desire to learn and experience. Bapchule often remarked, "Wisely choose path you walk be good path be bad path always lead person away from where first stand on path."

Leaving Edna's office in Sacaton, it is also the only town where the Greyhound bus from Utah stops, they drove to San Tan Village. He had not been to Edna's small but very pleasant looking home. Light sand color stucco trimmed in blue with newly planted flowers in between the exploding roses. It struck him odd at first; the front yard had no grass, it was bare dirt. The most interesting note about the bare dirt is that it was cement smooth; cement compacted and swept clean with a broom.

"Of course," he thought, "cement hard caliche requires no water and no mowing."

When they entered the home, it was late afternoon. The house was a thick walled adobe with cement plaster covering most of the inner wall and all of the outer. Sitting in the living room, he could see areas of smooth adobe bricks laced with straw were left exposed. It was a very comfortable room and offered a similar feeling of sitting or riding in the desert, except it was much cooler.

The two women sat together, as he related word for word and feeling for feeling his experience with death, life, spirit, father, mother and horse. Even in the retelling for the second time he shook with emotion and tears streamed from his eyes. When he was able to focus again he saw both women weeping.

"What a grand experience, we are so happy you were rescued, we are so sad you lost your faithful horse and we are thrilled to learn that your mother is alive and we are so pleased that you have had this great learning experience. What can we do to help?"

He was impressed and a little stunned. He had been so worried.

"What are they going to think? Will they believe? Do I believe my own experience or was it a mere dream?"

They sat in reverence for a moment.

"If I repeated this story to the average person they would scoff at the idea of spirits talking and the body and spirit separated, yet, these two women accepted my experience as if it had happened to them."

Edna wiped her eyes. Reached for Victoria's hand, "Now young lady, tell us your story. Why are you here?"

"About four days ago I had a dream in which GRC disappeared into darkness. I reached for him but the adversary had more strength. I saw his calloused hand reaching up for help and I could not help. I did not have enough strength."

Tears began flowing.

"Oh Momma, that is a terrible feeling so I began fasting from all food and prayed constantly for more strength. I was attending an early morning class and a small humming bird flew into the windowpane near where I was sitting, I saw it fall to the ground and I ran out to see if it were injured. The poor little bird lay motionless on the cold ground. I reached down to hold it my hands to offer warmth. As I cupped her in my hands and talked trying to calm her little nerves an extremely strong feeling filled my own soul and I felt a very distinct impression that my George was in a life-threatening situation. I was already on my knees when I began to plead in prayer. I know that my Father in Heaven desires that his children seek solutions and asked for his help; for some reason I opened my hand and the precious little bird did not attempt to fly away. She stood as stiff as a soldier waiting for a command. I spoke with a plea, not a command."

She pointed to George.

"I requested that this precious little creation go help you until I could get there."

I re-entered the class, so I could formally excuse myself; the professor and most of my classmates had tears flowing down their faces. The professor took my hand and commented,

"We all know that something extraordinary spiritual happened, we could feel and we saw you talking to the little bird and we experienced spiritually that the little humming bird understood. This is a class in which we study the revelations of past and present prophets. If it would be overly personal we'll understand, but if you would be willing, please share."

"I had not considered that the experience was related to revelation. I too have thought that revelation came to great and important people. When that thought passed through my mind, my heart was suddenly filled with a more refined feeling, 'You, my daughter, are great and important to me'. When that entered my heart it once again opened the gate to my tear ducts."

She held George's hand.

"My classmates and professor sat motionless even when it was time to dismiss they would not move. I related the feelings of the experience then I told them I did not have the reasons or answers as to what the problem was, but that I was leaving as quickly as possible for Arizona."

She choked up and for a long moment was unable to speak as tears of emotions streamed down her cheeks with small puddles forming in her deep dimples.

"Then a most amazing occurrence; one of the students stood and asked if those who wanted would be allowed to kneel in prayer, oh Momma, they all kneeled in prayer. I have never been aware of the mighty power of prayer that is generated by a group of young people completely united in thought. The same student that asked permission became the spokes person for the group. He expressed gratitude, then these precious words were uttered, 'Father, we know not the problem and we know not the answer, however we invoke Thee to save Brother George, whom we know only through Thy daughter Victoria, protect and save him, thus allowing him to fulfill the full measure of his creation.'"

They all sat in spiritual silence and spiritual glory that is a scarce experience in our fast paced society. Then Edna wrapped her daughter in her arms, much like she had done as a baby. Kissed her forehead and motioned for George to join the embrace.

"Now, I know the problem and why I came from Utah; please tell us more. Tell us of your inner feelings during the experience and your current feelings when you retell the experience."

"Each time I relate the experience it becomes more meaningful. I know for centuries Indians had no written words, telling stories to the children was the method for passing history and legends from generation to generation. I hope I will always make and take time to tell stories each evening to our children."

No discussion had taken place between Victoria and George yet her heart jumped at the sound of "our children."

Victoria knew deep within that she loved this man, she did not know him, she had not been out with him; yet she knew from her heart that she loved this gentle, yet great, spirit housed in a mortal body that often seemed bent on destroying itself. Even she was amazed at how strong these feelings were and by the way her heart was pounding. She wanted to say something; but more than anything, she wanted to hear more about this man that unknowingly had captured her heart.

He continued. "My mother would tell me stories or read from good books. Each evening she would announce, 'Story time in ten minutes' and that meant in ten minutes she would be sitting on the chair near my bed reading whether I was in bed or not. She never told me to go to bed, she just announced, 'Story time'. If I were not in bed she would start the story and have the very best part right at the beginning and when I would get into bed she just continued the story, not upset nor with a scowl on her face. I quickly learned that if I wanted to hear the whole story I had better be in bed within the ten-minute period. Gosh, I am just talking like a parrot; maybe I should let Victoria tell us of her trip or classes."

"No" Edna spoke, "Please continue because we sincerely want to know all about you and your mother."

"That conversation continued even through my teenage years, naturally the stories changed and most of the evenings were a recap of the day's activities or sometimes with long periods of laughter at the mishaps of the day."

They smiled. They both knew that George could generate plenty of mishaps.

"That is where I learned that most events society considers mistakes are not really mistakes; they are a part of life, an experience to learn from and most frequently should be laughed away without embarrassment. Often my mother would ask how many experiences that others might consider mistakes I had made that day? If I said none she would raise her finger and teasingly tell me that I must not be doing enough; those who don't try something new each day are the only ones who do not make mistakes."

He realized that he was deeply longing for his mother. His father had appeared to him many times in dreams after his death; yet, never once has his mother paid him a visit.

Almost in unison Edna and Victoria spoke, "Let's get to the office and start searching the Internet for articles. Let's find your mother."

They drove directly to the Tribal Office and logged in with "Big Mac." Within a short time they were able to find information concerning Beth Ann's death, information concerning how her remains were identified with dental records and the scarce few body parts remaining were cremated.

His nerves tightened,

George pondered, "After reading those articles, those written proofs and knowing there was a funeral, would Edna and Victoria continue to believe that his father's spirit had spoke to him? Would they believe what he felt, saw and heard? No one was there to witness the occurrence and the only partial proof was that Thunderbolt was missing. Was all of this an imagined incidence that only took place in my mind? I know the mud was real, I know Thunderbolt died in the mud but what about my father, what about the knowledge gained while out of the physical, what about…?"

His thoughts were interrupted by the sweet voice of Humming Bird.

"George, look, we found an old newspaper article where a female survived under the name of Mary Potts in a comatose state, when her family arrived a week later it was determined that this person in the coma was not Mary Potts. Months later it was reported that Mary Potts had indeed died in the bus accident and the person in the coma remained a mystery."

Edna, Victoria and George spent most of the night trying to locate the whereabouts of the person last reported to be in a coma. They could not find any new information but they did at least know the last known hospital.

When George stepped outside of the Sacaton office the two ladies were hugging each other and shedding tears of joy for a person they were learning to love. They also shed tears of pain. They did not relate to him that they had read another article that explained that both the car and the bus had burned and most occupants and all documentation were burned beyond recognition.

Victoria agonized, "Oh mother, what if he finds her alive and cannot even recognize her? What if she does not recognize her son?"

"My little Humming Bird, I would want to find you, hold you and talk with you know matter how you looked and I know that no matter your condition or my own condition, a mother knows her child," Edna lovingly responded.

That calmed all of Victoria's fears. She thought, "I would want the same and she felt that her George…" She stopped, embarrassed at her own thoughts, "her George," that was the second time she referred to him in that manner.

Edna wondered aloud, "Maybe we should contact the DEA and let them know she might be alive?"

When she mentioned this to George he abruptly stiffened, he did not know why.

"No, no don't let the DEA know, I cannot tell you why, maybe a spirit, maybe a cowboy hunch, but we must find her on our own."

Early the next morning they called the hospital, nobody seemed to remember and they were not very cooperative. He mentioned that the larger cities in the East often forget that patients are people. Too often, it seems that many people become a part of a worldly mechanism of work, reporting, home, reporting, sleep and returning to work. George, Edna and Victoria were trying to reach a decision as to what to do next when the phone rang. It was nine o'clock in the morning, Arizona time. A woman's voice on the other end of the line spoke with a heavy Mexican accent.

"You for look for a Beth Ann, lady be in coma many year. Nosotros we never for know her nombre; excuse to me, for to me speak no so good

Ingles, no registros doctor. She stay mucho dormir, sleep mucho years y porque because no insurance bueno be sent to institution of the state. We learn she no lady other people say she be. Nosotros nunca to learn she who be lady, no able talk to family, porque nunca find name of lady. I no remember mas. If remember yo happy call to you."

"Thank you so very much, you have been a great help."

"May ask I porque you look por this lady?"

Edna answered, "I have come across certain information that leads us to believe that her son is in Arizona and is looking for her. He was informed of her death years ago but now believes she is alive and needing his help."

"Oh my, que terrible. I look more for to find lady, por favor me promise to you tell to me when find good lady. Me tell when son find mother. Mi nombre es Roberta, trabajo del dia in Cooperstown Medical Center."

With tears flowing like water from a garden hose, the two ladies jumped up, hugged each other and hugged George. They felt that she was alive due to George's experience and now seemingly verified by the lady at the hospital. They knew that she possibly was in the area of Cooperstown, New York.

"I will fly to Albany and rent a car to drive down to Cooperstown or maybe I should fly to New York and check on my old house in Mahwah, New Jersey or maybe I should fly into Dulles and check on my property there. I could even try to find Lt. Col. Bones and see what help he could offer."

Victoria spoke, "I think you should fly to Albany and find your mother. Afterwards, if there is time, then you should check on your properties, anything else and contact Lt. Col. Bones for assistance, if necessary."

She realized that she just had a fleeting jealous thought that George might want to stop and check on his old girlfriend, however, it was a fleeting thought that quickly gave way to the concern for his mother. It was, however, a new feeling that was a little intriguing.

"We will continue to search with the computer. If we find her location or additional information, we will call you. You will be, hopefully, within a short distance of where she is."

He caught a "red-eye" flight through Pittsburgh and would be in Albany by morning. As he passed through the Sky Harbor terminals, he smiled recalling his first visit about a year ago. How much he had learned, how much he had experienced, and how much he loved the rawness of the desert. It was such a tremendous but stern professor. He was not looking forward to the seven hours required to get to Albany yet he was nervous and excited to possibly find his mother. He smiled to himself.

Arriving in Albany he laughed to himself, "I must be like the rednecks in so many jokes. I am already missing my truck."

Albany was just starting to thaw and there were still many hills covered with snow. He smiled,

"Just last week I was on horseback riding through the desert, now I am in near freezing climate."

As if that was not shock enough, "I am driving a midsize Chrysler after having spent the past several months in my F-350 Ford Power Stroke whose running boards were almost as high as the top of this car."

He reached Cooperstown and called Victoria.

"Your mother might possibly be working at the "Lakeshore Inn."

"Hey young lady," George chided, "how come you are not in class today?"

"I called and told my professors that I was in the middle of a Social Studies project and could not possibly leave. By the way George, last night you were about to tell me something when the computer interrupted us."

"Well, it will have to wait. I am pulling into Cooperstown as we speak. So, I am interrupted once again."

He found a map at the service station and was beginning to spread it out over the hood of the rented car when a van with the name and logo of the Lakeshore Inn stopped at the light, made a right hand turn and drove away. He did not know if the van was coming or going. It did not matter. He was going to follow it. It soon pulled up in front of a very elegant lodge. His heart was pounding at the prospect that he might have found his mother after many years.

George entered, "Excuse me, I am looking for a woman called Beth Ann Slade Chattit." The young female clerk looked suspiciously at him and eyed the dark tan, rough hands and solid muscles.

"Just a minute sir." She departed and the manager appeared.

"May I help you?"

"Yes sir, I am looking for a woman named Beth Ann…" Before George could finish the man interrupted,

"And who might you be?"

"If you have Beth Ann, and if she is the Beth Ann, and I hope she is, then I am her son." He was trembling with excitement.

"We have been caring for her for some time now, she owes quite a bit of back rent."

George was not physically measured amongst big men. He simply was not very tall, but with the constant loading and unloading of the hundred and fifty pound bales of hay he had muscled from about one hundred and forty pounds to one hundred and seventy five pounds. He had fully developed his shoulders and biceps. His shoulders were broad and his biceps swelled under the tight western shirt he wore. He recalled a thought by Bapchule when a couple of bullies were poking fun at his shortness.

"GRC, the Scorpion is very small and seldom sting yet people run, scream and even faint at the sight, not because it is big, he have big reputation."

With that thought he stood up, faced the manager, and made a direct challenge in a way that they knew he was serious, but also in a way that they could back down without losing their own pride. "Sir, this is neither the time, nor the place to be negotiating for money. Please take me to the woman now," he spoke authoritatively. The tone and command of his voice surprised George. He had never spoken in this fashion. It was not a belligerent tone, but it was confident and seemed to come from some previously unknown place deep in George's chest. He finished by saying; "I know that you will take me directly to the woman."

The manager led him down the hall and into a small room. There on the single bed lay a small woman with dry skin stretched over her bony frame. At the moment, it did not matter if this were his mother or not. She was somebody's mother, daughter, sister or even grandmother. Now she lay dying in a small room with inadequate ventilation, poor heat and no windows.

He had boots with approximately two-inch heels, he slipped on his hat, a gray Stetson stained with a sweat ring visible from the outside, a few specks of dried blood from dehorning some calves and he stood like a giant. The manager, even though much larger, knew he did not want to tangle with this cowboy.

"Why do you keep this woman in this dungeon?"

The manager stuttered and tried to excuse the deed,

"I have only been here a few months and they told me that she would be working to pay for her room and board. She did alright for awhile, but then she got sick and has been unable to work for over two weeks."

George knelt down beside the woman, he looked at her face, her chapped lips, dry sunken eyes and mats of sweat soaked hair covering her forehead; he was unable to recognize if this really was his mom or not. She gazed up with filmed covered eyes and reached to touch his face,

"J. J., is that you?"

He openly sobbed as he held his mother in his arms.

The young girl from the front desk asked, "If that is your mother and your name is George, why did she call you J.J.?"

"My Father's name was Jay John and my mother always called him J.J."

He gently lifted the emaciated body; a young room maid covered her with a blanket, followed them out and opened the rear door.

"Here let me get in," The young maid offered, "I will go with you and hold her head in my lap."

George was pleased that there was at least one person that cared for another for no particular reason except to care.

The young girl in the back seat knew the area and gave direction on how to quickly drive to the nearest hospital. The doctors diagnosed Beth Ann with pneumonia, dehydration, and severe malnutrition. She was given injections of antibiotics and connected with intravenous tubes to get nutrition and liquids back into her body.

After visiting with the young maid, and hearing what had happened and what was continuing to happen at the Lakeshore Inn, the doctor called the local police. In a very short time, the manager was brought to the hospital with hands cuffed behind his back.

"According to the doctor, this woman would have been dead by morning, I believe you will be charged with attempted murder, or unintentional manslaughter. Alternatively, I might just turn you lose and let this cowboy deal with you. I understand that hanging is still acceptable in Arizona." The Police stated to the spiritless manager.

The manager was white as a clean sheet that was seldom seen at the Inn.

"I am sorry, I will pay all hospital expenses and I will pay all Mrs. Chattit's back wages."

"And," the police officer interjected, "You will not discount her so called room and board."

"Agreed," the trembling man said as he left with his police escort.

A short time later the manager brought a pile of twenties to compensate for his unjust abuse. The Police asked George whether he wanted to file a complaint. He and the Police had already discussed a plan.

"No, I do not desire to file a complaint. My mother will be able to be alone for a while in the morning and I would enjoy having a quiet visit with this scoundrel so why not just let him go free."

With that comment the police captain excused the police escort and waved good-bye as the ex-manager vanished. Probably never to be seen again in Cooperstown.

George called Edna and she in turn notified Victoria to let her know. His mother and he would be arriving in Phoenix the following Thursday evening.

Before leaving he visited the Cooperstown Medical Center and met with Roberta, a short plump woman of Mexican descent. George related to her the happenings of the previous day. She notified her superior that she would be gone for awhile or maybe a day. Her Latin emotions were easily noted as she knelt by the bed, held Beth Ann's hand and wept,

"I be so 'appy for de both of you, you to find after muchos (many) year, I be so 'appy for you." Her sincere emotions and her Spanish accent were delightful.

On the flight home Beth Ann tried to recall a part of her life during the last years. It had been just little over a year, which she had been conscious and even then she could not remember who she was, where she was or what had happened. Tears would slip from under her closed eyelids. When her eyes would open she would affix them on her son.

"My grown son, my rancher son, my son again living in Arizona, and my son that somehow found me." Each time she spoke or each time they touched each other's hands, tears flowed.

"Tell me all about Miss Victoria. My how your eyes light up when you speak her name. Why, after all these years did you begin to look for me?"

He related the entire experience and again tears flowed freely. Passengers close by asked the stewardess what was the event or problem. They related in brief how the mother supposedly had died and after many years in some miraculous way the son, living in Arizona, found his dying mother in New York. With that small bit of information and with the powerful presence of the Great Spirits, most of the passengers were deeply touched.

"When you do good thing, good spread to others so others feel good thing then can do good thing," A quote from his friend Bapchule.

He was thrilled to be traveling with his mother; the mother he thought to be dead. When they arrived at Sky Harbor International Airport, the passengers in some unspoken communication all stood, applauded and waited for Beth Ann, still very weak, and her son to deplane. A wheel chair was waiting at the door and the attendants from Sky Harbor were kind beyond the call of duty. Beth Ann Slade Chattit was again enjoying Arizona after many years of separation.

"Mother, you have not talked much about your accident. Does it hurt to recall? If you do not want to talk it is okay."

"Son," She smiled at the use of the word. "Son, I really do not remember much of anything. They said I was a passenger on a bus but I do not recall being on a bus, I do not recall an accident. I vaguely remember standing in front of a man I knew but he was angry with me... Wait, I remember that he hit me or someone hit me."

"It is okay mother, if it is important to remember then you will remember. That is what my friend Bapchule says. Oh my dear mother, you are going to like Bapchule, Chula and Jesse. When you feel better, I'll take you to meet the Riggs clan, a family that I know you will like and they will love you."

Back at the Gila River Cattle Ranch House, Edna, the Riggs family, and many neighbors were busy doing spring-cleaning and spring planting. It appeared to be more of a giant party than a workday. Everyone knew when Gila River Cowboy was returning and that he was bringing his lost mother. Many tears of joy were shed upon relating that news. They all seemed to understand that, while George was a good man, he was an exceedingly poor housekeeper. They wanted the ranch house to be clean and filled with joy when they arrived. The only sad note was that the horse corral stood empty.

Edna called a good friend of hers and explained the situation,

"Shumway, I need a good horse that will be used on a desert ranch, and I need it brought down to the Gila River Cattle Ranch today." Even though it really was a request there is little doubt that the person on the other end of the telephone conversation received a direct order.

By the time George and his mother filed through the long terminals and reached the roadside exit of Sky Harbor she was exhausted and needed to lie down. With perfect timing, the big red F-350, seemingly without a driver, pulled up to the curb. Up and from behind the steering wheel Victoria emerged and flashed her gregarious smile. Naturally, the male police officers let her park for a few minutes while they all helped Beth Ann onto the bed made in the back seat of the truck.

Beth Ann smiled at Victoria,

"It certainly is a pleasure to meet you after such an enormous amount of enjoyable conversation concerning Miss Victoria that I have heard these past few days." Victoria beamed and let her sparkling eyes connect with those of "her George."

Victoria had the truck equipped with cool water, apples, oranges, nuts, cookies, cold milk and about anything else a person might need.

"What did you do, buy out the Circle K market?"

They all laughed. George could see a loving bond being formed between his mother and this beautiful Humming Bird.

"I am not sure where my mother should stay? The ranch house is such a mess?"

Victoria assured him that the Ranch House would be the proper place for Beth Ann to recuperate and that it would be clean.

"My mother Edna is a good 'General' when it comes to organizing a clean-up committee and that is what they are doing at this very moment."

He was dreading the drive over the rutted entrance; the bumps would cause pain to his mother. To his surprise, when he pulled off the blacktop the rutted road was smooth. It was smoother than the blacktop. It had been graded.

"How, why?" were the only words that came from his mouth.

"Remember when you rescued the family from the flood? The father of that family is Superintendent of road maintenance and he has wanted to do something to show his appreciation, you now have a smooth road to your ranch."

"What is this about a rescue?"

"Oh Beth Ann, May I call you Beth Ann or do you prefer Mrs. Chattit?"

"Please Victoria call me Beth Ann," then with a small smile Beth Ann revealed how much she knew about this young lady.

"Shall I call you Victoria or Little Humming Bird?"

Victoria blushed openly with her radiant smile and looked directly at George.

"We are almost at the Ranch House, I will talk to you later about the exploits and experiences of this rascal son of yours."

Over the poles of the front gate hung a paper banner, "WELCOME HOME BETH ANN."

When Beth Ann saw the banner, tears of joy flowed around the corners of her wide smile displaying the perfect teeth that were a blessing and a curse. If she had been to a dentist they might have been able to find her more quickly from dental imprints. She always felt, however, that good things happen for a reason and she felt she was experiencing a giant reason at the moment.

It was a glorious early spring day; a huge shade had been set up outside, the dry ground was well sprinkled and tables piled with good food including a twenty-seven pound turkey.

"Do you know all of these people?" Beth Ann was amazed.

Small little girls dressed like cowgirl dolls and little cowboys with boots and hats. Indian families, cowboys on horses, a used pickup parking lot seemed to appear and women standing on the porch.

"Who are all of these people? Why are they here?"

Victoria waved her hand, "These are your son's friends and now they are your friends."

They had a large leather recliner on the front porch, an electric fan and a small table with a glass of lemonade so Beth Ann could sit and enjoy the friendship and the activity.

She watched as the teenagers played a game of volleyball, while the younger kids played "cowboy and Indians" with real Indians. She gasped as little children climbed to the top of the haystack or walked through the corral with cattle milling around. One young man with his admiring followers proudly displayed a large scorpion he caught in a glass jar. Another came up with a desert gopher snake wrapped around his arm.

George was alarmed when he saw tears in his mother's eyes,

"What's wrong mother?" He jumped to her side.

"Nothing, nothing at all my son. I was just remembering my own youth in northern Arizona and the joy we had as youngsters. I am so happy for you and I know that your Dad is happy. I can just imagine him sitting over on that fence post with his big joyous smile watching this whole event."

To most of the people she was known as George's mom or GRC's mom, then one young Indian boy came over,

"Are you Gila River Cowboy's mom?" She had not associated the initials until that particular moment. She had wondered why her son was called GRC by some of his friends instead of George. She assumed it was the abbreviation of his name.

"Was it foreordained for him to own the Gila River Cattle Ranch that so perfectly fit this young man?" She pondered in her mind.

Days passed quickly and there is always much spring work. Beth Ann was recovering well and was taking long walks around the desert. The huge German Sheppard given to GRC to protect his chickens against the coyotes became a constant and loyal companion for Beth Ann and where she went, he went. GRC could always tell if she were in the house because the big dog would be resting on the front porch. His new job was not just to protect the ranch, but he assumed the special task of protecting Beth Ann. GRC pitied the person who dared to harm his mother.

Beth Ann hurriedly ran into the ranch house after a short morning walk in the desert.

20—UGLY BUT JUST

"**M**OTHER, WHAT'S WRONG. You're white as a ghost."

"I am remembering more of my accident. This morning as I was walking in the foothills I saw a couple of cars. I thought maybe they needed help. They didn't see me. I, however, overheard them talking then I distinctly heard one of the men speaking."

She shook with fright as she relayed the event. George embraced her.

As they sat at the kitchen table, George clasp her trembling hands as she recounted a portion of the events that took place that apparently was to cause her death. His mother explained, "I recognized the voice and fell to my knees in the sand wash. George, I could not move I was so frightened. Then I got better control of my feelings and when I was certain that it was he, I became angry. George, I heard him say that I was supposed to have died in the crash. He tried to have me killed, now he is back."

George knew it was not an appropriate time to ask a lot of questions. He quickly dialed his friends in the police department. "Hern," with the cell phone booster installed in his truck he could now call anytime, "this is GRC. I think you better head to the ranch in a hurry? My mother recognized one of the men you have been looking for and she knows who he is, and what he tried to do to her."

Twenty-five minutes later Hern (Gila River Police) and George were studying the car tracks and trash left vandalizing the desert.

They studied two sets of tire tracks made from two cars. Hern spoke, "These are the same tracks left from last time. These are new, not been here before. The new tracks are from a bigger and heavier vehicle. See where it turned around, the chaparral is smashed from extra weight. Also, notice how the front tires slip a little while turning sharp, means four-wheel drive engaged. Sharp turn make universal joints tight, cause tire slip on dirt."

George was impressed with this Indian officer. The next thing Hern did, however, impressed George even more. Hern held a branch and a few leaves, placed his hand on the tire tracks in the sand, and then looked towards heaven, as if receiving a genuine Indian vision.

"Looks to me be Cadillac Escalade, light tan in color, big chrome wheels with three occupants, two sitting on front seat, one sitting back seat on driver side."

George was almost speechless, "How could you possible know all of that from the tracks? Did you see paint on the bushes? Was one side heavier than the other?"

"No tell from tracks, saw car in Sacaton earlier today. Hern maybe know first tracks. Made by car that buy sell drug, see many time but no catch yet do wrong. Maybe new tracks from car that visit DEA officer this morning. Escalade belong to DEA important man. Now Hern have question? Is DEA man good or turn ugly?"

If it were as Hern suspected, they decided they would keep the information within the Indian Police rather than risk alerting the DEA, especially since the Indian Police had reported other findings, but never had enough proof. Working with the DEA in the past, each time the Indian Police thought they would catch a drug exchange in the act, the drug people seemed to know ahead of time.

A few mornings later Beth Ann felt much better. She decided she would go for her early morning walk. She stepped out on the porch and missed her usual canine morning greeting.

"George, have you seen Dog?" She always smiled at the thought of naming a dog "Dog."

"No."

They called for him but no response.

"I heard him several times last night growling. He is probably chasing coyotes or rabbits. I'm going to check the fence line so I will look for him."

For some reason she felt uneasy going for a walk without Dog.

"If it's okay, I think I will take the truck and go visit Edna."

"Sure, it is okay. If you just want to go for a ride, why don't you go to R Country and get some salt and a few bags of grain."

Less than thirty minutes later George received a terrible shock. He found the big German shepherd, shot to death. The tracks indicated a fight with someone wearing smooth leather shoes with a deep scuff probably from slipping on a rock. George had been learning details on tracking and recognizing signs people left behind. In the dirt were impressions showing a deep scuff on the sole of the right shoe that obviously was worn by the person that had shot Dog. It was apparent that before he had been shot, Dog had done severe damage to the man. There were torn pieces of clothing, probably from dress pants, and sufficient blood to indicate that Dog's large teeth had found their mark more than once.

George lifted this faithful animal onto his horse to take him back to the ranch for a proper burial. He tried to call Hern, but without the cell phone booster in his truck there was no reception. He remembered how even in the most difficult occasions, such as the rescue of the stranded family, his Indian friends would never let themselves get so serious or concerned about their self-importance that made them where they could not laugh a little. So even with his dog "Dog" lying astraddle his lap, George smiled at the non-use of his cell phone and wondered if Hern could be reached with an Indian smoke signal?

Meanwhile, Beth Ann who had been driving slowly along the highway, thinking and worrying about Dog was suddenly passed by a speeding, light tan Escalade.

"No," she screamed to herself. Not believing her sudden deep inner fear. She dared not stop. So, she sped up the last few miles and slid to a stop in front of R-Country feed store. She then sat trembling as tears of fright mixed with rage ran down her face.

The tall dark haired lady, one of the daughters-in-law, saw Beth Ann crying and rushed out to the truck, "What is the matter, you look scared to death."

"Please, I can't talk. Please, help me get back to our ranch. Please call George."

The tall daughter-in-law, Carin did not hesitate. "Move over, I will drive." She then called her husband with her cell phone.

"Honey, something is wrong at the Gila River Cattle Ranch. I am taking Beth Ann back, but I can't reach George. Please come as soon as possible. Thank you."

They left the black top and the dust from the dirt road leading to the ranch formed two small horizontal tornados starting behind the rear tires that could be seen for miles. They pulled into the ranch yard without ever having exchanged a word. Beth Ann was noticeably shaken but was under more control. A Gila River Police car and a four-wheel drive short wheel base pickup with two or three officer and dogs were there.

Beth Ann could not move. Then George, back from checking fence and finding Dog, ran out of the house. The moment he saw the tear streaked face of his mother he rushed to the pickup.

"Mother, what's wrong?"

"I saw Herbert Addison. He passed me in a light tan Escalade."

"Herbert Addison, wasn't he your boss? Wasn't he the one you were going to work with on some big drug bust when you had your accident?"

"It was no accident. He tried to kill me. He thought he had killed me. I found out that he was not only stealing drugs, he had killed two dealers to get more. Then he tried to kill me. I remember his angry face when he asked me for the floppy that recorded the evidence. I had hid it. When I told him, he hit me with his gun. That is all I remember."

Beth Ann trembled once again as thoughts and scenes reappeared in her mind. Suddenly she lit up with a good memory. "The disc is sewn in the bottom of the old fake leather purse. Where is the purse?" She asked aloud.

Hern was standing next to GRC and heard the entire story. "From story of car fire, purse maybe burnt. Maybe big drug man think Miss Beth Ann still have. Good for us, maybe make big mistake and try find. He reminded George that he had seen a light tan Escalade in town early this morning."

George nodded agreeably.

Hern spoke with a deep troubled voice, "Now understand why GRC no like word drug, no let Edna call DEA when finding mother. What do now?"

"Hern," George spoke, "We need to investigate the status of Addison and do it without the use of the DEA organization."

George slapped his hand on his dusty Wrangles. "I have a friend that I can call."

Before he could turn his mother inquired, "George, did you find Dog?"

He hesitated to add additional worry to his mother. He knew she would find out, anyway. It would be better for her to learn what happened from him than from another. He rehearsed where he found Dog and what he had found beside Dog.

"Mother, I wonder if this Addison character had someone spying on the house to see if it were really you."

George decided it was time to call in a favor and asked for help on a grand scale. It took several calls to locate Lt. Colonel Bones, George's steel-jawed, marine escort from Dulles to Sky Harbor. George finally found him through American Airlines. When he called American Airlines, he said there was an emergency situation and that he needed to talk to Miss Bee Hardy. The airline representative said the airline did not have a Bee Hardy working. The representative asked what the "B" stood for. George explained that it was not the letter "B," but the name B, E, E.

The representative then said, "The computer shows a Mrs. Bee Hardy Bones, if that is any help?"

"Yes, yes" was all he could manage at the thought of Miss Hardy now being Mrs. Bones." George noted the number and was overjoyed that it was a 602 prefix, which is a Phoenix number. He immediately dialed.

"John Paul here,"

Before George could even answer the first response the second echoed.

"Bones here, who's calling?"

George answered.

"John Paul," George was embarrassed at repeating the first name. "Lt. Colonel Bones this is George Ribit..."

Before he could finish the statement of introduction the deep military voice rang through the lines.

"Well I'll be a monkey's uncle. How are you doing? I am surprised to hear from you and surprised that you are still alive? What trouble are you in?" It was spoken in jest but little did Bones know just how much trouble George was in.

George briefly explained about his mom, the attempt to kill her, and what was currently happening. It didn't take Bones long to make his decision to jump in to help his friend.

In full commander voice he bellowed over the phone, "I am picking up Bee in about thirty minutes. You probably don't know, but we are married. After I pick her up, we'll be right down. We will need a good computer? Do you know where one is? Can we meet there?"

While George was planning how to save his mother, Bones was forming alliances. Addison, who liked to think of himself a legitimate commander, was meeting at a freeway rest stop with a ruthless, paid assassin. They met to conspire to kill George's mother.

"Ernesto, I am Herbert Addison, you have not met me before. However, I am your boss. I am the one that pays, you comprende? Yes you have been reporting to Raul but I am the big boss."

Addison inwardly smiled. This short Colombian turned Mexican man looked the part with his macho mustache, squinted eyes and patent leather hand sewn boots. He just lacked the large cross ammunition belts hanging from both his shoulders, similar to pictures of the famous Poncho Villa.

Ernesto was working with a Mexican family and had recently helped move about two thousand kilos of heroin paste across the U.S./ Mexico border. Ernesto did not personally know Addison but he knew the name, knew of his power, and knew of his ruthlessness and political connections. Ernesto had been at the Gila River Cattle Ranch to observe, and to make sure that a certain lady was there. And, if possible take pictures, so Addison could see for himself.

"Let me see the pictures."

With hateful eyes, he examined the photo of the only person that would and could attempt to destroy his illegal, but well organized, empire and put him behind bars. Even if she did not have sound evidence, the fact that he let her slip out of his hands would cause doubts with his drug-dealing counterparts. They are always looking for reasons to eliminate.

"Yes," he said with a grimace that would make bulldog's face look happy, "that is the lady. Was there any trouble?"

"No sir, I did have to shoot some miserable mutt roaming loose on the reservation. Look, he bit my arm, tore my pants, and actually had me on the ground before I shot him. Even after he was dead, he would not turn loose of my arm. He was a devil."

"Did anyone see or hear?"

"No, it was still dark and I was off the ranch before sunrise."

"What about her son?"

"He is a nobody and a genuine fool. He gets himself into trouble almost on a daily basis. He actually caused me to laugh on a few occasions because of his stupid mistakes. He talks to himself, the trees, and his animals. I think he is cracking up."

"Why hasn't he left that pile of dirt he calls a ranch? Have you warned him?"

"Yes, we have killed animals, wrecked fence and finally talked to him face to face. He is just too dumb. He thinks he is John Wayne or Clint Eastwood."

"Well I don't care how you do it. Get her out of that house and into the canyons of the San Tan Mountains and make sure this time she disappears permanently. I can't believe she lived through the crash. She was not even buckled in. The little car was on fire and the bus going seventy-five miles an hour at the moment of the collision."

"But Jefe (boss), surely you checked?"

"Yes, you Columbian imbecile, I checked. She was crumpled in the seat, and was burned beyond recognition. I couldn't even check her pulse because her body was fried, burned like bad bacon."

The Mexican/Columbian laughed.

"Then why is she here and alive?" probed Ernesto. A question that didn't get an answer.

Addison and Ernesto finalized their plans.

George discussed with his mom about going into Sacaton to the Tribal Office to meet with Lt. Colonel Bones and Edna. He encouraged her to come with him but she insisted she was too tired and that she felt safe at the ranch house with Carin. George, Edna, Bones and Bone's new wife Bee all met at Edna's office. It took Bones, Bee and Edna only a short time to enter the computer's data systems. They found some relevant phone numbers and then made a few phone calls. They learned that shortly after Beth Ann's accident the DEA Director and Addison made a trip through Mexico, Columbia and even into Bolivia. They gave the pretence of being unmanageably angry at the drug cartel. They also claimed that they were seeking revenge.

It appeared that Addison did indeed rid the world of several drug leaders. In reality, he was simply eliminating the competition. While

Addison's methods were questionable, not much was said as to the legality of his actions. The DEA was sure he was doing them a huge favor and was waiting for his return to Washington, D.C. He was in constant contact with several of the agents that had access to records and transactions. The Agency thought they could give him a slight slap on the wrist for the small wrong doings and deaths. Before he returned to the states, however, he mysteriously disappeared. Shortly thereafter, much to the puzzlement of the DEA, the drug sales and distribution in the U.S. greatly increased. The DEA leadership discussed the increase in sales on several occasions in recent years. The sales and other activities seemed to indicate that the drug bosses knew every move the DEA was trying to make, before they ever made the moves.

At the same time that Bones, Bee and Edna were reviewing information concerning Addison's rise in power within the drug cartel, Beth Ann had been visiting with Carin, who had driven her home from the store. When they saw one of the Riggs sons pull up, and asked, "Everything okay?" He asked as he got out of his truck. Together they fed the animals, checked on the windmill and attempted to look busy.

Beth Ann spoke softly, "I am alright now. I so appreciate your help but I know you have much work at the store and George will be here soon. "Why don't you two go on home and take care of your own family. Again, thank you so much for calming my nerves."

Addison, knowing it was Ernesto, who had only left the rest stop only thirty minutes ago, was irritated as he grabbed his cell phone, "Hey boss, this is Ernersto again. It looks like the lady you so very much hate is now alone in this old house. Addison went from irritated to delight quicker than the speed of sound. I parked my pickup about a mile beyond the hill so no one will see. The dog is dead so I can pick her up and get her into the San Tan canyons. I have time to 'play' with the lady before she 'accidentally' gets buried under a pile of large rocks. I know the perfect place. Earlier, I left a pry bar. One push and a dozen boulders will fall."

"Listen you imported, incompetent, imbecile," Addison responded, close to the boiling point, "get her out and bury her. You can play another time and place with another lady."

Ernesto silently slipped into the house to find Beth Ann resting. Before she could react he grabbed and pinned her to the bed. "Lady,

Ernesto would like to spend much time with you, but big boss say I take you for a mountain hike." He tied her hands with gray duct tape and placed a large strip over her mouth. He and another man, who apparently was never allowed to take a shower, picked her up and roughly threw her in the back seat of a car.

It was very difficult for Beth Ann to walk; she had regained much strength, but not enough to fight these "animals" and not enough to climb. She collapsed the moment they got out of the car. She had an idea where she was, even though she was held down in the seat, she recognized the thumping sound caused from cracked cement slabs crossing the Olberg Bridge. They made no fast turns and drove much slower on a very rough dirt road with what she could imagine was filled with rocks left sticking out of the ground after the infrequent, but hard desert rains. The car bumped the rocks several times and she had inwardly hoped it would damage the oil pan. She determined that they were straight north of the Olberg Store on a little dirt road. George had taken her down this road to show some of the ancient hieroglyphics that had been almost completely destroyed by vandals.

At least she thought, "George and his friends know this area. Now if they can only determine that she is in the area. This is a mighty big desert."

George was riding with Bones and Bee when they pulled into the ranch house yard; he felt something was wrong at the house. They all rushed into the empty house. George turned to run outside.

"Bapchule, what are you doing here?" asked George.

"Bapchule feel much evil, much angry in air. What problem have brother George?"

Bapchule did not smile and did not chuckle, as was his custom. He seemed to have felt before any words were spoken and quite possibly before he came to the ranch that this was not a laughing problem.

Bapchule could see the gravity on the face of his young friend. Bapchule attempted to lift his burden. Bapchule knew that this situation was not like George tangled in a tree or his face-to-face meeting with a diamond back rattlesnake. There was something dreadfully wrong. The evilness of the situation was enough to fill the universe. Anyone who tuned into the correct channel could have felt the great evil that was about to happen. "Young brother George, tell some to Bapchule."

Before George could begin, Bones and his wife Bee stepped out of the ranch house.

"Who this man, who this woman. Bapchule no feel evil to them, why here at ranch?"

George explained briefly how he had met Bones and Bee. He then explained a little what was happening and his concern for his mother.

Bapchule took George by the arm. Just then, George heard, "Little brother George, why Bapchule here? Mother in big danger. Bapchule hear Beth Ann cry. Soon come Jesse, sure Jesse hear cry."

Bones and Bee stood as if they were petrified tree trunks. They said nothing. Their eyes and uplifted eyebrows were filling with unanswered questions about spirit, universe, Jesse and Beth Ann's cries for help.

"Bapchule tell to George, no Bapchule tell to GRC who now be man, call to Riggs, tell to them, bring horse and big rifle come maybe to Sacaton road and wait. Tell to oldest son, listen to universe, he know."

As George finished the call, Jesse and Chula walked in.

"Jesse tell Hern big problem at ranch, many time problem but now big problem, Jesse not know problem but very big problem. GRC mom much trouble."

They all headed out the door.

"Stop, Bapchule feel very much evil close. Go by post office. Go to Ira Hayes Park."

They pulled into the station across the road from the park so they could see the park and also fill GRC's tank with diesel. They were each studying recent photos of the men possibly involved.

Suddenly, Bones seemed to double in size, as he rumbled, "There he is, the scum at the bottom side of pile of four day old fish guts."

They all looked, not at the park but towards Lt. Colonel Bones and his colorful description of what and whom he saw. On two previous occasions doing guard work for different embassies Lt. Colonel Bones had encountered serious trouble in which he knew the root of the troubles was Herbert Addison. Bones had done in depth studies of the man and knew of his cruel methods but had never been able to get hard evidence that would hold up in a U.S. Court.

"Go ahead and get diesel," Bones suggested. Addison does not know that all of you know him. I don't have my uniform, so he may not recognize me either. I will walk over to look at the monument and try to hear what he is saying. I will also try to avoid breaking his poison-ivy twig neck."

While hiding behind the truck in his uniform, Hern received a call. "Hello, is this the police?"

"Yes, this Hern, head of the police department."

"Oh Hern, I am glad that you answered. This is Steve over at the Olberg Trading Post. Remember, you asked me to call you if any strange or unauthorized vehicles passed on the way to the hieroglyphics, well one just bounced past here like he didn't care if he tore his car up. I think there were two of them. The passenger kept looking into the back seat."

"Thanks Steve, you have been a great help, I'll explain later."

"Bapchule think Beth Ann in much danger, maybe bad men take Beth Ann to San Tan cliffs."

George called the Riggs family to let them know that they suspected Beth Ann was in the San Tan Canyons near Hieroglyphic Pass. He asked them to take their horses and meet him near the canyons. Hern made similar calls to the Indian officers who had horses.

It was difficult for the group to look at the diesel pump, clean the windshield and kick the tires without looking towards the monument. They were curious and wanted to know of the relationship between Lt. Colonel Bones and Addison. They could see that Bones stood behind Addison. He was close enough that he could overhear the conversations.

Before Bones could get closer Addison's cell rang and he answered with a rage.

"You imported, incompetent, idiot, I told you not to call anymore. I will be at the Eloy Airport when the deed is done. The two of you can get your twenty-five grand anytime so the sooner the better. Just make sure it is over and final this time."

Addison had just flipped the cover when a big hand grabbed the phone.

"Herbert Addison, you hog slurp pig crap, I dare you to struggle or try to run away. Better yet, go ahead and pull that automatic from your belt. That would give me reason to snap your neck against my boss's orders."

Addison stiffened. He did not recognize the voice or the man. "Who is your boss? Who are you? Whatever Tarriba is paying I'll pay double"?

Bones smiled and thought to himself, "These drug people are so violent and tough until the tables are turned."

The Tarriba group is headquartered in Sinaloa, Mexico and is a competitive drug family. Addison has been trying to trick them into a partnership for years. Bones decided to play along. He thought, "Maybe get to scum's with one snort."

"Yeah, where's the money?" Bones fired the questions. Not giving Addison much time to think. "What will you do with Tarriba?"

"They are meeting at the rest stop between Phoenix and Casa Grande. I'll call and put a hit on them."

"Yeah, big deal, I already knew that." Lt. Colonel bluffed, "Tell me something I don't know and give me a reason not to break your neck."

"I need their business and I know where the powder is hidden."

"Big deal, maybe I or even the DEA knows where the powder is hidden."

"Hey wait a minute, how would you know? How would they know?"

"I truly would like to break your neck; however you might be my new boss someday. Don't you think your informant might be our informant? Now, dirt bag, give me a real reason. First, where and second how."

"Under the Olberg Bridge, the powder is on the south side in one of the metal gate panels. Some of the cash in under a mesquite stump near the teepee monument where the road Y's."

It was so very tempting for Bones, with his ample training, to simply make a swift turn of his arm and twist the neck so this man would be forever out of the drug business and out of the lives of people who didn't want him in their lives. Bones thought, "He's just not worth the effort."

"So, you're going to pay me big bucks?" asked Bones.

"Yes, Yes, I will double whatever you make."

"Well, one more thing, how are you going to kill em?"

Addison, thinking this strong-arm man was now working for him instead of the Tarriba's explained how the Tarriba's top gun men would meet their fate at the rest stop near Casa Grande.

"What color will the hit van be?" Bones inquired. After Bones got as much information he thought necessary he turned Addison, "See that red truck over there?" Bones pointed. "Slowly walk over to that red pickup. You told me something, so I will tell you something. I have information that will be of great interest to you."

Hern had stepped out of sight behind the big F-350 Ford before the whole experience had started. He had radioed for additional trucks with men and two horses. Of the various riders and horses, he knew which ones were best suited for the situation. He named the horses and the riders that he wanted to assist him. These horses and riders could handle mountain rocks and cholla cactus. Hern ordered them to head in the direction of Olberg. (Horses not accustomed to the cholla 'Jumping Cactus' will soon have themselves and their riders covered with little prickly balls of cactus that, with their invisible miniature hooks hang fastened to the skin and with every twitch of the muscle, the needles penetrate deeper into and under the skin.)

"Hey, have we met before?" Addison asked as he looked into the George's eyes. He had indeed met the very young boy in Washington D.C. once with Beth Ann.

Before there were any other verbal exchanges, and to prevent a physical confrontation, Hern stepped from behind the truck and two other officers stepped out from behind an unmarked van. Addison started to run but with Bones holding him around the neck and lifting up there was not much traction.

"What do you think you are doing? I have done nothing wrong. I have a permit for this gun. I have no drugs so release me this instance."

Big Cecil walked up behind Addison and lifted him at least two feet from the hot asphalt.

"Hern, you want I should scalp him like other man who lie to Hern."

That seemed to stop the flow of conversation.

Bones made a number of calls to friends in the DEA in whom he had total confidence. He told his friends that Eduardo Tarriba was at the Casa Grande rest stop on the south side of the freeway, the drug and money exchange would occur at the Eloy Airport. Bones had also overheard about an informant called Neal Gorbach.

"Neal Gorbach?" The cell phone seemed to scream. The DEA agent and friend of Lt. Colonel Bones spoke so loudly all could hear. "Neal Gorbach is the south west director of drug enforcement. No wonder we have met with so many dead end attempts."

"Well, I suggest you do this on your own. We'll take care of business on this end, also in our own way."

The agent visited over the cell with Bones, "Thanks, someday you will explain to me how all of this came to be. By the way, from your description of the other two fellows, the one cross breed called Ernesto is as mean as they come. He has a dozen killings on his record and more female mutilations. When you find him, waste him please. We have determined from other informants that he was responsible for the brutal death of an outstanding female agent in New York a few years ago. Reports say he pushed her burning car in front of a loaded passenger bus and watched them burn. Bones, what we have determined was that upon impact the unbelted agent was thrown from the car and an innocent female passenger was thrown through the windshield of the bus into the seat and burned in the small convertible VW. So please, get him, he does not need to be tried. The young female agent disappeared. We presumed Addison found her and finished the job that Ernesto had screwed up."

With Addison hand cuffed in the back seat of a police Bronco, Hern spoke out, "Just got a call, nine Riggs on horseback and four on quads are headed up the hill. They have found trail, see two men dragging woman. Sorry GRC."

The cell of Addison's rang and Bones recognized the number, "You imported, incompetent, imbecile." Addison was unable to say more.

Bones grabbed the cell phone as the voice continued.

"Boss, I do not know who this lady is but there is a whole army on horseback and quads coming up the hill. Behind them is another army of white pickups and a couple more horses."

Bones' life had often depended on quick thinking.

"Damn battery," he mimicked Addison's voice and clicked the phone off.

It rang back, but he did not answer.

"Bosses battery must be low." Ernesto spoke to Raul. "Let's get up to the canyon, dump the dame, climb up the hidden trail, pry the rocks to cover her up and block the trail, then we will drop over the back side of the mountain to the truck and go get our money."

One of the Riggs spotted them.

"They're heading for the box. They must know of the trail and have a truck on the backside. Call and have Noble, a cousin that lives on the north side of the mountain, check it out."

The Riggs' had stopped a few moments to breathe their horses and survey the situation. The lead rider spoke, "The varmints and Beth Ann are about two miles ahead of us but they are on foot. Ray, you have the fastest and best-conditioned horse and Jay is the best shot…"

"No, David is best shot."

They all turned to see two Indians sitting astride lathered horses.

"David shot eye of rabbit 600 yard and no touch eyelash."

There could have been a good laugh but all seemed to sense it was quite possibly true.

Ray, David and Ruben headed up the hill at almost a dead run. It was rough on horseflesh and dangerous for the rider, but in these moments when another life is at risk nothing else seems important.

"Ernesto, look at those crazy cowboys running their horses up the hill. Those horses are throwing white lather ten feet on each side."

"Quit jabbering and start shooting."

"All I have is a stub .38, it won't reach a third of the way."

"Let's shoot the woman and get out of here."

"Stupid, if we shoot the woman they will look but won't stop, if we leave her here they will have to stop and give her water, care for her knees and bandage her head."

They literally threw the weakened Beth Ann into a small ravine and ran up the hill to save their own hides. They stayed low in a small wash to keep out of sight of those "idiotic" cowboys. They were at least five or six hundred yards away from the riders and were only a few hundred yards from safety. They almost tasted their success, only one large crevice to pass through, which was deep enough to keep them well out of sight of any rider who might try to take a wild shot.

"Besides," Ernesto spoke, "at least two of the riders were a couple of dumb Indians that probably still use a bow and arrow."

The three jumped from their horses and ran down the side of the ravine to offer care and water to a hurt, scratched, but relieved and joyful Beth Ann.

Some distance behind GRC's truck, Hern with other police officers raced along the road. They went as fast as the old white Police pickup would allow. All were heading to the area of Olberg relying on the reports from the storeowner.

With a savage smirk, "What are you going to do with me?" Addison chided the officers. "You cannot hold me on anything. I have broken no laws."

"We all charge you with the attempted death of a DEA agent."

"Oh really, won't you need a witness?"

Lucky for Addison, he was not riding in the same truck with Cecil or George. That remark might have ended his life.

George's big truck was churning dust on both sides of the blacktop. The truck slid around the turns and flew over a very old and narrow road. Most of the trees along the road had branches that had grown almost to the center of the abandoned road. Both truck mirrors traveling at eighty-plus miles an hour were savagely pruning the overhanging branches.

True to the Indian form, there is never any real crisis that cannot be enjoyed.

"Chula think GRC send bill to Indian tribe for trimming trees. Chula maybe tell Edna, GRC cut special plants no permit. Edna make GRC pay fine."

Even with all that was on George's mind, he had a small chuckle.

Soon after turning up the narrow dirt/rock vehicle trail past the Olberg store, and past the remains of the hieroglyphics he could see where most of the horses and men were grouped.

The three men on a death-defying ride up the rock laden slope stopped to get a clear look up the mountainside.

"David," Ray spoke, "If those guys reach the old miner's trail we may never catch them."

David, a cross between Pima and Apache Indian was studying the canyon walls. He had been a decorated sniper during the Vietnam conflict and served recently in the Gulf War on "special assignment." Yet, with all the service, it only took a few weeks to pick up the Pima accent and direct way of speaking. He once told a Marine buddy of his, "You guys talk so much about him, he, his, hers, she and they that I forget to whom or for whom you are talking. Why don't you use the given name?"

"David saw something interesting. Top of canyon wall is big pry bar. David thinks maybe snake pee (bad men) maybe leave hurt lady at bottom, push big bar and cause much rock slide down and fill small canyon. David think big 30-06 rife with special steel jacket shell do same as pry bar. David have big scope." A steel jacket shell has a bullet that has steel wrapped around the lead bullet, rather than just a lead bullet that most bullets have. This keeps the bullet from fragmenting on impact and allows for deeper penetration. When a steel shell fired from a 30-06 hunting rifle strikes a fair size boulder, the boulder will literally explode.

"David, that is a least 800 yards away." Ruben and Ray both commented.

"Yeah, no challenge shot for David. Maybe shoot tip of pry bar and let pry bar move rock."

"That is fine David, just shoot the rock and bury the snake pee." Ray thought the term very logical.

David calculated the upward shot and the slight side breeze, laid the rifle across a large boulder, took a deep breath and unconsciously rolled his lips into a devilish smile that had been acquired from the years as a Special Forces sniper. Once again, David knew that an enemy would die. Once again along with the absolute steadiness of the rifle was the same steady devil's grin. The trigger gently moved backward, no jerk or flinch, just a slow calculated squeeze that would end the life of two renegade varmints.

"David" speaking to himself, "is good Boy Scout, do a good deed today, rid world of two varmints. Send to Great God, maybe He do something."

The rifle shot filled the air and echoed. The steel jacket shell found the perfect spot in the small crevice between the solid mountain and the thousands of pounds of rocks. The rocks were carefully balanced in a vertical position. They were just waiting for the right moment to begin their descent into a large hungry open mouth crevice. The crevice indeed had the dry devilish look of hunger. The crevice was hungry to add to the ever-changing living desert. The canyon walls were oblivious to the two men that might appear as small-infected tonsils in the large canyon cavern. The canyon was ready to swallow the thousand tons of rocks and the two men as a hungry teenage boy would swallow cheeseburgers.

When a giant 747 comes in for a landing, it is so large that it appears to be flying in slow motion. The same is true when the side of a canyon begins to fall. The side appears to be in slow motion as it slides and rumbles down the mountain. However, to a person or persons standing directly under the descending canyon wall it is without doubt falling at high velocity. Over the echo of the shot could be heard a couple of "death screams" from Ernesto and Raul.

George heard both the shot and the falling rock. "Did you hear that? George asked fearfully. Did they execute my mother? What is happening?"

All nodded. They had heard the shot and the rocks. A shot from a large rifle rang and echoed through the canyons followed by a roar that sounded more like a large exploding bomb or a large building collapsing. They all held their breath. The question that loomed in the forefront of every man's mind was, "Where is Beth Ann?"

The three men, shirts torn, arms scratched and bleeding from riding through trees, bushes and rocks were holding Beth Ann in their arms. They knew that she was hurt but safe. They also knew, without hesitation, that the end of the drug lord's guards had come. These guards were distastefully credited with many deaths. Their death was fast and did not allow for much suffering. The end, however, was permanent.

David sat the warm rifle on a nearby rock. "It over, new trail need be made."

He took no pleasure in ending another life; even if he felt the life to be "no good." It was still a human life. Yet he knew of the calm feeling that followed knowing that his special training and special skill might save the lives of hundreds of others, especially the lives of the innocent youth that became addicted to drugs.

David carefully lifted Beth Ann and held her against his sweaty shirt. Ray silently picked up the rifle. Ray and Ruben both knew that David would carry Beth Ann to the bottom of the rocky mountain; it was his way of reconnecting to life after calculatingly taking the life of another. It was his form of repentance. Ray and Ruben led the tired horses silently down the hill. They had not and never would ask David how many lives he had ended. It was his duty and it was their duty to offer silent support.

The reunion of mother and son was heartfelt.

Then Beth Ann saw Herbert Addison.

"Why Herbert?"

"Business is business," He offered a wicked smile. He realized too late that the smile and the words that followed would cost him his life. "You know with my connections and money, you will never convict me and even if you do I will only get a few years and will be out to find you and your Charles Bronson son."

It seems that when a person who works for the law chooses to work against the law, he or she becomes totally bad. It seems that, when they abuse the law, they then feel there is no law. It seems that, when that type of person becomes wickedly wealthy, they assume they can buy anything including freedom with that wealth. It seems Addison forgot he was in a separate nation with separate laws where a guilty person really is a guilty person. He was on the Pima Indian Nation. When Addison flashed that wicked smile and looked at Beth Ann with all the evil contempt that one man might have, Hern made the decision and knew that this man would never leave his custody. Addison was temporarily locked in the Sacaton jail until Hern could devise a plan.

Police, friends and Riggs families all met at the Casa Blanca restaurant. Bones and Bee were so full of questions, but offered or expressed no ridicule at the spiritual experiences that this group had prior to the Bones' involvement. They had seen and more importantly, they had felt enough occurrences in life to simply believe.

Edna, acting judge, Hern, acting police chief and Cecil, acting bodyguard, all walked in together.

"Where did you take Addison?" Edna queried.

"Let us first congratulate Lt. Colonel Bones before we talk of evil," responded Hern. Hern smiled as he shook Lt. Colonel Bones' strong hand. "With the information you furnished to the DEA many of the Tarriba group and Neal Gorbach have been apprehended. We met with legal counsel concerning Addison and he was right. Even though he admitted trying to kill Beth Ann, even though there was evidence on his person about other killings and even though his cell phone recorded call numbers, he would have received about five years and be out in one or two with his pay off system."

Beth Ann turned pale and trembled.

"Not to worry mom of Gila River Cowboy. Maybe Addison, when we try and give him food, maybe trip and fall. No hurt anyone anymore. Maybe take some money with him to learn money no good with Great God."

They all looked at each other with a silent puzzle on each face. They somehow knew that Addison would never make it to a Phoenix judge or a white man's court.

None of the group were thinking or trying to extract a personal revenge. Yet each was certain that if Herbert Addison made it into the Arizona court system he would be back in operation in a matter of years.

One of the Riggs' suggested dropping Addison down an old abandoned irrigation well maybe five hundred feet deep. There were a few other ideas.

Somehow or someway, Addison would soon be face to face with death. The general feeling was that Hern and his committee would endeavor to make it natural, painful and memorable for the ex-DEA director and if at all possible, legal.

21—NATURE'S EXECUTIONERS

"**Y**OU SCUM OF the earth, do you really think you are going to keep me in jail, especially in this half buried piece of aborted landscape."

Herbert Addison was locked in the Sacaton jail. The lower half of the building's outer walls is covered with mounds of dirt pushed up to the walls, partly for the landscape design and partly for cooling.

"You just tell me how much you make. Tell me how much you want. I can get my hands on hundreds of thousands of green backs within thirty minutes. The money is not far from this pile of garbage."

"Him talk much and say nothing," the jail guard commented.

Addison had spent two nights and was entering his third day. He had utilized his right to a phone call and he talked in length to an attorney in Phoenix. Holding the old style black phone,

Hey you so called officer of the law, can I receive phone calls?"

"Maybe, if you have own cell phone."

"Well, I had one until that ape of a Green Beret stole it from me at that make shift monument of some dead so called Indian war hero. What was the Indian's name? Oh yes, Hayes."

"Then you no receive phone call."

Gripping tightly the black landline phone that had been handed to Addison by the guard, Addison yelled as if he were talking directly to his Phoenix lawyer without the use of the phone, the self-proclaimed powerhouse made his demands.

"Bring me a cell phone pronto. Oh, don't get cute with me. I might temporarily be in this hole surrounded by half burnt offerings but I still have enough power to reach out and have someone break your scrawny neck. I told you earlier, you get paid when I say you get paid and that won't be until you get me out of here. Post the bail you dimwitted lawyer."

That afternoon an attorney with his spotless white shirt, dazzling crimson silk tie, faded denim jeans and new Wellington black shinning boots approached Ruth, office manager for the Tribal Police department.

"Ma'am, I am here to visit with Mr. Herbert Addison, I am his legal representative."

A full two minutes passed before Ruth finished reading the article from the Arizona Highways magazine.

"Excuse me, maybe you didn't hear, I am the…"

"Ruth hear very good, Ruth finish article, Addison no go anywhere, he in jail."

"John," Addison hollered from the jail when he heard his attorney's voice, part plea and a part demand, "Get me out of this god-forsaken place. It was bad enough the first night, and then they decided to put the worthless drunks in with me. I swear on my mother's grave, some of the Indian drunks seem to have a key to the jail; they just show up, no paper work, no fines, and no nothing. They just walk in, speak to the jailer and he lets them spend the night in the tank. One jailer said, 'Joe, glad you come here instead of drive home, maybe cause bad car crash.' Get me out of here. Get me to someplace natural where money means something, where money talks and talks loudly."

"I'll talk to them, maybe a good contribution to a school or church will soften them enough to speed the papers and get you transferred. Hang in there and try not to antagonize them. They do hold your future."

"John, you educated legal idiot, where is my cell phone?"

"I'll be down tomorrow and bring a special cell that has a scrambling device. Don't want the whole world to hear what you are saying."

"I don't care if these over baked brown cookie dough boys hear me talking. If I talk fast I doubt they could understand. It takes them ten minutes to say hello."

The lawyer and Addison visited for just a few minutes. "Addison, I will get you out soon but I must meet with a few people and get a little more cash. I'll be back as quickly as possible. Try not to cause any more trouble."

George had been busy on the ranch. Even if life on the outside is in shambles, life on a ranch continues. The good and the bad of any form of agriculture is that you cannot turn off the lights and shut the doors, the cattle still eat, fences still fall down and horses need water even if the outside world crumbles.

George was still George to his mom as he spoke, "How are you feeling today Mom? That was quite an ordeal and quite a scare."

"I am doing alright, a few bruises and scratches that will soon mend but I am still scared. I know Herbert Addison and saw the look in his eyes. He will not quit hunting me until one or the other of us is dead. Son, both your dad and the DEA has given me some training in the use of handguns. Do you have any guns in the house? Don't you think we should have some guns in the house?"

George responded, "It wouldn't hurt for us to have some guns even in the truck. You can practice with Victoria until you get comfortable again with guns and your aim returns. She is a much better shot than I with a rifle or pistol and has been shooting since she was a little girl." George had not realized that his mom had been previously trained in the use of all types of firearms. "Victoria will be home from school, this is her last semester thank goodness, and she can help. I am sure that Edna will allow you to get a permit to shoot on the reservation. There are signs posted at every entrance but very few people pay any attention."

"George," Beth Ann commented, "I could not believe the shot that David made. They had been running and were breathing immensely hard. David knelt beside me on the mountain, held my hand and looked at me with reverent and extremely respectful eyes. Then he looked upwards toward the area where Ernesto and Raul had disappeared and his face and eyes began to change. Ray told him it was about 800 yards and the bullet would have to hit within a one-inch circle to be successful. I heard him tell Ray and Ruben with fearsome confidence, 'I will hit the mark.' I couldn't see exactly where David was aiming because I was on the ground but I could see his face. Son, he knew he would hit the mark and he knew he was going to kill both men. His face changed, his eyes changed and his slight smile was alarming to me. Yet I was so appreciative of his skill. How long has he been shooting?"

"Oh Mother, they told me he has been shooting all his life and that in the service he was trained by the very best. Then after the formal training each day he would practice many extra hours while in the service. Hern said he was one of the best."

"Son, the bullet had scarcely left the rifle when he laid the gun down. He didn't wait for the few seconds needed to see if he had hit the mark. He knew. His face instantly changed and he bent over me as if I were a small child. When he picked me up the other two never said a word or offered to carry me. They both knew something that I didn't know. When he so carefully and lovingly laid me on the back seat of your truck he looked skyward, I saw enormous tears fall from this man's eyes and with a reverence I have never felt in any church or temple. Then he whispered, "We're even my good brother.""

"I don't know why he said that." George replied, "I will ask Edna or Hern. They both know him well."

"Please talk with them, I really want to know and understand his feelings."

Ruth, sitting at her desk inside the police headquarters and from years of habit subconsciously heard tires crunching on the graveled parking lot. She guessed it was the high-class lawyer returning with, he thought, all the answers. He entered the room with his hat in his hands as if to show a great respect for Ruth.

"Ma'am, how are you this fine day?"

"I tell you, I no ma'am, I Ruth. You maybe have bad memory?"

"I'm sorry ma'am, I mean Ruth, I will remember in the future. Could I please visit with Mr. Addison outside of his cell?"

"No problem, you stand outside cell."

He slowly folded a fifty-dollar bill in his hand so she could easily see the numbers. He was certain that she would accept the fifty. She did. She simply took the bill, thanked him, folded it and stuck it in the dresser drawer. She just looked out the window as she spoke,

"Thank you, this make next dinner for police Christmas dinner much better. Who those men outside?"

"They are just a couple of fellows that rode with me, they wanted to visit the reservation and better understand their Indian neighbors."

"Ruth no like when fancy lawyer make bullshit, maybe get all over floor. Ruth no have boots today. No like men outside, maybe cause trouble."

"No Ms. Ruth, they cause no trouble, they just want to better understand Indians..." He decided not to spread more "bullshit" as Ruth had so aptly explained.

"If want visit with Indian, why stay outside? Why not come inside where Indian?"

"Ms. Ruth, may I please visit with Mr. Addison?"

"Why always hurry, he no go nowhere. He still in jail." She then allowed the legal representative to enter the hallway leading to the cell.

"John, what in the blazes do you and Ruth talk about? I saw you come in ten minutes ago. Do you have the papers? When am I leaving?"

"I should have the papers tomorrow, it isn't as easy as it used to be to find a judge that will negotiate a price but I did locate one. He accepted our offer and will give us his account number to transfer funds. He wants half now and half when he gives me the necessary documents. To make the transfer, I need your power of attorney. I have the document prepared and will make the transfer this afternoon. You should be out of here in two days tops. I know there is a federal law about an initial appearance within forty-eight hours, however you need to remember that you do not even have U.S. documentation with you so they and I are having to determine your legal status."

Addison did not like the idea of giving a power of attorney for his "undocumented account" but he knew it was one of the two ways he was going to get out. He still had confidence in his own ability to "negotiate" with these slow speaking people. He also knew that when he got out the power of attorney would be revoked.

"You know that there are a couple of people near here that I must visit one last time before I leave the country. There are actually four or five but I will settle for two."

"Herbert, please listen to me, it would be better if you just forgot about revenge or elimination for a few months. I understand that the woman, Mrs. Chattit is still sick so she won't be going anywhere and the trial date isn't even set, it will be at least two years away. The judge has agreed to set bail after he receives the first payment so you will not spend one more day in this jail. You will be transferred. The judge will say that you are not a flight risk because of your long tenure as past Director of the DEA and bail is justified because of your flawless service record. The judge had misunderstood that you had had an accident and had disappeared; I assured him that you were still in full control and had been undercover for a lengthy period. Herbert you need to understand that even having bail set for someone who is charged with felony-murder is very unusual."

The high priced Phoenix lawyer continued to try and reason with his client. "You need to understand that even if you are not the person who actually killed Ernesto and Raul, you can still be charged with felony-murder. Their deaths occurred during the commission of a felony and you are accused of participating and conspiring in those actions. As evidence, they have phone records and voice conversations."

Hern and his partner pulled up to the police station and saw the two rough looking characters leaning against the Escalade. Hern noticed the special tread from mud grip tires purchased only in Mexico. He mentioned to his partner, "Be careful, this same car leave tire print in wash near Gila River Ranchouse."

Hern walked to the front door, "Ruthie, who those men outside?"

"Ruth ask Addison attorney, he say friends came to see and visit Indians in Sacaton. Ruth no like. Look like carry big gun under windbreaker. Ha, who wear windbreaker in Arizona when this hot?"

Both officers looked out the window at the two men.

"Ruthie, did you listen good to what attorney and Addison speak?"

"Yes, they speak that soon Addison be gone from Sacaton jail. Lawyer say no stay in jail when not in Sacaton. Fancy lawyer say judge in Phoenix make legal papers for much money. Ruth think lawyer no want Addison out. Get more money from special account. Addison say before leave country must visit with Mrs. Chattit. No sound like visit."

"Ruth, Hern and partner go outside and visit two men, maybe they want meet Indian police, maybe they do something wrong, go to jail. Maybe like Monopoly Game, get card say go straight to jail. Call to Cecil, Cecil big brother and call to four other officer. Maybe bad men no like card." They all chuckled. "Hern think big trouble come too soon from two men. Think maybe they break law."

"Howdy gentlemen." Hern spoke as he exited the building.

"How," the bigger of the two spoke mockingly as they laughed. "We are not sure how to speak to Indian chief?" They laughed again. Both men were taller, stouter and heavier by thirty percent than Hern.

"Hey little Indian Chief can we help you in some way?" They continued to mock.

"No Indian Chief, my name Hern." Hern deliberately talked with an exaggerated Pima Indian accent. "Come to visit with big men from out-of-town. You maybe important men from out-of-town?"

"Well we are very important to certain people."

"Look like important men have good big gun under jacket. It okay you have permit for gun?"

"Yes we have permits."

Hern pulled out his 44 automatic (not standard issue) and pointed to a stop sign about 25 yards across the parking lot. Without warning he fired four rounds.

"Hern not so good, one time last year hit beer bottle at 10 yards."

Hern was certain that the two larger men could not resist the challenge. However, to maintain some degree of legality, Hern warned the men that without a permit, shooting on the reservation was against the law. The bigger man knowing he had an Arizona permit pulled out a Smith and Wesson .357 with a longer than normal barrel then pulled out a special built long silencer (which he temporarily forgot was illegal) and carefully screwed it on the barrel and fired four shots. All four hit within the O of STOP.

"Hey chief, you better learn to shoot straight if you're going to be a police officer."

The other, rising to the challenge, removed his jacket to reveal a small .38 in a back holster and an automatic .44 with about six loaded clips hanging on the holster belt.

"Anybody can shoot in the same spot, I'll put four shots and follow the curve of the S."

Almost within the blink of an eye four shots were fired and the S had four perfectly matched holes.

"You are both excellent shots. Maybe Hern need much practice. May Hern look at the long silver gun? It is most handsome and must shoot very straight."

Hern examined the still warm 44 as the other man showed his special S & W 357 with fine threads on the end of the barrel so as to easily attach the silencer. The two big white gun totting bodyguards were proud of their guns, slowly came the realization that they no longer held these fine weapons in their hands. They had not noticed that four other officers had appeared and two Indians that stood at least six foot eight and together weighed over a quarter of a ton were walking towards them. They also noticed that these two were not fat, they were big as any professional lineman in the NFL.

Cecil spoke first.

"What is all the shooting? Why did those men shoot Indian property?"

With the officers standing close and big Cecil and his bigger brother walking up behind the two men Hern stepped closer to them.

"You under arrest."

The one reached for his small handgun from his back holster but only felt a vice grip hand coming from Cecil wrap around his arm above the wrist that reminded him of the pipe vise his father had in the plumber's workshop. The more he tried to move, the more the muscle from the Indian seemed to screw tighter.

"Oh yeah, what are the charges? We have permits."

"Maybe you have permits for Arizona. When you come on Indian land there is big sign say 'No firearms'. Same sign say illegal to destroy Indian property. Indian law say no shoot in town unless authorized. You break three laws. Now all here see you reach for gun to maybe shoot Indian officer. That big rule."

Ruth could hear the Phoenix lawyer yelling his head off trying to get her back inside to unlock the inner door. She was in no hurry. When she returned to open the door the lawyer rushed out of the building to observe the problem.

"What is going on out here? What was all the shooting? How come my friends are in cuffs? Turn them loose at this moment or I will..."

"You maybe obstruct justice? That maybe what you say?"

"No, no of course not. I am an attorney and duty bound to uphold the law."

It was clearly explained that the two had broken four laws, which now included resisting arrest, so they were going to spend some time in the Sacaton jail.

"How much is the bond? I will post it immediately."

"Sorry, do not know amount of bond. Judge set bond after hear what happen, maybe will be next day. Judge out of town. Maybe no bond because he try to get gun maybe to shoot officer."

"He says he was reaching to hand the gun to you."

"Maybe that be truth, maybe Judge believe, maybe no believe. Maybe lawyer better leave."

After a moment of consulting with his two bodyguards the attorney very politely asked, "My client said you were shooting in town and shot the sign. What right do you have to shoot a STOP sign then arrest my clients for doing the same?"

"Hern have permission to shoot in town. Your men tell to you that each shot four times. Lawyer look at sign and find eight holes. Hern no shoot at sign. Hern shoot at bale of hay over there. Maybe lucky, Hern hit haystack. Hearn also tell big man no legal shoot gun. That right big man?"

"Where is the Judge? If she is not here who is in charge?"

"Hern in charge of police. Tribal council in charge of laws."

"Hern, I would like to visit with you and the Judge or a Tribal leader to see if we might reach a mutual understanding concerning Addison and these two."

Hern assured the lawyer that he would arrange for a meeting. The next morning, Edna, three tribal council members and Hern met. They reviewed all that had happened, confessions and threats. One tribal leader summarized the problem.

"If drug man leaves Sacaton jail, maybe kill Beth Ann and GRC then leave country, will not be punished for the crime and then kill many more innocent children with evil drugs."

"We seem to all agree," Edna spoke. "Now what do we do. We just can't shoot him or hang him like some wild west even though that would be my preference."

Hern was laughing as he spoke. "Maybe play Indian and General Custer only this time Addison be Custer."

The next afternoon the group that had met the previous afternoon met with the attorney and Addison. The attorney initiated the conversation but soon Addison dominated all communication.

"Do you understand how much money I can get in just a matter of minutes?"

The Tribal leaders, Edna and others are for the most part very well educated but when confronted with the absolute ignorance and arrogance of people such as Addison and his lawyer it becomes more of a game to the Indians to simply play the presupposed part of a flunky. Because they have grown up with the Indian accent it is easy to mock. So with heavy accents and lazy tongues they each took their turn in talking as dumb as Addison considered them to be.

"We Indian not understand all white man law but poor Indian understand much money. Also need show much drug find, make good report, maybe DEA not be suspicious."

George had come into town and was talking with Edna. She filled him in on Addison's attempts to bribe anyone or all. He told his lawyer that the moment he was out he was going to visit your mom. Edna said they were going to visit with Addison one more time then confer to see if there were any legal ideas or ways to detain him in the Sacaton jail.

The group sat with Addison and his lawyer. Addison's eyes were sparkling with delight. He whispered to his lawyer John,

"These dumb Indians are just as greedy as most whites, did you see how they almost drooled at the mouth when I told them how much money and drugs were stashed on their precious land?"

They all visited for a few minutes before the Indian leaders and police officers excused themselves for a moment and walked a distance to visit with George. It was decided that Hern and Edna would ride with Addison to see if he really had the money and drugs on Tribal lands. George would return to the ranch, get some needed items and stay with his mom at the Riggs home. They all concluded that something might go wrong.

George did not like the idea of putting additional risk on the Riggs family. He took some comfort as he recalled the many hunting stories they had related. He was sure this family was equivalent to a small army.

About thirty minutes later, the tribal leader returned to visit with Addison.

"Okay chief, what's the plan?" Addison blurted.

Hern carefully spoke with a highly exaggerated Indian accent. Hern had realized that this self important ex-DEA leader was thinking about the "Dumb Indians" so he would help the man, if one really feels the other is dumb, mistakes are most often made, Hern was depending on this very thought.

Thus he spoke, "Many Indian leader think maybe Addison need show where is much money and maybe much drug. Then Addison tell to Hern and Edna where all money and all drug may be hid. Hern send other policeman to find. When all good, Hern take Addison to Olberg Bridge like maybe we investigate where Mrs. Chattit was captured. Important, maybe DEA watch. Indian police much proud of Bridge and want to show Addison. When stop to show big bronze plaque Addison maybe jump over small ridge on east side maybe into old water ditch with no water, dry ditch that Indian no use no more for irrigation, run fast through ditch to old rusted gate, jump over gate and escape maybe to freedom. Maybe plenty long walk. If Indian police no find all money, Hern find fast Addison walking in desert, must maybe shoot for escape. Hern know very hard for Addison tell to truth. Maybe Addison think life worth telling truth. Once jump over first ridge, Indian police no see Addison. Much plant, much tree, no see. Important for Indian make look accident. Maybe DEA watch, no want DEA get mad. Addison make escape look much like accident."

"How do I know that you won't just shoot me after I show you the money?"

"We not shoot, maybe DEA have big eye look down maybe from sky, big trouble for Indian to shoot white man. More big trouble to shoot white man with much money and much important like maybe Mr. Addison. Also, attorney be in car behind Indian, if Addison get shot, attorney call Pinal Sheriff, cause big trouble for little Indian Chief."

Addison talked to his lawyer about paying the Phoenix judge. Addison was concerned about the loyalty of this lawyer. He talked the night guard into letting him make a couple of phone calls. He was unable to sleep much that night. Not from the noise of the drunks but from his own inner laughter. He remembered once a young boy turned to his young companion after a hilarious mishap, looked him squarely in the face and yelled, "How dumb is you." That is what kept him inwardly laughing much of the night, the thought of how easily these "dumb" Indians were going to let him escape.

That evening George had met with Edna and Hern. Among other topics, George asked them both about the sniper that with one shot brought down half a mountain, George said his mother had felt a certain connection with this man and wondered if they knew much about David's history.

Hern explained, "Not know many details. David have mixed blood. Know very well how fight and shoot even when very young. Join Marine, maybe son of hero Ira Hayes. David say get good training how to shoot enemy long way from hiding spot, David good sniper they say. Same Marine that give good training sent to Viet Nam to help soldier Marine. Group of soldier Marine get in big trouble. Same Marine that teach shoot in safe place, yet Marine go back and get many solider so solider not get killed. Same Marine that teach to David be good shot rescue David. Same Marine get shot and die. David never say name of Marine. When Hern talk to David about big problem for George, David ask all name. When I tell to him George Ribit Chattit, David act like dirt in eye, hide tear and say David go to help, maybe save Beth Ann Chattit. David say many time the name Chattit. Hern never tell David mother name. David already know all Hern know."

George related to his mother all what Hern had said about David.

"Son, do you know his full name?"

"I think Edna called him David Everett Soke."

Beth Ann bent over with her head in her lap and George could hear and see her sobs even though she was trying to conceal her emotions.

"Mother, please tell me why you are sobbing. Please tell me."

"Your father was killed in action trying to save all the marines in his group. Three were seriously wounded and were unable to walk. The report said that your father led the group to safety, then, returned to bring all three to safety one at a time under heavy enemy fire. However on the last trip with the soldier over his shoulder an enemy bullet entered his back and went through his heart. They said he carried the man another thirty yards to safety before he collapsed and died. The commander witnessed your father's actions. Along with the Medal of Honor he explained in detail how your father, with his heart devastated from the bullet carried his comrade to safety. He then related that only once in his lifetime had he seen something similar, he then explained.

"While hunting Elk in Colorado, I came upon an exceptionally large bull elk that was standing in the shade of a large pine. I took careful aim and shot. The huge bull turned and trotted off. Needless to say, I was stunned. I considered myself an excellent shooter. I walked to the spot where the elk had been standing a saw blood on the bark of the pine just behind where the elk had been standing. When I found the elk about one hundred fifty yards away I later discovered that his heart and been shattered from my bullet. Jay John Chattit was as strong and as durable as a bull elk."

After the meeting, I asked a few question to the commander. He told me,

"You might know the last soldier he saved, he was from Arizona. His name was David Everett Soke."

"Now I understand why he took such good care of me, chanced crippling his fine horse, risked his own life and alone carried me to your pickup. He then looked upward and whispered, 'We're even friend.' He had paid his lifelong debt to your father."

The next morning about 8:00 a.m. Edna with one Tribal councilman, Hern with his partner, and Addison left in a dusty white Ford Expedition. The attorney with his fully charged cell phones followed alone about fifty yards behind. Not far from the Gila River Cattle Ranch headquarters they stopped near a super large dark gray boulder that had centuries earlier rolled down from a nearby mountain. Moving some dried grass and parting a large green creosote bush a small hole, looking much like a badger hole could be seen. Addison, leery of possible rattlesnakes or badgers in the hole poked with a stick then put on heavy leather gloves before reaching in to pull out a metal box packed with 100 dollar bills in neatly vacuumed wrapped in water proof packages of $10,000 each.

"Here is $500,000 now let's go get some white powder and get me to the north end of the bridge."

About five miles away was the collapsed ruins of an old adobe church built in the 1700's by Spanish Fathers trying to "help correct the Indian way of life." Inside the crumbling chimney, covered with dirt was a flat shale rock. Addison pointed to the place.

Hern spoke, "You want I go get powder. You maybe need much energy for long hot walk after escape."

Addison was so certain that because these Indians were "apparently so dumb" they would not suspect that he had made arrangements thru the attorney to have a pickup truck waiting for him about three miles from the bridge. The truck would have rifle, pistol, water and a camera.

He smiled at what he was planning to do with the no good woman that has caused so much trouble in his life and is like a cat with nine lives. This time she would not escape, not be rescued and she would most assuredly die. It would be so delightful that he wanted pictures to later remind him of the pleasure he had in killing this aggravating woman. That is why he asked for the camera.

"It looks like it is all here. Maybe $750,000 street value. Maybe only report half. Maybe sell other half to drug dealer, get money, arrest drug man and paint school. What say Edna?" Hern was speaking and asking, however he needed no answer. These comments were mostly for Addison. Only Hern had an idea of what would transpire in the next few hours. The others knew that an arrangement had been made with Addison, that is why he was giving up the money and the drugs.

"Give him a canteen of water, that is the least we can do for his generosity." Edna said, "He has a long way to walk."

The Expedition rumbled across the old cement bridge with potholes developing and Graffiti along the tan cement railings. Now, about 200 yards behind trailed the new Escalade driven by an exceptionally nervous attorney. He had taken large sums of money out of Addison's account and the lawyer feared the repercussions. That is why it was taking so long to post bail or get him out. John, the lawyer, did not want his client out of jail until John could fi gure out how to get the money replaced. He knew that Addison would not hesitate to have him killed once Addison discovered the missing money. John was calculating,

"I am sure that Addison has given the Indian police enough money and or drugs to more than repay the debt." John's plan was to watch the escape, while the Indians are making a show of looking for the escaped criminal, he would return and get the two bodyguards out of jail. Bring them back to the bridge and kill Edna and the officers with Addison's own personal gun. Then Addison would be blamed for killing officers of the law. All enforcement agencies would then hunt to kill. He was proud of his grand plan. He smiled at the long walk Addison would have, due to the fact that the pickup that was promised was still sitting at the Sacaton jail parking lot. If Addison did manage to walk to freedom, John could easily say the Indian Police must have found the truck and brought it to the station. All of this would make it certain the money could be replaced in the event Addison actually escaped. Chances are, when John himself reported the killings at the bridge the police would find Addison still in the desert. This would leave the "fancy lawyer" with power of attorney and millions of dollars. The lawyer again chuckled at his superb plan.

Addison was getting both irritated at the slow speed and excited for having out foxed the Indians so he couldn't help from making small comments such as, "Why don't you take some of the money and fix this old relic of a bridge you cherish so much?"

"Maybe do just that. Maybe bridge become famous. Big rich man escape from Indian Chief at bridge."

They stopped at the north end of the bridge. As they stepped out Addison motioned for the attorney to stay a safe distance behind in case there was some trouble.

Addison thought to himself, "These are the dumbest people alive. No wonder they lost the west to the U.S. Calvary."

"Okay important drug man, here is big plaque, I now show to you then maybe you push me so smart attorney make good report he saw important drug man push and saw jump over ridge. Indian police think of everything, right?"

Addison thought, "Yeah you red skinned Arizona native, you think of everything." Then he grinned, "This will my last chance to shove this jerk. The next time we meet one or the other will die and I know which one."

Addison greedily spoke, "Get these cuffs off of me and give me the canteen."

He again laughed to himself. "Got to carry the canteen so it will look good. They have no idea that a fully equipped four-wheel drive pickup waits for me about fifteen or twenty minutes away."

Hern spoke. Mainly to put in a report that Addison had been warned, that he voluntarily chose the desert rather than go to jail. "Mr. Addison, I must warn you that the desert is dangerous. If you want I can take you back to jail and you can stand trail."

Addison mockingly laughed. "Yeah, you would like me to go back to jail."

Together they walked to the bronze plate and removed the handcuffs. Addison shoved Hern with full force, causing him to fall to the hot cement.

"Adios you dumb suckers." He raised a finger to the attorney, the same type of gesture that George felt was indication that his pickup was number one, then the ex-DEA jumped over the ridge and slid down the embankment and disappeared under the foliage.

The attorney was sure that his services would no longer be required. With that thought he sped away in his newly acquired tan Escalade. Little did the "very smart lawyer" understand that all his great plans including his life's work would soon end, partly due to a so-called "dumb Indian."

Following behind the Lawyer, two deputies stepped out of their old International four-door pickup and allowed Addison's two gunmen to get out of the police truck and into the Escalade. The two officers simply believed there was not sufficient evidence to prosecute.

Addison landed in the dry dirt ditch, abandoned fifty years earlier. Occasionally water seeped into the ditch so there was ample vegetation and ample buzzing insects. From the jail Addison had made arrangements to have an explosive specialist install a bomb under the Escalade with a timed detonation. He disliked having to lose his new specially equipped Escalade but business is business.

Once he was fully concealed in the heavy foliage of the trees, he stopped to make a call on his cell with the special scrambler that the lawyer himself had purchased for his client. This call activated the timer, which would in approximately fifteen minutes detonate the bomb. He had to make the call right then or the Escalade would be out of range. Addison had no doubt that John, the criminal lawyer, had ulterior motives. Of course, in the life of a criminal, the only way to sever a relationship or contract without future problems is to eliminate the person. The arrangement with John would soon be severed.

When the bomb exploded, he was certain most of the Indian police would hurry to the scene of the explosion leaving plenty of time for him to take care of mother and son at the so called Gila River Cattle Ranch. His last reports were that they both stayed at the Ranch. He looked back towards the bridge and determined that he could not climb up the embankment and that he was indeed out of sight of the police. He guesstimated that the pickup was about twenty minutes away.

He thought aloud, "To make it look like a real escape." He recalled the constant concern of Hern that the DEA would be looking and might catch the Indian police doing something wrong. Thus he said to himself, "The police will return to Sacaton to organize a search party with dogs, the Escalade will explode, the police will divert their attention and I will be in the safety of the pickup and on my way to finish what I should have finished years earlier."

He prided himself in knowing his business and knowing what other people, especially these "dumb Indians" were thinking and planning, he spoke aloud as if cursing.

About ten minutes from the bridge as he was studying the dry ditch littered with green grass as well as dead branches, carefully watching his steps so as to not trip or sprain an ankle. Then something hit him, at first it felt like a lightweight BB Gun, then each area hit began to sting. Big yellow dive-bombing hornets began to strike at their moving target. "What the...?" The first struck, then five then a dozen.

Addison was wildly running through the brush, swatting at hornets until he came to a rusted metal gate historically used to let a portion of the water flow in different ditches. Blindly he jumped over and lay on the moist caliche mud. The dive-bombers had done much damage but at least had ceased making their attacks. The damp mud felt good.

"That was sheer bad luck, who would have ever known of a wasp nest right in middle of my path--a thousand to one odds." He thought to himself, no one would have known.

Well just a few more minutes and I will leave this damned desert once and for all. He lay motionless for a brief moment to catch his breath then moved his leg to get up.

"Maldito," He thought in Spanish as a never felt before pain seared his leg. "What the chupacabra was that?" (Chupacabra is a Mexican folklore demon.) It felt like a two prong pitchfork had jabbed his leg. He started to reach down to find what had jabbed him when another sharp pain hit is bicep. He rolled to his side and was struck in the neck two times, the sharp pains continued. The buzzing of a dozen rattles on a dozen angry Arizona Diamondback Rattlesnakes brings a fear not known to many and most of whom might have experienced that deadly sound have not lived to tell about it. Neither would Herbert Addison.

"Those dumb Indian Police. Yeah, dumb like a fox. Hern knows this country like the back of his hand. I don't suppose that 'dumb' Hern had any idea that there was a large hornets nest along the abandoned canal that would cause me to frantically run and jump over the rusted gate without so much as a second to look? I don't suppose that 'ignorant' Indian knew that just behind the rusted gate in the moist shady caliche was a den of Arizona Diamond Rattlesnakes? Yeah, dumb like a fox. I bet that the pickup that was supposed to be waiting for me is most likely parked at the police station at this very moment."

He crawled away from the den and leaned against the weed covered ditch bank. The deadly snakes seemed to sense there was no need to waste more venom. The numerous double puncture fang marks began to swell and the areas discolored as the venom moved quickly through the body.

"It is a strange feeling, sitting all alone, knowing that I am going to die watching the swelling and feeling the mounting pain. I have never wanted to believe in a God yet now I sense there really is a God and do not want to meet Him. Forty minutes ago I thought I was powerful, wealthy and super intelligent. Oh God, how long will this swelling continue. Now, I am a piece of earth returning to its creator. I am sure that the immeasurable pain I am now suffering will be but a drop in the ocean compared to what I will suffer for the lives of youth, mothers, parents and babies born or unborn that I personally have destroyed. Oh God, Why do I suddenly believe? Yes, yes, I will change my ways, just please stop the pain. Yes, yes, honestly I will make amends. I am still hurting. Don't You believe me? Remember, I have been to church, my mother used to go to church. Really God, I will change. I don't want to meet You at this time. Please!"

In the distance he heard an explosion, which he assumed, was his ex-attorney. What he did not know was that Hern had released Addison's two guards and allowed them to ride with the attorney. Hern (the dumb Indian) had suspected that Addison would eliminate the attorney one way or another. If the two thugs happened to be in the same car, so be it.

"Three birds with one stone pretty good work."

Herbert Addison's last thoughts, as he slipped into the subconscious state which stores all truths, was that all his previous pleadings were in vain. Before entering into the eternal damnation of blackness that he so ruthlessly earned in his mortal probation his subconscious thoughts were about Beth Ann Chattit.

"You were the best of all agents. That is why you discovered my double life." Even though he had momentarily gained a new appreciation for a supreme being, old habits are not forgotten on deathbed repentance. Even though Addison desperately tried to stop his last devil prompted thought, he could not. It was as if the devil feared losing this soul so Addison opened his now blue mouth and permanently sealed his eternal damnation with his last breath.

"Beth Ann, I really hope you and your son cook and rot in this Arizona desert. That you meet the same miserable fate that I am facing from this damnable desert that is my executioner."

The desert sighed with relief as one so evil left its presence. The buzzards quickly gathered. It mattered not to them who this evil man was, once the spirit leaves the body, what remains is just food. Bite by bite and tear-by-tear they would enjoy their meal.

Hern did not intend to file a report that was untrue. Thus the official report that read as follow:

1. Two suspects, possibly known as Ernesto and Raul, disappeared in the San Tan mountain range. Covered up tracks so even Indian not find. Certain they have left the country at this time and maybe not return.
2. Phoenix attorney John and two bodyguards killed in a car bomb explosion most likely under orders of Herbert Addison, well-known drug lord.
3. Herbert Addison, well-known drug smuggler and past narcotics officer died of multiple hornet and snakebites while trying to escape. Not certain if in Pima Indian or Pinal County jurisdiction, however, nature was executioner.

"Seriously Hern," inquired Edna, "Did you know about the hornets and the snakes? How did you figure it all?"

"Well, GRC told me about his experience with the hornets at the bridge so he and I went out to investigate. We did not want to jump over the ridge because there is no way back up the embankment so we decided to come from the other direction. We drove around the hill and walked up the old ditch. We were easing along the underbrush when GRC mentioned, 'This is a good place for rattlesnakes.' With that thought I became much more alert. With fair warnings the snakes began to buzz. We decided the hornet's nest could wait. Later GRC mentioned that he certainly was glad that we had not jumped down the ridge. We would have been so busy swatting and running that we would have never heard the snakes warning and jumped right into the middle of the den. So, even though I would like to claim credit, it actually goes to our Gila River Cowboy."

22—SUNRISE, SUNSET

UNDAY MORNINGS HAD almost become a ritual for the Gila River Cowboy. Before sunrise he would saddle his horse and ride to the same desert, rock-laden mountain, climb to the highest boulder and watch the sun at turtle speed climb over the mountains. He would let tears of gratitude freely fall; he would express his thanks aloud and always ask to be alerted if any neighbor needed help. He only once asked for a personal favor, which was help to locate his mother. That favor was granted. Now he was timid in asking for one more favor. He was as happy as any one man could possibly be. His physical experiences continued, even now his arm was in a sling supporting a dislocated shoulder from a fall off his horse. What he most appreciated were the spiritual teachings he received from friends, Bapchule and from his Heavenly Father.

He was shy in asking for another favor, however he considered Jesus Christ, not only as his Savior, but also as a good friend. George knew that he had been taught to always be ready to help a friend so he felt that his friend Jesus would also be ready to help him. So looking towards the heavens he expressed his desire to share his life with someone. He wondered.

"Why did I say someone? Sacred request needs to be specific." He repeated his plea out loud.

"I want to share my life with Victoria, give me the courage to ask and give her the courage to say yes." He fell to his knees in humble prayer.

"Yes" The audible voice resounded.

He jumped; he had never had such a quick and audible answer to a prayer. He turned to look in the direction from where the answer had been heard.

There in perfect harmony with the rising sun stood the most beautiful person he had ever seen. He could not distinctly see her face because the sun was directly behind, which was creating an exquisite glow. The sun seemed to stand still for a brief moment. Not by sight but by feeling he knew he loved this person more that life itself and he wanted her to be with him for all eternity.

"Yes, I have the courage to say yes. Do you have the courage to ask?"

George Ribit Chattit had planned a dozen romantic ways he was going to propose to his beautiful "Humming Bird." Now standing in front of her all he seemed to be able to do was fall to his knees with a mind blank as an unblemished piece of white paper. His mind had gone into a "screen saver mode" and some undetermined bit of information just bounced from one side to the other with no apparent meaning. His knees were obedient but had no eye to guide them to a safe landing, so in front of the woman he loved his knee sent his non-functional brain a message in the form of a sharp pain. It took a few moments for the brain to move back into a slow pace recognition. His left knee had collided with a sharp rock.

Yet, disregarding the knee pain or the pain from the shoulder he dislocated when falling from his horse. He raised his good arm and reached for her hand. Holding her small hand he looked up into those earth-shattering perfect blue eyes,

"Victoria, my dear little Humming Bird would you…"

"George," she jumped back, "get up quick…"

"It's okay, it is just a small cut." He softly spoke as the blood trickled from the open wound.

She stood waving and pointing her arms as she repeated with high anxiety, "George, George."

George moved closer to show her it was not a big cut on his leg but she backed away and that caused George to freeze in his tracks.

"Did she not want to marry him? Was it bad timing?" Thoughts now bounce back and forth at an accelerated rate.

"George, your leg!" She spoke with a slight tremble in her otherwise sweet voice.

He was about to explain once again that a little cut was not going to stop the Gila River Cowboy from completing what he started out to accomplish. Then he felt something like blood slowly crawling up his leg above the cut. Before he could look or determine the extent of this new problem Victoria finally completed her sentence.

"George, there's a large brown scorpion crawling on and up your pant leg."

It is amazing how the mind can make so many shifts in such a millisecond of time. Perfect romance turned once again to the all-American western stomp. When a larger than life pre-historic looking monster appears on thin material protecting a cowboy's leg, that leg can easily perform 4,000 ups and downs in less than a minute.

However, the difference between actuality and what is envisioned in the brain varies greatly. In George's mind, standing in front of the woman he loved, he calmly stood up and brushed the scorpion to the ground. In reality, he did not notice the dust, rolling rocks or scattering wildlife caused from his new version of the cowboy stomp. The slashed knee not in the slightest bothered him. At this moment, his complete focus and dedication to life was the stomping/dancing movements to remove the scorpion from his leg.

Eventually, he collected himself. He concluded that using a rock or a stiff limb he could expertly brush the scorpion off his pant leg. Of course, after the dancing and jumping, the scorpion had long departed the pant leg and was safely hidden under a rock.

Victoria was normally quite calm about most events. As a young girl, however, she had been stung a few times by scorpions. So she naturally reacted with fear.

Victoria noticed the blood soaking the pant leg that George had evidently forgotten. "Sit down," she commanded in a soft but authoritative way. She stepped toward "her George" and with one smooth movement she pulled a rather large knife from the scabbard strapped to her waist. He had never noticed any bump or bulge that could have hidden a knife.

George was completely convinced that the Gods of this earth have a delightful sense of humor and often allow events to happen for the Gods' own personal amusement.

The knife, growing much larger as it approached its desired target. Then just to add to the humor of the moment one of the early morning rays of sun was actually and physically bent so as to reflect off the shiny blade and redirect its increased lightning power directly into George's wide eyes, causing momentary blindness.

His mind's eye was already whirling searching in an absolute blank database so the only useless thoughts were. "All I was going to do was ask her to marry me. Is there an Indian culture that I don't know about? Do we become blood brother and sister? Is she going to cut my tongue out for openly asking?"

She calmly placed her hand on the not so calm head. She had seen the reflection from the blade and knew he was temporarily blind. She closed her hand over a batch of hair and tilted his head back.

At first he was petrified, and then a pleasant calm filled his heart and mind. "What a way to die. Having my throat slit by the most beautiful woman in the world would be an honor." Maybe, he thought, "This is how the Prophet Abraham's son felt. What an honor."

Then to his delightful surprise very soft and moist lips touched his dried and weather cracked lips. He thought for a moment that he was dead because when his eyes focused once again, they were gazing into the dark blue expanse of the heavens. He thought it strange that he had not even felt the slightest pain from the knife. Then even more to his surprises was the soft voice of Victoria. He instantly remembered a beautiful song about two young Indian lovers that swam to the middle of the river to die in each other's arms.

"Maybe?" He thought, "She took my life then hers so we could both be in heaven together?" No he thought again, "That would be murder and lovely Humming Bird could not ever commit mur…" He was in the middle of that thought. He felt it. It was physical. There is a powerful difference between the touch of the spirit and a physical touch. This feeling was no spirit. He focused again and realized the blue heavenly sight was definitely a look into the expanse of heaven but this blue belonged to Victoria's eyes. Now his brain was really swirling.

"She is kissing me. She is kissing me. She is kis…" Before he finished that thought.

She bent down, picked up his leg, propped his boot on her leg just above the knee, then expertly slit his pant leg and up past the injured knee. She displayed her very radiant smile. "Only the Gila River Cowboy would propose with a dislocated shoulder, a new cut on the knee bleeding profusely that will undoubtedly require stitches and a five inch scorpion crawling up his wounded leg."

She leaned down and once again kissed him angelically on his dry and cracked lips.

"George Ribit Chattit and/or the Gila River Cowboy, I accept your most romantic proposal. Now let's get you to the doctor, AGAIN."

Not a person who had seen Victoria and George together was surprised at the announcement. When he told Bapchule about the proposal he smiled,

"Bapchule right about Humming Bird and Thunderbolt. Thunderbolt knew what to do, no have courage so humming bird gives incentive and great horse jump into mud to save George. George know he love Victoria, no have courage to ask so Humming Bird give incentive."

Both men laughed at the comparison and both knew it was most likely true.

When George told Chula and Jesse it was no surprise. "Chula" George looked into her round brown eyes, "when Peggy, from my hometown visited the Ranch and was frightened at the presence of you and Jesse, you turned and walked away but I distinctly heard you say, 'Maybe now find Chupa Rosa.'" I had no idea if it was someone or something I should find? I looked up the Spanish words Chupa and Rosa and found that chupa meant suck and rosa was a rose flower.

Jesse roared with laughter as Chula teased. "Chula explain dat' Chupa Rosa, very pretty lady. Many moons back Chula think maybe Chupa Rosa maybe perfect for our George. Maybe was George but now GRC that find Victoria. Chula not know who love GRC most, Victoria or Chupa Rosa. Chula no can tell, think maybe George should tell Victoria about how much Chupa Rosa love, maybe George be honest man. Maybe good to tell to Victoria." Chula's eyes danced with delight. "Just other day Miss Chupa Rosa say how much she love George. Not good have two lady love same man."

George was perplexed but was determined to be always open and honest with Victoria and the next morning they were going horseback riding to check on the calves.

Early the next morning as they were saddling the horses GRC gathered enough courage. "Victoria you know my love for you is without limits and I have been and will always be honest with you because of that love. So…" even now he was hesitant. "So I need to talk with you about this girl that Chula says you know. This girl apparently has told Chula that she loves me. I don't even know her, how could she say such things?"

Victoria walked over to George and spoke briskly, "What, there is another woman in your life?"

"Oh no Victoria, there is no other woman in my life. I do not know if this girl is one month old or fifty years old. I don't even know who she is or anything about her."

"Surely you know her name?"

"Yes, her name is Chupa Rosa."

Victoria moved within inches of his red bewildered face. "Hah, you said you didn't know her but yet you know her name."

George was becoming more baffled. He didn't know much about girls. He knew less about young ladies. At this point, he realized he knew nothing about anything, except for the obvious truth that telling truth wasn't working as he thought it might work.

Victoria was sure her George had not been kidded when he was growing up so she teased him just a bit more. Soon she saw that her little hoax had gone far enough; she loved this man too much to watch him be saddened. She stood on her tiptoes, put her hand behind his head and softly placed a long kiss on his puzzled lips. "Do you like the way your Humming Bird kisses?"

It took him a full, long, and tense minute to recover. He had experienced a few one hundred eighty- degree turns before but none quite as fast as this. "Yes," was all that came out of his mouth and before he could react, Victoria once again offered a long and passionate kiss.

"My GRC, do you like the way Chupa Rosa kisses?"

They were indeed two different types of kisses. His mind was frantically searching for an answer. "Wait just a minute, you said, then you said, what did you say?"

Victoria explained, "Humming Bird in Spanish is Chupa Rosa. When I was but a baby, Chula decided that Chupa Rosa had a more suitable sound so they have always called me Chupa Rosa. Now, answer my question."

He smiled, picked her up and sat her on the open tailgate of his pickup. "I liked them both," then he kissed her.

"Hey," their mothers in unison spoke, "Aren't you two supposed to be checking on the calves?"

Edna and Beth Ann had become good friends and while Victoria and George were riding horses, checking calves and mending fences the two mothers preferred the F-350 bouncing across the desert or down the freeway towards a new shopping mall. Now they were together even more with the planning of a wedding.

It had been decided that the wedding reception would be an old fashion type gathering with dancing and plenty of food and it would take place at the Gila River Cattle Ranch House the first day of June. It did not give them much time but they were certain that with the many friends of Victoria and George, they would have plenty of help.

Three weeks before the reception the desert received an unusually long slow drizzle that soaked into the dry desert soil. It only takes a few days for some desert plants to respond to the moisture, some within a week but all within three weeks display brilliant arrays of color. Then surprisingly, two days before the reception the desert flowers and then again dry soil received a slow drizzle that settles the dust, freshens the leaves and causes flowers to maintain their brilliance.

Jesse claimed God was happy with this marriage so He gave the gift of rain.

Beth Ann was amazed and impressed how the Riggs family could so easily and enjoyably bring tables, chairs and an undetermined amount of fourteen inch and sixteen inch Dutch Ovens. A Dutch Oven is a large cast iron cooking pot used for biscuits or delicious cherry, peach, mixed berries or apple cobbler. She wondered how they could have any more fun at the fiesta than what they were having setting up. All the children, from two years to eighty years, helped with something, but when they weren't helping, they were chasing, catching, climbing or in some other way having the time of their lives.

The night of the fiesta was perfect. The sun spent almost forty-five minutes painting the sky with brilliant colors displaying the world renowned Arizona Sunset. Even the birds seemed to sing louder than ever as the Bride and Groom having been married for time and eternity stood on the porch. Bapchule stood,

"Bapchule say to this people, the Great God, the Creator of all is very happy today. Humming Bird and Gila River Cowboy make good thoughts, make much good for friends and soon make many good children."

Victoria squeezed her husband's hand.

"Man or woman not complete until much love between two. Then children to teach man and woman much more bout love and patience."

After much dancing and eating, a few games and saying hi or hugging everybody it was time for the bride and groom to leave. The younger children had printed the usual just married on the red F-350, tied cans to the bumper making it ready for the departure.

Victoria, radiantly beautiful stood on the porch once again and began dancing to a western song that no one will ever remember. She stunned her friends and her mother as George sat on a chair directly in front of his beautiful bride. George watched intently.

"GRC told me that he would not leave as long as I wore this delicate wedding gown. It is beautiful. I do, however, wish to fulfill my new husband's desire."

She stood on the porch and to the rhythm of western music she slowly began to unzip her dress. Her eyes were bright as stars dancing on a warm night. Her dazzling smile captivated all and her glistening coal black hair contrasted over her beautifully laced wedding gown. It slipped off her shoulders and in seemingly slow motion fell to the floor. Even the crickets were silent. George stood up and took her hand that wore a sparkling diamond ring. There they stood as eternal husband and wife. Under her hand sewn wedding dress she had put on matching western shirt, matching belt buckle, matching black Wrangler's, matching gray boots and both reached and placed on each other's head matching light Sandstone color Stetsons hats. They walked joyously through the crowd, kissing and hugging and mounted their horses that had been saddled by one of the Riggs family members. Silhouetted by the bright light of a clear night with a full moon, they, side by side rode into the Arizona Desert they both loved.

The last words spoken as they rode into their new life,

"Top this Mr. John Wayne or Mr. Clint Eastwood."

EPILOGUE

Victoria and George were confronted with threatening conflicts. They live at the Gila River Ranch House and have six children, four boys and two girls.

Beth Ann met a marine friend of Jay John whose name is David, one of the men J.J. rescued. They married and live in Payson, Arizona.

Edna became Governor of the Gila River Community

Bapchule spent many hours and days with GRC and Victoria, then helped with and taught some of their children, one evening he told them his work was finished and walked into the sunset and has never returned.

Chula and Jesse continue to live near Black Water and are the greatest baby sitters.

Cecil lifted an overturned car to save two trapped babies. The same evening he died from a massive heart attack

The Riggs family still operates R-Country Store along with other enterprises.

Lt. Colonel Jones and Bee live on Riggs Ranch Drive and visit the Gila River Cattle Ranch often.

Hern and the other officers are still serving their community

The Northeast part of the Gila River Ranch was sold for a new development.

The Gila River Basin still gets to 120 degrees in the summer shade.

The Olberg Bridge still stands as a monument to ingenuity. There are still bees, hornets and rattlesnakes.

If you are a round peg with square surroundings, be strong and develop your inner talents, not rebellious attitudes.

All were created spiritually before physically.

There is a life before mortality, there is life after mortality.

Good comes to those who seek good.

Hear, see and feel that which is not physically heard, seen or felt.